Kelly Campbell

About the Author

BERNARD CORNWELL is the author of the acclaimed and bestselling Saxon Novels, which began with *The Last Kingdom*; the Richard Sharpe novels; the Grail Quest series; the Nathaniel Starbuck Chronicles; the Warlord Trilogy; and many other novels, including *Stonehenge* and *Gallows Thief*. He lives with his wife on Cape Cod.

Books by Bernard Cornwell

THE SAXON NOVELS
THE LAST KINGDOM
THE PALE HORSEMAN

THE SHARPE NOVELS
(in chronological order)

SHARPE'S TIGER*
*Richard Sharpe and the Siege of
Seringapatam, 1799*

SHARPE'S TRIUMPH*
*Richard Sharpe and the Battle of Assaye,
September 1803*

SHARPE'S FORTRESS*
*Richard Sharpe and the Siege of
Gawilghur, December 1803*

SHARPE'S TRAFALGAR*
*Richard Sharpe and the Battle of
Trafalgar, 21 October 1805*

SHARPE'S PREY*
*Richard Sharpe and the Expedition to
Copenhagen, 1807*

SHARPE'S RIFLES
*Richard Sharpe and the French Invasion
of Galicia, January 1809*

SHARPE'S HAVOC*
*Richard Sharpe and the Campaign in
Northern Portugal, Spring 1809*

SHARPE'S EAGLE
*Richard Sharpe and the Talavera
Campaign, July 1809*

SHARPE'S GOLD
*Richard Sharpe and the Destruction of
Almeida, August 1810*

SHARPE'S ESCAPE*
*Richard Sharpe and the Bussaco
Campaign, 1810*

SHARPE'S BATTLE*
*Richard Sharpe and the Battle of Fuentes
de Onoro, May 1811*

SHARPE'S COMPANY
*Richard Sharpe and the Siege of Badajoz,
January to April 1812*

SHARPE'S SWORD
*Richard Sharpe and the Salamanca
Campaign, June and July 1812*

SHARPE'S ENEMY
*Richard Sharpe and the Defense of
Portugal, Christmas 1812*

SHARPE'S HONOUR
*Richard Sharpe and the Vitoria
Campaign, February to June 1813*

SHARPE'S REGIMENT
*Richard Sharpe and the Invasion of
France, June to November 1813*

SHARPE'S SIEGE
*Richard Sharpe and the Winter
Campaign, 1814*

SHARPE'S REVENGE
*Richard Sharpe and the Peace
of 1814*

SHARPE'S WATERLOO
*Richard Sharpe and the Waterloo
Campaign, 15 June to 18 June 1815*

SHARPE'S DEVIL*
*Richard Sharpe and the Emperor,
1820–21*

* Published by HarperCollins*Publishers*

SHARPE'S ESCAPE

Richard Sharpe

and the Bussaco Campaign,

1810

Bernard Cornwell

Harper

An Imprint of HarperCollinsPublishers

Sharpe's Escape *is for CeCe*

Originally published in 2003 in Great Britain by HarperCollins Publishers.

A hardcover edition of this book was published in the U.S. in 2004 by HarperCollins Publishers.

HarperCollins books may be purchased for educational, business, or sales promotional use. For information please write: Special Markets Department, HarperCollins Publishers, 10 East 53rd Street, New York, NY 10022.

FIRST HARPER PAPERBACK PUBLISHED 2006.

Map by Ken Lewis

Library of Congress Cataloging-in-Publication Data is available upon request.

ISBN 0-06-053047-2
ISBN-10: 0-06-056155-6 (pbk.)
ISBN-13: 978-0-06-056155-0 (pbk.)

08 09 10 ❖/RRD 10 9 8 7 6

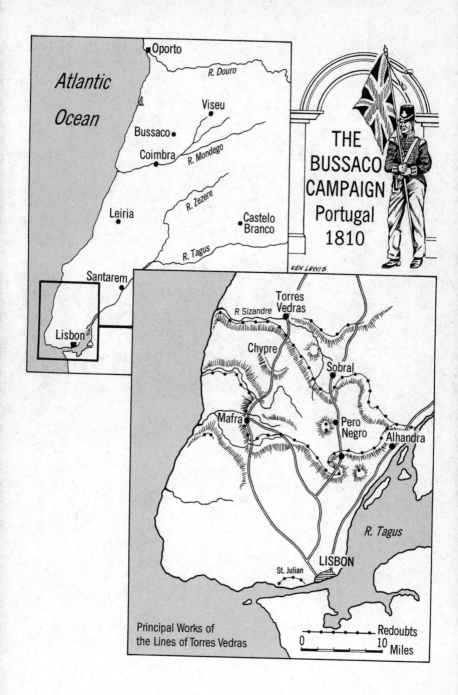

Atlantic Ocean

Oporto

R. Douro

Viseu

Bussaco

Coimbra

R. Mondego

R. Zezere

Leiria

Castelo Branco

R. Tagus

Santarem

Lisbon

THE BUSSACO CAMPAIGN Portugal 1810

KEN LEWIS

Torres Vedras

R Sizandre

Chypre

Sobral

Mafra

Pero Negro

Alhandra

R. Tagus

LISBON

St. Julian

Principal Works of the Lines of Torres Vedras

Redoubts

0   10   Miles

PART ONE

MISTER SHARPE WAS IN A BAD MOOD. A filthy mood. He was looking for trouble in Sergeant Harper's opinion, and Harper was rarely wrong about Captain Sharpe, and Sergeant Harper knew well enough not to engage his Captain in conversation when Sharpe was in such a black temper, but on the other hand Harper liked to live dangerously. "I see your uniform's been mended, sir," he said cheerily.

Sharpe ignored the comment. He just marched on, climbing the bare Portuguese slope under the searing sun. It was September 1810, almost autumn, yet the heat of late summer hammered the landscape like a furnace. At the top of the hill, another mile or so ahead of Sharpe, stood a barn-like stone building next to a gaunt telegraph station. The station was a black timber scaffolding supporting a high mast from which signaling arms hung motionless in the afternoon's heat.

"It's a rare nice piece of stitching on that jacket," Harper went on, sounding as though he did not have a care in the world, "and I can tell you didn't do it yourself. It looks like a woman's work, so it does?" He inflected the last three words as a question.

Sharpe still said nothing. His long, straight-bladed cavalry sword banged against his left thigh as he climbed. He had a rifle slung on his shoulder. An officer was not supposed to carry a longarm like his men, but Sharpe had once been a private and he was used to carrying a proper gun to war.

"Was it someone you met in Lisbon, now?" Harper persisted.

Sharpe simmered, but pretended he had not heard. His uniform jacket, decently mended as Harper had noticed, was rifle green. He had been a rifleman. No, he still thought of himself as a rifleman, one of the elite men who carried the Baker rifle and wore the dark green instead of the red, but the tides of war had stranded him and a few of his men in a redcoat regiment and now he commanded the light company of the South Essex who were following him up the hill. Most wore the red jackets of the British infantry and carried smoothbore muskets, but a handful, like Sergeant Harper, still kept their old green jackets and fought with the rifle.

"So who was she?" Harper finally asked.

"Sergeant Harper," Sharpe was finally goaded into speaking, "if you want bloody trouble then keep bloody talking."

"Yes, sir," Harper said, grinning. He was an Ulsterman, a Catholic and a sergeant, and as such he was not supposed to be friends with an Englishman, a heathen and an officer, but he was. He liked Sharpe and knew Sharpe liked him, though he was wise enough not to say another word. Instead he whistled the opening bars of the song "I Would That the Wars Were All Done."

Sharpe inevitably thought of the words that accompanied the tune; "In the meadow one morning, all pearly with dew, a fair pretty maiden plucked violets so blue," and Harper's delicate insolence forced him to laugh aloud. He then swore at the Sergeant, who was grinning with triumph. "It was Josefina," Sharpe admitted.

"Miss Josefina now! How is she?"

"She's well enough," Sharpe said vaguely.

"I'm glad to hear that," Harper said with genuine feeling. "So you took tea with her, did you, sir?"

"I took bloody tea with her, Sergeant, yes."

"Of course you did, sir," Harper said. He walked a few paces in silence, then decided to try his luck again. "And I thought you were sweet on Miss Teresa, sir?"

"Miss Teresa?" Sharpe said, as though the name were quite unknown to him, though in the last few weeks he had hardly stopped thinking about the hawk-faced girl who rode across the frontier in Spain with the partisan forces. He glanced at the Sergeant, who had a look of placid innocence on his broad face. "I like Teresa well enough," Sharpe went on defensively, "but I don't even know if I'll ever see her again!"

"But you'd like to," Harper pointed out.

"Of course I would! But so what? There are girls you'd like to see again, but you don't behave like a bloody saint waiting for them, do you?"

"True enough," Harper admitted. "And I can see why you didn't want to come back to us, sir. There you were, drinking tea while Miss Josefina's sewing, and a fine time the two of you must have been having."

"I didn't want to come back," Sharpe said harshly, "because I was promised a month's bloody leave. A month! And they gave me a week!"

Harper was not in the least sympathetic. The month's leave was supposed to be Sharpe's reward for bringing back a hoard of gold from behind enemy lines, but the whole of the light company had been on that jaunt and no one had suggested that the rest of them be given a month off. On the other hand Harper could well understand Sharpe's moroseness, for the thought of losing a whole month in Josefina's bed would make even a bishop hit the gin.

"One bloody week," Sharpe snarled, "bastard bloody army!" He stepped aside from the path and waited for the company to close up. In truth his foul mood had little to do with his truncated leave, but he could not admit to Harper what was really causing it. He stared back down the column, seeking out the figure of Lieutenant Slingsby. That was the problem. Lieutenant bloody Cornelius bloody Slingsby.

As the company reached Sharpe they sat beside the path. Sharpe commanded fifty-four rank and file now, thanks to a draft from England, and those newly arrived men stood out because they had bright-red coats. The uniforms of the other men had paled under the sun and were so liberally patched with brown Portuguese cloth that, from a distance, they looked more like tramps than soldiers. Slingsby, of course, had objected to that. "New uniforms, Sharpe," he had yapped enthusiastically, "some new uniforms will make the men look smarter. Fine new broadcloth will put some snap into them! We should indent for some." Bloody fool, Sharpe had thought. The new uniforms would come in due time, probably in winter, and there was no point in asking for them sooner and, besides, the men liked their old, comfortable jackets just as they liked their French oxhide packs. The new men all had British packs, made by Trotters, that griped across the chest until, on a long march, it seemed that a red-hot band of iron was constricting the ribs. Trotters' pains, that was called, and the French packs were far more comfortable.

Sharpe walked back down the company and ordered each of the new arrivals to give him their canteen and, as he had expected, every last one was empty. "You're bloody fools," Sharpe said. "You ration it! A sip at a time! Sergeant Read!"

"Sir?" Read, a redcoat and a Methodist, doubled to Sharpe.

"Make sure no one gives them water, Sergeant."

"I'll do that, sir, I'll do that."

The new men would be dry as dust by the time the afternoon was done. Their throats would be swollen and their breath rasping, but at least they would never be so stupid again. Sharpe walked on down the column to where Lieutenant Slingsby brought up the rearguard. "No stragglers, Sharpe," Slingsby said with the eagerness of a terrier thinking it had deserved a reward. He was a short man, straight-backed, square-shouldered, bristling with efficiency. "Mister Iliffe and I coaxed them on."

Sharpe said nothing. He had known Cornelius Slingsby for one week and in that week he had developed a loathing for the man that verged on being murderous. There was no reason for that hatred, unless disliking a man on sight was good reason, yet everything about Slingsby annoyed Sharpe, whether it was the back of the man's head, which was as flat as a shovel blade, his protuberant eyes, his black mustache, the broken veins on his nose, the snort of his laughter or the strut of his gait. Sharpe had come back from Lisbon to discover that Slingsby had replaced his Lieutenant, the reliable Robert Knowles, who had been appointed Adjutant to the regiment. "Cornelius is by way of being a relation," Lieutenant Colonel the Honorable William Lawford had told Sharpe vaguely, "and you'll find him a very fine fellow."

"I will, sir?"

"He joined the army late," Lawford had continued, "which is why he's still a lieutenant. Well, he was brevetted captain, of course, but he's still a lieutenant."

"I joined the army early, sir," Sharpe had said, "and I'm still a lieutenant. Brevetted captain, of course, but still a lieutenant."

"Oh, Sharpe." Lawford had sounded exasperated. "There is no one more cognizant of your virtues than I. If there was a vacant captaincy..." He left that notion hanging, though Sharpe knew the answer. He had been made into a lieutenant, and that was something of a miracle for a man who had joined the army as an illiterate private, and he had been brevetted a captain, which meant he was paid as such even though his true rank remained lieutenant, but he could only get the real promotion if he either purchased a vacant captaincy or, much less likely, was promoted by Lawford. "I value you, Sharpe," the Colonel had continued, "but I also have hopes for Cornelius. He's thirty. Or maybe thirty-one. Old for a lieutenant, but he's keen as mustard, Sharpe, and has experience. Lots of experience." That was the trouble. Before joining the South Essex Slingsby had been in the 55th, a regiment serving in the West Indies, and the yellow fever had decimated the officers' ranks and so Slingsby had been brevetted a captain, and captain, moreover, of the 55th's light company, and as a result he reckoned he knew as much about soldiering as Sharpe. Which might have been true, but he did not know as much about fighting. "I want you to take him under your wing," the Colonel had finished. "Bring him on, Sharpe, eh?"

Bring him to an early grave, Sharpe had thought sourly, but he had to hide his thoughts, and was still doing his best to conceal the hatred as Slingsby pointed up to the telegraph station. "Mister Iliffe and I saw men up there, Sharpe. A dozen of them, I think. And one looked as if he was wearing a blue uniform. Shouldn't be anyone up there, should there?"

Sharpe doubted that Ensign Iliffe, an officer newly come from England, had seen a thing, while Sharpe himself had noticed the men and their horses fifteen minutes earlier and he had been wondering ever since what the strangers were doing on the hilltop, for officially the telegraph station had been abandoned. Normally it was manned by a handful of soldiers who guarded the naval Midshipman who operated the black bags which were hoisted up and down the tall mast to send messages from one end of Portugal to the other. But the French had already cut the chain further north and the British had retreated away from these hills, and somehow this one station had not been destroyed. There was no point in leaving it intact for the Frogs to use, and so Sharpe's company had been detached from the battalion and given the simple job of burning the telegraph. "Could it be a Frenchman?" Slingsby asked, referring to the blue uniform. He sounded eager, as if he wanted to charge uphill. He was three inches over five feet, with an air of perpetual alertness.

"Doesn't matter if it is a bloody Crapaud," Sharpe said sourly, "there's more of us than there are of them. I'll send Mister Iliffe up there to shoot him." Iliffe looked alarmed. He was seventeen and looked fourteen, a raw-boned youngster whose father had purchased him a commission because he did not know what else to do with the boy. "Show me your canteen," Sharpe ordered Iliffe.

Iliffe looked scared now. "It's empty, sir," he confessed, and cringed as though he expected Sharpe to punish him.

"You know what I told the men with empty canteens?" Sharpe asked. "That they were idiots. But you're not, because you're an officer, and there aren't any idiot officers."

"Quite correct, sir," Slingsby put in, then snorted. He always snorted when he laughed and Sharpe suppressed an urge to cut the bastard's throat.

"Hoard your water," Sharpe said, thrusting the canteen back at Iliffe. "Sergeant Harper! March on!"

It took another half-hour to reach the hilltop. The barn-like building was evidently a shrine, for a chipped statue of the Virgin Mary was mounted in a niche above its door. The telegraph tower had been built against the shrine's eastern gable which helped support the lattice of thick timbers that carried the platform on which the Midshipman had worked his arcane skill. The tower was deserted now, its tethered signal ropes banging against the tarred mast in the brisk wind that blew around the summit. The black-painted bladders had been taken away, but the ropes used to hoist and lower them were still in place and from one of them hung a square of white cloth and Sharpe wondered if the strangers on the hilltop had raised the makeshift flag as a signal.

Those strangers, a dozen civilians, were standing beside the shrine's door and with them was a Portuguese infantry officer, his blue coat faded to a color very close to the French blue. It was the officer who strode forward to meet Sharpe. "I am Major Ferreira," he said in good English, "and you are?"

"Captain Sharpe."

"And Captain Slingsby." Lieutenant Slingsby had insisted on accompanying Sharpe to meet the Portuguese officer, just as he insisted on using his brevet rank even though he had no right to do so any longer.

"I command here," Sharpe said laconically.

"And your purpose, Captain?" Ferreira demanded. He was a tall man, lean and dark, with a carefully trimmed mustache. He had the manners and bearing of privilege, but Sharpe detected an uneasiness in the Portuguese Major that Ferreira attempted to cover with a brusque manner that tempted Sharpe to insolence. He fought the temptation and told the truth instead.

"We're ordered to burn the telegraph."

Ferreira glanced at Sharpe's men who were straggling onto the hill's summit. He seemed taken aback by Sharpe's words, but then smiled unconvincingly. "I shall do it for you, Captain. It will be my pleasure."

"I carry out my own orders, sir," Sharpe said.

Ferreira scented the insolence and gave Sharpe a quizzical look. For a second Sharpe thought the Portuguese Major intended to offer him a reprimand, but instead Ferreira nodded curtly. "If you insist," he said, "but do it quickly."

"Quickly, sir!" Slingsby intervened enthusiastically. "No point in waiting!" He turned on Harper. "Sergeant Harper! The combustibles, if you please. Quick, man, quick!"

Harper glanced at Sharpe for approval of the Lieutenant's orders, but Sharpe betrayed nothing, and so the big Irishman shouted at the dozen men who were burdened with cavalry forage nets that were stuffed full of straw. Another six men carried jars of turpentine, and now the straw was heaped about the four legs of the telegraph station and then soaked with the turpentine. Ferreira watched them work for a while, then went back to join the civilians who appeared worried by the arrival of British soldiers. "It's all ready, sir," Harper called to Sharpe, "shall I light her up?"

Slingsby did not even give Sharpe time to answer. "Let's not dilly-dally, Sergeant!" he said briskly. "Fire it up!"

"Wait," Sharpe snarled, making Slingsby blink at the harshness of his tone. Officers were expected to treat each other courteously in front of the men, but Sharpe had snapped angrily and the look he gave Slingsby made the Lieutenant step backwards in surprise. Slingsby frowned, but said nothing as Sharpe climbed the ladder to the mast's platform that stood fifteen feet above the hilltop. Three pock marks in the boards showed where the Midshipman had placed his tripod so he could stare at the neighboring telegraph stations and read their messages. The station to the north had already been destroyed, but looking south Sharpe could just see the next tower somewhere beyond the River Criz and still behind British lines. It would not be behind the lines for long, he thought. Marshal Masséna's army was flooding into central Portugal and the British would be retreating to their newly built defensive lines at Torres Vedras. The plan was to retreat to the new fortifications, let the French come, then either kill their futile attacks or watch them starve.

And to help them starve, the British and Portuguese were leaving them nothing. Every barn, every larder, every storehouse was being emptied. Crops were being burned in their fields, windmills were being destroyed and wells made foul with carcasses. The inhabitants of every town and village in central Portugal were being evicted, taking their livestock with them, ordered to go either behind the Lines of Torres Vedras or else up into the high hills where the French would be reluctant to follow. The intention was that the enemy would find a scorched land, bare of everything, even of telegraph ropes.

Sharpe untied one of the signal ropes and pulled down the white flag that turned out to be a big handkerchief of fine linen, neatly hemmed with the initials PAF embroidered in blue into one corner. Ferreira? Sharpe looked down on the Portuguese Major who was watching him. "Yours, Major?" Sharpe asked.

"No," Ferreira called back.

"Mine then," Sharpe said, and pocketed the handkerchief. He saw the anger on Ferreira's face and was amused by it. "You might want to move those horses," he nodded at the beasts picketed beside the shrine, "before we burn the tower."

"Thank you, Captain," Ferreira said icily.

"Fire it now, Sharpe?" Slingsby demanded from the ground.

"Not till I'm off the bloody platform," Sharpe growled. He looked round one last time and saw a small mist of gray-white powder smoke far off to the southeast. He pulled out his telescope, the precious glass that had been given to him by Sir Arthur Wellesley, now Lord Wellington, and he rested it on the balustrade and then knelt and stared towards the smoke. He could see little, but he reckoned he was watching the British rearguard in action. French cavalry must have pressed too close and a battalion was firing volleys, backed up by the cannons of the Royal Horse Artillery. He could just hear the soft thump of the far-off guns. He swept the glass north, the lens traveling over a hard country of hills, rocks and barren pasture, and there was nothing there, nothing at all, until suddenly he saw a hint of a different green and he jerked the glass back, settled it and saw them.

Cavalry. French cavalry. Dragoons in their green coats. They were at least a mile away, in a valley, but coming towards the telegraph station. Reflected sunlight glinted from their buckles, bits and stirrups as Sharpe tried to count them. Forty? Sixty men perhaps, it was hard to tell for the squadron was twisting between rocks in the valley's deep heart and going from sunshine to shadow. They looked to be in no particular hurry and Sharpe wondered if they had been sent to capture the telegraph station which would serve the advancing French as well as it had served the British.

"We've got company, Sergeant!" Sharpe called down to Harper. Decency and courtesy demanded that he should have told Slingsby, but he could barely bring himself to talk to the man, so he spoke to Harper instead. "At least a squadron of green bastards. About a mile away, but they could be here in a few minutes." He collapsed the telescope and went down the ladder and nodded at the Irish Sergeant. "Spark it off," he said.

The turpentine-soaked straw blazed bright and high, but it took some moments before the big timbers of the scaffold caught the flame. Sharpe's company, as ever fascinated by willful destruction, looked on appreciatively and gave a small cheer as the high platform at last began to burn. Sharpe had walked to the eastern edge of the small hilltop, but, denied the height of the platform, he could no longer see the dragoons.

Had they wheeled away? Perhaps, if they had hoped to capture the signal tower intact, they would have decided to abandon the effort when they saw the smoke boil off the summit.

Lieutenant Slingsby joined him. "I don't wish to make anything of it," he said in a low tone, "but you spoke very harshly to me just now, Sharpe, very harshly indeed."

Sharpe said nothing. He was imagining the pleasure of disemboweling the little bastard.

"I don't resent it for myself," Slingsby went on, still speaking softly, "but it serves the men ill. Very ill indeed. It diminishes their respect for the King's commission."

Sharpe knew he had deserved the reproof, but he was not willing to give Slingsby an inch. "You think men respect the King's commission?" he asked instead.

"Naturally." Slingsby sounded shocked at the question. "Of course!"

"I didn't," Sharpe said, and wondered if he smelled rum on Slingsby's breath. "I didn't respect the King's commission," he went on, deciding he had imagined the smell, "not when I marched in the ranks. I thought most jack-puddings were overpaid bastards."

"Sharpe," Slingsby expostulated, but whatever he was about to say dried on his tongue, for he saw the dragoons appear on the lower slope.

"Fifty or so of them," Sharpe said, "and coming this way."

"We should deploy, perhaps?" Slingsby indicated the eastern slope that was dotted with boulders which would hide a skirmish line very efficiently. The Lieutenant straightened his back and snapped his boot heels together. "Be an honor to lead the men down the hill, Sharpe."

"It might be a bloody honor," Sharpe said sarcastically, "but it would still be bloody suicide. If we're going to fight the bastards," he went on, "then I'd rather be on a hilltop than scattered halfway down a slope. Dragoons like skirmish lines, Slingsby. It gives them sword practice." He turned to look at the shrine. There were two small shuttered windows on the wall facing him and he reckoned they would make good loopholes if he did have to defend the hilltop. "How long till sunset?"

"Ten minutes less than three hours," Slingsby said instantly.

Sharpe grunted. He doubted the dragoons would attack, but if they did he could easily hold them off till dusk, and no dragoon would linger in hostile country after nightfall for fear of the partisans. "You stay here," he ordered Slingsby, "watch them and don't do anything without asking me. Do you understand that?"

Slingsby looked offended, as he had every right to be. "Of course I understand it," he said in a tone of protest.

"Don't take men off the hilltop, Lieutenant," Sharpe said, "and that's an order." He strode towards the shrine, wondering whether his men would be able to knock a few loopholes in its ancient stone walls. They did not have the right tools, no sledgehammers or crowbars, but the stonework looked old and its mortar was crumbling.

To his surprise his path to the shrine door was barred by Major Ferreira and one of the civilians. "The door is locked, Captain," the Portuguese officer said.

"Then I'll break it down," Sharpe answered.

"It is a shrine," Ferreira said reprovingly.

"Then I'll say a prayer for forgiveness after I've knocked it down," Sharpe said and he tried to get past the Major who held up a hand to stop him. Sharpe looked exasperated. "There are fifty French dragoons coming this way, Major," Sharpe said, "and I'm using the shrine to protect my men."

"Your work is done here," Ferreira said harshly, "and you should go." Sharpe said nothing. Instead he tried once more to get past the two men, but they still blocked him. "I'm giving you an order, Captain," the Portuguese officer insisted. "Leave now."

The civilian standing with Ferreira had taken off his coat and rolled up his shirtsleeves to reveal massive arms, both tattooed with fouled anchors. So far Sharpe had taken little notice of the man, other than to be impressed by his imposing physical size, but now he looked into the civilian's face and saw pure animosity. The man was built like a prizefighter, tattooed like a sailor, and there was an unmistakable message in his scarred, brutish face which was astonishing in its ugliness. He had a heavy brow, a big jaw, a flattened nose, and eyes that were like a beast's eyes. Nothing showed there except the desire to fight. And he wanted the fight to be man to man, fist against fist, and he looked disappointed when Sharpe stepped a pace backwards.

"I see you are sensible," Ferreira said silkily.

"I'm known for it," Sharpe said, then raised his voice. "Sergeant Harper!"

The big Irishman appeared around the side of the shrine and saw the confrontation. The big man, broader and taller than Harper, who was one of the strongest men in the army, had his fists clenched. He looked like a bulldog waiting to be unleashed, and Harper knew how to treat mad dogs. He let the volley gun slip from his shoulder. It was a curious weapon, made for the Royal Navy, and intended to be used from the deck of a ship to clear enemy marksmen from their fighting tops. Seven half-inch barrels were clustered together, fired by a single flintlock, and at sea the gun had proved too powerful, as often as not breaking the shoulder of the man who fired it, but Patrick Harper was big enough to make the seven-barrel gun look small and now he casually pointed it at the vast brute who blocked Sharpe's path. The gun was not cocked, but none of the civilians seemed to notice that. "You have trouble, sir?" Harper asked innocently.

Ferreira looked alarmed, as well he might. Harper's appearance had prompted some of the other civilians to draw pistols, and the hillside was suddenly loud as flints were clicked back. Major Ferreira, fearing a bloodbath, snapped at them to lower their guns. None obeyed until the big man, the bare-fisted brute, snarled at them and then they hurriedly lowered their flints, holstered their weapons and looked scared of the big man's disapproval. All the civilians were hard-looking rogues, reminding Sharpe of the cutthroats who ruled the streets of East London where he had spent his childhood, yet their leader, the man with the brutish face and muscled body, was the oddest and most frightening of them. He was a street fighter, that much was obvious from the broken nose and the scars on his forehead and cheeks, but he was also wealthy, for his linen shirt was of fine quality, his breeches cut from the best broadcloth and his gold-tasseled boots were made from soft expensive leather. He looked to be around forty years old, in the prime of life, confident in his sheer size. The man glanced at Harper, evidently judging the Irishman as a possible opponent, then unexpectedly smiled and picked up his coat which he brushed down before putting on. "What is in the shrine," the big man stepped towards Sharpe, "is my property." His English was heavily accented and spoken in a voice like gravel.

"And who are you?" Sharpe demanded.

"Allow me to name Senhor . . ." Ferreira began to answer.

"My name is Ferragus," the big man interrupted.

"Ferragus," Ferreira repeated, then introduced Sharpe. "Capitão Sharpe." He offered Ferragus a shrug as if to suggest that events were beyond his control.

Ferragus towered over Sharpe. "Your work is done here, Captain. The tower is no more, so you may go."

Sharpe stepped back out of the huge man's shadow, sideways to get around him and then went to the shrine and heard the distinctive sound of the volley gun's ratchet scraping as Harper cocked it. "Careful, now," the Irishman said, "it only takes a tremor for this bastard to go off and it would make a terrible mess of your shirt, sir." Ferragus had plainly turned to intercept Sharpe, but the huge gun checked him.

The shrine door was unlocked. Sharpe pushed it open and it took a moment for his eyes to adjust from the bright sunlight to the shrine's black shadows, but then he saw what was inside and swore.

He had expected a bare country shrine like the dozens of others he had seen, but instead the small building was heaped with sacks, so many sacks that the only space left was a narrow passage leading to a crude altar on which a blue-gowned image of the Virgin Mary was festooned with little slips of paper left by desperate peasants who came to the hilltop in search of a miracle. Now the Virgin gazed sadly on the sacks as Sharpe drew his sword and stabbed one. He was rewarded by a trickle of flour. He tried another sack further down and still more flour sifted to the bare earth floor. Ferragus had seen what Sharpe had done and harangued Ferreira who, reluctantly, came into the shrine. "The flour is here with my government's knowledge," the Major said.

"You can prove that?" Sharpe asked. "Got a piece of paper, have you?"

"It is the business of the Portuguese government," Ferreira said stiffly, "and you will leave."

"I have orders," Sharpe countered. "We all have orders. There's to be no food left for the French. None." He stabbed another sack, then turned as Ferragus came into the shrine, his bulk shadowing the doorway. He moved ominously down the narrow passage between the sacks, filling it, and Sharpe suddenly coughed loudly and scuffed his feet as Ferreira squeezed into the sacks to let Ferragus past.

The huge man held out a hand to Sharpe. He was holding coins, gold coins, maybe a dozen thick gold coins, bigger than English guineas and probably adding up to three years' salary for Sharpe. "You and I can talk," Ferragus said.

"Sergeant Harper!" Sharpe called past the looming Ferragus. "What are those bloody Crapauds doing?"

"Keeping their distance, sir. Staying well off, they are."

Sharpe looked up at Ferragus. "You're not surprised there are French dragoons coming, are you? Expecting them, were you?"

"I am asking you to go," Ferragus said, moving closer to Sharpe. "I am being polite, Captain."

"Hurts, don't it?" Sharpe said. "And what if I don't go? What if I obey my orders, *senhor*, and get rid of this food?"

Ferragus was plainly unused to being challenged for he seemed to shiver, as if forcing himself to be calm. "I can reach into your little army, Captain," he said in his deep voice, "and I can find you, and I can make you regret today."

"Are you threatening me?" Sharpe asked in astonishment. Major Ferreira, behind Ferragus, made some soothing noises, but both men ignored him.

"Take the money," Ferragus said.

When Sharpe had coughed and scuffed his feet he had been making enough noise to smother the sound of his rifle being cocked. It hung from his right shoulder, the muzzle just behind his ear, and now he moved his right hand back to the trigger. He looked down at the coins and Ferragus must have thought he had tempted Sharpe for he thrust the gold closer, and Sharpe looked up into his eyes and pressed the trigger.

The shot slammed into the roof tiles and filled the shrine with smoke and noise. The sound deafened Sharpe and it distracted Ferragus for half a second, the half second in which Sharpe brought up his right knee into the big man's groin, following it with a thrust of his left hand, fingers rigid, into Ferragus's eyes and then his right hand, knuckles clenched, into his Adam's apple. He reckoned he had stood no chance in a fair fight, but Sharpe, like Ferragus, reckoned fair fights were for fools. He knew he had to put Ferragus down fast and hurt him so bad that the huge man could not fight back, and he had done it in a heartbeat, for the big man was bent over, filled with pain and fighting for breath, and Sharpe cleared him from the passage by dragging him into the space in front of the altar and then walked past a horrified Ferreira. "You got anything to say to me, Major?" Sharpe asked, and when Ferreira dumbly shook his head Sharpe made his way back into the sunlight. "Lieutenant Slingsby!" he called. "What are those damned dragoons doing?"

"Keeping their distance, Sharpe," Slingsby said. "What was that shot?"

"I was showing a Portuguese fellow how a rifle works," Sharpe said. "How much distance?"

"At least half a mile. Bottom of the hill."

"Watch them," Sharpe said, "and I want thirty men in here now. Mister Iliffe! Sergeant McGovern!"

He left Ensign Iliffe in nominal charge of the thirty men who were to haul the sacks out of the shrine. Once outside, the sacks were slit open and their contents scattered across the hilltop. Ferragus came limping from the shrine and his men looked confused and angry, but they were hugely outnumbered and there was nothing they could do. Ferragus had regained his breath, though he was having trouble standing upright. He spoke bitterly to Ferreira, but the Major managed to talk some sense into the big man and, at last, they all mounted their horses and, with a last resentful look at Sharpe, rode down the westwards track.

Sharpe watched them retreat then went to join Slingsby. Behind him the telegraph tower burned fiercely, suddenly keeling over with a great splintering noise and an explosion of sparks. "Where are the Crapauds?"

"In that gully." Slingsby pointed to a patch of dead ground near the bottom of the hill. "Dismounted now."

Sharpe used his telescope and saw two of the green-uniformed men crouching behind boulders. One of them had a telescope and was watching the hilltop and Sharpe gave the man a cheerful wave. "Not much bloody use there, are they?" he said.

"They could be planning to attack us." Slingsby suggested eagerly.

"Not unless they're tired of life," Sharpe said, reckoning the dragoons had been beckoned westwards by the white flag on the telegraph tower, and now that the flag had been replaced by a plume of smoke they were undecided what to do. He trained his glass farther south and saw there was still gun smoke in the valley where the main road ran beside the river. The rearguard was evidently holding its own, but they would have to retreat soon for, farther east, he could now see the main enemy army that showed as dark columns marching in fields. They were a very long way off, scarce visible even through the glass, but they were there, a shadowed horde coming to drive the British out of central Portugal. *L'Armée de Portugal*, the French called it, the army that was meant to whip the redcoats clear to Lisbon, then out to sea, so that Portugal would at last be placed under the tricolor, but the army of Portugal was in for a surprise. Marshal Masséna would march into an empty land and then find himself facing the Lines of Torres Vedras.

"See anything, Sharpe?" Slingsby stepped closer, plainly wanting to borrow the telescope.

"Have you been drinking rum?" Sharpe asked, again getting a whiff of the spirit.

Slingsby looked alarmed, then offended. "Put it on the skin," he said gruffly, slapping his face, "to keep off the flies."

"You do what?"

"Trick I learned in the islands."

"Bloody hell," Sharpe said, then collapsed the glass and put it into his pocket. "There are Frogs over there," he said, pointing southeast, "thousands of goddamn bloody Frogs."

He left the Lieutenant gazing at the distant army and went back to chivvy the redcoats who had formed a chain to sling the sacks out onto the hillside which now looked as though it were ankle deep in snow. Flour drifted like powder smoke from the summit, fell softly, made mounds, and still more sacks were hurled out the door. Sharpe reckoned it would take a couple of hours to empty the shrine. He ordered ten riflemen to join the work and sent ten of the redcoats to join Slingsby's piquet. He did not want his redcoats to start whining that they did all the work while the riflemen got the easy jobs. Sharpe gave them a hand himself, standing in the line and tossing sacks through the door as the collapsed telegraph burned itself out, its windblown cinders staining the white flour with black spots.

Slingsby came just as the last sacks were being destroyed. "Dragoons have gone, Sharpe," he reported. "Reckon they saw us and rode off."

"Good." Sharpe forced himself to sound civil, then went to join Harper who was watching the dragoons ride away. "They didn't want to play with us, Pat?"

"Then they've more sense than that big Portuguese fellow," Harper said. "Give him a headache, did you?"

"Bastard wanted to bribe me."

"Oh, it's a wicked world," Harper said, "and there's me always dreaming of getting a wee bribe." He slung the seven-barrel gun on his shoulder. "So what were those fellows doing up here?"

"No good," Sharpe said, brushing his hands before pulling on his mended jacket that was now smeared with flour. "Mister bloody Ferragus was selling that flour to the Crapauds, Pat, and that bloody Portuguese Major was in it up to his arse."

"Did they tell you that now?"

"Of course they didn't," Sharpe said, "but what else were they doing? Jesus! They were flying a white flag to tell the Frogs it was safe up here and if we hadn't arrived, Pat, they'd have sold that flour."

"God and his saints preserve us from evil," Harper said in amusement, "and it's a pity the dragoons didn't come up to play."

"Pity! Why the hell would we want a fight for no purpose?"

"Because you could have got yourself one of their horses, sir," Harper said, "of course."

"And why would I want a bloody horse?"

"Because Mister Slingsby's getting one, so he is. Told me so himself. The Colonel's giving him a horse, he is."

"No bloody business of mine," Sharpe said, but the thought of Lieutenant Slingsby on a horse nevertheless annoyed him. A horse, whether Sharpe wanted one or not, was a symbol of status. Bloody Slingsby, he thought, and stared at the distant hills and saw how low the sun had sunk. "Let's go home," he said.

"Yes, sir," Harper said. He knew precisely why Mister Sharpe was in a bad mood, but he could not say as much. Officers were supposed to be brothers in arms, not blood enemies.

They marched in the dusk, leaving the hilltop white and smoking. Ahead was the army and behind it the French.

Who had come back to Portugal.

✧

MISS SARAH FRY, she had always disliked her last name, rapped a hand on the table. "In English," she insisted, "in English."

Tomas and Maria, eight and seven respectively, looked grumpy, but obediently changed from their native Portuguese to English. "'Robert has a hoop,'" Tomas read. "'Look, the hoop is red.'"

"When are the French coming?" Maria asked.

"The French will not come," Sarah said briskly, "because Lord Wellington will stop them. What color is the hoop, Maria?"

"*Rouge*," Maria answered in French. "So if the French are not coming why are we loading the wagons?"

"We do French on Tuesdays and Thursdays," Sarah said briskly, "and today is?"

"Wednesday," said Tomas.

"Read on," Sarah said, and she gazed out of the window to where the servants were putting furniture onto a wagon. The French were coming and everyone had been ordered to leave Coimbra and go south towards Lisbon. Some folk said the French approach was just a rumor and were refusing to leave, others had already gone. Sarah did not know what to believe, only that she had surprised herself by welcoming the excitement. She had been the governess in the Ferreira household for just three months and she suspected that the French invasion might be the means to extricate herself from a position that she now understood had been a mistake. She was thinking about her uncertain future when she realized that Maria was giggling because Tomas had just read that the donkey was blue, and that was nonsense, and Miss Fry was not a young woman to tolerate nonsense. She rapped her knuckles on the crown of Tomas's head. "What color is the donkey?" she demanded.

"Brown," Tomas said.

"Brown," Sarah agreed, giving him another smart tap, "and what are you?"

"A blockhead," Tomas said, and then, under his breath, added, "*Cadela*."

It meant "bitch," and Tomas had said it slightly too loudly and was rewarded with a smart crack on the side of his head. "I detest bad language," Sarah said angrily, adding a second slap, "and I detest rudeness, and if you cannot show good manners then I will ask your father to beat you."

The mention of Major Ferreira snapped the two children to attention and a gloom descended over the schoolroom as Tomas struggled with the next page. It was essential for a Portuguese child to learn English and French if, when they grew up, they were to be accounted gentlefolk. Sarah wondered why they did not learn Spanish, but when she had suggested it to the Major he had looked at her with utter fury. The Spanish, he had answered, were the offspring of goats and monkeys, and his children would not foul their tongues with their savage language. So Tomas and Maria were being schooled in French and English by their governess who was twenty-two years old, blue-eyed, fair-haired and worried for her future.

Her father had died when Sarah was ten and her mother a year later, and Sarah had been raised by an uncle who had reluctantly paid for her schooling, but refused to provide any kind of dowry when she had reached eighteen, and so, cut off from the more lucrative part of the marriage market, she had become a nursery maid for the children of an English diplomat who had been posted to Lisbon and it was there that Major Ferreira's wife had encountered her and offered to double her salary if she would school her two children. "I want our children to be polished," Beatriz Ferreira had said.

And so Sarah was in Coimbra, polishing the children and counting the heavy ticks of the big clock in the hall as, Tomas and Maria took turns to read from *Early Joys for Infant Souls*. " 'The cow is sabbler,' " Maria read.

"Sable," Sarah corrected her.

"What's sable?"

"Black."

"Then why doesn't it say black?"

"Because it says sable. Read on."

"Why aren't we leaving?" Maria asked.

"That is a question you must put to your father," Sarah said, and she wished she knew the answer herself. Coimbra was evidently to be abandoned to the French, but the authorities insisted that the enemy should find nothing in the city except empty buildings. Every warehouse, larder and shop was to be stripped as bare as Mother Hubbard's cupboard. The French were to enter a barren land and there starve, but it seemed to Sarah, when she took her two young charges for their daily walks, that most of the storehouses were still full and the riverside quays were thickly heaped with British provisions. Some of the wealthy folk had gone, transporting their possessions on wagons, but Major Ferreira had evidently decided to wait until the last moment. He had ordered his best furniture packed onto a wagon in readiness, but he was curiously reluctant to take the decision to leave Coimbra. Sarah, before the Major had ridden north to join the army, had asked him why he did not send the household to Lisbon and he had turned on her with his fierce gaze, seemed puzzled by her question, then dismissively told her not to worry.

Yet she did, and she was worried about Major Ferreira too. He was a generous employer, but he did not come from the highest rank of Portuguese society. There were no aristocrats in Ferreira's ancestry, no titles and no great landed estates. His father had been a professor of philosophy who had unexpectedly inherited wealth from a distant relative, and that legacy enabled Major Ferreira to live well, but not magnificently. A governess was judged not by how effectively she managed the children in her care, but by the social status of the family for whom she worked, and in Coimbra Major Ferreira possessed neither the advantages of aristocracy, nor the gift of great intelligence which was much admired in the university city. And as for his brother! Sarah's mother, God rest her soul, would have described Ferragus as being common as muck. He was the black sheep of the family, the willful, wayward son who had run away as a child and come back rich, not to settle, but to terrorize the city like a wolf finding a home in the sheep pen. Sarah was frightened of Ferragus; everyone except the Major was frightened of Ferragus, and no wonder.

The gossip in Coimbra said Ferragus was a bad man, a dishonest man, a crook even, and Major Ferreira was tarred by that brush, and in turn Sarah was smeared by it.

But she was trapped with the family, for she did not have enough money to pay her fare back to England and even if she got there, how was she to secure a new post without a glowing testimonial from her last employers? It was a dilemma, but Miss Sarah Fry was not a timid young woman and she faced the dilemma, as she faced the French invasion, with a sense that she would survive. Life was not to be suffered, it was to be exploited.

" 'Reynard is red,' " Maria read.

The clock ticked on.

※

IT WAS NOT WAR as Sharpe knew it. The South Essex, withdrawing westwards into central Portugal, was now the army's rearguard, though two regiments of cavalry and a troop of horse gunners were behind them, serving as a screen to deter the enemy's forward cavalry units. The French were not pressing hard and so the South Essex had time to destroy whatever provisions they found, whether it was the harvest, an orchard or livestock, for nothing was to be left for the enemy. By rights every inhabitant and every scrap of food should already have gone south to find refuge behind the Lines of Torres Vedras, but it was astonishing how much remained. In one village they found a herd of goats hidden in a barn, and in another a great vat of olive oil. The goats were put to the bayonet and their corpses hurriedly buried in a ditch, and the oil was spilled onto the ground. French armies famously lived off the land, stealing what they needed, so the land was to be ravaged.

There was no evidence of a French pursuit. None of the galloper guns fired and no wounded cavalrymen appeared after a brief clash of sabers. Sharpe continually looked to the east and thought he saw the smear of dust in the sky kicked up by an army's boots, but it could easily have been a heat haze. There was an explosion at mid-morning, but it came from ahead where, in a deep valley, British engineers had blown a bridge. The South Essex grumbled because they had to wade through the river rather than cross it by a roadway, but if the bridge had been left they would have grumbled at being denied the chance to scoop up water as they waded the river.

Lieutenant Colonel the Honorable William Lawford, commanding officer of the first battalion of the South Essex regiment, spent much of the day at the rear of the column where he rode a new horse, a black gelding, of which he was absurdly proud. "I gave Portia to Slingsby," he told Sharpe. Portia was his previous horse, a mare that Slingsby now rode and thus appeared, to any casual onlooker, to be the commander of the light company. Lawford must have been aware of the contrast because he told Sharpe that officers ought to ride. "It gives their men something to look up to, Sharpe," he said. "You can afford a horse, can't you?"

What Sharpe could or could not afford was not something he intended to share with the Colonel. "I'd prefer they looked up to me instead of at the horse, sir," Sharpe commented instead.

"You know what I mean." Lawford refused to be offended. "If you like, Sharpe, I'll cast about and find you something serviceable? Major Pearson of the gunners was talking about selling one of his hacks and I can probably squeeze a fair price from him."

Sharpe said nothing. He was not fond of horses, but he nevertheless felt jealous that bloody Slingsby was riding one. Lawford waited for a response and, when none came, he spurred the gelding so that it picked up its hooves and trotted a few paces ahead. "So what do you think, Sharpe, eh?" the Colonel demanded.

"Think, sir?"

"Of Lightning! That's his name. Lightning." The Colonel patted the horse's neck. "Isn't he superb?"

Sharpe stared at the horse, said nothing.

"Come, Sharpe!" Lawford encouraged him. "Can't you see his quality, eh?"

"He's got four legs, sir," Sharpe said.

"Oh, Sharpe!" the Colonel remonstrated. "Really! Is that all you can say?" Lawford turned to Harper instead. "What do you make of him, Sergeant?"

"He's wonderful, sir," Harper said with genuine enthusiasm, "just wonderful. Would he be Irish now?"

"He is!" Lawford was delighted. "He is! Bred in County Meath. I can see you know your horses, Sergeant." The Colonel fondled the gelding's ears. "He takes fences like the wind. He'll hunt magnificently. Can't wait to get him home and set him at a few damn great hedgerows." He leaned towards Sharpe and lowered his voice. "He cost me a few pennies, I can tell you."

"I'm sure he did, sir," Sharpe said, "and did you pass on my message about the telegraph station?"

"I did," Lawford said, "but they're busy at headquarters, Sharpe, damned busy, and I doubt they'll worry too much about a few pounds of flour. Still, you did the right thing."

"I wasn't thinking of the flour, sir," Sharpe said, "but about Major Ferreira."

"I'm sure there's an innocent explanation," Lawford said airily, then rode ahead, leaving Sharpe scowling. He liked Lawford, whom he had known years before in India and who was a clever, genial man whose only fault, perhaps, was a tendency to avoid trouble. Not fighting trouble: Lawford had never shirked a fight with the French, but he hated confrontations within his own ranks. By nature he was a diplomat, always trying to smooth the corners and find areas of agreement, and Sharpe was hardly surprised that the Colonel had shied away from accusing Major Ferreira of dishonesty. In Lawford's world it was always best to believe that yapping dogs were really sleeping.

So Sharpe put the confrontation of the previous day out of his mind and trudged on, half his thoughts conscious of what every man in the company was doing and the other half thinking of Teresa and Josefina, and he was still thinking of them when a horseman rode past him in the opposite direction, wheeled around in a flurry of dust and called to him. "In trouble again, Richard?"

Sharpe, startled out of his daydream, looked up to see Major Hogan looking indecently cheerful. "I'm in trouble, sir?"

"You do sound grim," Hogan said. "Get out of bed the wrong side, did you?"

"I was promised a month's leave, sir. A bloody month! And I got a week."

"I'm sure you didn't waste it," Hogan said. He was an Irishman, a Royal Engineer whose shrewdness had taken him away from engineering duties to serve Wellington as the man who collected every scrap of information about the enemy. Hogan had to sift rumors brought by peddlers, traders and deserters, he had to appraise every message sent by the partisans who harried the French on both sides of the frontier between Spain and Portugal, and he had to decipher the dispatches, captured by the partisans from French messengers, some of them still stained with blood. He was also an old friend of Sharpe, and one who now frowned at the rifleman. "A gentleman came to headquarters last night," he said, "to lodge an official complaint about you. He wanted to see the Peer, but Wellington's much too busy fighting the war, so the man was fobbed off on me. Luckily for you."

"A gentleman?"

"I stretch the word to its uttermost limits," Hogan said. "Ferragus."

"That bastard."

"Illegitimacy is probably the one thing he cannot be accused of," Hogan said.

"So what did he say?"

"That you hit him," Hogan said.

"He can tell the truth, then," Sharpe admitted.

"Good God, Richard!" Hogan examined Sharpe. "You don't seem hurt. You really hit him?"

"Flattened the bastard," Sharpe said. "Did he tell you why?"

"Not precisely, but I can guess. Was he planning to sell food to the enemy?"

"Close on two tons of flour," Sharpe said, "and he had a bloody Portuguese officer with him."

"His brother," Hogan said, "Major Ferreira."

"His brother!"

"Not much alike, are they? But yes, they're brothers. Pedro Ferreira stayed home, went to school, joined the army, married decently, lives respectably, and his brother ran away in search of sinks of iniquity. Ferragus is a nickname, taken from some legendary Portuguese giant who was reputed to have skin that couldn't be pierced by a sword. Useful, that. But his brother is more useful. Major Ferreira does for the Portuguese what I do for the Peer, though I fancy he isn't quite as efficient as I am. But he has friends in the French headquarters."

"Friends?" Sharpe sounded skeptical.

"More than a few Portuguese joined the French," Hogan said. "They're mostly idealists who think they're fighting for liberty, justice, brotherhood and all that airy nonsense. Major Ferreira somehow stays in touch with them, which is damned useful. But as for Ferragus!" Hogan paused, staring uphill to where a hawk hovered above the pale grass. "Our giant is a bad lot, Richard, about as bad as they come. You know where he learned English?"

"How would I?"

"He joined a ship as a seaman when he ran away from home," Hogan said, ignoring Sharpe's surly response, "and then had the misfortune to be pressed into the Royal Navy. He learned lower-deck English, made a reputation as the fiercest bare-knuckle fighter in the Atlantic fleet, then deserted in the West Indies. He apparently joined a slave ship and rose up through the ranks. Now he calls himself a merchant, but I doubt he trades in anything legal."

"Slaves?"

"Not any longer," Hogan said, "but that's how he made his money. Shipping the poor devils from the Guinea coast to Brazil. Now he lives in Coimbra where he's rich and makes his money in mysterious ways. He's quite an impressive man, don't you think, and not without his advantages?"

"Advantages?"

"Major Ferreira claims his brother has contacts throughout Portugal and western Spain, which sounds very likely."

"So you let him get away with treason?"

"Something like that," Hogan agreed equably. "Two tons of flour isn't much, not in the greater scheme of things, and Major Ferreira persuades me his brother is on our side. Whatever, I apologized to our giant, said you were a crude man of no refinement, assured him that you would be severely reprimanded, which you may now consider done, and promised that he would never see you again." Hogan beamed at Sharpe. "So the matter is closed."

"So I do my duty," Sharpe said, "and land in the shit."

"You have at last seized the essence of soldiering," Hogan said happily, "and Marshal Masséna is landing in the same place."

"He is?" Sharpe asked. "I thought we were retreating and he was advancing?"

Hogan laughed. "There are three roads he could have chosen, Richard, two very good ones and one quite rotten one, and in his wisdom he chose this one, the bad one." It was indeed a bad road, merely two rutted wheel tracks either side of a strip of grass and weeds, and littered with rocks large enough to break a wagon or gun wheel. "And this bad road," Hogan went on, "leads straight to a place called Bussaco."

"Am I supposed to have heard of it?"

"A very bad place," Hogan went on, "for anyone attacking it. And the Peer is gathering troops there in hope of giving Monsieur Masséna a bloody nose. Something to look forward to, Richard, something to anticipate." He raised a hand, kicked back his heels and rode ahead, nodding to Major Forrest who came the other way.

"Two ovens in the next village, Sharpe," Forrest said, "and the Colonel would like your lads to deal with them."

The ovens were great brick caves in which the villagers had baked their bread. The light company used pickaxes to reduce them to rubble so the French could not use them. They left the precious ovens destroyed and then marched on.

To a place called Bussaco.

CHAPTER 2

ROBERT KNOWLES AND RICHARD SHARPE stood on the Bussaco ridge and stared at l'Armée de Portugal that, battalion by battalion, battery by battery and squadron by squadron, streamed from the eastern hills to fill the valley.

The British and Portuguese armies had occupied a great ridge that ran north and south and so blocked the road on which the French were advancing towards Lisbon. The ridge, Knowles guessed, was almost a thousand feet above the surrounding countryside, and its eastward flank, which faced the French, was precipitously steep. Two roads zigzagged their way up that slope, snaking between heather, gorse and rocks, the better road reaching the ridge's crest towards its northern end just above a small village perched on a ledge of the ridge. Down in the valley, beyond a glinting stream, lay a scatter of other small villages and the French were making their way along farm tracks to occupy those lower settlements.

The British and Portuguese had a bird's-eye view of the enemy who came from a wooded defile in the lower hills, then marched past a windmill before turning south to take up their positions. They, in turn, could look up the high, bare slope and see a handful of British and Portuguese officers watching them. The army itself, with most of its guns, was hidden from the French. The ridge was ten miles long, a natural rampart, and General Wellington had ordered that his men were to stay well back from its wide crest so that the arriving French would have no idea which part of the high ground was most heavily defended. "Quite a privilege," Knowles said reverently.

"A privilege?" Sharpe asked sourly.

"To see such a thing," Knowles explained, gesturing at the enemy, and it was, in truth, a fine sight to see so many thousands of men at one time. The infantry marched in loose formations, their blue uniforms pale against the green of the valley, while the horsemen, released from the discipline of the march, galloped beside the stream to leave plumes of dust. And still they came from the defile, the might of France. A band was playing close to the windmill and, though the music was too far away to be heard, Sharpe fancied he could hear the thump of the bass drum like a distant heartbeat. "A whole army!" Knowles enthused. "I should have brought my sketching pad. It would make a fine picture."

"What would make a fine picture," Sharpe said, "is to see the buggers march up this hill and get slaughtered."

"You think they won't?"

"I think they'd be mad to try," Sharpe said, then frowned at Knowles. "Do you like being Adjutant?" he asked abruptly.

Knowles hesitated, sensing that the conversation was approaching dangerous ground, but he had been Sharpe's Lieutenant before becoming Adjutant and he liked his old company commander. "Not excessively," he admitted.

"It's always been a captain's job," Sharpe said, "so why is he giving it to you?"

"The Colonel feels the experience will be advantageous to me," Knowles said stiffly.

"Advantageous," Sharpe said bitterly. "It ain't your advantage he wants, Robert. He wants that piece of gristle to take over my company. That's what he wants. He wants bloody Slingsby to be Captain of the light company." Sharpe had no evidence for that, the Colonel had never said as much, but it was the only explanation that made sense to him. "So he had to get you out of the way," Sharpe finished, knowing he had said too much, but the rancor was biting at him and Knowles was a friend who would be discreet about Sharpe's outburst.

Knowles frowned, then flapped at an insistent fly. "I truly believe," he said after thinking for a moment, "that the Colonel believes he's doing you a favor."

"Me! A favor? By giving me Slingsby!"

"Slingsby has experience, Richard," Knowles said, "much more than I do."

"But you're a good officer and he's a jack-pudding. Who the hell is he anyway?"

"He's the Colonel's brother-in-law," Knowles explained.

"I know that," Sharpe said impatiently, "but who is he?"

"The man who married Mrs. Lawford's sister," Knowles said, refusing to be drawn.

"That tells you everything you bloody need to know," Sharpe said grimly, "but he doesn't seem the kind of fellow Lawford would want as a brother-in-law. Not enough tone."

"We don't choose our relatives," Knowles said, "and I'm sure he's a gentleman."

"Bloody hell," Sharpe grumbled.

"And he must have been delighted to get out of the 55th," Knowles went on, ignoring Sharpe's moroseness. "God, most of that regiment died of the yellow fever in the West Indies. He's much safer here, even with those fellows threatening." Knowles nodded down at the French troops.

"Then why the hell didn't he purchase a captaincy?"

"Six months short of requirements," Knowles said. A lieutenant was not allowed to purchase a captaincy until he had served three years in the lower rank, a newly introduced rule that had caused much grumbling among wealthy officers who wanted swifter preferment.

"But why did he join up so late?" Sharpe asked. If Slingsby was thirty then he could not have become a lieutenant before he was twenty-seven, by which age some men were majors. Most officers, like young Iliffe, joined long before they were twenty and it was odd to find a man coming to the army so late.

"I believe . . ." Knowles said, then reddened and checked his words. "New troops," he said instead, pointing down the slope to where a French regiment, its blue coats unnaturally bright, marched past the windmill. "I hear the Emperor has sent reinforcements to Spain," Knowles went on. "The French have nowhere else to fight these days. Austrians out of the war, Prussians doing nothing, which means Boney only has us to beat."

Sharpe ignored Knowles's summation of the Emperor's strategy. "You believe what?" he asked.

"Nothing. I said too much."

"You didn't say a bloody thing," Sharpe protested and waited, but Knowles still remained silent. "You want me to slit your skinny throat, Robert," Sharpe asked, "with a very blunt knife?"

Knowles smiled. "You mustn't repeat this, Richard."

"You know me, Robert, I never tell anyone anything. Cross my heart and hope to die, so tell me before I cut your legs off."

"I believe Mrs. Lawford's sister was in trouble. She found herself with child, she wasn't married and the man concerned was apparently a rogue."

"Wasn't me," Sharpe said quickly.

"Of course it wasn't you," Knowles said. He could be pedantically obvious at times.

Sharpe grinned. "So Slingsby was recruited to make her respectable?"

"Exactly. He's not from the topmost drawer, of course, but his family is more than acceptable. His father's a rector somewhere on the Essex coast, I believe, but they're not wealthy, and so Lawford's family rewarded Slingsby with a commission in the 55th, with a promise to exchange into the South Essex as soon as there was a vacancy. Which there was when poor Herrold died."

"Herrold?"

"Number three company," Knowles said, "arrived on a Monday, caught fever on Tuesday and was dead by Friday."

"So the idea," Sharpe said, watching a French gun battery being dragged along the track by the stream below, "is that bloody Slingsby gets quick promotion so that he's a worthy husband for the woman what couldn't keep her knees together."

"I wouldn't say that," Knowles said indignantly, then thought for a second. "Well, yes, I would say that. But the Colonel wants him to do well. After all, Slingsby did the family a favor and now they're trying to do one back."

"By giving him my bloody job," Sharpe said.

"Don't be absurd, Richard."

"Why else is the bugger here? They move you out of the way, give the bastard a horse and hope to God the French kill me." He fell silent, not only because he had said too much, but because Patrick Harper was approaching.

The big Sergeant greeted Knowles cheerfully. "We miss you, sir, we do."

"I can say the same, Sergeant," Knowles responded with real pleasure. "You're well?"

"Still breathing, sir, and that's what counts." Harper turned to look down into the valley. "Look at those daft bastards. Just lining up to be murdered."

"They'll take one look at this hill," Sharpe said, "and find another road."

Yet there was no sign that the French would take that good advice for the blue-uniformed battalions still marched steadily from the east and French gun batteries, dust flying from their big wheels, continued to arrive at the lower villages. Some French officers rode to the top of a spur which jutted east from the ridge and gazed through their telescopes at the few British and Portuguese officers visible where the better road crossed the ridge top. That road, the farther north of the two, zigzagged up the slope, climbing at first between gorse and heather, then cutting through vineyards beneath the small village perched on the slope. That was the road which led to Lisbon and to the completion of the Emperor's orders, which were to hurl the British out of Portugal so that the whole coastline of continental Europe would belong to the French.

Lieutenant Slingsby, his red coat newly brushed and his badges polished, came to offer his opinion of the enemy, and Sharpe, unable to stand the man's company, walked away southwards. He watched the French cutting down trees to make fires or shelters. Some small streams fell from the far hills to join and make a larger stream that flowed south towards the Mondego River which touched the ridge's southern end, and the bigger stream's banks were being trampled by horses, some from the gun teams, some cavalry mounts and some the officers' horses, all being given a drink after their march.

The French were concentrating in two places. One tangle of battalions was around the village from which the better road climbed to the northern end of the ridge, while others were two miles to the south, gathering at another village from which a track, passable to packhorses or men on foot, twisted to the ridge's crest. It was not a proper road, there were no ruts from carts, and in places the track almost vanished into the heather, but it did show the French that there was a route up the steep slope, and French batteries were now deploying either side of the village so that the guns could rake the track ahead of their advancing troops.

The sound of axes and falling trees came from behind Sharpe. One company from each battalion had been detailed to make a road just behind the ridge's crest, a road that would let Lord Wellington shift his forces anywhere along the hill's ten-mile length. Trees were being felled, bushes uprooted, rocks being rolled away and the soil smoothed so that British or Portuguese guns could be pulled swiftly to any danger point. It was a huge piece of work and Sharpe suspected it would all be wasted for the French would surely not be mad enough to climb the hill.

Except some were already climbing. A score of mounted officers, wanting a closer view of the British and Portuguese position, had ridden their horses along the summit of the spur which jutted out from the long ridge. The spur was less than half the height of the ridge, but it provided a platform on which troops could gather for an assault and the British and Portuguese gunners had plainly marked it as a target for, as the French horsemen neared the place where the spur joined the ridge, a cannon fired. The sound was flat and hard, startling a thousand birds up from the trees which grew thick on the ridge's reverse slope. The gun's smoke roiled in a gray-white cloud that was carried east on the small wind. The shell left a trace of powder smoke from its burning fuse as it arced down to explode a few paces beyond the French horsemen. One of the horses panicked and bolted back the way it had come, but the others seemed unworried as their riders took out telescopes and stared at the enemy above them.

Then two more guns fired, their sound echoing back from the eastern hills. One was evidently a howitzer for the smoke of its burning fuse went high in the sky before dropping towards the French. This time a horse was flung sideways to leave a smear of blood on the dry, pale heather. Sharpe was watching through his telescope and saw the unsaddled and evidently unwounded Frenchman get to his feet. He brushed himself down, drew a pistol and put his twitching horse out of its misery, then struggled to release the precious saddle. He trudged back eastwards, carrying saddle, saddlecloth and bridle.

More French, some mounted and some on foot, were coming to the spur. It seemed a madness to go where the guns were aiming, but dozens of French were wading through the stream and then climbing the low hill to stare up at the British and Portuguese. The gunfire continued. It was not the staccato fire of battle, but desultory shots as the gunners experimented with powder loads and fuse lengths. Too much powder and a shot would scream over the spur to explode somewhere above the stream, while if the fuse was cut too long the shell would land, bounce and come to rest with the fuse still smoking, giving the French time to skip out of the way before the shell exploded. Each detonation was a puff of dirty smoke, surprisingly small, but Sharpe could not see the deadly scraps of broken shell casing hiss away from each blast.

No more French horses or men were struck. They were well spread out and the shells obstinately fell in the gaps between the small groups of men who looked as carefree as folk out for a walk in a park. They stared up at the ridge, trying to determine where the defenses lay thickest, though it was surely obvious that the places where the two roads reached the summit would be the places to defend. Another score of cavalrymen, some in green coats and some in sky blue, splashed through the stream and spurred up the lower hill. The sun glinted on brass helmets, polished scabbards, stirrups and curb chains. It was, Sharpe thought, as though the French were playing cat and mouse with the sporadic shell fire. He saw a shell burst close by a group of infantrymen, but when the smoke cleared they were all standing and it seemed to him, though they were very far away, that they were laughing. They were confident, he thought, sure they were the best troops in the world, and their survival of the gunfire was a taunt to the defenders on the ridge's top.

The taunting was evidently too much, for a battalion of brown-jacketed Portuguese light troops appeared on the crest and, scattered in a double skirmish chain, advanced down the ridge's slope towards the spur. They went steadily downhill in two loose lines, one fifty paces behind the other, both spread out, giving a demonstration of how skirmishers went to war. Most troops fought shoulder to shoulder, but skirmishers like Sharpe went ahead of the line and, in the killing ground between the armies, tried to pick off the enemy skirmishers and then kill the officers behind so that when the two armies clashed, dense line against massive column, the enemy was already leaderless. Skirmishers rarely closed ranks. They fought close to the enemy where a bunch of men would make an easy target for enemy gunners, and so the light troops fought in loose formation, in pairs, one man shooting and then reloading as his comrade protected him.

The French watched the Portuguese come. They showed no alarm, nor did they advance any skirmishers of their own. The shells went on arcing down the slope, their detonations echoing dully from the eastern hills. The vast mass of the French were making their bivouacs, ignoring the small drama on the ridge, but a dozen cavalrymen, seeing easy meat in the scattered Portuguese skirmishers, kicked their horses up the hill.

By rights the cavalrymen should have decimated the skirmishers. Men in a loose formation were no match for swift cavalry and the French, half of them dragoons and the other half hussars, had drawn their long swords or curved sabers and were anticipating some practice cuts on helpless men. The Portuguese were armed with muskets and rifles, but once the guns were fired there would be no time to reload before the surviving horsemen reached them, and an empty gun was no defense against a dragoon's long blade. The cavalry were curving around to assault the flank of the line, a dozen horsemen approaching four Portuguese on foot, but the ridge was too steep for the horses, which began to labor. The advantage of the cavalry was speed, but the ridge stole their speed so that the horses were struggling and a rifle cracked, the smoke jetting above the grass, and a horse stumbled, twisted away and collapsed. Another two rifles fired and the French, realizing that the ridge was their enemy, turned away and galloped recklessly downhill. The unhorsed hussar followed on foot, abandoning his dying horse with its precious equipment to the Portuguese who cheered their small victory.

"I'm not sure the *cazadores* had orders to do that," a voice said behind Sharpe, who turned to see that Major Hogan had come to the ridge. "Hello, Richard," Hogan said cheerfully, "you look unhappy." He held out his hand for Sharpe's telescope.

"Cazadores?" Sharpe asked.

"Hunters. It's what the Portuguese call their skirmishers." Hogan was staring at the brown-coated skirmishers as he spoke. "It's rather a good name, don't you think? Hunters? Better than greenjackets."

"I'll stay a greenjacket," Sharpe said.

Hogan watched the cazadores for a few moments. Their riflemen had begun firing at the French on the spur, and that enemy prudently backed away. The Portuguese stayed where they were, not going down to the spur where the horsemen could attack them, content to have made their demonstration. Two guns fired, the shells falling into the empty space between the cazadores and the remaining French. "The Peer will be very unhappy," Hogan said. "He detests gunners firing at hopeless targets. It just reveals where his batteries are placed and it does no damn harm to the enemy." He turned the telescope to the valley and spent a long time looking at the enemy encampments beyond the stream. "We reckon Monsieur Masséna has sixty thousand men," he said, "and maybe a hundred guns."

"And us, sir?" Sharpe asked.

"Fifty thousand and sixty," Hogan said, giving Sharpe back the telescope, "and half of ours are Portuguese."

There was something in his tone that caught Sharpe's attention. "Is that bad?" he asked.

"We'll see, won't we?" Hogan said, then stamped his foot on the turf. "But we do have this." He meant the ridge.

"Those lads seem eager enough." Sharpe nodded at the cazadores who were now retreating up the hill.

"Eagerness in new troops is quickly wiped away by gunfire," Hogan said.

"I doubt we'll find out," Sharpe said. "The Crapauds won't attack up here. They're not mad."

"I certainly wouldn't want to attack up this slope," Hogan agreed. "My suspicion is that they'll spend the day staring at us, then go away."

"Back to Spain?"

"Good Lord, no. If they did but know it there's a fine road that loops round the top of this ridge," he pointed north, "and they don't need to fight us here at all. They'll find that road eventually. Pity, really. This would be a grand place to give them a bloody nose. But they may come. They reckon the Portuguese aren't up to scratch, so perhaps they'll think it's worth an attempt."

"Are the Portuguese up to scratch?" Sharpe asked. The gunfire had ended, leaving scorched grass and small patches of smoke on the spur. The French, denied their game of dare, were drifting back towards their lines.

"We'll find out about the Portuguese if the French decide to have at us," Hogan said grimly, then smiled. "Can you come for supper tonight?"

"Tonight?" Sharpe was surprised by the question.

"I spoke with Colonel Lawford," Hogan said, "and he's happy to spare you, so long as the French aren't being a nuisance. Six o'clock, Richard, at the monastery. You know where that is?"

"No, sir."

"Go north," Hogan pointed up the ridge, "until you see a great stone wall. Find a gap in it, go downhill through the trees until you discover a path and follow that till you see rooftops. There'll be three of us sitting down."

"Three?" Sharpe asked suspiciously.

"You," Hogan said, "me and Major Ferreira."

"Ferreira!" Sharpe exclaimed. "Why's that slimy piece of traitorous shit having supper with us?"

Hogan sighed. "Has it occurred to you, Richard, that the two tons of flour might have been a bribe? Something to exchange for information?"

"Was it?"

"Ferreira says so. Do I believe him? I'm not sure. But whatever, Richard, I think he regrets what happened and wants to make his peace with us. It was his idea to have supper, and I must say I think it decent of him." Hogan saw Sharpe's reluctance. "Truly, Richard. We don't want resentments to fester between allies, do we?"

"We don't, sir?"

"Six o'clock, Richard," Hogan said firmly, "and try to convey the impression that you're enjoying yourself." The Irishman smiled, then walked back to the ridge's crest where officers were pacing off the ground to determine where each battalion would be positioned. Sharpe wished he had found a good excuse to miss the supper. It was not Hogan's company he wanted to avoid, but the Portuguese Major, and he felt increasingly bitter as he sat in the unseasonable warmth, watching the wind stir the heather beneath which an army, sixty thousand strong, had come to contest the ridge of Bussaco.

SHARPE SPENT the afternoon bringing the company books up to date, helped by Clayton, the company clerk, who had the annoying habit of saying the words aloud as he wrote them. "Isaiah Tongue, deceased," he said to himself, then blew on the ink. "Does he have a widow, sir?"

"Don't think so."

"He's owed four shillings and sixpence halfpenny is why I ask."

"Put it in the company fund."

"If we ever gets any wages," Clayton said gloomily. The company fund was where stray money went, not that there ever was much stray money, but wages owed to the dead were put there and, once in a while, it was spent on brandy, or to pay the company wives for the laundry. Some of those wives had come to the ridge's crest where, joined by scores of civilians, they were gazing down at the French. The civilians had all been ordered to go south, to find the safety of the countryside around Lisbon that was protected by the Lines of Torres Vedras, but plainly many had disobeyed for there were scores of Portuguese folk gawping at the invaders. Some of the spectators had brought bread, cheese and wine and now sat in groups eating and talking and pointing at the French, and a dozen monks, all with bare feet, were among them.

"Why don't they wear shoes?" Clayton asked.

"God knows."

Clayton frowned disapprovingly at a monk who had joined one of the small groups eating on the ridge. "*Déjeuner à la fourchette*," he said, sniffing with disapproval.

"Day-jay what?" Sharpe asked.

"Dinner with a fork," Clayton explained. He had been a footman in a great house before he joined the South Essex, and had a great knowledge of the gentry's strange ways. "It's what people of quality do, sir, when they don't want to spend a lot of money. Give 'em food and a fork and let 'em wander round the grounds sniffing the bloody flowers. All titter and giggle in the garden." He frowned at the monks. "Shoeless bloody papist monks," he said. The gowned men were not monks at all, but friars of the Discalced Carmelite order, two of whom were gravely inspecting a nine-pounder cannon. "And you should see inside their bloody monastery, sir," Clayton went on. "The altar in one of the chapels is smothered with wooden tits."

Sharpe gaped at Clayton. "It's smothered with what?"

"Wooden tits, sir, all painted to look real. Got nipples and everything! I took the ration returns down there, sir, and one of the guards showed me. I couldn't believe my eyes! Mind you, them monks ain't allowed the real things, are they, so perhaps they make do as best they can. Punishment book now, sir?"

"See if you can scuff up some tea instead," Sharpe suggested.

He drank the tea on the crest. The French were plainly not planning to attack this day for their troops were scattered about the bivouacs near the villages. Their numbers had grown so that the low ground was now dark with men, while nearer the ridge shirt sleeved gunners were piling shot beside the newly placed batteries. The position of those batteries suggested where the French would attack, if indeed they did, and Sharpe saw that the South Essex would be just to the left of any assault aimed up the rough southern track that had been barricaded near its top with felled trees, presumably to deter the French from dragging their artillery up towards the crest. More French guns were crowded close to the road at the northern end of the ridge, which suggested there would be two assaults, and Sharpe supposed they would be like every other French attack he had ever endured: great columns of men advancing to the beat of massed drums, hoping to batter their way through the Anglo-Portuguese line like giant rams. The vast columns were supposed to overawe inexperienced troops and Sharpe looked to his left where the officers of a Portuguese battalion were watching the enemy. Would they stand? The Portuguese

army had been reorganized in the last few months, but they were endur-
ing the third invasion of their country in three years, and so far no one
could pretend that the Portuguese army had covered itself in glory.

There was a parade and inspection of kit in the late afternoon, and
when it was done Sharpe walked north along the ridge until he saw the
high stone wall enclosing a great wood. The Portuguese and British soldiers, wanting passage through the wall, had knocked gaps in it and
Sharpe negotiated one such breach and went into the trees, eventually
finding a path which led downhill. There were odd-looking brick sheds
beside the path, equally spaced, each about the size of a gardener's pot-
ting shed, and Sharpe stopped at the first to peer through the door which
was made of iron bars. Inside were clay statues, life-size, showing a group
of women clustered about a half-naked man and then Sharpe saw the
crown of thorns and realized the central figure must be Jesus and that the
brick sheds had to be part of the monastery. All of the small buildings had
the eerie statues, and at several of the shrines shawled women were
kneeling in prayer. A very pretty girl was beside another, listening shyly to
an impassioned Portuguese officer who paused, embarrassed, as Sharpe
walked by. The officer began his harangue again as soon as Sharpe had
gone down a flight of stone steps that led to the monastery. An ancient
and gnarled olive tree grew by the entrance and a dozen saddled horses
were tethered to its branches, while two redcoats stood guard by the doorway. They ignored Sharpe as he ducked through the low archway into a
dark passageway lined with doors that were covered with thick layers of
cork. One of the doors was open and Sharpe looked inside to see a shirt
sleeved surgeon in a monk's small cell. The surgeon was sharpening a
scalpel. "I'm open for trade," he said cheerfully.

"Not today, sir. Do you know where I'll find Major Hogan?"

"End of the passage, door on the right."

The supper was awkward. They ate in one of the small cells that was
lined with cork to keep out the cold of the coming winter, and their meal
was a stew of goat and beans, with coarse bread, cheese and a plentiful
supply of wine. Hogan did his best to keep the conversation moving, but
Sharpe had little to say to Major Ferreira who never referred to the events
on the hilltop where Sharpe had burned the telegraph tower. Instead he

talked of his time in Brazil where he had commanded a fort in one of the Portuguese settlements. "The women are beautiful!" Ferreira exclaimed. "The most beautiful women in all the world!"

"Including the slaves?" Sharpe asked, causing Hogan, who knew Sharpe was trying to turn the subject to the Major's brother, to roll his eyes.

"The slaves are the prettiest!" Ferreira said. "And so obliging."

"Not much choice," Sharpe observed sourly. "Your brother didn't give them any, did he?"

Hogan tried to intervene, but Major Ferreira stilled his protest. "My brother, Mister Sharpe?"

"He was a slaver, yes?"

"My brother has been many things," Ferreira said. "As a child he was beaten because the monks who taught us wanted him to be pious. He is not pious. My father beat him because he would not read his books, but the beating did not make him a reader. He was happiest with the servants' children, he ran wild with them until my mother could take his wildness no longer and so he was sent to the nuns of Santo Espírito. They tried to beat the spirit from him, but he ran away. He was thirteen then, and he came back sixteen years later. He came back rich and quite determined, Mister Sharpe, that no one would ever beat him again."

"I did," Sharpe said.

"Richard!" Hogan remonstrated.

Ferreira ignored Hogan, staring at Sharpe across the candles. "He has not forgotten," he said quietly.

"But it's all cleared up," Hogan said. "An accident! Apologies have been made. Try some of this cheese, Major." He pushed a chipped plate of cheese across the table. "Major Ferreira and I, Richard, have been questioning deserters all afternoon."

"French?"

"Lord, no. Portuguese." Hogan explained that, following the fall of Almeida, scores of that fortress's Portuguese garrison had volunteered into the Portuguese Legion, a French unit. "It seems they did it," Hogan explained, "because it gave them a chance to get near our lines and desert. Over thirty came in this evening. And they're all saying that the French will attack in the morning."

"You believe them?"

"I believe they are telling the truth as they know it," Hogan said, "and their orders were to make ready for an attack. What they don't know, of course, is whether Masséna will change his mind."

"Monsieur Masséna," Ferreira remarked acidly, "is too busy with his mistress to think sensibly about battle."

"His mistress?" Sharpe asked.

"Mademoiselle Henriette Leberton," Hogan said, amused, "who is eighteen years old, Richard, while Monsieur Masséna is what? Fifty-one? No, fifty-two. Nothing distracts an old man so effectively as young flesh, which makes Mademoiselle Leberton one of our more valued allies. His Majesty's government should pay her an allowance. A guinea a night, perhaps?"

When the supper was eaten Ferreira insisted on showing Hogan and Sharpe the shrine where, as Clayton had said, wooden breasts lay on an altar. A score of small candles flickered around the weird objects and dozens of other candles had burned down to wax puddles. "Women bring the breasts," Ferreira explained, "to be cured of diseases. Women's diseases." He yawned, then pulled a watch from his waistcoat pocket. "I must get back to the ridge top," he said. "An early night, I think. Perhaps the enemy will come at dawn."

"Let's hope so," Hogan said.

Ferreira made the sign of the cross, bowed to the altar and left. Sharpe listened as the sound of the Major's spurred boots faded down the passage. "What the hell was that all about?" he asked Hogan.

"What was what about, Richard?"

"That supper!"

"He was being friendly. Showing you there are no hard feelings."

"But there are! He said his brother hadn't forgotten."

"Not forgotten, but persuaded to let the matter rest. And so should you."

"I wouldn't trust that bugger as far as I can spit," Sharpe said, then had to step back because the door had been pushed wide open and a noisily cheerful group of British officers stepped into the small room. One man alone was not in uniform, wearing instead a blue top coat and a white silk stock. It was Lord Wellington, who glanced at Sharpe, but appeared not to notice him.

Instead the General nodded to Hogan. "Come to worship, Major?" he asked.

"I was showing Mister Sharpe the sights, my lord."

"I doubt Mister Sharpe needs to see replications," Wellington said. "He probably sees more of the real article than most of us, eh?" He spoke genially enough, but with an edge of scorn, then looked directly at Sharpe. "I hear you did your duty three days ago, Mister Sharpe," he said.

Sharpe was confused, first by the sudden change of tone and then by the statement, which seemed strange after Hogan's earlier reproof. "I hope so, my lord," he answered carefully.

"Can't leave food for the French," the General said, turning back to the modeled breasts, "and I would have thought I had made that stratagem entirely clear." The last few words were said harshly and left the other officers silent. Then Wellington smiled and gestured at the votive breasts. "Can't quite imagine these things in Saint Paul's," he went on, "can you, Hogan?"

"They might improve the place, my lord."

"Indeed they might. I shall advert the matter to the Dean." He gave his horse neigh of a laugh, then abruptly looked at Hogan again. "Any news from Trant?"

"None, my lord."

"Let us hope that is good news." The General nodded at Hogan, ignored Sharpe again and led his guests back to wherever they were having supper.

"Trant?" Sharpe asked.

"There's a road round the top of the ridge," Hogan said, "and we have a cavalry vedette there and, I trust, some Portuguese militia under Colonel Trant. They are under orders to alert us if they see any sign of the enemy, but no word has come, so we must hope Masséna is ignorant of the route. If he thinks his only road to Lisbon is up this hill, then up this hill he must come. I must say, unlikely as it seems, that he probably will attack."

"And maybe at dawn," Sharpe said, "so I must get some sleep." He grinned at Hogan. "So I was right about bloody Ferragus and you were wrong?"

Hogan returned the grin. "It is very ungentlemanly to gloat, Richard."

"How did Wellington know?"

"I suppose Major Ferreira complained to him. He said he didn't, but . . ." Hogan shrugged.

"You can't trust that Portuguese bugger," Sharpe said. "Get one of your nasties to slit his throat."

"You're the only nasty I know," Hogan said, "and it's past your bedtime. So good night, Richard."

It was not late yet, probably no more than nine o'clock, but the sky was black dark and the temperature had fallen sharply. A wind had come from the west to bring cold air from the distant sea and a mist was forming among the trees as Sharpe climbed back to the path where the strange statues were housed in their brick huts. The path was deserted now. The bulk of the army was up on the ridge and any troops bivouacking behind the line were encamped around the monastery where their fires offered some small light that filtered through the wood to throw Sharpe's monstrous shadow flickering across tree trunks, but that small light faded as Sharpe climbed higher. There were no fires on the ridge top because Wellington had ordered that none were to be lit so that their glow could not betray to the French where the allied army was concentrated, though Sharpe suspected the enemy must have guessed. The lack of campfires made the upper hill bleakly dark. The mist thickened. Far off, beyond the wall that encircled the monastery and its forest, Sharpe could hear singing coming from the British and Portuguese encampments, but the loudest noise was his own footsteps on the pine needles that carpeted the path. The first of the shrines came into sight, lit from inside by votive candles that cast a small hazy glow through the chill mist. A black-gowned monk knelt in prayer by the last shrine and, as Sharpe passed, he thought of offering the man a greeting, then decided against interrupting the monk's devotions, but just then the cowled man lashed out, catching Sharpe behind his left knee, and two more men came from behind the shrine, one with a cudgel that smacked into Sharpe's belly. He went down hard, his metal scabbard clanging against the ground. He twisted away, trying to draw the sword, but the two men who had come from behind the shrine seized his arms and dragged him into the building where there was a small space in front of the statues. They kicked some candles aside to make more room. One drew Sharpe's sword and tossed it onto the path outside, while the cowled monk pushed back his hood.

It was Ferragus, vast and tall, filling the shrine with his menace. "You cost me a lot of money," he said in his strongly accented English. Sharpe was still on the ground. He tried to stand up, but one of Ferragus's two companions kicked him in the shoulder and forced him back. "A lot of money," Ferragus said heavily. "You wish to pay me now?" Sharpe said nothing. He needed a weapon. He had a folding knife in one pocket, but he knew he would never have time to pull it out, let alone extract the blade. "How much money do you have?" Ferragus asked. Sharpe still said nothing. "Or would you rather fight me?" Ferragus went on. "Bare knuckles, Captain, toe to toe."

Sharpe made a curt suggestion of what Ferragus could do and the big man smiled and spoke to his men in Portuguese. They attacked with their boots, kicking Sharpe, who drew up his knees to shield his belly. He guessed they were ordered to disable him and thus leave him to Ferragus's mercies, but the shrine was small, the space left by the statues cramped and the two men got in each other's way. Their kicks still hurt. Sharpe tried to lunge up at them, but a boot caught him on the side of the face and he fell back heavily, rocking the kneeling image of Mary Magdalene, and that gave him his weapon. He hammered the statue with his right elbow, smacking its knee so hard that the clay shattered and Sharpe snatched up one shard that was nearly a foot long and ended in a wicked point. He stabbed the makeshift dagger at the nearest man, aiming at his groin, but the man twisted aside so that the clay sliced into his inner thigh. The man grunted. Sharpe was up from the floor now, using his head as a battering ram that he thumped into the wounded man's belly. A fist caught him on the side of the nose, a boot slammed into his ribs, but he lunged the clay dagger at Ferragus, slicing it along the big man's jawbone, then a mighty blow on the side of his head threw him back and he fell against Christ's clay lap. Ferragus ordered his men to get out of the shrine, to give him room, and he punched Sharpe again, delivering a ringing blow on the temple, and Sharpe let go of his makeshift knife, put his arm round the Son of God's neck and jerked it hard so that the whole head came clean off. Ferragus threw a straight left jab and Sharpe dodged it, then came off the ground to ram the broken head with its crown of thorns up into Ferragus's face. The hollow clay skull cracked apart as it hit, its jagged edges gouging deep cuts in the big man's cheeks, and Sharpe twisted to his left as Ferragus recoiled. Sharpe scrambled through the door, trying to reach his sword, but the two men were outside and they fell on him. Sharpe heaved, managed to half turn over, and then got a kick in the belly that drove all the wind out of him.

Ferragus had kicked him, and now he ordered his two men to pull Sharpe up. "You can't fight," he told Sharpe, "you're feeble," and he began punching, using short, hard blows that looked to have little force in them, but they felt to Sharpe as if he was being kicked by a horse. The blows started at his belly, worked up his chest, then one slammed into his cheek and blood started inside Sharpe's mouth. He tried to free himself from the two men's grip, but they held him too tight and he was dazed, confused, half conscious. A fist caught him in the throat and now he could hardly breathe, gagging for air, and Ferragus laughed. "My brother said I shouldn't kill you, but why not? Who'll miss you?" He spat into Sharpe's face. "Let him go," he said to the two men in Portuguese, then changed to English. "Let's see if this Englishman can fight."

The two men stepped away from Sharpe who spat blood, blinked, and staggered two paces backwards. His sword was out of reach, and even if he could have fetched it he doubted he would have the strength to use it. Ferragus smiled at his weakness, stepped towards him and Sharpe staggered again, this time half falling sideways, and he put his hand down to steady himself and there was a stone there, a big stone, the size of a ration biscuit, and he picked it up just as Ferragus threw a right fist intended to knock Sharpe down for ever. Sharpe, still half aware, reacted instinctively, blocking the fist with the stone, and Ferragus's knuckles cracked on the rock and the big man flinched and stepped back, astonished by the sudden pain. Sharpe tried to step towards him and use the stone again, but a left jab banged into his chest and threw him back down onto the path.

"Now you're a dead man," Ferragus said. He was massaging his broken knuckles, and was in such pain from them that he wanted to kick Sharpe to death. He began by aiming a massive boot at Sharpe's groin but the blow landed short, on the thigh, because Sharpe had managed to twist feebly to one side, and Ferragus kicked his leg away, drew his boot back again and suddenly there was a light on the path behind him and a voice calling.

"What's going on!" the voice shouted. "Hold still! Whoever you are, hold still!" The boots of two or three men sounded on the path. The approaching men must have heard the fight, but they could surely see nothing in the thickening mist and Ferragus did not wait for them. He shouted at his two men and they ran past Sharpe, down through the trees, and Sharpe curled up on the ground, trying to squeeze the pain from his ribs and belly. There were thick gobs of blood in his mouth and his nose was bleeding. The light came nearer, a lantern held by a redcoat. "Sir?" one of the three men asked. He was a sergeant and had the dark-blue facings of the provosts, the army's policemen.

"I'm all right," Sharpe grunted.

"What happened?"

"Thieves," Sharpe said. "God knows who they were. Just thieves. Jesus. Help me up."

Two of them lifted him while the Sergeant retrieved his sword and shako. "How many were there?" the Sergeant asked.

"Three. Bastards ran away."

"You want to see a surgeon, sir?" The Sergeant flinched as he saw Sharpe's face in the lantern light. "I think you should."

"Christ, no." He sheathed the sword, put his shako on his bruised skull and leaned against the shrine. "I'll be all right," he said.

"We can take you to the monastery, sir."

"No. I'll make my way up to the ridge." He thanked the three men, wished them a peaceful night, waited until he had recovered some strength, and then limped back uphill, through the wall and down the ridge to find his company.

Colonel Lawford had pitched a tent close to the new road that had been hacked along the ridge top. The tent flaps were open, revealing a candlelit table on which silver and crystal gleamed, and the Colonel heard a sentry challenge Sharpe, heard Sharpe's muffled response and shouted through the open flaps, "Sharpe! Is that you?"

Sharpe thought briefly about pretending not to have heard, but he was plainly within earshot so he turned towards the tent. "Yes, sir."

"Come and have some brandy." Lawford was entertaining Majors Forrest and Leroy, and with them was Lieutenant Slingsby. All had on greatcoats for, after the last few days of brutal heat, the night was suddenly winter cold.

Forrest made space on a bench made out of wooden ammunition crates, then stared up at Sharpe. "What happened to you?"

"Took a tumble, sir," Sharpe said. His voice was thick, and he leaned to one side and spat out a glutinous gobbet of blood. "Took a tumble."

"A tumble?" Lawford was gazing at Sharpe with an expression of horror. "Your nose is bleeding."

"Mostly stopped, sir," Sharpe said, sniffing blood. He remembered the handkerchief that had been used as a white flag at the telegraph station and fished it out. It seemed a pity to stain the fine linen with blood, but he put it over his nose, flinching at the pain. Then he noticed his right hand was cut, presumably by the makeshift clay dagger.

"A tumble?" Major Leroy echoed the Colonel's question.

"Treacherous path down there, sir."

"You've got a black eye too," Lawford said.

"If you're not up to scratch," Slingsby said, "then I'll happily command the company tomorrow, Sharpe." Slingsby was high-colored and sweating, as if he had drunk too much. He looked to Colonel Lawford and, because he was nervous, gave a snort of laughter. "Be honored to command, sir," he added quickly.

Sharpe gave the Lieutenant a look that would have killed. "I was hurt worse than this," he said icily, "when Sergeant Harper and I took that damned Eagle on your badge."

Slingsby stiffened, appalled at Sharpe's tone, and the other officers looked embarrassed.

"Have some brandy, Sharpe," Lawford said emolliently, pouring it from a decanter and pushing the glass across the trestle table. "How was Major Hogan?"

Sharpe was hurting. His ribs were like strips of fire and it took him a moment to comprehend the question and find an answer. "He's confident, sir."

"I should hope so," Lawford said. "Aren't we all? Did you see the Peer?"

"The Peer?" Slingsby asked. He stumbled slightly on the word, then tossed down the rest of his brandy and helped himself to more.

"Lord Wellington," Lawford explained. "So did you see him, Sharpe?"

"Yes, sir."

"I hope you remembered me to him?"

"Of course, sir." Sharpe told the required lie and forced himself to add another. "And he asked me to present his regards."

"Very civil of him," Lawford said, plainly pleased. "And does he think the French will come up and dance tomorrow?"

"He didn't say, sir."

"Perhaps this fog will deter them," Major Leroy said, peering out of the tent where the haze was perceptibly thickening.

"Or it will encourage them," Forrest said. "Our gunners can't aim into fog."

Leroy was watching Sharpe. "Do you need a doctor?"

"No, sir," Sharpe lied. His ribs hurt, his skull was throbbing and one of his upper teeth was loose. His belly was a mass of pain, his thigh hurt and he was angry. "Major Hogan," he forced himself to change the subject, "thinks the French will attack."

"Then we'd best keep a keen eye in the morning," Lawford said, hinting that the evening was over. The officers took the hint, standing and thanking the Colonel, who held out a hand to Sharpe. "Stay a moment, if you will, Sharpe."

Slingsby, who looked the worse for drink, drained his glass, banged it down and clicked his heels. "Thank you, William," he said to Lawford, presuming on their relationship to use the Colonel's Christian name.

"Good night, Cornelius," Lawford said, and waited until the three officers had gone from the tent and were lost in the mist. "He drank rather a lot. Still, I suppose on the eve of a man's first battle a little fortification isn't out of order. Sit, Sharpe, sit. Drink some brandy." He took a glass himself. "Was it really a tumble? You look as if you've been in the wars."

"Dark in the trees, sir," Sharpe said woodenly, "and I missed my footing on some steps."

"You must take more care, Sharpe," Lawford said, leaning forward to light a cigar from one of the candles. "It's gone damned cold, hasn't it?" He waited for a response, but Sharpe said nothing and the Colonel sighed. "I wanted to talk to you," he went on between puffs, "about your new fellows. Young Iliffe shaping up well, is he?"

"He's an ensign, sir. If he survives a year he might have a chance of growing up."

"We were all ensigns once," Lawford said, "and mighty oaks from tiny acorns grow, eh?"

"He's still a bloody small acorn," Sharpe said.

"But his father's a friend of mine, Sharpe. He farms a few acres near Benfleet and he wanted me to look after his son."

"I'll look after him," Sharpe said.

"I'm sure you will," Lawford said, "and what about Cornelius?"

"Cornelius?" Sharpe asked, wanting time to think. He swilled his bloody mouth out with brandy, spat it onto the ground, then drank some and fancied it took away some of the hurt.

"How's Cornelius doing?" Lawford asked pleasantly. "Being useful, is he?"

"He has to learn our ways," Sharpe said warily.

"Of course he must, of course. But I particularly wanted him to be with you."

"Why, sir?"

"Why?" The Colonel seemed taken aback by the direct question, but then waved the cigar as if to say the answer was obvious. "I think he's a capital fellow, and I'll be honest with you, Sharpe, I'm not sure young Knowles possesses the right verve for skirmishing."

"He's a good officer," Sharpe said indignantly, and then wished he had not spoken so forcibly for the pain in his ribs seemed to stab right to his heart.

"Oh, none finer!" Lawford agreed hastily. "And an admirable character, but you skirmishers aren't dull fellows, are you? You're the whippers-in! I need my light company to be audacious! Aggressive! Astute!" Each quality was accompanied by a thump that rattled the glass and silverware on the table, but the Colonel paused after the third, evidently realizing that astuteness lacked the force of audacity and aggression. He thought for a few seconds, trying to find a more impressive word, then carried on without thinking of it. "I believe Cornelius has those qualities and I look to you, Sharpe, to bring him on." Lawford paused again, as if expecting Sharpe to respond, but when the rifleman said nothing the Colonel looked acutely embarrassed. "The nub of the matter is, Sharpe, that Cornelius seems to think you don't like him."

"Most people think that, sir," Sharpe said woodenly.

"Do they?" Lawford looked surprised. "I suppose they might. Not everyone knows you as well as I do." He paused to draw on his cigar. "Do you ever miss India, Sharpe?"

"India," Sharpe responded cautiously. He and Lawford had served there together when Lawford had been a lieutenant and Sharpe a private. "I liked it well enough."

"There are regiments in India that could use an experienced officer," Lawford said casually and Sharpe felt a stab of betrayal because the words suggested the Colonel did want to be rid of him. He said nothing, and Lawford seemed unaware of having given any offence. "So I can reassure Cornelius that all is well?"

"Yes, sir," Sharpe said, then stood. "I must go and inspect the picquets, sir."

"Of course you must," Lawford said, not hiding his frustration with the conversation. "We should talk more often, Sharpe."

Sharpe took his battered shako and walked out into the fog-shrouded night. He picked his way through the thick darkness, going across the ridge's wide crest and then some short way down the eastern slope until he could just see the mist-blurred string of enemy fires in the valley's deep darkness. Let them come, he thought, let them come. If he could not murder Ferragus then he would take out his anger on the French. He heard footsteps behind him, but did not turn round. "Evening, Pat," he said.

"What happened to you?" Harper must have seen Sharpe inside the Colonel's tent and had followed him down the slope.

"That bloody Ferragus and two of his coves."

"Tried to kill you?"

Sharpe shook his head. "Bloody nearly succeeded. Would have done, except three provosts came along."

"Provosts! Never thought they'd be useful. And how is Mister Ferragus?"

"I hurt him, but not enough. He beat me, Pat. Beat me bloody."

Harper thought about that. "And what did you tell the Colonel?"

"That I had a tumble."

"So that's what I'll tell the lads when they notice you're better-looking than usual. And tomorrow I'll keep an eye open for Mister Ferragus. You think he'll be back for more?"

"No, he's buggered off."

"We'll find him, sir, we'll find him."

"But not tomorrow, Pat. We're going to be busy tomorrow. Major Hogan reckons the Frogs are coming up this hill."

Which was a comforting thought to end the day, and the two sat, listening to the singing from the dark encampments behind. A dog began barking somewhere in the British lines and immediately dozens of others echoed the sound, prompting angry shouts as the beasts were told to be quiet, and slowly peace descended again, all but for one dog that would not stop. On and on it went, barking frantically, until there was the sudden harsh crack of a musket or pistol.

"That's the way to do it," Harper said.

Sharpe said nothing. He just gazed down the hill to where the French fires were a dull, hazed glow in the mist. "But what will we do about Mister Ferragus?" Harper asked. "He can't be allowed to get away with assaulting a rifleman."

"If we lose tomorrow," Sharpe said, "we'll have to retreat through Coimbra. That's where he lives."

"So we'll find him there," Harper said grimly, "and give him what he deserves. But what if we win tomorrow?"

"God only knows," Sharpe said, and nodded down the hill to the misted firelight. There were thousands of fires. "Follow those bastards back to Spain, I suppose," he went on, "and fight them there." And go on fighting them, he thought, month after month, year after year, until the very crack of doom. But it would begin tomorrow, with sixty thousand Frenchmen who wanted to take a hill. Tomorrow.

※

MARSHAL NEY, second in command of l'Armée de Portugal, reckoned the whole of the enemy army was on the ridge. There were no fires in the high darkness to betray their presence, but Ney could smell them. A soldier's instinct. The bastards were laying a trap, hoping the French would stroll up the hill to be slaughtered, and Ney reckoned they should be obliged. Send the Eagles up the hill and beat the bastards into mincemeat, but Ney was not the man to make that decision and so he summoned an aide, Captain D'Esmenard, and told him to find Marshal Masséna. "Tell his highness," Ney said, "that the enemy's waiting to be killed. Tell him to get back here fast. Tell him there's a battle to be fought."

Captain D'Esmenard had a journey of more than twenty miles and he had to be escorted by two hundred dragoons who clattered into the small town of Tondella long after nightfall. A tricolor flew above the porch of the house where Masséna lodged. Six sentries stood outside, their muskets tipped by bayonets that reflected the firelight of the brazier that offered a small warmth in the sudden cold.

D'Esmenard climbed the stairs and hammered on the Marshal's door. There was silence.

D'Esmenard knocked again. This time there was a woman's giggle followed by the distinct sound of a hand slapping flesh, then the woman laughed. "Who is it?" the Marshal called.

"A message from Marshal Ney, your highness." Marshal André Masséna was Duke of Rivoli and Prince of Essling.

"From Ney?"

"The enemy has definitely stopped, sir. They're on the ridge."

The girl squealed.

"The enemy has what?"

"Stopped, sir," D'Esmenard shouted through the door. "The Marshal believes you should come back." Masséna had been in the valley beneath the ridge for a few moments in the afternoon, given his opinion that the enemy would not stand and fight, and ridden back to Tondela. The girl said something and there was the sound of another slap followed by more giggling.

"Marshal Ney believes they are offering battle, sir," D'Esmenard said.

"Who are you?" the Marshal asked.

"Captain D'Esmenard, sir."

"One of Ney's boys, eh?"

"Yes, sir."

"Have you eaten, D'Esmenard?"

"No, sir."

"Go downstairs, Captain, tell my cook to give you supper. I shall join you."

"Yes, sir." D'Esmenard paused. He heard a grunt, a sigh, then the sound of bedsprings rhythmically squeaking.

"Are you still there, Captain?" the Prince of Essling shouted.

D'Esmenard crept downstairs, timing his steps on the creaking stair treads to the regular bounce of the bedsprings. He ate cold chicken. And waited.

PEDRO AND LUIS FERREIRA had always been close. Luis, the oldest, the rebel, the huge, uncontrollable boy, had been the brighter of the two, and if he had not been exiled from his family, if he had not been sent to the nuns who beat and mocked him, if he had not run away from Coimbra to see the world, he might have secured an education and become a scholar, though in truth that would have been an unlikely fate for Luis. He was too big, too belligerent, too careless of his own and other men's feelings, and so he had become Ferragus. He had sailed the world, killed men in Africa, Europe and America, had seen the sharks eat the dying slaves thrown overboard off the Brazilian coast, and then he had come home to his younger brother and the two of them, so different and yet so close, had embraced. They were brothers. Ferragus had come home rich enough to set himself up in business, rich enough to own a score of properties about the city, but Pedro insisted that he have a room in his house to use when he wished. "My house is your house," he had promised Ferragus, and though Major Ferreira's wife might wish otherwise she dared not protest.

Ferragus rarely used the room in his brother's house, but on the day when the two armies faced each other at Bussaco, after his brother had promised to lure Captain Sharpe to a beating among the trees, Ferragus had promised Pedro that he would return to Coimbra and there guard the Ferreira household until the pattern of the French campaign was clear. Folk were supposed to be fleeing the city, going to Lisbon, but if the French were stopped then no such flight would be necessary, and whether they were stopped or not, there was unrest in the streets because people were unhappy with the orders to abandon their homes. Ferreira's house, grand and rich, bought with the legacy of his father's wealth, would be a likely place for thieves to plunder, though none would dare touch it if Ferragus and his men were there and so, after his failure to kill the impudent rifleman, the big man rode to keep his promise.

The journey from the ridge of Bussaco to the city of Coimbra was less than twenty miles, but the mist and the darkness slowed Ferragus and his men, so it was just before dawn that they rode past the imposing university buildings and down the hill to his brother's house. There was a squeal from the hinges of the gates to the stable yard where Ferragus dismounted, abandoned his horse and pushed into the kitchen to thrust his injured hand into a vat of cool water. Sweet Jesus, he thought, but the damned rifleman had to die. Had to die. Ferragus brooded on the unfairness of life as he used a cloth to wipe the wounds on his jawbone and cheeks. He winced at the pain, though it was not as bad as the throbbing in his groin that persisted from their confrontation at the shrine. Next time, Ferragus promised himself, next time he would face Mister Sharpe with nothing but fists and he would kill the Englishman as he had killed so many other men, by pulverizing him into a bloody, whimpering mess. Sharpe had to die, Ferragus had sworn it, and if he did not keep the oath then his men would think he was weakening.

He was being weakened anyway. The war had seen to that. Many of his victims had fled Coimbra and its surrounding farmlands, gone to take shelter in Lisbon. That temporary setback would pass, and, anyway, Ferragus hardly needed to go on extorting money. He was rich, but he liked to keep cash flowing for he did not trust the banks. He liked land, and the vast profits of his slaving years had been invested in vineyards, farms, houses and shops. He owned every brothel in Coimbra and scarcely a student at the university did not live in a house owned by Ferragus. He was rich, rich beyond his childhood dreams, but he could never be rich enough. He loved money. He yearned for it, loved it, caressed it, dreamed of it.

He rinsed his jaw again and saw how the water dripped pink from the cloth. Capitâo Sharpe. He said the name aloud, feeling the pain in his mouth. He looked at his hand that was hurting. He reckoned he had cracked some knuckle bones, but he could still move his fingers so the damage could not be that bad. He dipped the knuckles in the water, then turned suddenly as the kitchen door opened and his brother's governess, Miss Fry, dressed in a nightdress and a heavy woolen gown, came into the kitchen. She was carrying a candle and gave a small start of surprise when she saw her employer's brother. "I am sorry, *senhor*," she said, and made to leave.

"Come in," Ferragus growled.

Sarah would rather have gone back to her room, but she had heard the horses clattering in the stable yard and, hoping it might be Major Ferreira with news of the French advance, she had come to the kitchen. "You're hurt," she said.

"I fell from my horse," Ferragus said. "Why are you up?"

"To make tea," Sarah said. "I make it every morning. And I wondered, *senhor*," she took a kettle off the shelf, "whether you have news of the French."

"The French are pigs," Ferragus said, "which is all you need to know, so make your tea and make some for me too."

Sarah put down the candle, opened the stove and fed kindling onto the embers. When the kindling was blazing she put more wood onto the fire. By the time the fire was properly burning there were other servants busy around the house, opening shutters and sweeping the corridors, but none came into the kitchen where Sarah hesitated before filling the kettle. The water in the big vat was bloodstained. "I'll draw some from the well," she said.

Ferragus watched her through the open door. Miss Sarah Fry was a symbol of his brother's aspirations. To Major Ferreira and his wife an English governess was as prized a possession as fine porcelain or crystal chandeliers or gilt furniture. Sarah proclaimed their good taste, but Ferragus regarded her as a priggish waste of his brother's money. A typical, snobbish Englishwoman, he reckoned, and what would she turn Tomas and Maria into? Little stuck-up copies of herself? Tomas did not need manners or to know English; he needed to know how to defend himself. And Maria? Her mother could teach her manners, and so long as she was pretty, what else mattered? That was Ferragus's view, anyway, but he had also noticed, ever since Miss Fry had come to his brother's house, that she was pretty, more than just pretty, beautiful. Fair-skinned, fair-haired, blue-eyed, tall, elegant. "How old are you?" he asked as she came back to the kitchen.

"Is it any business of yours, *senhor*?" Sarah asked briskly.

Ferragus smiled. "My brother sent me here to protect you all. I like to know what I'm protecting."

"I'm twenty-two, *senhor*." Sarah set the kettle on the stove, then stood the big brown English teapot close by so that the china would warm. She took down the tin caddy, then had nothing to do because the pot was still cold and the kettle would take long minutes to boil on the newly awakened fire so, abhorring idleness, she began polishing some spoons.

"Are Tomas and Maria learning properly?" Ferragus addressed her back.

"When they apply themselves," Sarah said briskly.

"Tomas tells me you hit him."

"Of course I hit him," Sarah said, "I am his governess."

"But you don't hit Maria?"

"Maria does not use bad language," Sarah said, "and I detest bad language."

"Tomas will be a man," Ferragus said, "so he will need bad language."

"Then he may learn it from you, *senhor*," Sarah retorted, looking Ferragus in the eye, "but I shall teach him not to use it in front of ladies. If he learns that alone then I shall have been useful."

Ferragus gave a grunt that might have been amusement. He was challenged by her gaze, which showed no fear of him. He was accustomed to his brother's other servants shrinking when he passed; they dropped their eyes and tried to become invisible, but this English girl was brazen. But also beautiful, and he marveled at the line of her neck which was shadowed by unruly fair hair. Such white skin, he thought, so delicate. "You teach them French. Why?" he asked.

"Because the Major's wife expects it," Sarah said, "because it is the language of diplomacy. Because possession of French is a requisite of gentility."

Ferragus made a growling noise in his throat that was evidently a verdict on gentility, then shrugged. "The language will at least be useful if the French come here," he said.

"If the French come here," Sarah said, "then we should be long gone. Is that not what the government has ordered?"

Ferragus flinched as he moved his right hand. "But perhaps they won't come now. Not if they lose the battle."

"The battle?"

"Your Lord Wellington is at Bussaco. He hopes the French will attack him."

"I pray they do," Sarah said confidently, "because then he will beat them."

"Perhaps," Ferragus said, "or perhaps your Lord Wellington will do what Sir John Moore did at La Coruña. Fight, win and run away."

Sarah sniffed to show her opinion of that statement.

"*Os ingleses*," Ferragus said savagely, "*por mar.*"

The English, he had said, are for the sea. It was a general belief in Portugal. The British were opportunists, looking for victory, but running from any possible defeat. They had come, they had fought, but they would not stay to the end. *Os ingleses por mar.*

Sarah half feared Ferragus was right, but would not admit it. "You say your brother sent you to protect us?" she asked instead.

"He did. He can't be here. He has to stay with the army."

"Then I shall rely on you, *senhor*, to make certain I am long gone to safety if, as you say, the English take to the sea. I cannot stay here if the French come."

"You cannot stay here?"

"Indeed not. I am English."

"I shall protect you, Miss Fry," Ferragus said.

"I am glad to hear it," she said briskly and turned back to the kettle.

Bitch, Ferragus thought, stuck-up English bitch. "Forget my tea," he said and stalked from the kitchen.

And then, from far off, half heard, there was a noise like thunder. It rose and fell, faded to nothing, came again, and at its loudest the windows shook softly in their frames. Sarah stared into the yard and saw the cold gray mist and she knew it was not thunder she heard from so far away.

It was the French.

Because it was dawn and, at Bussaco, the guns were at work.

CHAPTER 3

SHARPE SLEPT BADLY. The ground was damp, it got colder as the night wore on and he was hurting. His damaged ribs stabbed like knives every time he moved, and when he finally abandoned sleep and stood in the pre-dawn darkness, he wanted to lie down again because of the pain. He fingered his ribs, wondering if the injury was worse than he feared. His right eye was swollen, tender to the touch and half shut.

"You awake, sir?" a voice called from nearby.

"I'm dead," Sharpe said.

"Mug of tea, then, sir?" It was Matthew Dodd, a rifleman in Sharpe's company who had been newly made up to corporal while Sharpe was away. Knowles had given Dodd the extra stripe and Sharpe approved of the promotion.

"Thanks, Matthew," Sharpe said and grimaced with pain as he stooped to collect some damp scraps of wood to help make a fire. Dodd had already used a steel and flint to light some kindling that he now blew into bright flame.

"Are we supposed to have fires, sir?" Dodd asked.

"We weren't supposed to last night, Matthew, but in this damned fog who could see one? Anyway, I need some tea, so get her going." Sharpe added his wood, then listened to the crack and hiss of the new flames as

Dodd filled a kettle with water and threw in a handful of tea leaves that he kept loose in his pouch. Sharpe added some of his own, then fed the fire with more wood.

"Damp old morning," Dodd said.

"Bloody mist." Sharpe could see the fog was still thick.

"Be reveille soon," Dodd said, settling the kettle in the flames.

"Can't even be half past two yet," Sharpe said. Here and there along the ridge other men were lighting fires that made glowing, misted patches in the fog, but most of the army still slept. Sharpe had picquets out at the ridge's eastern edge, but he did not need to check them for another few minutes.

"Sergeant Harper said you fell down some steps, sir," Dodd said, looking at Sharpe's bruised face.

"Dangerous things, steps, Matthew. Especially in the dark when it's slippery."

"Sexton back home died like that," Dodd said, his gaunt face lit by the flames. "He went up the church tower to fasten a new rope on the big tenor bell and he slipped. Some said he was pushed, mind, because his wife was sweet on another man."

"You, Matthew?"

"Mister Sharpe!" Dodd said, shocked. "Not me, no!"

The tea brewed quickly enough and Sharpe scooped some out with his tin mug and then, after thanking Dodd, went across the ridge top towards the French. He did not go down the slope, but found a small spur that jutted out close to the road. The spur, which protruded like a bastion from the ridge's top, extended out for a hundred paces before ending in a knoll crowned with a ragged jumble of scattered boulders and it was there he expected to find the sentries. He stamped his feet as he went, wanting to alert the picquets to his presence.

"Who's there?" The challenge came smartly enough, but Sharpe had expected it because Sergeant Read was doing duty.

"Captain Sharpe."

"Countersign, Captain?" Read demanded.

"A sip of hot tea, Sergeant, if you don't shoot me," Sharpe said.

Read was a stickler for following the rules, but even a Methodist could be persuaded to ignore a missing password by an offer of tea. "The password's Jessica, sir," he told Sharpe reprovingly.

"The Colonel's wife, eh? Mister Slingsby forgot to tell me." He handed Read the mug of tea. "Anything nasty about?"

"Not a thing, sir, not a thing."

Ensign Iliffe, who was nominally in charge of the picquet, though under standing orders to do nothing without his Sergeant's agreement, came and gawped at Sharpe.

"Good morning, Mister Iliffe," Sharpe said.

"Sir," the boy stammered, too scared to make conversation.

"All quiet?"

"I think so, sir," Iliffe said and stared at Sharpe's face, not quite sure he believed the damage he saw in the half light and much too nervous to ask what had caused it.

The eastern slope dropped into the fog and darkness. Sharpe crouched, wincing at the pain in his ribs, closed his eyes and listened. He could hear men stirring on the slope above him, the clang of a kettle, the crackle of small fires being revived. A horse thumped the ground with its foot and somewhere a baby cried. None of those sounds concerned him. He was listening for something from below, but all was quiet. "They won't come till dawn," he said, knowing that the French needed some light to find the track up the hill.

"And you think they will come, sir?" Read asked apprehensively.

"That's what their deserters say. How's your priming?"

"In this fog? I don't trust it," Read said, then frowned at Sharpe. "You hurt yourself, sir?"

"I fell down some steps," Sharpe said. "Wasn't watching out. You'd best blow the guns out at reveille," he went on, "and I'll warn the battalion." The six men of the picquet had stood guard on the rocky promontory through the darkness with loaded muskets and rifles. By now the damp air would have penetrated the priming in the lock pans and the odds were that the sparks would not light the powder. So, when the army was woken by bugle calls, the picquets would put a fresh pinch of dry powder in their pans and fire the musket to clear out the old charge and, if folk were not warned, they might think the shots meant the French had climbed through the fog. "Keep your eyes open till then," he said.

"We're being relieved at reveille?" Read asked anxiously.

"You can get a couple of hours' sleep after stand-to," Sharpe said. "But sharpen your bayonets before you put your heads down."

"You think . . ." Ensign Iliffe started the question, but did not finish it.

"I don't know what to expect," Sharpe answered him anyway, "but you don't face battle with a blunt blade, Mister Iliffe. Show me your saber."

Iliffe, as befitted an officer in a skirmishing company, wore a light cavalry saber. It was an old one, bought cheap back home, with a tarnished hilt and a worn leather grip. The Ensign gave the weapon to Sharpe who ran a thumb down its curved fore blade, then down the sharpened upper edge of the back blade. "Half a mile back," he told Iliffe, "there's a regiment of Portuguese dragoons, so when it's light go back there, find their smith, and give him a shilling to put an edge on that blade. You couldn't skin a cat with that saber." He gave the blade back, then half drew his own.

Sharpe, perversely, did not carry the light cavalry saber. Instead he wore a heavy cavalry sword, a long and straight-bladed weapon that was ill-balanced and too heavy, but a brutal instrument in a strong man's hands. It seemed sharp enough when he felt the fore blade, but he would still have a keener edge ground onto the sword. Money well spent, he reckoned.

He went back up to the ridge top and scrounged another mug of tea just a moment before the first bugle sounded. It was muffled, far off, for it came from the valley beneath, from the invisible French, but within a moment scores of bugles and trumpets were blasting the ridge with their clamor. "Stand to! Stand to!" Major Leroy shouted. He saw Sharpe through the mist. "Morning, Sharpe! Damned cold one, eh? What happened to summer?"

"I've told the picquets to empty their guns, sir."

"I won't be alarmed," Leroy said, then brightened. "Is that tea, Sharpe?"

"I thought Americans didn't drink tea, sir."

"The loyal Americans do, Sharpe." Leroy, the son of parents who had fled the rebel victory in the Thirteen Colonies, stole Sharpe's mug. "The rebellious sort feed their tea to the codfish." He drank and looked disgusted. "Don't you use sugar?"

"Never."

Leroy took a sip and grimaced. "It tastes like warm horse piss," he said, but drained the mug nonetheless. "Good morning, lads! Time to shine! Fall in!"

Sergeant Harper had led the new picquet towards the rocks on the small spur where Sergeant Read ordered his men to shoot their guns out into the foggy void. Leroy called that the sound should be ignored. Lieutenant Slingsby, despite having been drunk the night before, now looked as fresh and smart as though he were mounting guard on Windsor Castle. He came from his tent, plucked his red coat straight, adjusted the angle of his saber scabbard, then marched after the picquet. "You should have waited for me, Sergeant!" he called to Harper.

"I told him to go," Sharpe said.

Slingsby swiveled around, his bulging eyes showing surprise at seeing Sharpe. "Morning, Sharpe!" The Lieutenant sounded indecently cheerful. "My word, but that's a rare black eye! You should have put a beefsteak on it last night. Beefsteak!" Slingsby, finding that advice funny, snorted with laughter. "How are you feeling? Better, I trust?"

"Dead," Sharpe said, and turned back to the ridge top where the battalion was forming into line. They would stay there through the dull moments of dawn, through the dangerous time when the enemy might make a surprise attack. Sharpe, standing ahead of the light company, looked down the line and felt an unexpected surge of affection for the battalion. It was nearly six hundred men strong, most from the small villages of southern Essex, but a good few from London and a lot from Ireland, and they were mostly thieves, drunks, murderers and fools, but they had been hammered into soldiers. They knew each other's weaknesses, liked each other's jokes, and reckoned no battalion in God's world was half as good as theirs. They might not be as wild as the Connaught Rangers, who were now moving up to take post to the left of the South Essex, and they were certainly not as fashionable as the Guards battalions farther north, but they were dependable, stubborn, proud and confident. A ripple of laughter went through number four company and Sharpe knew, even without hearing its cause, that Horace Pearce had just made a jest and he knew his men would want the joke passed down. "Silence in the ranks!" he called and wished he had kept silent because of the pain.

A Portuguese unit was formed to the battalion's right and beyond them was a battery of Portuguese six-pounders. Useless guns, Sharpe thought, but he had seen enough nine-pounders on the ridge to know that the cannons could do some slaughter this day. He reckoned the mist was clearing, for he could see the small six-pounders more clearly with every passing minute, and when he turned north and stared at the tops of the trees beyond the monastery's far wall he saw the whiteness thinning and shredding.

They waited the best part of an hour, but no French came. The mist drained from the ridge top, but still filled the valley like a great white river. Colonel Lawford, mounted on Lightning, rode down the battalion's front, touching his hat in answer to the companies' salutes. "We shall do well today," he told each company, "and add luster to our reputation. Do your duty, and let the Frenchmen know they've met better men!" He repeated this encouragement to the light company at the left of the line, ignored the man who asked what luster was, then smiled down at Sharpe. "Come and have breakfast with me, will you, Sharpe?"

"Yes, sir."

"Good man." A bugle sounded from half a mile north and Lawford twisted in his saddle to find Major Forrest. "We can stand down, Major. Half and half, though, I think."

Half the men stayed in line, the others were released to make tea, to eat and relieve themselves, but none was permitted to go beyond the newly made road and so vanish from the battalion's sight. If the French came then the men were expected to be in line within half a minute. Two of the light company wives sat by a fire honing bayonets with sharpening stones and cackling with laughter at a joke told by Rifleman Hagman. Sergeant Read, off duty for the moment, was on one knee, a hand on his musket, praying. Rifleman Harris, who claimed to believe in none of the gods, was making certain that his lucky rabbit's foot was in his pouch, while Ensign Iliffe was trying to hide behind the Colonel's tent where he was being sick. Sharpe called to him. "Mister Iliffe!"

"Sir." Iliffe, strands of yellowish liquid straggling from his unshaven chin, came nervously to Sharpe, who drew his sword.

"Take that, Mister Iliffe," Sharpe said, pretending not to notice that the Ensign had been vomiting. "Find the Portuguese cavalry smith and have an edge put on it. A proper edge. One I can shave with." He gave the boy two shillings, realizing that his earlier advice, that Iliffe should pay a shilling himself, had been impractical because Iliffe probably did not have a penny to spare. "Go on with you. Bring it back to me as soon as you can."

Robert Knowles, stripped to his waist, was shaving outside Lawford's tent. The skin of his chest and back was milk white while his face was as dark as old wood. "You should grow a mustache, Robert," Sharpe said.

"What a ghastly notion," Knowles said, peering into the mirror that was propped against the water bowl. "I had an uncle with a mustache and he went bankrupt. How are you feeling?"

"Horrible."

Knowles paused, face half lathered, razor poised by his cheek, and stared at Sharpe. "You look horrible. You're to go in, Richard, the Colonel's expecting you."

Sharpe thought of borrowing the razor, but his jaw was still tender where he had been kicked and he reckoned he could go a day without a shave, though at the end of it his chin would be black as powder. He ducked into the tent to find Lawford sitting at a trestle table covered with fine linen and expensive porcelain. "Boiled eggs," the Colonel greeted him warmly. "I do so relish a properly boiled egg. Sit yourself down, Sharpe. The bread's not too hard. How are your wounds?"

"Hardly notice them, sir," Sharpe lied.

"Good man." The Colonel spooned some runny egg into his mouth, then gestured through the canvas towards the east. "Fog's lifting. You think the French will come?"

"Major Hogan seemed sure of it, sir."

"Then we shall do our duty," Lawford said, "and it will be good practice for the battalion, eh? Real targets! That's coffee, very good coffee as well. Do help yourself."

It seemed that Sharpe was to be Lawford's only guest, for there were no plates or silverware for another man. He poured himself coffee, helped himself to an egg and a slice of bread, and ate in silence. He felt uncomfortable. He had known Lawford for over ten years, yet he could think of nothing to say. Some men, like Hogan or Major Forrest, were never short of conversation. Put them down among a group of strangers and they could chatter away like magpies, but Sharpe was always struck dumb except with those he knew really well. The Colonel did not seem to mind the silence. He ate steadily, reading a four-week-old copy of *The Times*. "Good Lord," he said at one point.

"What's that, sir?"

"Tom Dyton's dead. Poor old chap. Of an advanced age, it says here. He must have been seventy if he was a day!"

"I didn't know him, sir."

"Had land in Surrey. Fine old fellow, married a Calloway, which is always a sensible thing to do. Consols are holding steady, I see." He folded the paper and pushed it across the table. "Like to read it, Sharpe?"

"I would, sir."

"All yours, then."

Sharpe would not read it, but the paper would be useful anyway. He cracked the top off another egg and wondered what Consols were. He knew they had something to do with money, but just what he had no idea.

"So you think the French will come?" Lawford asked, forcing a heartiness into his voice and apparently unaware that he had voiced the identical question just minutes before.

Sharpe sensed a nervousness in the Colonel and wondered what caused it. "I think we have to assume they'll come, sir."

"Quite so, quite so. Prepare for the worst, eh, and hope for the best? Very wise that, Sharpe." Lawford buttered a slice of bread. "So let's assume there's going to be a scrap, shall we? Wellington and Masséna playing King of the Castle, eh? But it shouldn't be a difficult day, should it?"

Was Lawford nervous of a battle? It seemed unlikely, for the Colonel had been in enough actions to know what must be coming, but Sharpe attempted to reassure him anyway. "It never does to underestimate the Crapauds, sir," he said carefully, "and they'll keep coming whatever we chuck at them, but no, it shouldn't be difficult. That hill will slow them and we'll kill them."

"That's rather what I thought, Sharpe," Lawford said, offering a dazzling smile. "The hill will slow them and then we'll kill them. So, all in all, the fox is running, the scent's high, we're mounted on a damned fine horse and the going's firm."

"We should win, sir," Sharpe said, "if that's what you mean. And if the Portuguese fight well."

"Ah yes, the Portuguese. Hadn't thought of them, but they seem fine fellows. Do have that last egg."

"I'm full, sir."

"You're sure? Very kind. I never say no to a well-boiled egg. My father, God rest him, always believed he would be met at the gates of heaven by an angel carrying two decently boiled eggs on a silver salver. I do hope it turned out that way for him." Sharpe decided there was nothing to say to that so stayed silent as the Colonel sliced off the egg's top, sprinkled it with salt and dug in his spoon. "The thing is, Sharpe," Lawford went on, but hesitantly now, "if the going is firm and we don't need to be over-anxious, then I'd like to spread some experience through the battalion. Know what I mean?"

"The French do that, sir," Sharpe said.

"Do they?" Lawford seemed surprised.

"Every time they fight us, sir, they shovel experience all over us."

"Ah, I see your drift!" Lawford ate some egg, then dabbed his lips with a napkin. "I mean real experience, Sharpe, the kind that will serve the regiment well. Fellows don't learn their duties by watching, do they? But by doing. Don't you agree?"

"Of course, sir."

"So I've decided, Sharpe," Lawford was not looking at Sharpe any more, but concentrating on his egg, "that Cornelius ought to command the light company today. He's not taking it over, don't think that for a moment, but I do want him to stretch his wings. Want to see how he does, eh? And if it ain't going to be a tricky business, then today will blood him gently." He spooned more egg into his mouth and dared to give Sharpe a quizzical look. Sharpe said nothing. He was furious, humiliated and helpless. He wanted to protest, but to what end? Lawford had plainly made up his mind and to fight the decision would only make the Colonel dig in his heels. "And you, Sharpe," Lawford smiled now he felt the worst was over, "I think you probably need a rest. That tumble you took did some damage, eh? You look battered. So let Cornelius show us his stuff, eh? And you can use his horse and serve as my eyes. Advise me."

"My advice, sir," Sharpe could not help saying, "is to let your best man command the light company."

"And if I do that," Lawford said, "I'll never know what potential Cornelius has. No, Sharpe, let him have his canter, eh? You've already proved yourself." Lawford stared at Sharpe, wanting his approval of the suggestion, but again Sharpe said nothing. He felt as though the bottom had dropped from his world.

And just then a gun fired from the valley.

The shell screamed through the fog, burst into sunlight above the ridge where, showing as a black ball against a clear sky, it arched over the troops to fall close beside the newly made road which linked the British and Portuguese troops along the ridge. It exploded after its first bounce, doing no harm, but a scrap of shell casing, almost spent, rapped against Lawford's tent, making the taut gray canvas shudder. "Time to go, Sharpe," Lawford said, throwing down his egg-stained napkin.

Because the French were coming.

THIRTY-THREE FRENCH BATTALIONS formed into four columns were launched across the stream and up the far slope that was thickly obscured by fog. This was only the first attack. The second attack was still assembling, their twenty-two battalions forming into two more great columns which would advance on either side of the better road that led towards the northern end of the ridge while a third, smaller column would follow behind them to exploit their success. Together the two attacks made a hammer and an anvil. The first assault, the heaviest, would follow the lesser road up to the lowest part of the ridge, capture its wide summit, then turn north to drive in the defenders desperately fending off the second blow. Marshal Masséna, waiting close to the troops who would deliver that second thunderous strike, imagined the English and Portuguese troops reduced to panic; he saw them fleeing from the ridge, throwing down packs and weapons, discarding anything that would slow them, and then he would release his cavalry to sweep across the ridge's northern end and slaughter the fugitives. He drummed his fingers against his saddle's pommel in time to the fog-muffled rhythm of the drums that sounded to the south. Those drums were driving the first attack up the slope. "What's the time?" he asked an aide.

"A quarter to six, sir."

"The fog's lifting, don't you think?" Masséna stared into the vapor with his one eye. The Emperor had taken the other in a shooting accident while they were hunting, and, ever since, Masséna had worn a patch.

"Perhaps a little, sir," the aide said doubtfully.

Tonight, Masséna thought, he would sleep in the monastery said to be on the ridge's far slope. He would send a troop of dragoons to escort Henriette from Tondela from where he had been so abruptly summoned the previous night, and he smiled as he recalled her white arms reaching playfully for him as he dressed. He had slept an hour or two with the army, and risen early to find a cold, foggy dawn, but the fog, he reckoned, was France's friend. It would let the troops get most of the way up the slope before the British and Portuguese could see them, and once the Eagles were close to the summit the business should not take long. Victory by midday, he thought, and he imagined the bells ringing out in Paris to announce the triumph of the Eagles. He wondered what new honors would come to him. He was already the Prince of Essling, but by tonight, he thought, he might have earned a dozen other royal titles. The Emperor could be generous in such things, and the Emperor expected great things of Masséna. The rest of Europe was at peace, cowed into submission by the armies of France, and so Napoleon had sent reinforcements into Spain, had formed this new Army of Portugal that had been entrusted to Masséna, and the Emperor expected Lisbon to be captured before the leaves fell. Victory, Masséna thought, victory by midday, and then the enemy's remnants would be pursued all the way to Lisbon.

"You're sure there's a monastery across the ridge?" he enquired of one of his Portuguese aides, a man who fought for the French because he believed they represented reason, liberty, modernity and rationality.

"There is, sir."

"We shall sleep there tonight," Masséna announced, and turned his one eye to another aide. "Have two squadrons ready to escort Mademoiselle Leberton from Tondela." That essential comfort assured, the Marshal spurred his horse forward through the fog. He stopped close to the stream and listened. A single cannon sounded to the south, the signal that the first attack was under way, and when the cannon's reverberating echo had died away Masséna could hear the drums fading in the distance as the four southern columns climbed the slope. It was the sound of victory. The sound of the Eagles going into battle.

It had taken over two hours to form the four columns. The men had been roused in the dark, and the reveille had been sounded an hour later to fool the British into thinking that the French had slept longer, but the columns had been forming long before the bugles sounded. Sergeants with flaming torches served as guides, and the men formed on them, company by company, but it had all taken much longer than expected. The fog confused the newly woken men. Officers gave orders, sergeants bellowed, shoved, and used their musket stocks to force men into the ranks, and some fools mistook their orders and joined the wrong column, and they had to be pulled out, cursed, and sent to their proper place, but eventually the thirty-three battalions were assembled in their four assault columns in the small meadows beside the stream.

There were eighteen thousand men in the four columns. If those men had been paraded in a line of three ranks, which was how the French made their lines, they would have stretched for two miles, but instead they had been concentrated into the four tight columns. The two largest led the attack, while the two smaller came behind, ready to exploit whatever opening the first two made. Those two larger columns had eighty men in their front ranks, but there were eighty more ranks behind and the great blocks made two battering rams, almost two miles of infantry concentrated into two moving squares that were designed to be hammered against the enemy line and overwhelm it by sheer weight.

"Stay close!" the sergeants shouted as they began to ascend the ridge. A column was no good if it lost cohesion. To work it had to be like a machine, every man in step, shoulder to shoulder, the rear ranks pushing the front rank on into the enemy guns. That front rank would probably die, as would the one behind, and the one behind that, but eventually the impetus of the massive formation should force it across its own dead and through the enemy line and then the real killing could begin. The battalions' drummers were concentrated at the center of each column and the boys played the fine rhythm of the charge, pausing every so often to let the men call out the refrain, "*Vive l'Empereur!*"

That refrain became breathless as the columns climbed. The ridge was horribly steep, lung-sapping, and men tired and so began to lag and stray. The fog was still thick. Scattered gorse bushes and stunted trees obstructed the columns which split to pass them, and after a while the fragments did not join up again, but just struggled up through the silent fog, wondering what waited for them at the summit. Before they were halfway up the hill both the leading columns had broken into groups of tired men, and the officers, swords drawn, were shouting at the groups to form ranks, to hurry, and the officers shouted from different parts of the hill and only confused the troops more so that they went first one way and then the other. The drummer boys, following the broken ranks, beat more slowly as they grew more tired.

Ahead of the columns, way ahead, and scattered in their loose formation, the French skirmishers climbed towards the light. The fog thinned as they neared the ridge's top. There was a swarm of French light troops, over six hundred *voltigeurs* in front of each column, and their job was to drive away the British and Portuguese skirmishers, force them back over the ridge top and then start shooting at the defending lines. That skirmish fire was designed to weaken those lines ready for the hammer blows coming behind.

Above the disordered columns, unseen in the fog, the Eagles flew. Napoleon's Eagles, the French standards, the gilt statuettes shining on their poles. Two had their tricolor flags attached, but most regiments took the flags off the poles and stored them at the depot in France, relying on the Emperor's Eagle to be the mark of honor. "Close on the

Eagle!" an officer shouted, and the scattered men tried to form their ranks and then, from above them, they heard the first staccato snapping as the skirmishers began their fight. A gun fired from the valley, then another, and suddenly two batteries of French artillery were firing blind into the fog, hoping their shells would rake the defenders at the ridge top.

"GOD'S TEETH!" The exclamation was torn from Colonel Lawford who, peering down the slope, saw the horde of French skirmishers break out of the fog. The voltigeurs far outnumbered the British and Portuguese light companies, but those redcoats, cazadores and greenjackets fired first. Puffs of smoke jetted from the hillside. A Frenchman twisted and fell back and then the voltigeurs went down onto one knee and aimed their muskets. The volley splintered the morning, thickening the fog with powder smoke, and Sharpe saw two redcoats and a Portuguese go down. The second men of the allied skirmishing pairs fired, but the voltigeurs were too numerous and their musket fire was almost continuous and the red, green and brown jackets were falling back. The voltigeurs advanced in short rushes, at least two of them for every allied skirmisher, and it was plain the French were winning this early contest by sheer weight of numbers.

Lieutenant Slingsby and the South Essex light troops had deployed ahead of the battalion and now found themselves on the flank of the French advance. Ahead of them was mostly empty hillside, but the voltigeurs were thick to their right and for a few moments the company was able to stand and drive in that enemy flank, but a French officer saw what was happening and shouted for two companies to chase the redcoats and greenjackets away. "Back away now," Sharpe muttered. He was mounted on Portia, Slingsby's horse, and the extra height gave him a clear view of the fight that was some three hundred paces away. "Back off!" he said louder, and the Colonel gave him an irritated look. But then Slingsby understood the danger and gave eight whistle blasts. That told the light company to retreat while inclining to their left, an order that would bring them back up the slope towards the battalion, and it was the right order, the one Sharpe would have given, but Slingsby had his blood up and did not want to fall too far back too soon and thus yield the fight to the French and so instead of slanting back up the hill as he had ordered he ran straight across the slope's face.

The men had started back up the ridge, but seeing the Lieutenant stay lower down, they hesitated. "Keep firing!" Slingsby shouted at them. "Don't bunch! Smartly now!" A ball struck a rock by his right foot and ricocheted up to the sky. Hagman shot the French officer who had led the move against the South Essex and Harris put down an enemy sergeant who fell into a gorse bush, but the other Frenchmen kept advancing and Slingsby slowly backed away, yet instead of being between the French and the South Essex he was now on the enemy's flank, and another French officer, reckoning that the South Essex's light company had been brushed aside, shouted at the voltigeurs to climb straight up the hill towards the right flank of the South Essex line. Cannon opened fire from the ridge top, shooting from the left of the battalion down into the fog behind the voltigeurs. "They must have seen something," Lawford said, patting Lightning's neck to calm the stallion, which had been frightened by the sudden crash of the six-pounders. "Hear the drums?"

"I can hear them," Sharpe said. It was the old sound, the French *pas de charge*, the noise of attacking Eagles. "Old trousers," he said. That was the British nickname for the *pas de charge*.

"Why do we call it that?"

"It's a song, sir."

"Do I want to hear it?"

"Not from me, sir. Can't sing."

Lawford smiled, though he had not really been listening. He took off his cocked hat and ran a hand through his hair. "Their main body can't be far off now," he said, wanting the confrontation over. The voltigeurs were no longer advancing, but shooting at the line to weaken it before the column arrived.

Sharpe was watching Slingsby who, seeing the French turn away from him, now seemed momentarily bereft. He had not done badly. All his men were alive, including Ensign Iliffe who, when he had returned Sharpe's sword, had been pale with nervousness. The boy had stood his ground, though, and that was all that could be expected of him, while the rest of Slingsby's men had scored some hits on the enemy, but now that enemy climbed away from the company. What Slingsby should do, Sharpe thought, was climb the hill and spread his men across the face of the South Essex, but just then the first of the columns came into view from the fog.

They were shadows first, then dark shapes, and Sharpe could make no sense of it, for the column was no longer a coherent mass of men, but rather groups of men who emerged ragged from the whiteness. Two more cannons opened fire from the ridge, their round shot banging through files of men to spray the fog with blood, and still more men came, hundreds of men, and as they came into the light they hurried together, trying to reform the column, and the cannons, reloaded with canister, blasted great jagged holes in the blue uniforms.

Slingsby was still out on the flank, but the sight of the column prompted him to order his men to open fire. The voltigeurs saw what was happening and dozens ran to cut off the light company. "For Christ's sake!" Sharpe said aloud, and this time Lawford did not look irritated, just worried, but Slingsby saw the danger and shouted at his men to retreat as quickly as they could. They scrambled up the slope. It was not a dignified withdrawal, they were not firing as they backed, but just running for their lives. One or two, farthest down the slope, ran downhill to hide in the fog, but the rest managed to scramble their way back to the ridge's summit where Slingsby barked at them to spread along the battalion's face.

"Too late," Lawford said quietly, "too damn late. Major Forrest! Call in skirmishers."

The bugle sounded and the light company, panting from their near escape, formed at the left of the line. The voltigeurs who had chased the light company off the column's flank were firing at the South Essex now and the bullets hissed close to Sharpe, for most of the Frenchmen were aiming at the colors and at the group of mounted officers clustered beside the two flags. A man went down in number four company. "Close ranks!" a sergeant shouted, and a corporal, appointed as a file closer, dragged the wounded man back from the ranks.

"Take him to the surgeon, Corporal," Lawford said, then watched as the great mass of Frenchmen, thousands of them now visible at the swirling margins of the fog, turned towards his ranks. "Make ready!"

Close to six hundred men cocked their muskets. The voltigeurs knew what was coming and fired at the battalion. Bullets twitched the heavy yellow silk of the regimental color. Two more men were hit in front of Sharpe and one was screaming in pain. "Close up! Close up!" a corporal shouted.

"Stop your bleeding noise, boy!" Sergeant Willetts of five company growled.

The column was two hundred paces away, still ragged, but in sight of the crest now. The voltigeurs were closer, just a hundred paces away, kneeling and firing, standing to reload and then firing again. Slingsby had let his riflemen go a few paces forward of the line and those men were hurting the voltigeurs, taking out their officers and sergeants, but a score of rifles could not blunt this attack. That would be a job for the redcoats. "When you fire," Lawford called, "aim low! Don't waste His Majesty's lead! You will aim low!" He rode along the right of his line, repeating the message. "Aim low! Remember your training! Aim low!"

The column was coalescing, the ranks shuffling together as if for protection. A nine-pounder round shot seared through it, sending up a long fast spray of blood. The drummers were beating frantically. Sharpe glanced left and saw the Connaught Rangers were closing on the South Essex, coming to add their volleys, then a voltigeur's bullet slapped off the top of his horse's left ear and twitched at the sleeve of his jacket. He could see the faces of the men in the column's front rank, see their mustaches, see their mouths opening to cheer their Emperor. A canister from a nine-pounder tore into them, twitching files red and ragged, but they closed up, stepped over the dead and dying, and came on with their long bayonets gleaming. The Eagles were bright in the new sunlight. Still more cannons opened fire, blasting the column with canisters loaded over round shot, and the French, sensing that there was no artillery off to their left, slanted that way, climbing now towards the Portuguese battalion on the right of the South Essex. "Offering themselves to us," Lawford said. He had ridden back to the battalion's center and now watched as the French turned away to reveal their right flank to his muskets. "I think we should join the dance, Sharpe, don't you? Battalion!" He took a deep breath. "Battalion will advance!"

Lawford marched the South Essex forward, only twenty yards, but the movement scared the voltigeurs who thought they might be the target of a regimental volley and so they hurried away to join the column that now marched slantwise across the front of the South Essex. "Present!" Lawford shouted, and nearly six hundred muskets went into men's shoulders.

"Fire!"

The massive volley pumped out a long cloud of gun smoke that smelled like rotting eggs, and then the musket stocks thumped onto the ground and men took new cartridges and began to reload. "Platoon fire now!" Lawford called to his officers, and he took off his hat again and wiped sweat from his forehead. It was still cold, the wind blowing chill from the far-off Atlantic, yet Lawford was hot. Sharpe heard the splintering crack of the Portuguese volley, then the South Essex began their own rolling fire, shooting half company by half company from the center of the line, the bullets never ending, the men going through the well-practiced motions of loading and firing, loading and firing. The enemy was invisible now, hidden from the battalion by its own gun smoke. Sharpe rode along the right of the line, deliberately not going left so no one could accuse him of interfering with Slingsby. "Aim low!" he called to the men. "Aim low!" A few bullets were coming back out of the smoke, but they were nearly all high. Inexperienced men usually shot high and the French, who were being flayed by the Portuguese and by the South Essex, were trying to fire uphill into a cloud of smoke and they were taking a terrible punishment from muskets and cannons. Some of the enemy must be panicking because Sharpe saw two ramrods go wheeling overhead, evidence that the men were too scared to remember their musket drill. He stopped by the grenadier company and watched the Portuguese and he reckoned they were firing as efficiently as any redcoat battalion. Their half-company volleys were steady as clockwork, the smoke rolling out from the battalion's center, and he knew the bullets must be striking hard into the disintegrating column's face.

More muskets flared as the 88th, the feared Connaught Rangers, wheeled forward of the line to blast at the wounded French column, but somehow the French held on. Their outer ranks and files were being killed and injured, but the mass of men inside the column still lived and more were climbing the hill to replace the dead, and the whole mass, in no good order, but crowding together, tried to advance into the terrible volleys. More red- and brown-jacketed troops were moving towards the fight, adding their musketry, but still the French pushed against the storm. The column was dividing again, torn by the slashing round shots and ripped by canister, so now it seemed as though disorganized groups of men were struggling uphill past piles of dead. Sharpe could hear the officers and sergeants shouting them on, could hear the rattle of the frantic drums, which was now challenged by a British band that was playing "Men of Harlech." "Not very appropriate!" Major Forrest had joined Sharpe and had to shout to make himself heard over the dense sound of musketry. "We're hardly in a hollow."

"You're wounded," Sharpe said.

"A scratch." Forrest glanced at his right sleeve, which was torn and bloodstained. "How are the Portuguese?"

"Good!"

"The Colonel was wondering where you were," Forrest said.

"Did he think I'd gone back to the light company?" Sharpe asked sourly.

"Now, now, Sharpe," Forrest chided him.

Sharpe clumsily turned his horse and kicked it back to Lawford. "The buggers aren't moving!" the Colonel greeted him indignantly. Lawford was leaning forward in his saddle, trying to see through the smoke and, between the half-company volleys, when the foul-smelling cloud thinned a little, he could just make out the huge groups of stubborn Frenchmen clinging to the hillside beneath the crest. "Will bayonets shift them?" he asked Sharpe. "By God, I've a mind to try steel. What do you think?"

"Two more volleys?" Sharpe suggested. It was chaos down the slope. The French column, broken again, was now clumps of men who fired uphill into the smoke, while more men, perhaps another column altogether or else stragglers from the first, were continually joining the groups. French artillery was adding to the din. They must have brought their howitzers to the foot of the slope and the shells, shot blind into the fog, were screaming overhead to crash onto the rear area where women, campfires, tents and tethered horses were the only casualties. A group of French voltigeurs had taken the rocky spur where Sharpe had placed his picquet in the night. "We should move those fellows away," Sharpe said, pointing to them.

"They're not harming us," Lawford shouted above the din, "but we can't let those wretches stay here!" He pointed to the smoke-wreathed Frenchmen. "That's our land!" He took a breath. "Fix bayonets! Fix bayonets!"

Colonel Wallace, commander of the 88th, must have had the same thought, for Sharpe was aware that the Irishmen had stopped firing, and they would only do that to fix the seventeen-inch blades on their muskets. Clicks sounded all along the South Essex line as the two ranks slotted their bayonets onto blackened muzzles. The French, with extraordinary bravery, used the lull in the musket fire to try and advance again. Men clambered over dead and dying bodies, officers shouted them forward, the drummers redoubled their efforts and suddenly the Eagles were moving again. The leading Frenchmen were among the bodies of the dead voltigeurs now and must have been convinced that one more hard push would break through the thin line of Portuguese and British troops, yet the whole hilltop must have seemed ripples of flame and rills of smoke to them. "South Essex!" Lawford shouted. "Advance!" The cannons jetted more powder smoke and flaming scraps of wadding deep into the tight French ranks. Sharpe could hear the screaming of wounded men now. Musket shots hammered from a knot of Frenchmen to the right, but the South Essex and the men of Connaught were going forward, bayonets bright, and Sharpe kicked the horse forward, following the battalion, which suddenly broke into the double and shouted their challenge. The Portuguese, seeing the redcoats advance, cheered and fixed their own blades.

The charge struck home. The French were not formed properly, most did not have loaded muskets and the British line closed on the clumps of blue-coated infantry and then wrapped around them as the redcoats lunged with bayonets. The enemy fought back and Sharpe heard the crack of muskets clashing, the scrape of blades, the curses and shouts of wounded soldiers. The enemy dead obstructed the British, but they clambered over the bodies to rip with long blades at the living. "Hold your lines! Hold your lines!" a sergeant bellowed, and in some places the companies had split because some files were attacking one French group and the rest another, and Sharpe saw two French soldiers break clear through such a gap and start uphill. He turned the horse towards them and drew his sword, and the two men, hearing the blade's long scrape against the scabbard's throat, immediately threw down their muskets and spread their hands. Sharpe pointed the sword uphill, indicating they were prisoners now and should go to the South Essex color party. One obediently set off, but the other snatched up his musket and fled downhill. Sharpe let him go. He could see the Eagles were being hurried down the slope, being carried away from the danger of capture, and more Frenchmen, seeing their standards retreat, broke from the unequal fight. The allied cannons had stopped their fire because their targets were masked by their own men, but the French guns still shot through the thinning fog and then, off to Sharpe's right, more cannons opened and he saw a second column, even larger than the first, appearing on the lower slope.

The first French attack broke from the back. Most of the men in the front ranks could not escape because they were trapped by their comrades behind, and those men were being savaged by Portuguese and British bayonets, but the French rear ranks followed the Eagles and, as the pressure eased, the remnants of the column fled. They ran, leaping over the dead and wounded that marked their passage up the hill, and the redcoats and Portuguese pursued them. A man from the grenadier company rammed his bayonet into the small of a Frenchman's back, stabbed him again when he fell, then kicked him and stabbed him a third time when the man obstinately refused to die. A drum, painted with a French Eagle, rolled downhill. A drummer boy, his arm shot off by a cannonball, hunched in misery beside a gorse bush. British redcoats and blue-jacketed Portuguese ran past him, intent on pursuing and killing the fleeing enemy. "Come back!" Lawford shouted angrily. "Come back!" The men did not hear him, or did not care; they had won and now they simply wanted to kill. Lawford looked for Sharpe. "Get them, Sharpe!" the Colonel snapped. "Fetch them back!"

Sharpe wondered how the hell he was to stop such a chaotic pursuit, but he obediently kicked his borrowed horse, which immediately bolted downhill so violently that he was nearly thrown off the back of the saddle. He yanked the reins to slow the mare and she swerved to her left and Sharpe heard a bullet flutter past him and looked up to see that scores of voltigeurs still held the rocky knoll and were firing at him. The horse ran on, Sharpe clinging to the saddle's pommel for dear life, then she stumbled and he felt himself flying. By a miracle his feet came clear of the stirrups and he landed on the slope with an almighty thump, rolled for a few yards and then banged against a boulder. He was sure he must have broken a dozen bones, but when he picked himself up he found he was only bruised. Ferragus had hurt him much worse, but the fall from the horse had exacerbated those injuries. He thought the mare must have been shot, but when he turned round to look for his fallen sword he saw the horse trotting calmly uphill without any apparent damage except her bullet-cropped ear. He swore at the mare, abandoned her, picked up his sword and rifle and went on downhill.

He shouted at redcoats to get back to the ridge. Some were Irishmen from the 88th, many of them busy plundering the bodies of French dead and, because he was an officer they did not know, they snarled, swore or simply ignored him, implicitly daring him to tangle with them. Sharpe let them be. If there was one regiment in the army that could look after itself it was the men of Connaught. He ran on down, shouting at troops to get the hell up to the ridge top, but most were halfway down the long slope, almost to where the fog had retreated, and Sharpe had to run hard to get within shouting distance and it was then, as the fog swirled away, that he saw two more French columns climbing from the valley. There was another column, he knew, somewhere near the summit, but these were new troops making a fresh attack. "South Essex!" he shouted. He had been a sergeant once and still had a voice that could carry halfway across a city, though using it caused his ribs to bang pain into his lungs

"South Essex! Back! Back!" A shell struck the hill not five paces away, bounced up and exploded in jets of hissing smoke. Two scraps of casing spun past his face so close that he felt the momentary warmth and the slap of the hot air. French cannon were at the foot of the slope, just visible in the thinning fog, and they were firing at the men who had pursued the broken column, but who now had checked their reckless downhill run to watch the new columns advance. "South Essex!" Sharpe roared, and the anger in his voice was harsh, and at last men turned to trudge uphill. Slingsby, his saber drawn, was watching the columns, but, hearing Sharpe, he suddenly snapped at men to turn around and go back to the ridge top. Harper was one of them and, seeing Sharpe, the big man angled across the slope. His seven-barreled gun was slung on his back and in his hand was his rifle with its twenty-three-inch sword bayonet reddened to its brass handle. The rest of the light company, at last aware that more columns were attacking, hurried after Harper.

Sharpe waited to make sure that every redcoat and rifleman had turned back. French shells and round shot were banging onto the hill, but using artillery against such scattered targets was a waste of powder. One cannonball, spent after its bouncing impact, rolled down the hill to make Harper skip aside, then he grinned at Sharpe. "Gave it to them proper, sir."

"You should have stayed up top."

"It's a hell of a climb," Harper said, surprised to see how far down the hill he had gone. He fell in beside Sharpe and the two climbed together. "Mister Slingsby, sir," the Irishman said, then fell silent.

"Mister Slingsby what?"

"He said you weren't well, sir, and he was taking command."

"Then he's a lying bastard," Sharpe said, careless that he ought not to say such a thing of another officer.

"Is he now?" Harper said tonelessly.

"The Colonel told me to step aside. He wants Mister Slingsby to have a chance."

"He had that right enough," Harper said.

"I should have been there," Sharpe said.

"And so you should," Harper said, "but the lads are all alive. Except Dodd."

"Matthew? Is he dead?"

"Dead or alive, I don't know," Harper said, "but I couldn't see him anywhere. I was keeping an eye on the boys, but I can't find Matthew. Maybe he went back up the hill."

"I didn't see him," Sharpe said. They both turned and counted heads and saw the light company were all present except for Corporal Dodd. "We'll look for him as we climb," Sharpe said, meaning they would look for his body.

Lieutenant Slingsby, red-faced and saber drawn, hurried over to Sharpe. "Did you bring orders, Sharpe?" he demanded.

"The orders are to get back to the top of the hill as quick as you can," Sharpe said.

"Quick, men!" Slingsby called, then turned back to Sharpe. "Our fellows did well!"

"Did they?"

"Outflanked the voltigeurs, Sharpe. Outflanked them, by God! We turned their flank."

"Did you?"

"Pity you didn't see us." Slingsby was excited, proud of himself. "We slipped past them, drove in their wing, then hurt them."

Sharpe thought the light company had been led to one side where it had been about as much use as a kettle with a hole in it, and had then been ignominiously chased away, but he kept silent. Harper unclipped his sword bayonet, cleaned the blade on the jacket of a French corpse, then quickly ran his hands over the man's pockets and pouches.

He ran to catch up with Sharpe and offered a half sausage. "I know you like Crapaud sausage, sir."

Sharpe put it into his pouch, saving it for dinner. A bullet whispered past him, almost spent, and he looked up to see puffs of smoke from the rocky knoll. "Pity the voltigeurs took that," he said.

"No trouble to us," Slingsby said dismissively. "Turned their flank, by God, turned their damn flank and then punished them!"

Harper glanced at Sharpe, looked as though he would start laughing, and managed to keep a straight face. The big British and Portuguese guns were hammering at the second big column, the one that had ar-

rived just after the first had been defeated. That column was fighting at
the top of the ridge and the two fresh columns, both smaller than the first
pair, were climbing behind. Another bullet from the voltigeurs in their
rocky nest whipped past Sharpe and he angled away from them.

"You still have my horse, Sharpe?" Slingsby demanded.

"Not here," Sharpe said, and Harper made a choking sound which
he turned into a cough.

"You said something, Sergeant Harper?" Slingsby demanded crisply.

"Smoke in my throat, sir," Harper said. "It catches something dreadful, sir. I was always a sickly child, sir, on account of the peat smoke in
our cottage. My mother made me sleep outside, God rest her soul, until
the wolves came for me."

"Wolves?" Slingsby sounded cautious.

"Three of them, sir, big as you'd like, with slobbery great tongues the
color of your coat, sir, and I had to sleep inside after that, and I just
coughed my way through the nights. It was all that smoke, see?"

"Your parents should have built a chimney," Slingsby said disapprovingly.

"Now why didn't we think of that?" Harper enquired innocently and
Sharpe laughed aloud, earning a vicious look from the Lieutenant.

The rest of the light company was close now and Ensign Iliffe was
among them. Sharpe saw the boy's saber was red at the tip. Sharpe nodded at it. "Well done, Mister Iliffe."

"He just came at me, sir." The boy had suddenly found his voice. "A
big man!"

"He was a sergeant," Harris explained, "and he was going to stick
Mister Iliffe, sir."

"He was!" Iliffe was excited.

"But Mister Iliffe stepped past him neat as a squirrel, sir, and gave
him steel in the belly. It was a good stroke, Mister Iliffe," Harris said, and
the Ensign just blushed.

Sharpe tried to recall the first time he had been in a fight, steel
against steel, but the trouble was he had been brought up in London and
almost born to that kind of savagery. But for Mister Iliffe, son of an im-
poverished Essex gentleman, there had to be a shock in realizing that

some great brute of a Frenchman was trying to kill him and Sharpe, re-membering how sick the boy had been, reckoned he had done very well. He grinned at Iliffe. "Only the one Crapaud, Mister Iliffe?"

"Only one, sir."

"And you an officer, eh? You're supposed to kill two a day!"

The men laughed. Iliffe just looked pleased with himself.

"Enough chatter!" Slingsby took command of the company. "Hurry up!" The South Essex colors had moved south along the ridge top, evi-dently going towards the fight with the second leading column, and the light company slanted that way. The French shells had stopped their fu-tile harassment of the slope and were instead firing at the ridge top now, their fuses leaving small pencil traces in the sky above the light company. The sound of the second column was loud now, a cacophony of drums, war cries and the stutter of the skirmishers' muskets.

Sharpe went with the light company to the ridge top where he re-luctantly let Slingsby take them again while he looked for Lawford. The fog, which had cleared almost to the valley bottom, was thickening again now, a great billow of it hiding the two smaller columns and rolling southwards to where, by the rough track that climbed the ridge, the sec-ond French column was advancing. That second column, larger than the first, had climbed more slowly, and had been given an easier time than their defeated comrades for they had been able to follow the track that twisted its way up the ridge's slope, and the track gave them a guide in the fog so that when they erupted into the sunlight they had managed to keep their ranks. Eight thousand men, driven by one hundred and sixty-three drummers, closed on the crest and there, under the flail of fire, they stopped.

The first battalion of the 74th Highlanders had been waiting and be-side them was a whole brigade of Portuguese and on their right flank were two batteries of nine-pounders. The guns struck first, flaying the column with round shot and canister, making the heather slick with blood, and then the Highlanders opened fire. The range was very long, more suited for riflemen than redcoats, but the bullets slapped home and then the Portuguese opened fire and the column, like a bull confused by an unexpected attack by terriers, stalled. Columns were again meeting lines and, though the column outnumbered the line, the line would always outshoot the column. Only the men at the front of the column and a handful along the edge could use their muskets, but every man in the British and Portuguese line could fire his weapon and the column was being driven in, turned red, hammered, yet it did not retreat. The voltigeurs, who had chased away the Scottish and Portuguese skirmishers, retreated to the column's front rank which now tried to return the musket fire. French officers shouted at the men to march, the drummers persisted with the *pas de charge*, but the front ranks would not press up into the relentless pelting of the musket balls. Instead, feebly, they returned the fire, but the men in the column's front rank were dying every second, and then more Portuguese cannons came to the right flank of the 74th. The guns slewed around, their horses were taken back out of musket range, and the gunners rammed canister over round shot. The new guns crashed back and the leading left corner of the column began to resemble the devil's butcher's shop. It was a sodden tangle of broken bodies, blood and screaming men. And still the guns recoiled, jetting a spew of smoke with every discharge, their barrels depressed to fire down into the crowded mass of Frenchmen. Every round shot had to be wedged in the barrel with a circle of rope to stop the ball trickling down the barrel, and the rope loops burned in the air like crazed fireballs as they spun in mad whorls. More allied troops were coming to the fight, marching along the newly made road from the southern end of the long ridge. That southern end was quiet, apparently under no threat from the French, and the arriving men formed south of the guns and added their own musket fire.

The column shuddered under the onslaught of the merciless guns and then began to edge northwards. The French officers could see there was an empty space on the ridge beyond the Portuguese brigade and they shouted at their men to go right. A voltigeur officer sent a company ahead to occupy the skyline as, behind them, the cumbersome mass edged its way towards the opening, leaving a right-angled line of bodies, the remnants of their left flank and front lines, thick on the rocky slope.

Lieutenant Colonel Lawford saw the column approaching and, more urgently, the voltigeurs running to claim the open ground. "Mister

Slingsby!" Lawford called. "You will deploy the light company! Send those miscreants back where they belong. Battalion! Battalion will move to the right!" Lawford was marching the South Essex into the open space, going to seal it off, and Slingsby had the job of throwing back the enemy skirmishers. Sharpe, back on Slingsby's horse which had been rescued by Major Forrest, rode behind the color party and counted the Eagles in the shuffling column. He could see fifteen. The noise of splintering dominated the air, the sound of muskets like dry thorns burning, and the incessant crackling was echoing from the distant side of the valley. The powder smoke drifted above the fog which had crept back up the slope almost to the ridge's top. Every now and then the great white vaporous mass twitched as a French round shot or shell punched through. The hillside was dotted with bodies, all blue-coated. A man crawled downhill, trailing a broken leg. A dog ran to and fro, barking, trying to rouse its dead master. A French officer, sword discarded, held his hands to his face as blood oozed between his fingers. The cannons hammered and bucked, and then came the distinctive crack of the rifles as Sharpe's company went into action. He hated just watching them, but he also admired them. They were good. They had taken the enemy voltigeurs by surprise and the riflemen had already put down two officers and now the muskets took up the fight.

Slingsby, holding his saber scabbard clear of the rough ground, strutted up and down behind them. He was doubtless snapping his orders and Sharpe felt a surge of hatred for the man. The bastard was going to take his job and all because he had married Lawford's sister-in-law. The hatred was like bile and Sharpe instinctively reached for his rifle, took it from his shoulder and pulled the flint to half cock. He used his thumb to push the strike plate forward and the frizzen leaped away on its spring. He felt in the pan, making certain the priming was still there after his tumble from the horse. He confirmed the powder was there, gritty under his dirty thumb and, staring all the while at Slingsby, he pulled the frizzen back into place and then cocked the gun fully. He raised it to his shoulder. The horse stirred and he growled at it to be still.

He aimed at Slingsby's back. At the small of his back. At the place where two brass buttons were sewn above the red jacket's vent. Sharpe wanted to pull the trigger. Who would know? The Lieutenant was a hundred paces away, a reasonable shot for a rifle. Sharpe imagined Slingsby arching his back as his spine was shot through, shuddering as he fell, the clang of his scabbard chains as he struck the ground and the quiver of life fighting to stay in a dying body. The strutting little bastard, Sharpe thought, and he tightened his finger on the rifle's trigger. No one was watching him, they were all staring at the column which edged ever closer, or if some men were watching him then they must assume he was aiming at a voltigeur. It would not be Sharpe's first murder and he doubted it would be his last, and then a sudden spasm of hatred coursed through him, a spasm so fierce that he shivered and, almost involuntarily, pulled the trigger all the way back. The rifle banged into his shoulder, startling his horse, which twitched away to one side.

The ball spun across the heads of number four company, missed Lieutenant Slingsby's left arm by an inch, struck a rock on the edge of the hillside and ricocheted up to hit a voltigeur beneath the chin. The man had managed to get very near to Slingsby and had just stood to shoot his musket at close range and Sharpe's bullet lifted him off the ground so that the dead man looked as if he was being propelled backwards by a jet of blood, then the Frenchman collapsed in a crash of musket, bayonet and body.

"Good God, Richard! That was fine shooting!" Major Leroy had been watching. "That fellow was stalking Slingsby! I've been watching him."

"So was I, sir," Sharpe lied.

"Bloody fine shooting! And from horseback! Did you see that, Colonel?"

"Leroy?"

"Sharpe just saved Slingsby's life. Damnedest piece of shooting I've ever seen!"

Sharpe slung the unloaded rifle. He was suddenly ashamed of himself. Slingsby might be an irritant, he might be a cocky man, but he had never set out to harm Sharpe. It was not Slingsby's fault that his laugh, his presence and his very appearance galled Sharpe to the quick, and a new misery descended on Sharpe, the misery of knowing he had let himself down, and even Lawford's energetic and undeserved congratulations did nothing to lift his spirits. He turned away from the battalion, staring blankly at the back area where two men were holding a wounded grenadier on the table outside the surgeon's tent. Blood sprang from the saw that was being whipped to and fro across the man's thigh bone. A few yards away a wounded man and two of the battalion's wives, all with French muskets, were guarding a dozen prisoners. A toddler played with a French bayonet. Monks were leading a dozen mules loaded with barrels of water that they were distributing to the allied troops. A Portuguese battalion, followed by five companies of redcoats, marched north on the new road, evidently going to reinforce the northern end of the ridge. A mounted galloper, carrying a message from one general to another, pounded along the new road, leaving a plume of dust in his wake. The toddler swore at the horseman who had scared him by riding too close and the women laughed. The monks dropped a water barrel behind the South Essex, then went on towards the Portuguese brigade.

"They're too far away to charge!" Lawford called to Sharpe.

Sharpe turned and saw that the column had stalled again. The ground they had wanted to take had been occupied by the South Essex and now the vast mass of men was content to spread slowly outwards to form a thick line and then trade musket shots with the troops on top of the hill. The attack had been stopped and not all the drumming in the world was going to start it back into motion. "We need a pair of guns here," Sharpe said and he looked to his left to see whether any batteries were nearby and he saw that the South Essex, in moving to block the column's advance, had left a great gap on the hilltop between themselves and the Connaught Rangers, and that the gap was being rapidly filled by a cloud of voltigeurs. Those voltigeurs had come from the rocky knoll and, seeing the ridge ahead deserted, they had advanced to occupy the abandoned ground. Then the fog shuddered, was swept aside by a gust of wind, and Sharpe saw it was not just voltigeurs who were filling the gap in the British line, but that the last two French columns had climbed to the same place. They had been shielded by the fog so the Portuguese and British gunners had spared them and now, hurrying, they were scrambling the last few yards to the ridge's empty crest. Their Eagles reflected the sun, victory was just yards away and there was nothing in front of the French but bare grass and vacancy.

And Sharpe was seeing disaster.

CHAPTER 4

STRANGELY, ON THE MORNING that the guns began to fire and make the windows, glasses and chandeliers vibrate throughout Coimbra, Ferragus announced that his brother's household, which had readied itself to go south to Lisbon, was to stay in Coimbra after all. He made the announcement in his brother's study, a gloomy room lined with unread books, where the family and the servants had gathered on Ferragus's summons.

Beatriz Ferreira, who was scared of her brother-in-law, crossed herself. "Why are we staying?" she asked.

"You hear that?" Ferragus gestured towards the sound of the guns that was like an unending muted thunder. "Our army and the English troops are giving battle. My brother says that if there is a battle then the enemy will be stopped. Well, there is a battle, so if my brother is right then the French will not come."

"God and the saints be thanked," Beatriz Ferreira said, and the servants murmured agreement.

"But suppose they do come?" It was Sarah who asked.

Ferragus frowned because he thought the question impertinent, but he supposed that was because Miss Fry was an arrogant English bitch who knew no better. "If they are not stopped," he said irritably, "then we shall know, because our army must retreat through Coimbra. We shall leave then. But for the moment you will assume we are staying." He nodded to show that his announcement was done and the household filed from the room.

Ferragus was uncomfortable in his brother's house. It was too full of their parents' belongings, too luxurious. His own quarters in Coimbra were above a brothel in the lower town where he kept little more than a bed, table and chair, but Ferragus had promised to keep a watchful eye on his brother's house and family, and that watchful eye extended past the battle. If it were won, then the French would presumably retreat, yet Ferragus was also plotting what he should do if the battle were lost. If Lord Wellington could not hold the great, gaunt ridge of Bussaco against the French, then how would he defend the lower hills in front of Lisbon? A defeated army would be in no mood to face the victorious French again, and so a loss at Bussaco would surely mean that Lisbon itself would fall inside a month. *Os ingleses por mar.* His brother had tried to deny that, to persuade Ferragus that the English would stay, but in his heart Ferragus knew that Portugal's allies would run back to the sea and go home. And why, if that happened, should he be trapped in Lisbon with the conquering French? Better to be caught here, in his own town, and Ferragus was planning how he would survive in that new world in which the French, at last, captured all of Portugal.

He had never discounted such a capture. Ferreira had warned him of the possibility, and the tons of flour that Sharpe had destroyed on the hill-top had been a token offer to the invaders, an offer to let them know that Ferragus was a man with whom negotiations could be conducted. It had been insurance, for Ferragus had no love for the French; he certainly did not want them in Portugal, but he knew it would be better to be a partner of the invaders rather than their victim. He was a wealthy man with much to lose, and if the French offered protection he would stay wealthy. If he resisted, even if he did nothing except flee to Lisbon, the French would strip him bare. He had no doubt that he would lose some of his wealth if the French came, but if he cooperated with them he would retain more than enough. That was just common sense and, as he sat in his brother's study and listened to the shudder of distant gunfire, he was thinking that it had been a mistake to even consider fleeing to Lisbon. If this battle were won then the French would never come here, and if it were lost, all would be lost. Best therefore to stay near his property and so protect it.

His elder brother was the key. Pedro Ferreira was a respected staff officer and his contacts stretched across the gap between the armies to those Portuguese officers who had allied themselves with the French. Ferragus, through his brother, could reach the French and offer them the one thing they most wanted: food. In his warehouse in the lower town he had hoarded six months' worth of hard biscuit, two months' supply of salt beef, a month's supply of salt cod and a stack of other food and materials. There was lamp oil, boot leather, linen, horseshoes and nails. The French would want to steal it, but Ferragus had to devise a way to make them buy it. That way Ferragus would survive.

He opened the study door, shouted for a servant and sent her to summon Miss Fry to the study. "I cannot write," he explained to her when she arrived, holding up his bruised right hand to prove the incapacity. In truth he could write, though his knuckles were still sore and to flex his fingers was painful, but he did not want to write. He wanted Sarah. "You will write for me," he went on, "so sit."

Sarah bridled at his abrupt tone, but obediently sat at the Major's desk where she pulled paper, inkwell and sand shaker towards her. Ferragus stood close behind her. "I am ready," she said.

Ferragus said nothing. Sarah looked at the wall opposite that was filled with leather-bound books. The room smelled of cigar smoke. The gunfire was persisting, a grumble from far away like thunder in the next county. "The letter," Ferragus said, startling her with his gravelly voice, "is for my brother." He moved even closer so that Sarah was aware of his big presence just behind the chair. "Give him my regards," Ferragus said, "and tell him that all is well in Coimbra."

Sarah found a steel-nibbed pen, dipped it in ink and began writing. The nib made a scratching noise. "Tell him," Ferragus went on, "that the matter of honor is not settled. The man escaped."

"Just that, *senhor*?" Sarah asked.

"Just that," Ferragus said in his deep voice. Damn Sharpe, he thought. The wretched rifleman had destroyed the flour, and so Ferragus's token gift to the French had stayed ungiven, and the French had been expecting the flour and they would now think Ferragus could not be trusted, and that left Ferragus and his brother with a problem. How to reassure the enemy? And would the enemy need reassurance? Would they even come? "Tell my brother," he went on, "that I rely on his judgment whether or not the enemy will be stopped at Bussaco."

Sarah wrote. As the ink began to thin on the nib she dipped the pen again and then froze because Ferragus's fingers were touching the nape of her neck. For a heartbeat she did not move, then she slapped the pen down. "*Senhor*, you are touching me."

"So?"

"So stop! Or do you wish me to call Major Ferreira's wife?"

Ferragus chuckled, but took his fingers away. "Pick up your pen, Miss Fry," he said, "and tell my brother that I pray the enemy will be stopped."

Sarah added the new sentence. She was blushing, not from embarrassment, but out of rage. How dare Ferragus touch her? She pressed too hard on the pen and the ink spattered in tiny droplets across the words. "But tell him," the harsh voice persisted behind her, "that if the enemy is not stopped, then I have decided to do what we discussed. Tell him he must arrange protection."

"Protection for what, *senhor*?" Sarah asked in a tight voice.

"He will know what I mean," Ferragus said impatiently. "You just write, woman." He listened to the pen's tiny noise and sensed, from the force of the nib on the paper, the extent of the girl's anger. She was a proud one, he thought. Poor and proud, a dangerous mixture, and Ferragus saw her as a challenge. Most women were frightened of him, terrified even, and he liked that, but Miss Fry seemed to think that because she was English she was safe. He would like to see terror replace that confidence, see her coldness warm into fear. She would fight, he thought, and that would make it even better and he considered taking her right there, on the desk, muffling her screams as he raped her white flesh, but there was still a terrible pain in his groin from the kick Sharpe had given him and he knew he would not be able to finish what he began and, besides, he would rather wait until his brother's wife was gone from the house. In a day or two, he thought, he would take Miss Fry's English pride and wipe his arse on it. "Read what you have written," he ordered her.

Sarah read the words in a small voice. Ferragus, satisfied, ordered her to write his name and seal the letter. "Use this." He gave her his own seal and, when Sarah pressed it into the wax, she saw the image of a naked woman. She ignored it, rightly suspecting that Ferragus had been trying to embarrass her. "You can go now," he told her coldly, "but send Miguel to me."

Miguel was one of his most trusted men and he was ordered to carry the letter to where the cannons sounded. "Find my brother," Ferragus instructed, "give this to him and bring me his answer."

The next few days, Ferragus thought, would be dangerous. Some money and lives would be lost, but if he was clever, and just a little bit lucky, much could be gained.

Including Miss Fry. Who did not matter. In many ways, he knew, she was a distraction and distractions were dangerous, but they also made life interesting. Captain Sharpe was a second distraction, and Ferragus wryly noted the coincidence that he was suddenly obsessed by two English folk. One, he was sure, would live and scream while the other, the one who wore the green jacket, must scream and die.

It would just take luck and a little cleverness.

THE FRENCH STRATEGY WAS SIMPLE. A column must gain the ridge, turn north and fight its way along the summit. The British and Portuguese, turning to meet that threat, would be hammered by the second attack at the ridge's northern end and, thus pincered, Wellington's troops would collapse between the two French forces. Masséna's cavalry, released to the pursuit, would harry the defeated enemy all the way to Coimbra. Once Coimbra was captured the march on Lisbon could not take long.

Lisbon would then fall. British shipping would be ejected from the Tagus and other French forces would advance north to capture Porto and so deny the British another major harbor. Portugal would belong to the French, and what remained of the British army would be marched into captivity and the forces that had defeated it would be free to capture Cadiz and maul the scattered Spanish armies in the south. Britain would face a decision then, whether to sue for peace or face years of futile war, and France, once Spain and Portugal were pacified, could turn her armies to whatever new lands the Emperor wished to bless with French civilization. It was all so very simple, really, just so long as a column reached the ridge of Bussaco.

And two columns were there. Both were small columns, just seven battalions between them, fewer than four thousand men, but they were there, on top, in the sunlight, staring at the smoky remnants of British campfires, and more Frenchmen were coming up behind, and the only immediate threat was a Portuguese battalion that was marching north on the new road made just behind the ridge's crest. That unsuspecting battalion was met by the closest French column with a blast of musketry and, because the Portuguese were in column of companies, in march order rather than fighting order, the volley drove into their leading troops, and the French, seeing an opportunity, began to deploy into a ragged line, thus unmasking the files in the center of the column who could now add their fire. Voltigeurs had advanced across the summit, almost to the newly made road, and they began firing at the flank of the embattled Portuguese. British and Portuguese women fled from the voltigeurs, scrambling away with their children.

The Portuguese edged back. An officer tried to deploy them into line, but a French general, mounted on a big gray stallion, ordered his men to fix bayonets and advance. *"En avant! En avant!"* The drums beat frantically as the French line lurched forward and the Portuguese, caught as they deployed, panicked as the leading companies, already decimated by the French volleys, broke. The rear companies kept their ranks and tried to shoot past their own comrades at the French.

"Oh, sweet Jesus," Lawford had said when he saw the French athwart the ridge. He had seemed stunned by the sight, and no wonder, for he was seeing a battle lost. He was seeing an enemy column occupy the land where his battalion had been posted. He was seeing disaster, even personal disgrace. The French General, Sharpe presumed he was a general for the man's blue coat had as much gold decoration as the frock of a successful Covent Garden whore, had hoisted his plumed hat on his sword as a signal of victory. "Dear God!" Lawford said.

"About turn," Sharpe said quietly, not looking at the Colonel and sounding almost as though he were talking to himself, "then right wheel 'em."

Lawford gave no sign of having heard the advice. He was staring at the unfolding horror, watching the Portuguese being cut down by bullets. For a change it was the French who outflanked an allied column and they were giving to the blue-coated troops what they themselves usually received. The French were not in proper line, not in their three ranks, it was more like a thick line of seven or eight ranks, but enough of them could use their muskets and the men behind jostled forward to fire at the hapless Portuguese. "Call in the skirmishers," Lawford said to Forrest, then gave an anxious glance at Sharpe. Sharpe remained expressionless. He had made his suggestion, it was unorthodox, and it was up to the Colonel now. The Portuguese were running now, some streaming down the reverse slope of the ridge, but most hurrying back to where a half-battalion of redcoats had halted. The French had more ground to exploit and, even better, they could attack the exposed left flank of the South Essex. "Do it now," Sharpe said, maybe not quite loud enough for the Colonel to hear.

"South Essex!" Lawford shouted loud above the splintering noise of muskets. "South Essex! About turn!"

For a second no one moved. The order was so strange, so unexpected, that the men did not believe their ears, but then the company officers took it up. "About turn! Smartly now!"

The battalion's two ranks about-turned. What had been the rear rank was now the front rank, and both ranks had their backs to the slope and to the big, stalled column that was still exchanging fire with the ridge top. "Battalion will right wheel on number nine company!" Lawford shouted. "March!"

This was a test of a battalion's ability. They would swing like a giant door, just two ranks thick, swing around across rough country and across the bodies of their wounded comrades and the dying fires, and they must do it holding their ranks and files while under fire, and when they had finished, if they finished at all, they would form a musket line facing the new French columns. Those Frenchmen, seeing the danger, had checked their charge and started firing at the South Essex, allowing the Portuguese to re-form on the half-battalion of redcoats who had been marching behind them on the road. "Dress on number nine!" Lawford shouted. "Start firing when you're in position!" Number nine company, which had been the battalion's left flank when it had been facing downhill, was now the right flank company and, because it formed the hinge of the door, it had the smallest distance to march. It took only seconds for the company to be re-formed and James Hooper, its Captain, ordered the men to load. The light company, which normally paraded outside number nine, was running be-hind the swinging battalion. "Get your fellows in front, Mister Slingsby!" Lawford shouted. "In front! Not behind, for God's sake!"

"Number nine company!" Hooper bellowed. "Fire!"

"Number eight company!" The next was in line. "Fire!"

The outer companies were running, holding on to open cartridge boxes as they scrambled over the uneven turf. A man was hurled back-wards, twitching from a bullet's strike. Lawford was riding up behind the swinging door, the colors following him. Musket balls hissed past him as the voltigeurs, closest to the battalion, shot at its officers. The light com-pany, slightly downhill and on the flank of the battalion, began firing at the French, who suddenly saw that the South Essex would form an out-flanking line that would soak them with dreaded British musketry, and the columns' officers began shouting at men to deploy into three ranks. The General on the white horse was shoving at men to hurry them into place and a ragged procession of French infantry, all of them remnants of the failed first attack, was coming up the hill to join the seven battalions that had breached the British line. The drummers were still beating their instruments and the Eagles had gained the heights.

"South Essex!" Lawford was standing in his stirrups. "Half-company fire from the center!"

The Portuguese who had broken in the face of the devastating French musketry were coming back to join the South Essex's line. Red-coats were also forming on that left flank. More battalions, brought from the peaceful southern end of the ridge, were hurrying towards the gap, but Lawford wanted to seal it himself. "Fire!" he shouted.

The South Essex had lost a score of men as they clumsily wheeled around on the summit's ridge, but they were in their ranks now and this was what they had been trained to do. To fire and reload. That was the essential skill. To tear off the ends of the thick cartridge paper, prime the gun, close the frizzen, upend the musket, pour the powder, put in the ball, ram the ball and paper, drop the ramrod into the barrel rings, bring the musket to the shoulder, pull the doghead to full cock, aim at the smoke, remember to aim low, wait for the order. "Fire!" The muskets smashed back into bruised shoulders and the men, without thinking, found a new cartridge, tore the end off with their blackened teeth, began again, and all the while the French balls came back and every now and then there would be a sickening thud as a ball found flesh, or a smack as it struck a musket stock, or a hollow pop as it punctured a shako. Then the musket was back up in the shoulder, the doghead was back, the command came, and the flint drove onto the strike plate, flying the frizzen open as the sparks flashed down and there would be a pause, less than the time it took for a sparrow's heart to beat, before the powder in the gun fired and the redcoat's cheek would be burning because of the scraps of fiery powder thrown up from the pan, and the brass stock would hammer back into his shoulder, and the corporals were bellowing behind, "Close up! Close up!" Which meant a man was dead or wounded.

All the while the sound of the musketry flared out from the center, an unending noise like breaking sticks, but louder, much louder, and the French muskets were banging away, but the men could not see those because the powder smoke was thicker than the fog that had wreathed the ridge at dawn. And every man was thirsty because when they bit open the cartridges they got scraps of saltpeter from the gunpowder in their mouths and the saltpeter dried a man's tongue and throat so that he had no spit at all. "Fire!" and the muskets flamed, making the cloud of powder smoke suddenly lurid with fire, and the hooves of the Colonel's horse thumped close behind the rearward rank as he tried to see across the smoke, and somewhere else, way behind the ranks, a band was playing "The Grenadiers' March," but no one was really aware of it, only of the need to pull a new cartridge out and tear off the tip and get the damn musket loaded and get the damn thing done.

They were thieves and murderers and fools and rapists and drunk-ards. Not one had joined for love of country, and certainly not for love of their King. They had joined because they had been drunk when the re-cruiting sergeant came to their village, or because a magistrate had of-fered them a choice between the gallows and the ranks, or because a girl was pregnant and wanted to marry them, or because a girl did not want to marry them, or because they were witless fools who believed the re-cruiter's outrageous lies or simply because the army gave them a pint of rum and three meals a day, and most had been hungry ever since. They were flogged on the orders of officers who were mostly gentlemen who would never be flogged. They were cursed as drunken halfwits, and they were hanged without trial if they stole so much as a chicken. At home, in Britain, if they left the barracks respectable people crossed the street to avoid them. Some taverns refused them service. They were paid pitifully, fined for every item they lost, and the few pennies they managed to keep they usually gambled away. They were feckless rogues, as violent as hounds and as coarse as swine, but they had two things.

They had pride.

And they had the precious ability to fire platoon volleys. They could fire those half-company volleys faster than any other army in the world. Stand in front of these redcoats and the balls came thick as hail. It was death to be in their way and seven French battalions were now in death's forecourt and the South Essex was tearing them to ribbons. One battal-ion against seven, but the French had never properly deployed into line and now the outside men tried to get back into the column's protection and so the French formation became tighter and the balls struck it re-lentlessly, and more men, Portuguese and British, had extended the South Essex line, and then the 88th, the Connaught Rangers, came from the north and the Frenchmen who had gained the ridge were being as-sailed on two sides by enemies who knew how to fire their muskets. Who had practiced musketry until they could do it blindfolded, drunk or mad. They were the red-coated killers and they were good.

"Can you see anything, Richard?" Lawford shouted over the sound of the volleys.

"They won't hold, sir." Thanks to a vagary of the wind, a small gust that had moved the sluggish smoke a few yards, he had a better view than the Colonel.

"Bayonet?"

"Not yet." Sharpe could see the French were being hit brutally. The South Essex alone was shooting close to fifteen hundred musket balls every minute and they were now one of four or five battalions who had closed on the two French columns. Smoke thickened above the ridge, ringing the Frenchmen who stubbornly stayed on the summit. As ever, Sharpe was astonished by the amount of punishment a column could endure. It seemed to shudder under the blows, yet it did not retreat, it just shrank as the outer ranks and files died, and die they did under the terrible flail of the British and Portuguese musketry.

A big man, dressed in a shabby black coat, with a stub of dead cigar between yellowed teeth and a grubby tasseled nightcap on his head, rode up behind the South Essex. He was followed by a half-dozen aides, the only sign that the big, disheveled man in civilian dress might be someone of importance. He watched the French die, watched the South Essex platoon fire, took the cigar from between his teeth, looked at it morosely and spat out a shred of tobacco. "You must have Welshmen in your bloody battalion, Lawford," he growled.

Lawford, surprised by the man's voice, turned and threw a hasty salute. "Sir!"

"Well, man? Do you have bloody Welshmen?"

"I'm sure we have some, sir."

"They're good!" the man in the nightcap said. He gestured at the ranks with his dead cigar. "Too good to be English, Lawford. Maybe there's a Welsh settlement in Essex?"

"I'm sure there is, sir."

"You're sure of nothing of the bloody sort," the big man said. His name was Sir Thomas Picton and he was the General commanding this portion of the ridge. "I saw what you did, Lawford," he went on, "and I thought you'd lost your bloody mind! About turn and right wheel, eh? In the middle of a bloody battle? Gone soft in the head, I thought, but you did well, man, bloody well. Proud of you. You must have Welsh blood. Do you have any fresh cigars, Lawford?"

"No, sir."

"Not much bloody use, are you?" Picton nodded curtly and rode off, followed by his aides who were as well uniformed as their master was ill clothed. Lawford preened, looked back to the French and saw they were crumbling.

Major Leroy had listened to the General, now he rode to Sharpe. "We've pleased Picton," he said, drawing his pistol, "pleased him so much that he reckons Lawford must have Welsh blood." Sharpe laughed. Leroy aimed the pistol and fired into the remnants of the nearest French column. "When I was a youngster, Sharpe," Leroy said, "I used to shoot raccoons."

Sharpe saw a musket fail to fire in four company. Shattered flint, he suspected, and he pulled a spare one from his pocket and shouted the man's name. "Catch it!" he bellowed, and tossed the flint over the rear rank before looking at Leroy. "What's a raccoon?"

"A useless damn animal, Sharpe, that God put on earth to improve a boy's marksmanship. Why don't the bastards move?"

"They will."

"Then they might take your company with them," Leroy said, and jerked his head towards the slope as if advising Sharpe to go and see for himself.

Sharpe rode to the flank of the line and saw that Slingsby had taken the company down the slope and to the north from where, in skirmish line, they were shooting uphill at the French left flank while a handful of his men were shooting downhill to prevent a scatter of hesitant Frenchmen from reinforcing the column. Did Slingsby want to be a hero? Did he think that the company could cut off the French column by itself? In a moment, Sharpe knew, the French would break and close to six thousand men would spill over the crest and rush down the hill to escape the slaughter and they would sweep the light company away like so much chaff. That moment came even closer when he heard the crack of a cannon from the far side of the fight. It was canister, the tin can that splintered apart at the cannon's mouth and spread its charge of musket balls like a blast from the devil's shotgun. Sharpe did not have a moment, he had seconds, and so he kicked the horse down the hill. "Back to the line!" he shouted at his men. "Back! Fast!"

Slingsby gave him an indignant look. "We're holding them," he protested, "can't go back now!"

Sharpe dropped from the horse and gave its reins to Slingsby. "Back to battalion, Slingsby, that's an order! Now!"

"But . . ."

"Do it!" Sharpe bellowed like a sergeant.

Slingsby reluctantly mounted and Sharpe shouted at his men. "Form on the battalion!"

And just then the French broke.

They had lasted longer than any general could ask. They had gained the hilltop and for a splendid moment it seemed as if victory had to be theirs, but they had not received the massive reinforcement they needed and the British and Portuguese battalions had reformed, outflanked them and then doused them with rolling volleys. No army in the world could have stood against those volleys, but the French had endured them until bravery alone would not suffice and their only impulse left was to survive and Sharpe saw the blue uniforms come like a breaking wave across the skyline. He and his men ran. Slingsby was well clear, kicking his horse up towards James Hooper's company, and the men who had been on the left of the skirmish line were safe enough, but most of the skirmishers could not escape the rush.

"Form on me!" Sharpe bellowed. "Rally square!"

It was a desperate maneuver, one that broken infantry used in their dying moments against rampaging cavalry, but it served. Thirty or forty men ran to Sharpe, faced outwards and fixed bayonets. "Edge south lads," Sharpe said calmly, "away from them."

Harper had unslung his volley gun. The tide of Frenchmen parted to avoid the clump of redcoats and riflemen, streaming to either side, but Sharpe kept the men moving, a yard at a time, trying to escape the torrent. One Frenchman did not see Sharpe's men and ran onto Perkins's sword bayonet and stayed there until the boy pulled the trigger to blow the man off the long blade with a gout of blood. "Go slow," Sharpe said quietly, "go slow," and just then the General on the white horse, his sword drawn and gold braid bright, came straight at the rally square and he seemed astonished to find an enemy in front of him and he instinctively lowered his sword to make the straight-armed lunge and Harper pulled his trigger, as did four or five other men, and the horse's head and the man behind vanished in a cockade of blood. Both went down, the horse sliding down the hill, hooves flailing, and Sharpe bellowed at his men to hurry leftwards and so just avoided the dying beast. The rider, a bullet hole in his forehead, slid to a halt at the men's feet. "He's a bloody general, sir," Perkins said in amazement.

"Just keep calm," Sharpe said, "edge left." They were out of the stream of Frenchmen now that was running desperately downhill, leaping over corpses, intent on nothing except escaping the musket balls. The British and Portuguese battalions were following them, not in pursuit, but to make a line on the crest from where they harried the fugitives, and some balls whistled over Sharpe's head. "Break now!" he told his men and they ran away from the square and up towards the battalion.

"That was close," Harper said.

"You were in the wrong bloody place."

"It wasn't healthy," Harper said, then looked to see if any man had been left behind. "Perkins! What the hell is that you've got?"

"It's a French general, Sergeant," Perkins said. He had dragged the corpse all the way up the hill and now knelt by the body and began searching the pockets.

"Leave that body alone!" It was Slingsby, back again, on foot now, striding towards the company. "Form on number nine company, look sharp now! I told you to leave that alone!" he snapped at Perkins who had ignored the order. "Take that man's name, Sergeant!" he ordered Huck-field.

"Perkins!" Sharpe said. "Search that body properly. Lieutenant!"

Slingsby looked wide-eyed at Sharpe. "Sir?"

"Come with me." Sharpe stalked off to the left, well out of earshot of the company, then turned on Slingsby and all his pent-up rage exploded. "Listen, you goddamn bastard, you bloody well nearly lost the company there. Lost them! Every damned man of them! And they know it. So shut your damned mouth until you've learned how to fight."

"You're being offensive, Sharpe!" Slingsby protested.

"I mean to be."

"I take exception," Slingsby said stiffly. "I will not be insulted by your kind, Sharpe."

Sharpe smiled and it was not a pretty smile. "My kind, Slingsby? I'll tell you what I am, you sniveling little bastard, I'm a killer. I've been killing men for damn near thirty years. You want a duel? I don't mind. Sword, pistol, knives, anything you bloody well like, Slingsby. Just let me know when and where. But till then, shut your damned mouth and bugger off." He walked back to Perkins who had virtually stripped the French officer naked. "What did you find?"

"Cash, sir." Perkins glanced at an outraged Slingsby, then back to Sharpe. "And his scabbard, sir." He showed Sharpe the scabbard that was sheathed in blue velvet studded with small golden N's.

"They're probably brass," Sharpe said, "but you never know. Keep half the cash and share the other half."

All the Frenchmen had retreated now, except those who were dead or wounded. The voltigeurs who had held the rocky knoll had stayed, though, and those men had been reinforced by some of the survivors from the defeated columns, the rest of whom had stopped halfway down the ridge from where they just stared upwards. None had gone all the way back to the valley that was now clear of fog so that the French gunners could aim their shells which came up the hill, trailing wisps of smoke, to bang among the scatter of dead bodies. British and Portuguese skirmish companies were going down among the shell bursts to form a picquet line, but Sharpe, without any orders from Lawford or anyone else, took his own men to where the hill jutted out towards the boulder-strewn promontory held by the French. "Rifles," he ordered, "keep their heads down."

He let his riflemen shoot at the French who, armed with muskets, could not reply. Meanwhile Sharpe searched the lower slopes with his telescope, looking for a green-jacketed body among the drifts of dead French, but he could see no sign of Corporal Dodd.

Sharpe's riflemen kept up their desultory target practice. He sent the redcoats back a few paces so they would not be an inviting target for the French gunners at the foot of the slope. The rest of the British troops had also marched back, denying the enemy artillery a plain target, but the presence of the skirmish chain on the forward slope told the defeated enemy infantry that the volleys were still waiting just out of sight. None tried to advance and then, one by one, the French cannon fell silent and the smoke slowly drifted off the hill.

Then the guns started a mile to the north. For a few seconds it was just one or two guns, and then whole batteries opened and the thunder started again. The next French attack was coming.

Lieutenant Slingsby did not rejoin the company, going back to the battalion instead. Sharpe did not care.

He rested on the hillside, watched the French, and waited.

⚜

"THE LETTER," Ferragus instructed Sarah, "is to a Senhor Verzi." He paced up and down behind her, the floorboards creaking beneath his weight. The sound of the guns reverberated softly on the big window through which, at the end of a street that ran downhill, Sarah could just see the River Mondego. "Tell Senhor Verzi that he is in my debt," Ferragus ordered her.

The pen scratched. Sarah, summoned to write a second letter, had wrapped a scarf about her neck so that no skin was exposed between her hair and the blue dress's high embroidered collar.

"Tell him he may discharge all his debts to me with a favor. I require accommodation on one of his boats. I want a cabin for my brother's wife, children and household."

"Not too fast, *senhor*," Sarah said. She dipped the nib and wrote. "For your brother's wife, children and household," she said as she finished.

"I am sending the family and their servants to Lisbon," Ferragus went on, "and I ask, no, I require Senhor Verzi to give them shelter on a suitable vessel."

"On a suitable vessel," Sarah repeated.

"If the French come to Lisbon," Ferragus continued, "the vessel may carry them to the Azores and wait there until it is safe to return. Tell him to expect my brother's wife within three days of receipt of this letter." He waited. "And say, finally, that I know he will treat my brother's people as though they were his own." Verzi had better treat them well, Ferragus thought, if he did not want his guts punched into a liquid mess in some

Lisbon alley. He stopped and stared down at Sarah's back. He could see her spine against the thin blue material. He knew she was aware of his gaze and could sense her indignation. It amused him. "Read me the letter."

Sarah read and Ferragus gazed out of the window. Verzi would oblige him, he knew that, and so Major Ferreira's wife and family would be far away if the French came. They would escape the rape and slaughter that would doubtless occur, and when the French had settled, when they had slaked their appetites, it would be safe for the family to return.

"You sound certain the French will come, *senhor,*" Sarah said when she had finished reading.

"I don't know whether they will or not," Ferragus said, "but I know preparations must be made. If they come, then my brother's family is safe; if they do not, then Senhor Verzi's services will not be needed."

Sarah sprinkled sand on the paper. "How long would we wait in the Azores?" she asked.

Ferragus smiled at her misapprehension. He had no intention of letting Sarah go to the Azores, but this was not the time to tell her. "As long as necessary," he said.

"Perhaps the French will not come," Sarah suggested just as a renewed bout of gunfire sounded louder than ever.

"The French," Ferragus said, giving her the seal, "have conquered every place in Europe. No one fights them now, except us. Over a hundred thousand Frenchmen have reinforced the armies in Spain. They have how many soldiers south of the Pyrenees? Three hundred thousand? Do you really believe, Miss Fry, that we can win against so many? If we win today then they will come back, even more of them."

He sent three men with the letter. The road to Lisbon was safe enough, but he had heard there was trouble in the city itself. The people there believed the British planned to abandon Portugal and so leave them to the French and there had been riots in the streets, so the letter had to be guarded. And no sooner was the letter gone than two others of his men came with more news of trouble. A *feitor* had arrived at the warehouse and was insisting the stores be destroyed.

Ferragus buckled on a knife belt, thrust a pistol into a pocket, and stalked across town. Many folk were in the streets, listening to the far-off gunfire as though they could tell from the rise and fall of the sound how the battle went. They made way for Ferragus, the men pulling off their hats as he passed. Two priests, loading the treasures of their church onto a handcart, made the sign of the cross when they saw him and Ferragus retaliated by giving them the devil's horns with his left hand, then spitting on the cobbles. "I gave thirty thousand *vinténs* to that church a year ago," Ferragus said to his men. That was a small fortune, close to a hundred pounds of English money. He laughed. "Priests," he sneered, "are like women. Give and they hate you."

"So don't give," one of his men said.

"You give to the church," Ferragus said, "because that is the way to heaven. But with a woman you take. That too is the way to heaven." He turned down a narrow alley and pushed through a door into a vast warehouse that was dimly lit by dusty skylights. Cats hissed at him, then scampered away. There were dozens of the beasts, kept to protect the warehouse's contents from rats. At night, Ferragus knew, the warehouse was a bloody battlefield as the rats fought against the hungry cats, but the cats always won and so protected the barrels of hard-baked biscuit, the sacks of wheat, barley and maize, the tin containers filled with rice, the jars of olive oil, the boxes of salt cod and the vats of salt meat. There was enough food here to feed Masséna's army all the way to Lisbon and enough hogsheads of tobacco to keep it coughing all the way back to Paris. He stooped to tickle the throat of a great one-eyed tom cat, scarred from a hundred fights. The cat bared its teeth at Ferragus, but submitted to the caress, then Ferragus turned to two of his men who were standing with the *feitor* who wore a green sash to show he was on duty. "What is the trouble?" Ferragus demanded.

A *feitor* was an official storekeeper, appointed by the government to make certain there were sufficient rations for the Portuguese army. Every sizable town in Portugal had a *feitor*, answerable to the Junta of Provisions in Lisbon, and Coimbra's storekeeper was a middle-aged, corpulent man called Rafael Pires who snatched off his hat when he saw Ferragus and seemed about to drop to one knee.

"Senhor Pires," Ferragus greeted him affably enough. "Your wife and family are well?"

"God be praised, *senhor*, they are."

"They are still here? You have not sent them south?"

"They left yesterday. I have a sister in Bemposta." Bemposta was a small place nearer to Lisbon, the kind of town the French might ignore in their advance.

"Then you are fortunate. They won't starve on the streets of Lisbon, eh? So what brings you here?"

Pires fidgeted with his hat. "I have orders, *senhor*."

"Orders?"

Pires gestured with his hat at the great heaps of food. "It is all to be destroyed, *senhor*. All of it."

"Who says so?"

"The Captain-Major."

"And you take orders from him?"

"I am directed to do so, *senhor*."

The Captain-Major was the military commander of Coimbra and its surrounding districts. He was in charge of recruiting and training the *ordenança*, the "armed inhabitants," who could reinforce the army if the enemy came, but the Captain-Major was also expected to enforce the government's decrees.

"So what will you do?" Ferragus asked Pires. "Eat it all?"

"The Captain-Major is sending men here," Pires said.

"Here?" Ferragus's voice was dangerous now.

Pires took a breath. "They have my files, *senhor*," he explained. "They know you have been buying food. How can they not know? You have spent much money, *senhor*. I am ordered to find it."

"And?" Ferragus asked.

"It is to be destroyed," Pires insisted and then, as if to show that he was helpless in this situation, he invoked a higher power. "The English insist."

"The English," Ferragus snarled. "*Os ingleses por mar*," he shouted at Pires, then calmed down. The English were not the problem. Pires was. "You say the Captain-Major took your papers?"

"Indeed."

"But he does not know where the food is stored?"

"The papers only say how much food is in the town," Pires said, "and who owns it."

"So he has my name," Ferragus asked, "and a list of my stores?"

"Not a complete list, *senhor*." Pires glanced at the massive stacks of food and marvelled that Ferragus had accumulated so much. "He merely knows you have some supplies stored and he says I must guarantee their destruction."

"So guarantee it," Ferragus said airily.

"He will send men to make sure of it, *senhor*," Pires said. "I am to bring them here."

"So you don't know where the stores are," Ferragus said.

"I am to make a search this afternoon, *senhor*, every warehouse in the city!" Pires shrugged. "I came to warn you," he said in helpless appeal.

"I pay you, Pires," Ferragus said, "to keep my food from being taken at a thief's price to feed the army. Now you will lead men here to destroy it?"

"You can move it, perhaps?" Pires suggested.

"Move it!" Ferragus shouted. "How, in God's name, do I move it? It would take a hundred men and twenty wagons."

Pires just shrugged.

Ferragus stared down at the *feitor*. "You came to warn me," he said in a low voice, "because you will bring the soldiers here, yes? And you do not want me to blame you, is that it?"

"They insist, *senhor*, they insist!" Pires was pleading now. "And if our own troops don't come, the British will."

"*Os ingleses por mar*," Ferragus snarled, and he used his left hand to punch Pires in the face. The blow was swift and extraordinarily powerful, a straight jab that broke the *feitor*'s nose and sent him staggering back with blood pouring from his nostrils. Ferragus followed fast, using his wounded right hand to thump Pires in the belly. The blow hurt Ferragus, but he ignored the pain because that was what a man must do. Pain must be endured. If a man could not take pain then he should not fight, and Ferragus backed Pires against the warehouse wall and systematically punched him, left and right, each blow traveling a short distance, but landing with hammer force. The fists drove into the *feitor*'s body, cracking his ribs and breaking his cheekbones, and blood spattered on Ferragus's hands and sleeves, but he was oblivious of the blood just as he was oblivious of the pain in his hand and groin. He was doing what he loved to do and he hit even harder, silencing the *feitor*'s pathetic screams and yelps, seeing the man's breath come bubbling and pink as his huge fists crunched the broken ribs into the lungs. It took awesome strength to do this. To kill a man with bare hands without strangling him.

Pires slumped against the wall. He no longer resembled a man, though he lived. His visible flesh was swollen, bloody, pulpy. His eyes had closed, his nose was destroyed, his face was a mask of blood, his teeth were broken, his lips were split to ribbons, his chest was crushed, his belly was pounded, yet still he managed to stay upright against the warehouse wall. His ruined face looked blindly from side to side, then a fist caught him on the jaw and the bone broke with an audible crack and Pires tottered, groaned and fell at last.

"Hold him up," Ferragus said, stripping off his coat and shirt.

Two men seized Pires under his arms and hauled him upright and Ferragus stepped in close and punched with a vicious intensity. His fists did not travel far, these were not wild swinging clouts, but short, precise blows that landed with sickening force. He worked on the man's belly, then moved up to his chest, pounding it so that Pires's head flopped with every strike and his bloody mouth sprayed drops of reddened spittle onto Ferragus's chest. He went on punching until the man's head jerked back and then flopped sideways like a puppet whose crown-string had snapped. There was a rattling noise from the battered throat, Ferragus hit him one last time and then stepped back. "Put him in the cellar," Ferragus ordered, "and slit his belly."

"Slit his belly?" one of the men asked, thinking he had misheard.

"Give the rats something to work on," Ferragus said, "because the sooner they're done with him, the sooner he's gone." He crossed to Miguel who gave him a rag with which he wiped the blood and spittle from his chest and arms that were covered in tattoos. There were anchors wrapped in chains on both his forearms, three mermaids on his chest, and snakes encircling his vast upper arms. On his back was a warship under full sail, its skyscrapers aloft, studding sails spread, and at its stern a British flag. He pulled on his shirt, then a coat, and watched the corpse being dragged to the back of the warehouse where a trapdoor opened into a cellar. There was already one belly-slitted corpse rotting in that darkness, the remnants of a man who had tried to betray Ferragus's hoard to the authorities. Now another had tried, failed and died.

Ferragus locked the warehouse. If the French did not come, he thought, then this food could be sold legally and at a profit, and if they did come, then it might mean a greater profit. The next few hours would reveal all. He made the sign of the cross, then went to find a tavern because he had killed a man and was thirsty.

No ONE CAME from battalion to give Sharpe orders, which suited him just fine. He was standing guard on the rocky knoll where, he reckoned, a hundred French infantry were keeping their heads well down because of his desultory rifle fire. He wished he had enough men to shift the voltigeurs off the hill, for their presence was an invitation to the enemy to try for the summit again. They could throw a couple of battalions up to the knoll and use them to attack along the spur, and such a move might be encouraged by the new French attack that was heating up a mile to the north. Sharpe went a small way along the spur, too far probably because a couple of musket shots whirred past him as he crouched and took out his telescope. He ignored the voltigeurs, knowing they were shooting far beyond a musket's accurate range, and he stared at the vast French columns climbing the better road that twisted up to the village just beneath the ridge's northern crest. A stone windmill, its sails and vanes taken away and machinery dismantled like every other mill in central Portugal, stood near the crest itself and there was a knot of horsemen beside the stumpy tower, but Sharpe could not see any troops except for the two French columns that were halfway up the road and a third, smaller column, some way behind. The huge French formations looked dark against the slope. British and Portuguese guns were blasting shot from the crest, blurring his view with their gray-white smoke.

"Sir! Mister Sharpe, sir!" It was Patrick Harper who called.

Sharpe collapsed the telescope and walked back, seeing as he went what had prompted Harper's call. Two companies of brown-coated cazadores were approaching the spur and Sharpe supposed the Portuguese troops had orders to clear the rocky knoll of the enemy. A pair of nine-pounders were being repositioned to support their attack, but Sharpe did not hold out much chance for it. The cazadores numbered about the same as the voltigeurs, but the French had cover and it would be a nasty fight if they decided to make a stand.

"I didn't want you in the way when those gunners started firing," Harper explained, jerking his head towards the pair of nine-pounders.

"Decent of you, Pat."

"If you died, sir, then Slingsby would take over," Harper said without a trace of insubordination.

"You wouldn't want that?" Sharpe asked.

"I'm from Donegal, sir, and I put up with whatever the good Lord sends to trouble me."

"He sent me, Pat, he sent me."

"Mysterious are the ways of the Lord," Harris put in.

The cazadores were waiting fifty paces behind Sharpe. He ignored them, instead asking again if any of the men had seen Dodd. Mister Iliffe, who had not heard Sharpe ask before, nodded nervously. "He was running, sir."

"Where?"

"When we were almost cut off, sir? Down the hill. Going like a hare." Which matched what Carter, Dodd's partner, had thought. The two men had very nearly been trapped by the voltigeurs and Dodd had elected the fast way out, downhill, while Carter had been lucky to escape uphill with nothing more serious than a musket ball in his pack, which he claimed had only helped him along. Sharpe reckoned Dodd would rejoin later. He was a countryman, could read ground, and doubtless he would avoid the French and climb up the southern part of the ridge. Whatever, there was nothing Sharpe could do about him now.

"So are we going to help the Portuguese boys?" Harper asked.

"Not on your bloody life," Sharpe said, "not unless they bring a whole bloody battalion."

"He's coming to ask you," Harper said in warning, nodding towards a slim Portuguese officer who approached the light company. His brown uniform had black facings and his high-fronted shako had a long black plume. Sharpe noted that the officer wore a heavy cavalry sword and, unusually, carried a rifle. Sharpe could think of only one officer who was so armed, himself, and he felt irritated that there should be another officer with the same weapons, but then the approaching man took off his black-plumed *barretina* and smiled broadly.

"Good God," Sharpe said.

"No, no, it's only me." Jorge Vicente, whom Sharpe had last seen in the wild country north east of Oporto, held out his hand. "Mister Sharpe," he said.

"Jorge!"

"Capitão Vicente now." Vicente clasped Sharpe and then, to the rifleman's embarrassment, gave his friend a kiss on both cheeks. "And you, Richard, a major by now, I expect?"

"Bloody hell, no, Jorge. They don't promote the likes of me. It might spoil the army's reputation. How are you?"

"I am—how do you say?—flourishing. But you?" Vicente frowned at Sharpe's bruised face. "You are wounded?"

"Fell down some steps," Sharpe said.

"You must be careful," Vicente said solemnly, then smiled. "Sergeant Harper! It is good to see you."

"No kissing, sir, I'm Irish."

Vicente greeted the other men he had known in the wild pursuit of Soult's army across the northern frontier, then turned back to Sharpe. "I've orders to knock those things out of the rocks." He gestured towards the French.

"It's a good idea," Sharpe said, "but there aren't enough of you."

"Two Portuguese are equal to one Frenchman," Vicente said airily, "and you might do the honor of helping us?"

"Bloody hell," Sharpe said, then evaded an answer by nodding at the Baker rifle on Vicente's shoulder. "And what are you doing carrying a rifle?"

"Imitating you," Vicente said frankly, "and besides, I am now the captain of a *atirador* company, the how do you say? marksmen. We carry rifles, the other companies have muskets. I transferred from the 18th when we raised the cazador battalions. So, shall we attack?"

"What do you think?" Sharpe countered.

Vicente smiled uncertainly. He had been a soldier for less than two years; before that he had been a lawyer and when Sharpe first met him the young Portuguese had been a stickler for the supposed rules of warfare. That might or might not have changed, but Sharpe suspected Vicente was a natural soldier, brave and decisive, no fool, yet he was still nervous of showing his skills to Sharpe who had taught him most of what he knew about fighting. He glanced at Sharpe, then shadowed his eyes to stare at the French. "They won't stand," he suggested.

"They might," Sharpe said, "and there are at least a hundred of the bastards. How many are we? A hundred and thirty? If it was up to me, Jorge, I'd send in your whole battalion."

"My Colonel ordered me to do it."

"Does he know what he's doing?"

"He's English," Vicente said dryly. The Portuguese army had been reorganized and trained in the last eighteen months and huge numbers of British officers had volunteered into its ranks for the reward of a promotion.

"I'd still send in more men," Sharpe said.

Vicente had no chance to answer because there was the sudden thump of hooves on the springy turf and a stentorian voice shouting at him. "Don't hang about, Vicente! There are Frogs to kill! Get on with it, Captain, get on with it! Who the devil are you?" This last question was directed at Sharpe and came from a horseman who had trouble curbing his gelding as he tried to rein in beside the two officers. The rider's voice betrayed he was English, though he was wearing Portuguese brown to which he had added a black cocked hat that sported a pair of golden tassels. One tassel shadowed his face that looked to be red and glistening.

"Sharpe, sir," Sharpe answered the man's bad-tempered question.

"95th?"

"South Essex, sir."

"That bloody mob of yokels," the officer said. "Lost a color a couple of years back, didn't you?"

"We took one back at Talavera," Sharpe said harshly.

"Did you now?" The horseman did not seem particularly interested.

He took out a small telescope and stared at the rocky knoll, ignoring some musket balls which, fired at extreme range, fluttered impotently by.

"Allow me to name Colonel Rogers-Jones," Vicente said, "my Colonel."

"And the man, Vicente," Rogers-Jones said, "who ordered you to turf those buggers out of the rocks. I didn't tell you to stand here and chatter, did I?"

"I was seeking Captain Sharpe's advice, sir," Vicente said.

"Reckon he's got any to offer?" The Colonel sounded amused.

"He took a French Eagle," Vicente pointed out.

"Not by standing around talking, he didn't," Rogers-Jones said. He collapsed his telescope. "I'll tell the gunners to open fire," he went on, "and you advance, Vicente. You'll help him, Sharpe." He added the order carelessly. "Winkle them out, Vicente, then stay there to make sure the bastards don't come back." He turned his horse and spurred away.

"Jesus bloody wept," Sharpe said. "Does he know how many of them there are?"

"I still have my orders," Vicente said bleakly.

Sharpe took the rifle off his shoulder and loaded it. "You want advice?"

"Of course."

"Send our rifles up the middle," Sharpe said, "in skirmish order. They're to keep firing, hard and fast, no patches, just keeping the bastards' heads down. The rest of our lads will come up behind in line. Bayonets fixed. Straightforward battalion attack, Jorge, with three companies, and hope your bastard Colonel is satisfied."

"Our lads?" Vicente picked those two words out of Sharpe's advice.

"Not going to let you die alone, Jorge," Sharpe said. "You'd probably get lost trying to find the pearly gates." He glanced northwards and saw the cannon smoke thickening as the French attack closed on the village beneath the ridge's summit, then the first of the guns close to the knoll fired and a shell banged smoke and casing scraps just beyond the rocky knoll. "So let's do it," Sharpe said.

It was not wise, he thought, but it was war. He cocked the rifle and shouted at his men to close up. Time to fight.

CHAPTER 5

THE VILLAGE OF SULA, which was perched on the eastward slope of the ridge very close to where the northernmost road crossed the summit, was a small and unremarkable place. The houses were cramped, the dung heaps large, and for a long time the village had not even possessed a church, which had meant that a priest must be fetched from Moura, at the ridge's foot, or else a friar summoned from the monastery, to give extreme unction to the dying, but the sacraments had usually arrived too late and so the dead of Sula had gone to their long darkness unshriven, which was why the local people liked to claim that the tiny hamlet was haunted by specters.

On Thursday, 27th September 1810, the village was haunted by skirmishers. The whole first battalion of the 95th Rifles were in and around the hamlet, and with them were the 3rd Cazadores, many of whom were also armed with the Baker rifle, which meant that more than a thousand skirmishers in green and brown opened fire on the two advancing French columns, which had deployed almost as many skirmishers themselves, but the French had muskets and were opposed by rifles, and so the voltigeurs were the first to die in the small walled paddocks and terraced vineyards beneath the village. The sound of the fight was like dry brush burning, an unending crackle of muskets and rifles, which was augmented by the bass notes of the artillery on the crest that fired shell and shrapnel over the Portuguese and British skirmishers to tear great holes in the two columns struggling up the slope behind the voltigeurs.

To the French officers in the column, scanning the ridge above, it seemed they were opposed only by skirmishers and artillery. The artillery had been placed on a ledge beyond the village and just below the sky-line, and near the guns was a scatter of horsemen who watched from beside the white-painted stump of the windmill's tower. The artillery was hurting the columns, smashing round shot through tight ranks and exploding shells above the files, but two batteries could never stop these great columns. The horsemen by the mill were no danger. There were only four or five riders visible when the cannon smoke thinned, and all wore cocked hats, which meant they were not cavalrymen, so it seemed that the British and Portuguese skirmishers, supported by cannon, were supposed to defeat the attack. Which meant the French must win, for there were no redcoats in sight, no damned lines to envelop a column with volley fire. The drummers beat the *pas de charge* and the men gave their war cry, *"Vive l'Empereur!"* One of the two columns divided into two smaller units to negotiate an outcrop of rock, then rejoined on the road as two shells exploded right over their front ranks. A dozen men were thrown down, the dusty road was suddenly red and sergeants dragged the dead and wounded aside so that the ranks behind would not be obstructed. Ahead of the column the sound of the skirmishing grew in intensity as the voltigeurs closed the range and opened on the riflemen with their muskets. There were so many skirmishers now that the noise of their battle was a continuous crackling. Smoke drifted off the hillside. *"Vive l'Empereur!"* the French shouted and the first riflemen began picking at the columns' front ranks. A bullet smacked an Eagle, ripping off the tip of a wing, and an officer went down in the front rank, gasping with pain as the files tramped round him. The voltigeurs, outranged by the rifles, were being driven back onto the columns and so Marshal Ney, who commanded this attack, ordered that more companies were to deploy as skirmishers to drive the riflemen and cazadores back up the slope.

The drummers kept up their monotonous rhythm. A round of shrapnel, designed to burst in the air and slam its load of bullets down and forward, exploded above the right-hand column and the drums momentarily ceased as a dozen boys went down and the men behind were spattered with their blood. "Close up!" a sergeant shouted and a shell banged behind him and a hat went spiraling up in the air and fell on the road with a heavy thump because half the man's head was still inside. A drummer boy, both legs broken and his belly slit by shell fragments, sat and kept up his drumming as the files went past him. The men patted his head for luck, leaving him to die among the vines.

Ahead of the columns the new French skirmishers deployed and their officers shouted them up the hill to close the range and so swamp the hated greenjackets with musket fire. The Baker rifle was a killer, but a slow one. To fire it accurately a man was supposed to wrap each ball in a greased leather patch, then ram it down on the charge, and ramming a patched bullet was hard work and made a rifle slow to load. A man could shoot a musket three times while a rifleman reloaded. Time could be saved by forgetting the patch, but then the ball did not grip the seven lands and grooves spiraling inside the barrel and the weapon became little more accurate than a musket. The reinforced voltigeurs climbed and the sheer weight of their fire forced the riflemen and cazadores back, then more Portuguese skirmishers joined the fight, the whole of the 1st cazadores, but the French countered with three more companies of blue-jacketed troops who ran out of the columns and broke down the vines to climb up to where the powder smoke dotted the hillside. Their muskets added more smoke and their bullets pressed the brown- and green-jacketed men back. A rifleman, shot in the lungs, was draped over one of the chestnut stakes holding the vines and a voltigeur drew his bayonet and stabbed the wounded man until he stopped twitching, then searched his pockets for coins or plunder. A sergeant pushed the voltigeur away from the corpse. "Kill the others first!" he shouted. "Get uphill!" The French fire was overwhelming now, a drenching of lead, and the cazadores and riflemen scrambled up to the village itself where they took cover behind low stone walls or in the windows of the small cottages from which shards of broken tiles cascaded as the roofs were spattered by French musketry and by the fragments of shell casing fired by the French guns in the valley. The voltigeurs were shouting, encouraging each other, advancing in rushes, pointing out targets. *"Sauterelle! Sauterelle!"*

a sergeant shouted, pointing at a rifleman of the 95th. The shout meant "grasshopper," the French nickname for the green pests who dodged and shot, moved and reloaded, shot and moved again. A dozen muskets fired at the man who vanished in an alley as the tile pieces clattered behind him.

The French skirmishers were all about the village's eastern margin, enveloping it in musketry, and small groups ran up to the houses and fired at shadows in the smoke. The road was blocked with handcarts where it entered the village, but a company of French troops charged the makeshift barricade which spat smoke and flame as rifles fired from behind the carts. Three Frenchmen went down, but the rest reached the obstacle and fired at the greenjackets. A shell exploded overhead, driving down two more Frenchmen and shattering tiles on a roof. The first handcart was pulled away and the French poured through the gap. Rifles and muskets spat at them from windows and doors. More voltigeurs climbed garden walls or charged into alleyways and over dung heaps. British, Portuguese and French shells were exploding among the houses, smashing walls and filling the narrow lanes with smoke and with shrieking shards of metal and broken tile, but the voltigeurs outnumbered the riflemen and the cazadores and, because they were inside the village, the rifles lost the advantage of long-range accuracy, and the blue-coated men pushed forward, advancing group by group, clearing houses and gardens. The road was cleared as the last carts were dragged away. The column was close to the village now and the voltigeurs were hunting the last cazadores and riflemen from the upper houses. One cazador, trapped in an alley, swung his unloaded musket like a club and put down two Frenchmen before a third lunged a bayonet into his belly. The village had been abandoned by its inhabitants and the voltigeurs plundered the small houses, taking whatever small possessions the villagers had left in their haste to leave. One man fought another for possession of a wooden bucket, a thing not worth a sou, and both died when cazadores shot them through a window.

The smoke from the British guns made leprous clouds on the ridge top as the columns reached the village. The shells banged at the columns, but the files closed up and the men marched on and the drummers worked their sticks, pausing only so that the shout of *"Vive l'Empereur"* could tell Marshal Masséna, down in the valley where the French gunners hammered their own shells up towards the ridge's crest, that the attack continued.

The windmill on the ledge below the crest lay a third of a mile from the village. The voltigeurs cleared the last enemy skirmishers from Sula's western edge, sending them scurrying up the more open ground that lay between the village and the mill. One column skirted the village, pushing down fences and clambering over two stone walls, but the other marched right through Sula's center. At least half a dozen roofs were burning, their rafters set alight by shells. Another shell exploded in the heart of the main street, flinging aside half a dozen infantrymen in smoke, blood and flame, and smearing the whitewashed walls of the houses with spatters of blood. "Close up!" the sergeants shouted. "Close up!" The drums echoed from the bloodied walls, while up on the ridge the British officers heard the rousing cheer, *"Vive l'Empereur!"* The voltigeurs were climbing ever closer, and were now so thick on the ground that their musketry was almost as dense as volley fire. The British and Portuguese skirmishers had vanished, gone northwards into some trees that crowned the northern crest, and all that seemed to be ahead of the French was the ledge where the horsemen stood close to the mill. Bullets began smacking against the mill's white-painted stones. One of the artillery batteries was near the mill and its smoke helped to hide the horsemen, among whom was a small, scowling, black-haired, dark-faced man who was perched atop an oversize saddle on a horse that seemed much too big for him. He stared indignantly at the French as if their very presence offended him. Musket balls hummed past him, but he ignored them. An aide, worried by the intensity of the voltigeurs' fire, considered suggesting that the small man should ride back a few paces, but checked himself from speaking. Such advice to Black Bob Craufurd, commander of the Light Division, would be construed as arrant weakness.

The columns were in the open ground beneath the mill now and the voltigeurs were being whipped by blasts of canister that flattened the grass as if a sudden gale gusted from the west. More canisters were fired, each taking its handful of casualties, and the voltigeur officers ordered their men back to the columns. Their job was done. The British and Portuguese skirmishers had been driven back and victory waited at the ridge top, and that victory was close, so very close, because the ridge was empty except for the two batteries of guns and the handful of horsemen.

Or so the French thought. But behind the ledge, where a path ran parallel to the ridge's top, was dead ground, invisible from below, and in the concealment, lying down to protect themselves from the French artillery, were the 43rd and the 52nd. They were two light infantry battalions, the 43rd from Monmouthshire and the 52nd from Oxfordshire, and they reckoned themselves the best of the best. They had a right to that opinion, for they had been drilled to a savage hardness by the small, black-jowled man who scowled at the French from beside the mill. A gunner spun back from the muzzle of his nine-pounder, struck in the ribs by a French musket ball. He spat up blood, then his Sergeant dragged him away from the gun's high wheel and rammed a canister home. "Fire!" the gun Captain shouted, and the huge weapon slammed back, bucking up on its trail to spew a thundercloud of smoke in which the canister was torn apart to loose its load of musket balls into the French ranks. "Close up," the French sergeants shouted, and wounded men, leaving snails' traces of blood, crawled back to the village where the stone walls would protect them from the gut-slitting blasts of canister. Yet there was not enough canister to finish the columns. They were too big. The outer ranks soaked up the punishment, left their dead and dying, while the ranks behind stepped over the corpses. The hidden redcoats could hear the drums getting closer, could hear the shouts of the infantry and the sound of the musket balls whickering close overhead. They waited, understanding from the swelling noise that Black Bob was letting the enemy get close, very close. This was not to be a firefight at extreme musket range, but a sudden, astonishing slaughter, and then they saw the gunners of one British battery, who were taking a drenching of musketry from the front rank of the left-hand column, abandon their pieces and run back to safety. There was an odd silence then. Not a real silence, of course, for the drums were still beating and the blue-coated French were shouting their war cry, but one British battery was deserted, its guns left to the enemy, and the other was reloading and so for a moment it seemed strangely quiet.

Then the French, who had been ripped by the round shot and torn by the dreadful canister, realized that the battery had been abandoned. They gave a great cheer and scrambled over rocks to touch the hot cannon, and officers shouted at them to ignore the guns. The guns could be taken away later, but for now all that mattered was to reach the crest and so win Portugal. Beneath them Marshal Masséna wondered whether Henriette would find the beds in the monastery comfortable, and whether he would be named Prince of Portugal and whether his cook could find something palatable among the discarded British rations to make for supper. Pertinent questions all, for the Army of Portugal was on the very brink of victory.

Then Black Bob took a breath.

"FORWARD!" SHARPE CALLED. He had concentrated the riflemen, British and Portuguese, on the spur's center from where they could pour an accurate fire on the voltigeurs crouching among the knoll's jumbled rocks. "Make it fast," he shouted. He knelt and fired his rifle, the smoke hiding whatever damage he did. "Forward! Forward!" If this damned attack was to be done, he thought, then do it quickly, and he chivvied the riflemen on, then beckoned at the redcoats and the rest of the Portuguese who advanced in a two-deep line behind. The guns helped. One was firing canister, the balls rattling on the rocks, while the second was cutting its fuses desperately short so that the shells exploded just above the knoll. It would be hell there, Sharpe thought. The French were being assailed by rifle fire, canister and shell fragments, yet they stubbornly clung to the promontory.

He slung his rifle. He did not have time to reload and, besides, he wanted the attack over quickly and so, in anticipation, he drew his sword. Why the hell did the bastards not run? "Forward!" he shouted and felt a ball smack past his cheek, the wind of it like a small hot puff of air. More smoke showed among the rocks as the voltigeurs opened on the riflemen, but none of the musket balls hit for the range was long. The rifles made a deeper, quicker noise than the muskets. "Forward!" Sharpe shouted again, conscious that Vicente had brought the three-company line close behind the skirmishers. The riflemen darted forward, knelt, aimed and fired, and a musket ball whipped through the heather to Sharpe's left. A Frenchman firing low, he thought, a man with experience, and he was a hundred paces from the knoll now and fear had dried his mouth. The enemy was hidden, his own men were in the open, and another ball went close enough for him to feel the wind of its passing. A cazador was down, clutching his right thigh, his rifle fallen in the heather. "Leave him!" Sharpe shouted at two men going to help the man. "Keep firing! Forward! Forward!" The noise of the big attack to the north was at full intensity, guns and muskets, then the two artillery pieces supporting Sharpe's attack fired together and he saw a shell burst right at the edge of the rocks and heard the canister strike stone and a Frenchman seemed to stand up slowly, his blue coat turning red before he jerked back down.

"Aim true!" Sharpe shouted at his men. In the excitement of battle there was a temptation to snatch at shots, to waste bullets, and he was close enough now to see the crouching enemy. Hagman fired, then took a loaded rifle from young Perkins and fired again. More musket smoke puffed from the rocks. God, they were stubborn! The riflemen ran another ten paces forward, knelt, fired and reloaded. Another cazador was hit, this time in the shoulder and the man stumbled down the spur's side. A ball hit Sharpe's shako, jerking it back on its cords so that it hung from his neck. Harper fired his rifle, then unslung the seven-barreled gun, anticipating the order to rush the rocks and Sharpe turned to find Vicente almost on his heels.

"Let me give one volley," the Portuguese said.

"Rifles!" Sharpe bellowed. "Down! Down!"

The riflemen flattened themselves, Vicente halted his men. "Present!" The orders in the Portuguese army were given in English, a concession to the many British officers. Sharpe edged into their ranks.

"Fire!" Vicente shouted, and the volley cracked on the spur, pumping out smoke, just as the two cannon fired and the knoll was suddenly a tangled hell of bullets, shell scraps and blood.

"Charge!" Sharpe shouted and he ran ahead, saw Ensign Iliffe off to his left with his saber drawn. The Portuguese were shouting as they advanced, their words indistinguishable, but plainly full of hate for the French. They all began to run. It was all fury now, fury and hate and terror and anger, and smoke showed in the rocks as the French fired and a man screamed behind Sharpe who found Harper beside him, the big man running clumsily, and they were just ten paces from the nearest rocks when suddenly a rank of a dozen Frenchmen stood up, an officer in their center, and presented muskets.

Harper had the volley gun low, at his hip, but he instinctively pulled the trigger and the seven bullets smacked into the row of Frenchmen, blasting a hole in the center of their small line. The officer was hit hard, falling backwards, and the others seemed more shocked by the noise of the gun than by its bullets, for suddenly they were turning and running. One or two shot first, but no bullet came anywhere near Sharpe who jumped onto the rocks and saw that the voltigeurs had taken enough. They were spilling over the spur's steep edges while the wounded French officer, who had been hit by Harper's bullet, was screaming at them to stay and fight. Sharpe silenced the man with a back blow of the sword that half stunned him. Cazadores and riflemen and redcoats were scrambling onto the knoll now, desperate to catch the French before they escaped. Some of the enemy were slow and they screamed as they were caught by the bayonets. A sergeant, reckoning escape was impossible, turned and lunged his own bayonet at Harper, who knocked it aside with the seven-barrel gun and then hit the man on the jaw with a fist and the French Sergeant went back as if he had been hit by a nine-pounder ball. Harper made sure of him by banging the volley gun's butt on his forehead.

A score of Frenchmen were still on the knoll, some trapped by fear of the drop off its eastern edge. "Put your guns down!" Sharpe roared at them, but none spoke English and instead they turned, bayonets leveled, and Sharpe cracked a musket aside with the heavy sword and then stabbed it forward into a man's belly, twisting the steel so the flesh did not grip the blade, and then yanking the weapon back so that blood splashed onto the stones. He slipped on the blood, heard a musket bang, swept the sword at another Frenchman and Vicente was there, his own big sword hacking down on a corporal. Sharpe pushed himself up, saw a Frenchman standing on the edge of the rocks and lunged the sword at the man's back so that he seemed to dive off the cliff. There was a heartbeat's silence after the man vanished, then a sound from far below like a sack of offal falling onto stone from a high roof.

And silence again, blessed silence, except for the percussive sound of the guns to the north. The French were gone from the knoll. They were running down the ridge, pursued by rifle fire, and Vicente's Portuguese began to cheer.

"Sergeant Harper!" Sharpe shouted.

"Sir?" Harper was searching a dead man's clothes.

"Butcher's bill," Sharpe ordered. He wiped his sword on a blue jacket, then thrust it back into its scabbard. A French shell exploded harmlessly below the rocks as Sharpe sat, suddenly tired, and remembered the half sausage in his pouch. He ate it, then pushed his bullet-riddled shako into some kind of order before putting the hat back on. It was strange, he thought, but in the last few minutes he had been quite unaware of his damaged ribs, but now the pain stabbed at him. There was a dead voltigeur at his feet and the corpse was wearing one of the old-fashioned short sabers that all French skirmishers used to carry, but had abandoned because the blades were useful for nothing except reaping crops. The man looked oddly peaceful, not a mark visible on his body, and Sharpe wondered if he was feigning death and prodded him with his boot. The man did not react. A fly crawled on the voltigeur's eyeball and Sharpe reckoned the man had to be dead.

Harper picked his way back through the rocks. "Mister Iliffe, sir," he said.

"What about him?"

"He's dead, sir," Harper said, "and none of the others are even scratched."

"Iliffe? Dead?" For some reason it did not make sense to Sharpe.

"He wouldn't have felt a thing, sir." Harper tapped his forehead. "Straight in."

Sharpe swore. He had not liked Iliffe until today, but in battle the boy had shown courage. He had been terrified, so terrified he had vomited at the prospect of fighting, but once the bullets began to fly he had conquered that fear and that was admirable. Sharpe walked to the body, took off his hat and stared down at Iliffe who looked vaguely surprised. "He would have made a good soldier," Sharpe said, and the men of the light company murmured agreement.

Sergeant Read took four men and carried Iliffe's body back to battalion. Lawford would not be pleased, Sharpe thought, then wondered why the hell it could not have been Slingsby shot through the forehead. That would have been a good morning's work for a voltigeur, Sharpe thought, and wondered why the hell his own bullet had missed. He glanced up at the sun and realized it was still mid-morning. He felt as if he had been fighting all day, but back in England some folk would not even have finished their breakfasts yet.

It was a pity about Iliffe, he thought, then drank some water, listened to the guns, and waited.

⚜

"NOW!" GENERAL CRAUFURD SHOUTED and the two battalions stood, appearing to the French as though they had suddenly sprung from the bare ground. "Ten paces forward!" Craufurd bellowed, and they marched smartly, hefting loaded muskets. "Fifty-second!" Craufurd called to the battalion nearest him in a voice that was raw with anger and savage with resolve. "Avenge Moore!" The 52nd had been at Corunna where, in defeating the French, they had lost their beloved general, Sir John Moore.

"Present!" the Colonel of the 52nd shouted.

The enemy were close, less than twenty-five yards away. They were staring upwards where the long red line had so unexpectedly appeared. Even the novices in the battered French ranks knew what was coming. The British line overlapped the columns, every musket was aimed at the leading French files, and a French officer made the sign of the cross as the red line seemed to take a quarter turn to the right as the guns went up into men's shoulders.

"Fire!"

The ledge vanished in smoke as over a thousand musket balls thumped into the columns. Dozens of men fell and the living, still marching upwards in obedience to the drumbeats, found they could not get across the writhing pile of injured men. Ahead of them they could hear the scrape of ramrods going into musket barrels. The British gunners of the remaining battery shot four barrel-loads of canister that tore into the survivors, clouding the columns' head with sprays of blood. "Fire by half companies!" a voice shouted.

"Fire!"

The volley fire began: the rippling, merciless, incessant clock-work drill of death. The British and Portuguese skirmishers had reformed on the left and added their own fire so that the heads of the columns were ringed by flame and smoke, pummeled by bullets, flayed by the canister spitting down from the ledge. A hundred fires began in the grass as flaming wadding spat from the barrels.

The fire was not just coming from the front. The skirmishers and the outer companies of the 43rd and the 52nd had wheeled down the slope to wrap themselves around the beleaguered French, who were now being shot at from three sides. The smoke of the half-company volleys rippled up and down the red lines, the balls slapped into flesh and banged into muskets, and the French advance had been stopped. No troops could advance into the bank of smoke that was ripped by flame as the volleys flared.

"Bayonets! Bayonets!" Craufurd shouted. There was a pause as men took out the seventeen-inch blades and slotted them over blackened musket muzzles. "Now kill them!" Black Bob shouted. He was feeling exultant, watching his hard-trained men tear four times their number into ruin.

The men with loaded muskets fired, and the redcoats were going down the hill, steadily at first, but then the two ranks met the French dead and they lost their cohesion as they negotiated the bodies, and there, just yards away, were the living. The British gave a great shout of rage and charged. "Kill them!" Black Bob was right behind the ranks, sword drawn, glaring at the French as the redcoats lunged with their blades.

It was slaughterhouse work. Most of the French in the leading ranks who had survived the musketry and the canister were wounded. They were also crammed together, and now the redcoats came at them with bayonets. The long blades stabbed forward, were twisted and pulled back. The loudest noise on the ridge was screaming now, men shouting for mercy, calling for God, cursing the enemy, and still the half-company volleys whipped in from the flanks so that no Frenchmen could deploy into line. They had been marched up a hill of death and were penned like sheep just below its summit and the bullets killed them from the flanks and the blades took them at the front, and the only escape from the torment was back down the hill.

They broke. One moment they were a mass of men cowering under an onslaught of steel and lead, and the next, starting with the rearmost ranks, they were a rabble. The front ranks, trapped by the men behind, could not escape and they were easy meat for the savage seventeen-inch blades, but the men at the back fled. Drums rolled down the hill, aban-doned by boys too terrified to do anything except escape, and, as they went, the British and Portuguese skirmishers came from the flanks to pur-sue them. The last of the Frenchmen broke, pursued by redcoats, and some were caught in the village where the blades went to work again and the cobbles and the white stones of the houses were painted with more blood and the screams could be heard down in the valley where Masséna watched, open-mouthed. Some Frenchmen became entangled in the vines and the cazadores caught them there and slit their throats. Rifle-men poured bullets after the fugitives. A man shouted for mercy in a vil-lage house and the shout turned into a terrible scream as two bayonets took his life.

And then the French were gone. They had been swamped by panic and the slope around the village was littered with abandoned muskets and bodies. Some of the enemy were fortunate. Two riflemen rounded up prisoners and prodded them up towards the windmill where the British gunners had reclaimed their battery. A French captain, who had only kept his life by pretending to be dead, yielded his sword to a lieu-tenant of the 52nd. The Lieutenant, a courteous man, bowed in ac-knowledgment and gave the blade back. "You will do me the honor of accompanying me up the hill," the Lieutenant said, and he then tried to make conversation in his school French. The weather had gone sud-denly cold, had it not? The French Captain agreed it had, but he also would have agreed if the Englishman had remarked how warm it was. The Captain was shaking. He was covered in blood, none of it his own, but all from wounds inflicted by canister on men who had climbed near him. He saw his men lying dead, saw others dying, saw them looking up from the ground and trying to call for help he could not give. He remembered the bayonets coming at him and the joy of the killing plain on the faces of the men who held them. "It was a storm," he said, not knowing what he said.

"Not now the heat's broken, I think," the Lieutenant said, misunderstanding his captive's words. The bandsmen of the 43rd and 52nd were collecting the wounded, almost all of them French, and carrying them up to the mill where those that survived would be put on carts and taken to the monastery where the surgeons waited. "We were hoping for a game of cricket if tomorrow stays fine," the Lieutenant said. "Have you had the privilege of watching cricket, monsieur?"

"Cricket?" The Captain gaped at the redcoat.

"The Light Division officers hope to play the rest of the army," the Lieutenant said, "unless war or the weather intervenes."

"I have never seen cricket," the Frenchman said.

"When you get to heaven, monsieur," the Lieutenant said gravely, "and I pray that will be many happy years hence, you will find that your days are spent in playing cricket."

Just to the south there was more sudden firing. It sounded like British volleys, for they were regular and fast, but it was four Portuguese battalions that guarded the ridge to the right of the Light Division. The smaller French column, meant to reinforce the success of the two that had climbed through Sula, had swung away from the village and found itself split from the main attack by a deep, wooded ravine, and so the men climbed on their own, going through a grove of pines, and when they emerged onto the open hillside above they saw nothing but Portuguese troops ahead. No redcoats. The column outnumbered the Portuguese. They also knew their enemy for they had beaten the Portuguese before and did not fear the men in brown and blue as they feared the British muskets. This would be a simple victory, a hammer blow against a despised enemy, but then the Portuguese opened fire and the volleys rippled like clockwork and the musket balls were fired low and the guns were reloaded swiftly and the column, like those to the north, found itself assailed from three sides and suddenly the despised enemy was driving the French ignominiously downhill. And so the last French column ran, defeated by men fighting for their homeland, and then the whole ridge was empty of the Emperor's men except for the dead and the wounded and the captured. A drummer boy cried as he lay in the vines. He was eleven years old and had a bullet in his lung. His father, a sergeant, was lying dead twenty paces away where a bird pecked at his eyes. Now that the guns had stopped the black feathered birds were coming to the ridge and its feast of flesh.

Smoke drifted off the hill. Guns cooled. Men passed round water bottles.

The French were back in the valley. "There is a road around the north of the ridge," an aide reminded Marshal Masséna, who said nothing. He just stared at what was left of his attacks on the hill. Beaten, all of them. Beaten to nothing. Defeated. And the enemy, hidden once more behind the ridge's crest, waited for him to try again.

※

"YOU REMEMBER MISS SAVAGE?" Vicente asked Sharpe. They were sitting at the end of the knoll, staring down at the beaten French.

"Kate? Of course I remember Kate," Sharpe said. "I often wondered what happened to her."

"She married me," Vicente said, and looked absurdly pleased with himself.

"Good God," Sharpe said, then decided that probably sounded like a rude response. "Well done!"

"I shaved off my mustache," Vicente said, "as you suggested. And she said yes."

"Never did understand mustaches," Sharpe said, "must be like kissing a blacking brush."

"And we have a child," Vicente went on, "a girl."

"Quick work, Jorge!"

"We are very happy," Vicente said solemnly.

"Good for you," Sharpe said, and meant it. Kate Savage had run away from her home in Oporto, and Sharpe, with Vicente's help, had rescued her. That had been eighteen months before and Sharpe had often wondered what had happened to the English girl who had inherited her father's vineyards and port lodge.

"Kate is still in Porto, of course," Vicente said.

"With her mother?"

"She went back to England," Vicente said, "just after I joined my new regiment in Coimbra."

"Why there?"

"It is where I grew up," Vicente said, "and my parents still live there. I went to the university of Coimbra, so really it is home. But from now on I shall live in Porto. When the war is over."

"Be a lawyer again?"

"I hope so." Vicente made the sign of the cross. "I know what you think of the law, Richard, but it is the one barrier between man and bestiality."

"Didn't do much to stop the French."

"War is above the law, which is why it is so bad. War lets loose all the things which the law restrains."

"Like me," Sharpe said.

"You are not such a bad man," Vicente said with a smile.

Sharpe looked down into the valley. The French had at last withdrawn to where they had been the previous evening, only now they were throwing up earthworks beyond the stream where infantry dug trenches and used the spoil to make bulwarks. "Those buggers think we're coming down to finish them off," he said.

"Will we?"

"Christ, no! We've got the high ground. No point in giving it up."

"So what do we do?"

"Wait for orders, Jorge, wait for orders. And I reckon mine are coming now." Sharpe nodded towards Major Forrest who was riding his horse along the spine of the spur.

Forrest stopped by the rocks and looked down at the French dead, then took off his hat and nodded to Sharpe. "The Colonel wants the company back," he said, sounding tired.

"Major Forrest," Sharpe said, "let me introduce you to Captain Vicente. I fought with him at Oporto."

"Honored," Forrest said, "honored." His red sleeve was dark with blood from the musket ball that had struck him. He hesitated, trying to think of something complimentary to say to Vicente, but nothing occurred to him, so he looked back to Sharpe. "The Colonel wants the company now, Sharpe," he said.

"On your feet, lads!" Sharpe stood himself and shook Vicente's hand. "Keep a look out for us, Jorge," he said, "we might need your help again. And give my regards to Kate."

Sharpe walked the company back across ground scorched by musket and rifle fire. The ridge was quiet now, no guns firing, just the wind sighing on the grass. Forrest rode beside Sharpe, but said nothing until they reached the battalion's lines. The South Essex were in ranks, but sitting and sprawling on the grass, and Forrest gestured to the left-hand end of the line as if to order the light company to take their place. "Lieutenant Slingsby will command them for the moment," Forrest said.

"He'll do what?" Sharpe asked, shocked.

"For the moment," Forrest said placatingly, "because right now the Colonel wants you, Sharpe, and I daresay he isn't pleased."

That was an understatement. The Honorable William Lawford was in a temper, though, being a man of exquisite politeness, the anger only showed as a slight tightening of the lips and a distinctly unfriendly glance as Sharpe arrived at his tent. Lawford ducked out into the sunlight and nodded at Forrest. "You'll stay, Major," he said, and waited as Forrest dismounted and gave his reins to Lawford's servant, who led the horse away. "Knowles!" Lawford summoned the Adjutant from the tent. Knowles gave Sharpe a sympathetic look, which only made Lawford angrier. "You had best stay, Knowles," he said, "but keep other folk away. I don't want what is said here bruited about the battalion."

Knowles put on his hat and stood a few yards away. Forrest hovered to one side as Lawford looked at Sharpe. "Perhaps, Captain," he spoke icily, "you can explain yourself?"

"Explain myself, sir?"

"Ensign Iliffe is dead."

"I regret it, sir."

"Good God! The boy is entrusted to my care! Now I have to write to his father and say the lad's life was tossed away by an irresponsible officer who committed his company to an attack without any authorization from me!" Lawford paused, evidently too angry to frame his next words, then slapped his hand against his sword scabbard. "I command this battalion, Sharpe!" he said. "Perhaps you have never realized that? Do you think you can swan around as you like, killing men as you see fit, without reference to me?"

"I had orders, sir," Sharpe said woodenly.

"Orders?" Lawford demanded. "I gave no order!"

"I was ordered by Colonel Rogers-Jones, sir."

"Who the devil is Colonel Rogers-Jones?"

"I believe he commands a battalion of cazadores," Forrest put in quietly.

"God damn it, Sharpe," Lawford snapped, "Colonel Rogers bloody Jones does not command the South Essex!"

"I had orders from a colonel, sir," Sharpe insisted, "and I obeyed." He paused. "And I recalled your advice, sir."

"My advice?" Lawford asked.

"Last night, sir, you told me you wanted your skirmishers to be audacious and aggressive. So we were."

"I also want my officers to be gentlemen," Lawford said, "to show courtesy."

Sharpe sensed that they had reached the real point of this meeting. Lawford, it was true, had a genuine grievance that Sharpe had committed the light company to an attack without his permission, but no officer could truly object to a man fighting the enemy. The complaint had been merely a ranging shot for the assault that was about to come. Sharpe said nothing, but just stared fixedly at a spot between the Colonel's eyes.

"Lieutenant Slingsby," the Colonel said, "tells me that you insulted him. That you invited him to a duel. That you called him illegitimate. That you swore at him."

Sharpe cast his mind back to the brief confrontation on the ridge's forward slope just after he had pulled the company out of the French panic. "I doubt I called him illegitimate, sir," he said. "I wouldn't use that sort of word. I probably called him a bastard."

Knowles stared westwards. Forrest looked down at the grass to hide a smile. Lawford looked astonished. "You called him what?"

"A bastard, sir."

"That is entirely unacceptable between fellow officers," Lawford said.

Sharpe said nothing. It was usually the best thing to do.

"Have you nothing to say?" Lawford demanded.

"I have never done a thing," Sharpe was goaded into speaking "except for the good of this battalion."

That vehement statement rather took Lawford aback. He blinked. "No one is decrying your service, Sharpe," he said stiffly. "I am, rather, attempting to inculcate the manners of an officer into your behavior. I will not tolerate crass rudeness to a fellow officer."

"You'd tolerate losing half your light company, sir?" Sharpe asked.

"Half my light company?"

"My fellow officer," Sharpe did not bother to hide his sarcasm, "had the light company in skirmish order underneath the French. When they broke, sir, which they did, he'd have lost them all. They'd have been swept away. Luckily for the battalion, sir, I was there and did what had to be done."

"That is not what I observed," Lawford said.

"It happened," Sharpe said bluntly.

Forrest cleared his throat and stared pointedly at a blade of grass by his right toe. Lawford took the hint. "Major?"

"I rather think Lieutenant Slingsby had taken the light company a bit too far, sir," Forrest observed mildly.

"Audacity and aggression," Lawford said, "are not reprehensible in an officer. I applaud Lieutenant Slingsby for his enthusiasm, and that is no reason, Sharpe, for you to insult him."

Time to bite his tongue again, Sharpe thought, so he kept quiet.

"And I will not abide dueling between my officers"—Lawford was back in stride—"and I will not abide gratuitous insults. Lieutenant Slingsby is an experienced and enthusiastic officer, an undoubted asset to the battalion, Sharpe, an asset. Is that understood, Sharpe?"

"Yes, sir."

"So you will apologize to him."

I bloody well will not, Sharpe thought, and kept staring at the spot between Lawford's eyes.

"Did you hear me, Sharpe?"

"I did, sir."

"So you will apologize?"

"No, sir."

Lawford looked outraged, but for a few seconds was lost for words. "The consequences, Sharpe," he finally managed to speak, "will be dire if you disobey me in this."

Sharpe shifted his gaze so that he was looking at Lawford's right eye. Looking straight at Lawford and making the Colonel feel uncomfortable. Sharpe saw weakness there, then decided that was wrong. Lawford was not a weak man, but he lacked ruthlessness. Most men did. Most men were reasonable, they sought accommodation and found mutual ground. They were happy enough to fire volleys, but shrank from getting in close with a bayonet. But now was the time for Lawford to wield the blade. He had expected Sharpe to apologize to Slingsby, and why not? It was a small enough gesture, it appeared to solve the problem, but Sharpe was refusing and Lawford did not know what to do about it. "I will not apologize," Sharpe said very harshly, "sir." And the last word had all the insolence that could be invested in a single syllable.

Lawford looked furious, but again said nothing for a few seconds. Then, abruptly, he nodded. "You were a quartermaster once, I believe?"

"I was, sir."

"Mister Kiley is indisposed. For the moment, while I decide what to do with you, you will assume his duties."

"Yes, sir," Sharpe responded woodenly, betraying no reaction.

Lawford hesitated, as though there was something more to be said, then crammed on his cocked hat and turned away.

"Sir," Sharpe said.

Lawford turned, said nothing.

"Mister Iliffe, sir," Sharpe said. "He fought well today. If you're writing to his family, sir, then you can tell them truthfully that he fought very well."

"A pity, then, that he's dead," Lawford said bitterly and walked away, beckoning Knowles to accompany him.

Forrest sighed. "Why not just apologize, Richard?"

"Because he damned well nearly had my company killed."

"I know that," Forrest said, "and the Colonel knows it, and Mister Slingsby knows it and your company knows it. So eat humble pie, Sharpe, and go back to them."

"He"—Sharpe pointed at the retreating figure of the Colonel—"wants rid of me. He wants his goddamned brother-in-law in charge of the skirmishers."

"He doesn't want rid of you, Sharpe," Forrest said patiently. "Good God, he knows how good you are! But he has to bring on Slingsby. Family business, eh? His wife wants him to make Slingsby's career, and what a wife wants, Sharpe, a wife gets."

"He wants rid of me," Sharpe insisted. "And if I apologize, Major, then sooner or later I'd still be out on my ear, so I might as well go now."

"Don't go far," Forrest said with a smile.

"Why not?"

"Mister Slingsby drinks," Forrest said quietly.

"He does?"

"Far too much," Forrest said. "He's holding it in check for now, hoping a new battalion will give him a new beginning, but I fear for him. I had a similar problem myself, Richard, though I'll thank you not to tell anyone. I suspect our Mister Slingsby will revert to his old behavior in the end. Most men do."

"You didn't."

"Not yet, Sharpe, not yet." Forrest smiled. "But think on what I've said. Mutter an apology to the man, eh? And let it all blow over."

When hell froze over, Sharpe thought. Because he would not apologize.

And Slingsby had the light company.

MAJOR FERREIRA HAD READ his brother's letter shortly after the last French column had been defeated. "He wants an answer, *senhor*," Miguel, Ferragus's messenger, had said. "One word."

Ferreira stared through the cannon smoke that hung in skeins over the hillside where so many French had died. This was a victory, he thought, but it would not be long before the French found the road looping about the ridge's northern end. Or perhaps the victorious British and Portuguese would sweep down Bussaco's long hillside and attack the French in the valley? Yet there was no sign of such an attack. No gallopers rode to give generals fresh instructions, and the longer Wellington waited the more time the French had to throw up earthworks beyond the stream. No, the Major thought, this battle was over and Lord Wellington probably intended to fall back towards Lisbon and offer another battle in the hills north of the city.

"One word," Miguel had prompted the Major again.

Ferreira had nodded. "*Sim*," he said, though he said it heavily. Yes, it meant, and once the fatal word was spoken he turned his horse and spurred northwards past the victorious Light Division, behind the windmill that was pocked with the marks left by musket balls and then down through the small trees growing on the northern end of the ridge. No one remarked his going. He was known to be an occasional explorer, one of the Portuguese officers who, like their British counterparts, rode out to scout the enemy's position, and besides, there were Portuguese militia in the Caramula hills north of the ridge and it was not surprising that an officer rode to check on their position.

Yet Ferreira, even though his departure from the army had appeared quite innocent, rode with trepidation. His whole future, the future of his family, depended on the next few hours. The Major had inherited wealth, but he had never made any. His investments had failed, and it had only been his brother's return that had restored his fortunes, and that fortune would be threatened if the French took over Portugal. What Major Ferreira must do now was change horses, leap from the patriotic saddle into a French one, yet do it in such a way that no one would ever know, and he would do it only to preserve his name, his fortune and his family's future.

He rode for three hours and it was past midday when he turned eastwards, climbing to a prominent hill. He knew that the Portuguese militia guarding the road about the northern end of the ridge were well behind him, and as far as he knew there were no British or Portuguese cavalry patrols in these hills, but he still made the sign of the cross and composed a silent prayer that he would not be seen by anyone from his own side. And he did think of the British and Portuguese army as his side. He was a patriot, but what use was a penniless patriot?

He stopped at the hilltop. Stopped there for a long time until he was certain that any French cavalry vedettes would have seen him, and then he rode slowly down the hill's eastern face. He stopped halfway down. Now, anyone approaching him could see that he was not luring them to an ambush. There was no dead ground behind him, nowhere for a cavalry unit to hide. There was just Major Ferreira on a long, bare hillside.

And ten minutes after he stopped, a score of green-coated dragoons appeared a half-mile away. The horsemen spread into a line. Some had their carbines out of their holsters, but most had drawn swords and Ferreira dismounted to show them that he was not trying to escape. The officer in charge of the dragoons stared upwards, searching for danger, and finally he must have concluded that all was well for he rode forward with a half-dozen of his men. The horses' hooves left puffs of dust on the dry hillside. Ferreira, as the dragoons came nearer, spread his arms to show he carried no weapons, then stood quite still as the horsemen surrounded him. A blade dipped near his throat, held by the officer, whose uniform had been faded by the sun. "I have a letter of introduction," Ferreira said in French.

"To whom?" It was the officer who answered.

"To you," Ferreira answered, "from Colonel Barreto."

"And who in the name of holy Christ is Colonel Barreto?"

"An aide to Marshal Masséna."

"Show me the letter."

Ferreira brought the piece of paper from a pocket, unfolded it and handed it up to the French officer, who leaned from his saddle to take it.

The letter, creased and dirty, explained to any French officer that the bearer could be trusted and should be given every help possible. Barreto had given Ferreira the letter when the Major had been negotiating the gift of the flour, but it came in more useful now. The dragoon officer read it swiftly, glanced once at Ferreira, then tossed the letter back. "So what do you want?"

"To see Colonel Barreto, of course," Ferreira said.

It took an hour and a half to reach the village of Moura where Ney's men, who had attacked towards the windmill above Sula, were resting. The surgeons were busy in the village and Ferreira had to steer his horse past a pile of severed arms and legs that lay just outside an open window. Next to the stream, where the flat stones provided a place for the village women to do their laundry, there was now a heap of corpses. Most had been stripped of their uniforms and their white skin was laced with blood. Ferreira averted his eyes as he followed the dragoons to a small hill just beyond the village where, in the shadow of Moura's windmill, Marshal Masséna was eating a meal of bread, cheese and cold chicken. Ferreira dismounted and waited as the dragoon officer threaded his way through the aides, and, as he waited, the Major stared at the ridge and wondered that any general would think to throw his men up such a slope.

"Major Ferreira!" The voice was sour. A tall man in the uniform of a French colonel of dragoons approached him. "Give me one reason, Major," the Colonel said, pointing to the mill, "why we shouldn't put you against that wall and shoot you." The Colonel, though dressed as a Frenchman, was Portuguese. He had been an officer in the old Portuguese army and had seen his home burned and his family killed by the *ordenança*, the Portuguese militia that had turned on the privileged classes in the chaos of the first French invasions. Colonel Barreto had joined the French, not because he hated Portugal, but because he saw no future for his country unless it was rid of superstition and anarchy. The French, he believed, would bring the blessings of modernity to Portugal, but only if the French forces were fed. "You promised us flour!" Barreto said angrily. "And instead there was British infantry waiting for us!"

"In war, Colonel, things go wrong," Ferreira said humbly. "The flour was there, my brother was there, and then a British company arrived. I tried to send them away, but they would not go." Ferreira knew he sounded weak, but he was terrified. Not of the French, but in case some officer on the ridge saw him through a telescope. He doubted that would happen. The ridge top was a long way away and his blue Portuguese jacket would look much like a French coat at that distance, but he was still frightened. Treachery was a hard trade.

Barreto seemed to accept the explanation. "I found the remnants of the flour," he admitted, "but it's a pity, Major. This army is hungry. You know what we found in this village? One half barrel of lemons. What damn good is that?"

"Coimbra," Ferreira said, "is full of food."

"Full of food, eh?" Barreto asked skeptically.

"Wheat, barley, rice, beans, figs, salt cod, beef," Ferreira said flatly.

"And how, in God's name, do we reach Coimbra, eh?" Barreto had switched to French because a group of Masséna's other aides had come to listen to the conversation. The Colonel pointed to the ridge. "Those bastards, Ferreira, are between us and Coimbra."

"There is a road around the ridge," Ferreira said.

"A road," Barreto said, "which goes through the defile of Caramula, and how many damn redcoats are waiting for us there?"

"None," Ferreira said. "There is only the Portuguese militia. No more than fifteen hundred. In three days, Colonel, you can be in Coimbra."

"And in three days," Barreto said, "the British will empty Coimbra of food."

"My brother guarantees you three months' supply," Ferreira said, "but only . . ." He faltered and stopped.

"Only what?" a Frenchman asked.

"When your army enters a town, monsieur," Ferreira spoke very humbly, "they do not behave well. There is plundering, theft, murder. It has happened every time."

"So?"

"So if your men get into my brother's warehouses, what will they do?"

"Take everything," the Frenchman said.

"And destroy what they cannot take," Ferreira finished the statement. He looked back to Barreto. "My brother wants two things, Colonel. He wants a fair payment for the food he will supply to you, and he wants his property guarded from the moment you enter the city."

"We take what we want," another Frenchman put in, "we don't pay our enemies for food."

"If I do not tell my brother that you agree," Ferreira said, his voice harder now, "then there will be no food when you arrive in Coimbra. You can take nothing, monsieur, or you can pay for something and eat."

There was a moment's silence, then Barreto nodded abruptly. "I will talk to the Marshal," he said and turned away.

One of the French aides, a tall and thin major, offered Ferreira a pinch of snuff. "I hear," he said, "that the British are building defenses in front of Lisbon?"

Ferreira shrugged as if to suggest the Frenchman's fears were trivial. "There are one or two new forts," he admitted, for he had seen them for himself when he was riding north from Lisbon, "but they are small works," he went on. "What they are also building, monsieur, is a new port at São Julião."

"Where's that?"

"South of Lisbon."

"They're building a port?"

"A new harbor, monsieur," Ferreira confirmed. "They fear trying to evacuate their troops through Lisbon. There might be riots. São Julião is a remote place and it will be easy for the British to take to their ships there without trouble."

"And the forts you saw?"

"They overlook the main road to Lisbon," Ferreira said, "but there are other roads."

"And how far were they from Lisbon?"

"Twenty miles," Ferreira guessed.

"And there are hills there?"

"Not so steep as that." Ferreira nodded towards the looming ridge.

"So they hope to delay us in the hills, yes, as they retreat to their new port?"

"I would think so, monsieur."

"So we will need food," the Frenchman concluded. "And what does your brother want besides money and protection?"

"He wants to survive, monsieur."

"It is what we all want," the Frenchman said. He was gazing at the blue bodies that lay on the ridge's eastern slope. "God send us back to France soon."

To Ferreira's surprise the Marshal himself returned with Colonel Barreto. The one-eyed Masséna stared hard at Ferreira who returned the gaze, seeing how old and tired the Frenchman looked. Finally Masséna nodded. "Tell your brother we will pay him a price and tell him Colonel Barreto will take troops to protect his property. You know where that property is, Colonel?"

"Major Ferreira will tell me," Barreto said.

"Good. It's time my men had a proper meal." Masséna walked back to his cold chicken, bread, cheese and wine while Barreto and Ferreira first haggled over the price to be paid, then made arrangements to safeguard the food. And when that was all done Ferreira rode back the way he had come. He rode in the afternoon sun, chilled by an autumn wind, and no one saw him and no one in the British or Portuguese army thought it strange that he had been away since the battle's end.

And on the ridge, and in the valley beneath, the troops waited.

COIMBRA

THE BRITISH AND PORTUGUESE ARMY stayed on the ridge all the next day while the French remained in the valley. At times the crackle of muskets or rifles started birds up from the heather as skirmishers contested the long slope, but mostly the day was quiet. The cannons did not fire. French troops, without weapons and dressed in shirtsleeves, climbed the slope to take away their wounded who had been left to suffer overnight. Some of the injured had crawled down to the stream while others had died in the darkness. A dead voltigeur just beneath the rocky knoll lay with his clenched hands jutting to the sky while a raven pecked at his lips and eyes. The British and Portuguese picquets let the enemy work undisturbed, only challenging the few voltigeurs who climbed too close to the crest. When the wounded had been taken away, the dead were carried to the graves being dug behind the entrenchments the French had thrown up beyond the stream, but the defensive bastions were a waste of effort, for Lord Wellington had no intention of giving up the high ground to take the fight into the valley.

Lieutenant Jack Bullen, a nineteen-year-old who had been serving in number nine company, was sent to the light company to replace Iliffe. Slingsby, Lawford decreed, was now to be addressed as Captain Slingsby. "He was brevetted as such in the 55th," Lawford told Forrest, "and it will distinguish him from Bullen."

"Indeed it will, sir."

Lawford bridled at the Major's tone. "It's merely a courtesy, Forrest. You surely approve of courtesy?"

"Indeed I do, sir, though I value Sharpe more."

"What on earth do you mean?"

"I mean, sir, that I'd rather Sharpe commanded the skirmishers. He's the best man for the job."

"And so he will, Forrest, so he will, just as soon as he learns to behave in a civilized manner. We fight for civilization, do we not?"

"I hope we do," Forrest agreed.

"And we do not gain that objective by behaving with crass discourtesy. That's what Sharpe's behavior is, Forrest, crass discourtesy! I want it eradicated."

Might as well wish to extinguish the sun, Major Forrest thought. The Major was a courteous man, judicious and sensible, but he doubted the fighting efficiency of the South Essex would be enhanced by a campaign to improve its manners.

There was a sullen atmosphere in the battalion. Lawford put it down to the casualties of the battle, who had either been buried on the ridge or carried away in carts to the careless mercies of the surgeons. This was a day, Lawford thought, when the battalion ought to be busy, yet there was nothing to do except wait on the long high summit in case the French renewed their attacks. He ordered all the muskets to be cleaned with boiling water, the flints to be inspected and replaced if they were too chipped, and every man's cartridge box to be replenished, but those useful tasks only took an hour and the men were no more cheerful at its end than they had been at the beginning. The Colonel made himself visible and tried to encourage the men, yet he was aware of reproachful glances and muttered comments, and Lawford was no fool and knew exactly what caused it. He kept hoping Sharpe would make the requisite apology, but the rifleman stayed stubbornly out of sight and finally Lawford sought out Leroy, the loyal American. "Talk to him," he pleaded.

"Won't listen to me, Colonel."

"He respects you, Leroy."

"It's kind of you to suggest as much," Leroy said, "but he's stubborn as a mule."

"Getting too big for his boots, that's the trouble," Lawford said irritably.

"Boots he took from a French colonel of chasseurs, if I remember," Leroy said, staring up at a buzzard that circled lazily above the ridge.

"The men are unhappy," Lawford said, deciding to avoid a discussion of Sharpe's boots.

"Sharpe's a strange man, Colonel," Leroy said, then paused to light one of the rough, dark brown cigars that were sold by Portuguese peddlers. "Most of the men don't like officers up from the ranks, but they're kind of fond of Sharpe. He scares them. They want to be like him."

"I can't see that scaring men is a virtue in an officer," Lawford said, annoyed.

"Probably the best one," Leroy said provocatively. "Of course he ain't an easy man in the mess," the American went on more placidly, "but he's one hell of a soldier. Saved Slingsby's life yesterday."

"That is nonsense." Lawford sounded testy. "Captain Slingsby might have taken the company a little too far, but he would have retrieved them, I'm sure."

"Wasn't talking about that," Leroy said. "Sharpe shot a fellow about to give Slingsby a Portuguese grave. Finest damned piece of shooting I've ever seen."

Lawford had congratulated Sharpe at the time, but he was in no mood to consider mitigating circumstances. "There was a good deal of firing, Leroy," he said airily, "and the shot could have come from anywhere."

"Maybe," the American said, sounding dubious, "but you have to admit Sharpe was damned useful yesterday."

Lawford wondered whether Leroy had overheard Sharpe's quiet advice to turn the battalion around and then wheel them onto the French flank. It had been good advice, and taking it had retrieved a distinctly unhealthy situation, but the Colonel had persuaded himself that he would have thought of turning and wheeling the battalion without Sharpe. He had also persuaded himself that his authority was being deliberately challenged by the rifleman, and that was quite intolerable. "All I want is an apology!" he protested.

"I'll talk to him, Colonel," Leroy promised, "but if Mister Sharpe says he won't apologize then you can wait till doomsday. Unless you get Lord Wellington to order him. That's the one man who scares Sharpe."

"I will not involve Wellington!" Lawford said in alarm. He had once been an aide to the General and knew how his lordship detested being niggled by minor concerns, and, besides, to make such a request would only betray Lawford's failure. And it was failure. He knew Sharpe was a far finer officer than Slingsby, but the Colonel had promised Jessica, his wife, that he would do all he could to press Cornelius's career and the promise had to be kept. "Talk to him," he encouraged Leroy. "Suggest a written apology, perhaps? He won't have to deliver it in person. I'll convey it myself and tear it up afterwards."

"I'll suggest it," Leroy said, then went down the reverse slope of the ridge where he found the battalion's temporary quartermaster sitting with a dozen of the battalion's wives. They were laughing, but fell silent as Leroy approached. "Sorry to disturb you, ladies." The Major took off his battered cocked hat as a courtesy to the women, then beckoned to Sharpe. "A word?" He led Sharpe a few paces down the hill. "Know what I'm here to say?" Leroy asked.

"I can guess."

"And?"

"No, sir."

"Reckoned as much," Leroy said. "Jesus Christ, who is that?" He was looking back at the women and Sharpe knew the Major had to be referring to an attractive, long-haired Portuguese girl who had joined the battalion the week before.

"Sergeant Enables found her," Sharpe explained.

"Christ! She can't be more than eleven," Leroy said, then stared at the other women for a moment. "Damn," he went on, "but that Sally Clayton is pretty."

"Pretty well married, too," Sharpe said.

Leroy grinned. "You ever read the story of Uriah the Hittite, Sharpe?"

"Hittite? A prizefighter?" Sharpe guessed.

"Not quite, Sharpe. Fellow in the Bible. Uriah the Hittite, Sharpe, had a wife and King David wanted her in his bed, so he sent Uriah to war and ordered the general to put the poor bastard in the front line so some other bastard would kill him. Worked, too."

"I'll remember that," Sharpe said.

"Can't remember the woman's name," Leroy said. "Weren't Sally. So what shall I tell the Colonel?"

"That he's just got himself the best damned quartermaster in the army."

Leroy chuckled and walked uphill. He paused and turned after a few paces. "Bathsheba," he called back to Sharpe.

"Bath what?"

"That was her name, Bathsheba."

"Sounds like another prizefighter."

"But Bathsheba hit below the belt, Sharpe," Leroy said, "well below the belt!" He raised his hat again to the battalion wives and walked on.

"He's thinking about it," he told the Colonel a few moments later.

"Let us hope he thinks clearly," Lawford said piously.

But if Sharpe was thinking about it, no apology came. Instead, as evening fell, the army was ordered to ready itself for a retreat. The French could be seen leaving, evidently going towards the road that looped about the ridge's northern end and so the gallopers pounded along the ridge with orders that the army was to march towards Lisbon before dawn. The South Essex, alone among the British battalions, received different orders. "It seems we're to retreat, gentlemen," Lawford said to the company commanders as his tent was taken down by orderlies. There was a murmur of surprise that Lawford stilled with a raised hand. "There's a route round the top of the ridge," he explained, "and if we stay the French will outflank us. They'll be up our backsides, so we're dancing backwards for a few days. Find somewhere else to bloody them, eh?" Some of the officers still looked surprised that, having won a victory, they were to yield ground, but Lawford ignored their puzzlement. "We have our own orders, gentlemen," he went on. "The battalion is to leave tonight and hurry to Coimbra. A long march, I fear, but necessary. We're to reach Coimbra with all dispatch and aid the commissary officers in the destruction of the army's supplies on the river quays. A Portuguese regiment is being sent as well. The two of us are the vanguard, so to speak, but our responsibility is heavy. The General wants those provisions brought to ruin by tomorrow night."

"We're expected to reach Coimbra tonight?" Leroy asked skeptically. The city was at least twenty miles away and, by any reckoning, that was a very ambitious march, especially at night.

"Wagons are being provided for baggage," Lawford said, "including the men's packs. Walking wounded will guard those packs, women and children go with the wagons. We march light, we march fast."

"Advance party?" Leroy wanted to know.

"I'm sure the quartermaster will know what to do," Lawford said.

"Dark night," Leroy said, "probably chaotic in Coimbra. Two battalions looking for quarters and the commissary people will mostly be drunk. Even Sharpe can't do that alone, sir. Best let me go with him."

Lawford looked indignant for he knew Leroy's suggestion was an expression of sympathy for Sharpe, but the American's objections had been cogent and so, reluctantly, Lawford nodded. "Do that, Major," he said curtly, "and as for the rest of us? I want to be the first battalion into Coimbra, gentlemen! We can't have the Portuguese beating us, so be ready to march in one hour."

"Light company to lead?" Slingsby asked. He was fairly bursting with pride and efficiency.

"Of course, Captain."

"We'll set a smart pace," Slingsby promised.

"Do we have a guide?" Forrest asked.

"We can find one, I'm sure," Lawford said, "but it's not a difficult route. West to the main road, then turn south."

"I can find it," Slingsby said confidently.

"Our wounded?" Forrest asked.

"More wagons will be provided. Mister Knowles? You'll determine those arrangements? Splendid!" Lawford smiled to show that the battalion was one happy family. "Be ready to leave in one hour, gentlemen, one hour!"

Leroy found Sharpe, who had not been invited to the company commanders' meeting. "You and I are for Coimbra, Sharpe," the Major said. "You can ride my spare horse and my servant can walk."

"Coimbra?"

"Billeting. Battalion's following tonight."

"You don't need to come," Sharpe said. "I've done billeting before."

"You want to walk there on your own?" Leroy asked, then grinned. "I'm coming, Sharpe, because the battalion is marching twenty goddamn miles in the twilight and it's going to be a shambles. Twenty miles at night? They'll never do it, and two battalions on one narrow road? Hell, I don't need that. You and I can go ahead, mark the place up, find a tavern, and ten guineas says the battalion won't be there before the sun's up."

"Keep your money," Sharpe said.

"And when they do get there," Leroy went on happily, "they're going to be in one hell of a God-awful temper. That's why I'm appointing myself as your assistant, Sharpe."

They rode down the hill. The sun was low and the shadows long. It was almost the end of September and the days were drawing in. The first wagons loaded with wounded British and Portuguese soldiers were already on the road and Leroy and Sharpe had to edge past them. They went through half-deserted villages where Portuguese officers were persuading the remaining folk to leave. The arguments were shrill in the dusk. A black-dressed woman, her gray hair covered in a black scarf, beat at an officer's horse with a broom, evidently screaming at the rider to go away. "You can't blame them," Leroy said. "They hear we won the battle, now they want to know why the hell they have to leave home. Nasty business leaving home."

His tone was bitter and Sharpe glanced at him. "You've done it?"

"Hell, yes. We were thrown out by the damned rebels. Went to Canada with nothing but the shirts on our backs. The bastards promised restitution after the war, but we never saw a goddamned penny. I was only a kid, Sharpe. I thought it was all exciting, but what do kids know?"

"Then you went to England?"

"And we thrived, Sharpe, we thrived. My father made his money trading with the men he once fought." Leroy laughed, then rode in silence for a few yards, ducking under a low tree branch. "So tell me about these fortifications guarding Lisbon."

"I only know what Michael Hogan told me."

"So what did he tell you?"

"That they're the biggest defenses ever made in Europe," Sharpe said. He saw Leroy's skepticism. "Over a hundred and fifty forts," Sharpe went on, "connected by trenches. Hills reshaped to make them too steep to climb, valleys filled with obstacles, streams dammed to flood the approaches, the whole lot filled with cannon. Two lines, stretching from the Tagus to the ocean."

"So the idea is to get behind them and thumb our noses at the French?"

"And let the bastards starve," Sharpe said.

"And you, Sharpe, what will you do? Apologize?" Leroy laughed at Sharpe's expression. "The Colonel ain't going to give in."

"Nor am I," Sharpe said.

"So you'll stay quartermaster?"

"The Portuguese want British officers," Sharpe said, "and if I join them I get a promotion."

"Hell," Leroy said, thinking about it.

"Not that I want to leave the light company," Sharpe went on, thinking about Pat Harper and the other men he counted as friends. "But Lawford wants Slingsby, he doesn't want me."

"He wants you, Sharpe," Leroy said, "but he's made promises. Have you ever met the Colonel's wife?"

"No."

"Pretty," Leroy said, "pretty as a picture, but about as soft as an angry dragoon. I watched her ream out a servant once because the poor bastard hadn't filled a flower vase with enough water, and by the time she'd done there was nothing left of the man but slivers of skin and spots of blood. A formidable lady, our Jessica. She'd make a much better commanding officer than her husband." The Major drew on a cigar. "But I wouldn't be in too much of a hurry to join the Portuguese. I have a suspicion that Mister Slingsby will cook his own goose."

"Drink?"

"He was liquored to the gills on the night of the battle. Staggering, he was. Fine next morning."

They reached Coimbra long after dark and it was close to midnight before they discovered the office of the Town Major, the British officer responsible for liaison with the town authorities, and the Major himself was not there, but his servant, wearing a tasseled nightcap, opened the door and grumbled about officers keeping unseasonable hours. "What is it you want, sir?"

"Chalk," Sharpe said, "and you've got two battalions arriving before dawn."

"Oh, Jesus Christ," the servant said, "two battalions? Chalk?"

"At least four sticks. Where are the commissary officers?"

"Up the street, sir, six doors on the left, but if it's rations you're after help yourself from the town quay. Bloody tons there, sir."

"A lantern would be useful," Major Leroy put in.

"Lantern, sir. There is one somewhere."

"And we need to stable two horses."

"Round the back, sir. Be safe there."

Once the horses were stabled and Leroy was equipped with the lantern they worked their way up the street chalking on the doors. SE, Sharpe chalked, meaning South Essex, 4-6, which said six men of number four company would be billeted in the house. They used the small streets close to the bridge over the Mondego, and after a half-hour they encountered two Portuguese officers chalking up for their battalion. Neither of the battalions had arrived by the time the work was done, so Sharpe and Leroy found a tavern on the quay where lights still glowed and ordered themselves wine, brandy and food. They ate salt cod and, just as it was served, the sound of boots echoed in the street outside. Leroy leaned over, pulled open the tavern door and peered out. "Portuguese," he said laconically.

"So they beat us?" Sharpe said. "Colonel won't be pleased."

"The Colonel is going to be one very unhappy man about that," Leroy said and was about to close the door when he saw the legend chalked on the woodwork. SE, CO, ADJ, LCO, it said, and the American grinned. "Putting Lawford and the light company officers in here, Sharpe?"

"I thought the Colonel might want to be with his relative, sir. Friendly like."

"Or are you putting temptation in Mister Slingsby's path?"

Sharpe looked shocked. "Good lord," he said, "I hadn't thought of that."

"You lying bastard," Leroy said, closing the door. He laughed. "I don't think I'd want you as an enemy."

They slept in the taproom and, when Sharpe woke at dawn, the South Essex had still not reached the city. A sad procession of wagons, all with men wounded on Bussaco's slope, was crossing the bridge and Sharpe, going to the quayside, saw that the sills of the wagon beds were stained where blood had dripped from the vehicles. He had to wait to cross to the river bank because the convoy of wounded was followed by a smart traveling coach, drawn by four horses and heaped with trunks, accompanied by a wagon piled with more goods on which a half-dozen unhappy servants clung, and both vehicles were escorted by armed civilian horsemen. Once they were gone Sharpe crossed to the vast heaps of army provisions that had been brought to Coimbra. There were sacks of grain, barrels of salt meat, puncheons of rum, boxes of biscuit, all unloaded from the river boats that were tied to the wharves. Each boat had a number painted on its bow beneath the owner's name and town. The Portuguese authorities had ordered the boats to be numbered and labeled, then listed town by town, so they could be sure that all the craft would be destroyed before the French arrived. The name Ferreira was painted on a half-dozen of the larger vessels, and Sharpe assumed that meant the craft belonged to Ferragus. The boats were all under the guard of redcoats, one of whom, seeing Sharpe, slung his musket and walked along the quay. "Is it true we're retreating, sir?"

"We are."

"Bloody hell." The man gazed at the vast heaps of provisions. "What happens to this lot?"

"We have to get rid of it. And those boats."

"Bloody hell," the man said again, then watched as Sharpe marked dozens of boxes of biscuit and barrels of meat as rations for the South Essex.

The battalion arrived two hours later. They were, as Leroy had forecast, irritable, hungry and tired. Their march had been a nightmare, with wagons obstructing the road, clouds across the moon and at least two wrong turns that had wasted so much time that in the end Lawford had ordered the men to get some sleep in a pasture until dawn gave them some light to find their way. Major Forrest, sliding wearily from his saddle, looked askance at Sharpe. "Don't tell me you and Leroy came straight here?"

"We did, sir. Had a night's sleep too."

"What a detestable man you are, Sharpe."

"Can't see how you could get lost," Sharpe said. "The road was pretty well straight. Who was leading?"

"You know who was leading, Sharpe," Forrest said, then turned to gaze at the great piles of food. "How do we destroy that lot?"

"Shoot the rum barrels," Sharpe suggested, "and sling the flour and grain into the river."

"Got it all worked out, haven't you?"

"That's what a good night's sleep does for a man, sir."

"Damn you, too."

The Colonel would dearly have liked to rest his battalion, but the brown-jacketed Portuguese troops were starting work and it was unthinkable that the South Essex should collapse while others labored, and so he ordered each company to start on the piles. "You can send men to make tea," he suggested to his officers, "but breakfast must be eaten as we work. Mister Sharpe, good morning."

"Good morning, sir."

"I hope you have had time to consider your predicament," Lawford said, and it took a deal of courage to say it for it stirred up an unhappy situation, and the Colonel would have been much happier if Sharpe had simply volunteered to apologize and so clear the air.

"I have, sir," Sharpe said with a surprising willingness.

"Good!" Lawford brightened. "And?"

"It's the meat that's the problem, sir."

Lawford stared incomprehensibly at Sharpe. "The meat?"

"We can shoot the rum barrels, sir," Sharpe said cheerfully, "throw the grain and flour into the river, but the meat? Can't burn it." He turned and stared at the huge barrels. "If you give me a few men, sir, I'll see if I can find some turpentine. Soak the stuff. Even the Frogs won't eat meat doused in turpentine. Or souse it in paint, perhaps?"

"A problem for you," Lawford said icily, "but I have battalion business to do. You have quarters for me?"

"The tavern on the corner, sir," Sharpe pointed, "all marked up."

"I shall see to the paperwork," Lawford said loftily, meaning he wanted to lie down for an hour, and he nodded curtly at Sharpe and, beckoning his servants, went to find his billet.

Sharpe grinned and walked down the vast piles. Men were slitting grain sacks and levering the tops from the meat barrels. The Portuguese were working more enthusiastically, but they had reached the city late at night and so managed to sleep for a few hours. Other Portuguese soldiers had been sent into the narrow streets to tell the remaining inhabitants to flee, and Sharpe could hear women's voices raised in protest. It was still early. A small mist clung to the river, but the west wind had gone around to the south and it promised to be another hot day. The sharp crack of rifles sounded, startling birds into the air, and Sharpe saw that the Portuguese were shooting the rum barrels. Closer by, Patrick Harper was stoving in the barrels with an axe he had filched. "Why don't you shoot them, Pat?" Sharpe asked.

"Mister Slingsby, sir, he won't let us."

"He won't let you?"

Harper swung the axe at another barrel, releasing a flood of rum onto the cobbles. "He says we're to save our ammunition, sir."

"What for? There's plenty of cartridges."

"That's what he says, sir, no shooting."

"Work, Sergeant!" Slingsby marched smartly down the row of barrels. "You want to keep those stripes, Sergeant, then set an example! Good morning, Sharpe!"

Sharpe turned slowly and examined Slingsby from top to bottom. The man might have marched all night and slept in a field, yet he was perfectly turned out, every button shining, his leather gleaming, the red coat brushed and boots wiped clean. Slingsby, uncomfortable under Sharpe's sardonic gaze, snorted. "I said good morning, Sharpe."

"I hear you got lost," Sharpe said.

"Nonsense. A detour! Avoiding wagons." The small man stepped past Sharpe and glared at the light company. "Put your backs into it! There's a war to win!"

"For Christ's sake come back," Harper said softly.

Slingsby swiveled, eyes wide. "Did you say something, Sergeant?"

"He was talking to me," Sharpe said, and he stepped towards the smaller man, towering over him. He forced Slingsby back between two heaps of crates, taking him to where no one from the battalion could overhear. "He was talking to me, you piece of shit," Sharpe said, "and if you interrupt another of my conversations I'll tear your bloody guts out of your arsehole and wrap them round your bleeding throat. You want to go and tell that to the Colonel?"

Slingsby visibly quivered, but then he seemed to shake off Sharpe's words as though they had never been spoken. He found a narrow passage between the crates, slipped through it like a terrier pursuing a rat, and clapped his hands. "I want to see progress!" he yapped at the men.

Sharpe followed Slingsby, looking for trouble, but then he saw that the Portuguese troops were from the same battalion that had taken the rocky knoll, for Captain Vicente was commanding the men shooting at the rum barrels and that was diversion enough to save Sharpe from more foolishness with Slingsby. He veered away and Vicente saw him coming and smiled a welcome, but before the two could utter a greeting, Colonel Lawford came striding across the cobbled quay. "Sharpe! Mister Sharpe!"

Sharpe offered the Colonel a salute. "Sir!"

"I am not a man given to complaint," Lawford complained, "you know that, Sharpe. I am as hardened to discomfort as any man, but that tavern is hardly a fit billet. Not in a city like this! There are fleas in the beds!"

"You want somewhere better, sir?"

"I do, Sharpe, I do. And quickly."

Sharpe turned. "Sergeant Harper! I need you. Your permission to take Sergeant Harper, sir?" he asked Lawford who was too bemused to question Sharpe's need of company, but just nodded. "Give me half an hour, sir," Sharpe reassured the Colonel, "and you'll have the best billet in the city."

"Just something adequate," Lawford said pettishly. "I'm not asking for a palace, Sharpe, just something that's barely adequate."

Sharpe beckoned Harper and walked over to Vicente. "You grew up here, yes?"

"I told you so."

"So you know where a man called Ferragus lives?"

"Luis Ferreira?" Vicente's face mingled surprise and alarm. "I know where his brother lives, but Luis? He could live anywhere."

"Can you show me his brother's house?"

"Richard," Vicente warned, "Ferragus is not a man to . . ."

"I know what he is," Sharpe interrupted. "He did this to me." He pointed to his fading black eye. "How far is it?"

"Ten minutes' walk."

"Will you take me there?"

"Let me ask my Colonel," Vicente said, and hurried off towards Colonel Rogers-Jones who was sitting on horseback and holding an open umbrella to shade him from the early sun.

Sharpe saw Rogers-Jones nod to Vicente. "You'll have your billet in twenty minutes, sir," he told Lawford, then plucked Harper's elbow so that they followed Vicente off the quays. "That bastard Slingsby," Sharpe said as they went. "The bastard, bastard, bastard, bastard."

"I'm not supposed to hear this," Harper said.

"I'll skin the bastard alive," Sharpe said.

"Who?" Vicente asked, leading them up narrow alleys where they were forced to negotiate knots of unhappy folk who were at last readying themselves to leave the city. Men and women were bundling clothes, hoisting infants onto their backs and complaining bitterly to anyone they saw in uniform.

"A bastard called Slingsby," Sharpe said, "but we'll worry about him later. What do you know about Ferragus?"

"I know most folk are frightened of him," Vicente said, leading them across a small square where a church door stood open. A dozen black-shawled women were kneeling in the porch and they looked around in fear as a sudden rumble, jangle and clatter sounded from a nearby street. It was the noise of an artillery battery heading downhill towards the bridge. The army must have marched long before dawn and now the leading troops had reached Coimbra. "He is a criminal," Vicente went on, "but he wasn't raised in a poor family. His father was a colleague of my father, and even he admitted his son was a monster. The bad one of the litter. They tried to beat the evil from him. His father tried, the priests tried, but Luis is a child of Satan." Vicente made the sign of the cross. "And few dare oppose him. This is a university town!"

"Your father teaches here, yes?"

"He teaches law," Vicente said, "but he is not here now. He and my mother went north to Porto to stay with Kate. But people like my father don't know how to deal with a man like Ferragus."

"That's because your father's a lawyer," Sharpe said. "Bastards like Ferragus need someone like me."

"He gave you a black eye," Vicente said.

"I gave him worse," Sharpe said, remembering the pleasure of kicking Ferragus in the crotch. "And the Colonel wants a house, so we'll find the Ferreira house and give it to him."

"It is not wise, I think," Vicente said, "to mix private revenge with war."

"Of course it's not wise," Sharpe said, "but it's bloody enjoyable. Enjoying yourself, Sergeant?"

"Never been happier, sir," Harper said gloomily.

They had climbed to the upper town where they emerged into a small, sunlit square and on its far side was a pale stone house with a grand front door, a side entrance that evidently led into a stable yard and three high floors of shuttered windows. The house was old, its stonework carved with heraldic birds. "That is Pedro Ferreira's house," Vicente said and watched as Sharpe climbed the front steps. "Ferragus is thought to have murdered many people," Vicente said unhappily, making one last effort to dissuade Sharpe.

"So have I," Sharpe said, and hammered on the door, keeping up the din until the door was opened by an alarmed woman wearing an apron. She chided Sharpe in a burst of indignant Portuguese. A younger man was behind her, but he backed into the shadows when he saw Sharpe while the woman, who was gray-haired and hefty, tried to push the rifleman down the steps. Sharpe stayed where he was. "Ask her where Luis Ferreira lives," he told Vicente.

There was a brief conversation. "She says Senhor Luis is staying here for the moment," Vicente said, "but he is not here now."

"He's living here?" Sharpe asked, then grinned and took a piece of chalk from a pocket and scrawled SE CO on the polished blue door. "Tell her an important English officer will be using the house tonight and he wants a bed and a meal." Sharpe listened to the conversation between Vicente and the gray-haired woman. "And ask her if there's stabling." There was. "Sergeant Harper?"

"Sir?"

"Can you find your way back to the quay?"

"Down the hill, sir."

"Bring the Colonel here. Tell him he's got the best billet in town and that there's stabling for his horses." Sharpe pushed past the woman to get into the hallway and glared at the man who backed still farther away. The man had a pistol in his belt, but he showed no sign of wanting to use it as Sharpe pushed open a door and saw a dark room with a desk, a portrait over the mantel and shelves of books. Another door opened into a comfortable parlor with spindly chairs, gilt tables and a sofa upholstered in rose-colored silk. The servant was arguing with Vicente who was trying to calm her.

"She is Major Ferreira's cook," Vicente explained, "and she says her master and his brother will not be happy."

"That's why we're here."

"The Major's wife and children have gone," Vicente went on translating.

"Never did like killing men in front of their family," Sharpe said.

"Richard!" Vicente said, shocked.

Sharpe grinned at him and climbed the stairs, followed by Vicente and the cook. He found the big bedroom and threw open the shutters. "Perfect," he said, looking at the four-poster bed hung with tapestry curtains. "The Colonel can get a lot of work done in that. Well done, Jorge! Tell that woman Colonel Lawford likes his food plain and well cooked. He'll provide his own rations, all it needs is to be cooked, but there are to be no damned foreign spices mucking it up. Who's the man downstairs?"

"A servant," Vicente translated.

"Who else is in the house?"

"Stable boys," Vicente interpreted the cook's answer, "kitchen staff, and Miss Fry."

Sharpe thought he had misheard. "Miss who?"

The cook looked frightened now. She spoke fast, glancing up to the top floor. "She says," Vicente interpreted, "that the children's governess is locked upstairs. An Englishwoman."

"Bloody hell. Locked up? What's her name?"

"Fry."

Sharpe climbed up to the attics. The stairs here were uncarpeted and the walls drab. "Miss Fry!" he shouted. "Miss Fry!" He was rewarded by an incoherent cry and the sound of a fist beating on a door. He pushed the door to find it was indeed locked. "Stand back!" he called.

He kicked the door hard, thumping his heel close to the lock. The whole attic seemed to shake, but the door held. He kicked again and heard a splintering sound, drew back his leg and gave the door one last almighty blow and it flew open and there, hunched under the window, her arms wrapped about her knees, was a woman with hair the color of pale gold. She stared at Sharpe, who stared back, then he looked hastily away as he remembered his manners because the woman, who had struck him as undoubtedly beautiful, was as naked as a new-laid egg. "Your servant, ma'am," he said, staring at the wall.

"You're English?" she asked.

"I am, ma'am."

"Then fetch me some clothes!" she demanded.

And Sharpe obeyed.

※

FERRAGUS HAD SENT his brother's wife, children and six servants away at dawn, but had ordered Miss Fry up to her room. Sarah had protested, insisting she must travel with the children and that her trunk was already on the baggage wagon, but Ferragus had ordered her to wait in her room. "You will go with the British," he told her.

Major Ferreira's wife had also protested. "The children need her!"

"She will go with her own kind," Ferragus snapped at his sister-in-law, "so get in the coach!"

"I will go with the British?" Sarah had asked.

"*Os ingleses por mar*," he had snarled, "and you can run away with them. Your time is done here. You have paper, a pen?"

"Of course."

"Then write yourself a character. I will sign it on my brother's behalf. But you can take refuge with your own people. So wait in your room."

"But my clothes, my books!" Sarah pointed to the baggage cart. Her small savings, all in coin, were also in the trunk.

"I'll have them taken off," Ferragus said. "Now go."

Sarah had gone upstairs and written a letter of recommendation in which she described herself as being efficient, hard-working, and good at instilling discipline in her charges. She said nothing about the children being fond of her, for she was not sure that they were, nor did she believe it part of her job that they should be. She had paused once in writing the letter to lean from the window when she had heard the stable-yard gates being opened, and she saw the coach and baggage wagon, escorted by four mounted men armed with pistols, swords and malevolence, clatter into the street. She sat again, and added a sentence which truthfully said she was honest, sober and assiduous, and she had just been writing the last word when she had heard the heavy steps climbing the stairs to the servants' rooms. She had instantly known it was Ferragus and an instinct told her to lock her door, but before she could even get up from behind her small table Ferragus had thrust the door open and loomed in the entrance. "I am staying here," he had announced.

"If you think that's wise, *senhor*," she said in a tone which suggested she did not care what he did.

"And you will stay with me," he went on.

For a heartbeat Sarah thought she had misheard, then she shook her head dismissively. "Don't be ridiculous," she said. "I will travel with the British troops." She stopped abruptly, distracted by gunshots coming from the lower town. The sound came from the rifles puncturing the first of the rum barrels, but Sarah could not know that and she wondered if the noise presaged the arrival of the French. Everything was so confusing. First had come news of the battle, then an announcement that the French had been defeated, and now everyone was ordered to leave Coimbra because the enemy was coming.

"You will stay with me," Ferragus repeated flatly.

"I most certainly will not!"

"Shut your bloody mouth," Ferragus said, and saw the shock on her face.

"I think you had better leave," Sarah said. She still spoke firmly, but her fear was obvious now and it excited Ferragus who leaned on her table, making its spindly legs creak.

"Is that the letter?" he asked.

"Which you promised to sign," Sarah said.

Instead he had torn it into shreds. "Bugger you," he said, "damn you," and he added some other words he had learned in the Royal Navy, and the effect of each was as though he had slapped her around the head. It might well come to that, he thought. Indeed, it almost certainly would and that was the pleasure of teaching the arrogant English bitch a lesson. "Your duties now, woman," he had finished, "are to please me."

"You have lost your wits," Sarah said.

Ferragus smiled. "Do you know what I can do with you?" he had asked. "I can send you with Miguel to Lisbon and he can have you shipped to Morocco or to Algiers. I can sell you there. You know what a man will pay for white flesh in Africa?" He paused, enjoying the horror on her face. "You wouldn't be the first girl I've sold."

"You will go!" Sarah said, clinging to her last shreds of defiance. She was looking for a weapon, any weapon, but there was nothing within reach except the inkpot and she was on the point of snatching it up and hurling it into his eyes when Ferragus tipped the table on its side and she had backed to the window. She had an idea that a good woman should rather die than be dishonored and she wondered if she ought to throw herself from the window and fall to her death in the stable yard, but the notion was one thing and the reality an impossibility.

"Take your dress off," Ferragus said.

"You will go!" Sarah had managed to say, and no sooner had she spoken than Ferragus punched her in the belly. It was a hard, fast blow and it drove the breath from her, and Ferragus, as she bent over, simply tore the blue frock down her back. She had tried to clutch to its remnants, but he was so massively strong, and when she did hold fast to her undergarments he just slapped her around the head so that her skull rang and she fell against the wall and could only watch as he threw her torn clothes out into the yard. Then, blessedly, Miguel had shouted up the stairs saying that the Major, Ferragus's brother, had arrived.

Sarah opened her mouth to scream to her employer for help, but Ferragus had given her another punch in the belly, leaving her incapable of making a sound. Then he had thrown her bedclothes out of the window. "I shall be back, Miss Fry," he said, and he had forced her thin arms apart to stare at her. She was weeping with anger, but just then Major Ferreira had shouted up the stairs and Ferragus had let go of her, walked from the room and locked the door.

Sarah shivered with fear. She heard the brothers leave the house and she thought of trying to escape out of the window, but the wall outside offered no handholds, no ledges, just a long drop into the stable yard where Miguel smiled up at her and patted the pistol at his belt. So, naked and ashamed, she had sat on the rope webbing of the bed and had been almost overcome with despair.

Then there had been footsteps on the stairs and she had hunched under the window, clutching her arms about her knees, and heard an English voice. The door had been hammered open and a tall man with a scarred face, a black eye, a green coat and a long sword was staring at her. "Your servant, ma'am," he had said, and Sarah was safe.

⁂

MAJOR FERREIRA, having arranged to sell the food to the French, wanted to reassure himself that the quantities he had promised to the enemy truly existed. They did. There was food enough in Ferragus's big warehouse to feed Masséna's army for weeks. Major Ferreira followed his brother down the dark alleys between the stacks of boxes and barrels, and again marveled that his brother had managed to amass so much. "They have agreed to pay for it," Ferreira said.

"Good," Ferragus said.

"The Marshal himself assured me."

"Good."

"And protection will be given when the French arrive."

"Good."

"The arrangement," Ferreira said, stepping over a cat, "is that we are to meet Colonel Barreto at the shrine of Saint Vincent south of Meal-hada." That was less than an hour's ride north of Coimbra. "And he will bring dragoons straight to the warehouse."

"When?"

Ferreira thought for a few seconds. "Today," he said, "is Saturday. The British could leave tomorrow and the French arrive on Monday. Possibly not until Tuesday? But they could come Monday, so we should be at Mealhada by tomorrow night."

Ferragus nodded. His brother, he thought, had done well, and so long as the rendezvous with the French went smoothly then Ferragus's future was safe. The British would flee back home, the French would capture Lisbon, and Ferragus would have established himself as a man with whom the invaders could do business. "So tomorrow," he said, "you and I ride to Mealhada. What about today?"

"I must report to the army," Ferreira said, "but tomorrow I shall find an excuse."

"Then I will guard the house," Ferragus said, thinking of the pale pleasures waiting on the top floor.

Ferreira examined a pair of wagons parked at the side of the ware-house. They were piled with useful goods, linen and horseshoes, lamp oil and nails, all things the French would value. Then, going farther back in the huge building, he grimaced. "That smell," he said, remembering a man whose death he had witnessed in the warehouse, "the body?"

"Two bodies now," Ferragus said proudly, then turned because a wash of light flooded into the warehouse as the outer door was dragged open. A man called his name and he recognized Miguel's voice. "I'm here!" he shouted. "At the back!"

Miguel hurried to the back where he bobbed his head respectfully. "The Englishman," he said.

"What Englishman?"

"The one on the hilltop, *senhor*. The one you attacked at the monastery."

Ferragus's good mood evaporated like the mist from the river. "What of him?"

"He is at the Major's house."

"Jesus Christ!" Ferragus's hand instinctively went to his pistol.

"No!" Ferreira said, earning a malevolent look from his brother. The Major looked at Miguel. "Is he alone?"

"No, *senhor*."

"How many?"

"Three of them, *senhor*, and one is a Portuguese officer. They say others are coming because a colonel will use the house."

"Billeting," Ferreira explained. "There will be a dozen men in the house when you get back, and you can't start a war with the English. Not here, not now."

It was good advice, and Ferragus knew it, then he thought of Sarah. "Did they find the girl?"

"Yes, *senhor*."

"What girl?" Ferreira asked.

"It doesn't matter," Ferragus said curtly, and that was true. Sarah Fry was not important. She would have been an amusement, but finishing Captain Sharpe would be a good deal more amusing. He thought for a few seconds. "The English," he said to his brother, "why are they staying here? Why do they not march straight to their ships?"

"Because they will probably offer battle again north of Lisbon," Ferreira said.

"But why wait here?" Ferragus insisted. "Why do they billet men here? Will they fight for Coimbra?" It seemed an unlikely prospect, for the city's walls had mostly been pulled down. It was a place for learning and trading, not for fighting.

"They're staying here," Ferreira said, "just long enough to destroy the supplies on the quays."

An idea occurred to Ferragus then, a risky idea, but one that might yield the amusement he craved. "What if they knew these supplies were here?" He gestured at the stacks in the warehouse.

"They would destroy them, of course," Ferreira said.

Ferragus thought again, trying to put himself into the Englishman's place. How would Captain Sharpe react? What would he do? There was a risk, Ferragus thought, a real risk, but Sharpe had declared war on Ferragus, that much was obvious. Why else would the Englishman have gone to his brother's house? And Ferragus was not a man to back down from a challenge, so the risk must be taken. "You say there was a Portuguese officer with them?"

"Yes, *senhor*. I think I recognized him. Professor Vicente's son."

"That piece of shit," Ferragus snarled, then thought again and saw the way clear to finishing the feud. "This," he said to Miguel, "is what we will do."

And laid his trap.

CHAPTER 7

"THIS IS SPLENDID, Sharpe, quite splendid." Colonel Lawford paced through his new quarters, opening doors and inspecting rooms. "The taste in furniture is a little florid, wouldn't you say? A hint of vulgarity, perhaps? But very splendid, Sharpe. Thank you." He stooped to look in a gilt-framed mirror and smoothed down his hair. "Is there a cook on the premises?"

"Yes, sir."

"And stabling, you say?"

"Out the back, sir."

"I shall inspect it," Lawford said grandly. "Lead on." It was evident from his loftily genial manner that he had received no new complaint from Slingsby about Sharpe's rudeness. "I must say, Sharpe, you make a very good quartermaster when you put your mind to it. Maybe we should confirm you in the post. Mister Kiley is not improving, the doctor tells me."

"I wouldn't do that, sir," Sharpe said as he led Lawford down through the kitchens, "on account that I'm thinking of applying to the Portuguese service. You'd only have to find someone to replace me."

"You were thinking of what?" Lawford asked, shocked by the news.

"The Portuguese service, sir. They're still asking for British officers, and so far as I can see they're not very particular. They probably won't notice my manners."

"Sharpe!" Lawford spoke brusquely, then stopped abruptly because they had gone into the stable yard where Captain Vicente was trying to calm Sarah Fry, who was now wearing one of Beatriz Ferreira's dresses, a concoction of black silk that Major Ferreira's wife had worn when mourning the death of her mother. Sarah had taken the dress gratefully enough, but was repelled by its ugliness and was only placated when she was assured that it was the only garment left in the house. Lawford, oblivious to the dress and noticing simply that she was damned attractive, took off his hat and bowed to her.

Sarah ignored the Colonel, turning on Sharpe instead. "They took everything!"

"Who?" Sharpe asked. "What?"

"My trunk! My clothes! My books!" Her money had disappeared too, but she said nothing of that, instead she demanded, in fluent Portuguese from a stable boy whether her trunk really had been left on the cart. It had "Everything!" she said to Sharpe.

"Allow me to present Miss Fry, sir," Sharpe said. "This is Colonel Lawford, miss, our commanding officer."

"You're English!" Lawford said brightly.

"They took everything!" Sarah rounded on the stable boy and screamed at him, though it was hardly his fault.

"Miss Fry, sir, was the governess here," Sharpe explained over the noise, "and somehow got left behind when the family left."

"The governess, eh?" Lawford's enthusiasm for Sarah Fry noticeably diminished as he understood her status. "You'd best ready yourself to leave the city, Miss Fry," he said. "The French will be here in a day or two!"

"I have nothing!" Sarah protested.

Harper, who had brought the Colonel and his entourage to the house, now led Lawford's four horses into the yard. "You want me to rub Lightning down, sir?" he asked the Colonel.

"My fellows will do that. You'd best get back to Captain Slingsby."

"Yes, sir, at once, sir, of course, sir," Harper said, not moving.

"Everything!" Sarah wailed. The cook came into the yard and shouted at the English girl to be silent and Sarah, in fury, turned on her.

"If you'll permit it, sir," Sharpe said, raising his voice over the din,

"Major Forrest told me to find some turpentine. He wants it to ruin the salt meat, sir, and Sergeant Harper will be a great help to me."

"A help?" Lawford, distracted by Sarah's grief and the cook's protest, was not really paying attention.

"He's a better sense of smell than me, sir," Sharpe said.

"He's a better sense of . . ." the Colonel began to ask, then frowned at Sarah who was shouting at the cook in Portuguese. "Do whatever you want, Sharpe," Lawford said, "whatever you want, and for God's sake take Miss whatever-her-name-is away, will you?"

"He promised to take the trunk off the wagon!" Sarah appealed to Lawford. She was angry and, because he was a colonel, she seemed to expect him to do something.

"I'm sure it can all be sorted out," Lawford said, "things usually can. Will you escort Miss, er, the lady away, Sharpe? Perhaps the battalion wives can assist her. You really do have to leave, my dear." The Colonel knew he would get no sleep while this woman protested about her missing possessions. Any other time he would have been happy enough to entertain her, for she was a pretty young thing, but he needed some rest. He ordered his servants to carry his valise upstairs, told Lieutenant Knowles to post a pair of sentries on the house and another pair in the stable yard, then turned away, immediately looking back. "And about that proposition of yours, Sharpe," he said. "Don't do anything rash."

"About the turpentine, sir?"

"You know exactly what I mean," Lawford said testily. "The Portuguese, Sharpe, the Portuguese. Oh, my God!" This last was because Sarah had begun to cry.

Sharpe tried to soothe her, but she was devastated by the loss of her trunk and her small savings. "Miss Fry," Sharpe said, and she ignored him. "Sarah!" He put his hands gently on her shoulders. "You'll get everything back!"

She stared up at him, said nothing.

"I'll sort Ferragus out," Sharpe said, "if he's still here."

"He is!"

"Then calm down, lass, and leave it to me."

"My name is Miss Fry," Sarah said, offended at the "lass."

"Then calm down, Miss Fry. We'll get your things back."

Harper rolled his eyes at the promise. "Turpentine, sir."

Sharpe turned to Vicente. "Where will we find turpentine?"

"The Lord alone knows," Vicente said. "A timber yard? Don't they treat timber with it?"

"So what are you doing now?" Sharpe asked him.

"My Colonel gave me permission to go to my parents' house," Vicente said, "just to make sure it's safe."

"Then we'll come with you," Sharpe said.

"There's no turpentine there," Vicente said.

"Bugger the turpentine," Sharpe said, then remembered a lady was present. "Sorry, miss. We're just keeping you safe, Jorge," he added, then turned back to Sarah. "I'll take you down to the battalion wives later," he promised her, "and they'll look after you."

"The battalion wives?" she asked.

"The soldiers' wives," Sharpe explained.

"There are no officers' wives?" Sarah asked, jealous of her precarious position. A governess might be a servant, but she was a privileged one. "I expect to be treated with respect, Mister Sharpe."

"Miss Fry," Sharpe said, "you can walk down the hill now and you can find an officer's wife. There are some. None in our battalion, but you can look, and you're welcome to try. But we're looking for turpentine and if you want protection you'd best stay with us." He put on his shako and turned away.

"I'll stay with you," Sarah said, remembering that Ferragus was loose somewhere in the city.

The four of them walked higher into the upper town, going into a district of big, elegant buildings that Vicente explained was the university. "It has been here a long time," he said reverently, "almost as long as Oxford."

"I met a man from Oxford once," Sharpe said, "and killed him." He laughed at the shocked expression on Sarah's face. He was in a strange mood, wanting to work mischief and careless of the consequences. Lawford could go to hell, he thought, and Slingsby with him, and Sharpe just wanted to be free of them. Damn the army, he thought. He had served it well and it had turned on him, so the army could go to hell as well.

Vicente's house was one of a terrace, all of them shuttered. The door was locked, but Vicente retrieved a key from beneath a big stone hidden in a space under the stone steps. "First place a thief would look," Sharpe said.

Yet no thief had been inside. The house smelled musty, for it had been closed up for some weeks, but everything was tidy. The bookshelves in the big front room had been emptied and their contents taken down to the cellar where they were stored in wooden crates, each crate carefully labeled with its contents. Other boxes held vases, pictures and busts of the Greek philosophers. Vicente carefully locked the cellar, hid its key under a floorboard, ignored Sharpe's advice that it was the first place a thief would look, and went upstairs where the beds lay bare, their blankets piled in cupboards. "The French will probably break in," he said, "but they're welcome to the blankets." He went into his old room and came out with a faded black robe. "My student gown," he said happily. "We used to attach a colored ribbon to show what discipline we studied and every year, at the end of lectures, we would burn the ribbons."

"Sounds like a barrel of fun," Sharpe said.

"They were good times," Vicente said. "I liked being a student."

"You're a soldier now, Jorge."

"Till the French are gone," he said, folding the gown away with the blankets.

He locked the house, hid the key and took Sharpe, Harper and Sarah through the university. The students and the teachers had all gone, fled to Lisbon or to the north of the country, but the university servants still guarded the buildings and one of them accompanied Sarah and the three soldiers, unlocking the doors and bowing them into the rooms. There was a library, a fantastic place of gilding, carving and leather-bound books that Sarah gazed at in rapture. She reluctantly left the old volumes to follow Vicente as he showed them the rooms where he had received his lectures, then climbed to the laboratories where clocks, balances and telescopes gleamed on shelves. "The French will love this lot," Sharpe said scornfully.

"There are men of learning in the French army," Vicente said. "They don't make war on scholarship." He stroked an orrery, a glorious device of curved brass strips and crystal spheres which imitated the movement of the planets. "Learning," he said earnestly, "is above war."

"It's what?" Sharpe asked.

"Learning is sacred," Vicente insisted. "It goes above boundaries."

"Quite right," Sarah chimed in. She had been silent ever since they had left Ferreira's house, but the university reassured her that there was a world of civilized restraint, far from threats of slavery in Africa. "A university," she said, "is a sanctuary."

"Sanctuary!" Sharpe was amused. "You think the Crapauds will get in here, take one look and say it's sacred?"

"Mister Sharpe!" Sarah said. "I cannot abide bad language."

"What's wrong with 'Crapaud'? It means toad."

"I know what it means," Sarah said, but blushed, for she had momentarily thought Sharpe had said something else.

"I think the French are only interested in food and wine," Vicente said.

"I can think of something else," Sharpe said, and received a stern look from Sarah.

"There is no food here," Vicente insisted, "just higher things."

"And the Crapauds will get in here," Sharpe said, "and they'll see beauty. They'll see value. They'll see something they can't have. So what will they do, Pat?"

"Mangle the bloody lot, sir," Harper said promptly. "Sorry, miss."

"The French will guard it," Vicente insisted. "They have men of honor, men who respect learning."

"Men of honor!" Sharpe said scornfully. "I was in a place called Seringapatam once, Jorge. In India. There was a palace there, stuffed with gold! You should have seen it! Rubies and emeralds, golden tigers, diamonds, pearls, more riches than you can dream of! So the men of honor guarded it. The officers, Jorge. They put a reliable guard on it to stop us heathens getting in and stripping it bare. And you know what happened?"

"It was saved, I hope," Vicente said.

"The officers stripped it bare," Sharpe said. "Cleaned it up properly. Lord Wellington was one of them and he must have made a penny or two out of that lot. There wasn't a tiger's golden whisker left by the time they'd all done."

"This will be safe," Vicente insisted, but unhappily.

They left the university, going back downhill into the smaller streets of the lower town. Sharpe had the impression that the folk of quality, the university people and most of the richer inhabitants, had left the city, but there were thousands of ordinary men and women left. Some were packing and leaving, but most had fatalistically accepted that the French would come and they just hoped to survive the occupation. A clock struck eleven somewhere and Vicente looked worried. "I must get back."

"Something to eat first," Sharpe said, and pushed into a tavern. It was crowded, and the people inside were not happy to see soldiers, for they did not understand why their city was being abandoned to the French, but they reluctantly made space at a table. Vicente ordered wine, bread, cheese and olives, then again made an attempt to leave. "Don't worry," Sharpe said, stopping him, "I'll get Colonel Lawford to explain to your Colonel. Tell him you were on an important mission. You know how to deal with senior officers?"

"Respectfully," Vicente said.

"Confuse them," Sharpe said. "Except for the ones who can't be confused like Wellington."

"But isn't he leaving?" Sarah asked. "Going back to England?"

"Lord love you, no, miss," Sharpe said. "He's got a surprise ready for the Frogs. A chain of forts, miss, clear across the land north of Lisbon. They'll break their heads there and we'll sit back and watch them. We're not leaving."

"I thought you were going back to England," Sarah said. She had conceived an idea of traveling with the army, preferably with a family of quality, and making a new start. Quite how she would do that without money, clothes or a written character, she did not know, but nor was she willing to give in to the despair she had felt earlier in the morning.

"We're not going home till the war's won," Sharpe said, "but what are we going to do with you? Send you home?"

Sarah shrugged. "I have no money, Mister Sharpe. No money, no clothes."

"You've got family?"

"My parents are dead. I have an uncle, but I doubt he'll be willing to help me."

"The more I see of families," Sharpe said, "the happier I am to be an orphan."

"Sharpe!" Vicente said reprovingly.

"You'll be all right, miss," Harper intervened.

"How?" Sarah demanded.

"Because you're with Mister Sharpe now, miss. He'll see you're all right."

"So why did Ferragus lock you in?" Sharpe asked.

Sarah blushed and looked down at the table. "He . . ." she began, but did not know how to finish.

"Was going to?" Sharpe asked, knowing exactly what she was reluctant to say. "Or did?"

"Was going to," she said in a low voice, then she recovered her poise and looked up at him. "He said he would sell me in Morocco. He said they give a lot of money for . . ." Her voice trailed away.

"That bastard has got a right bloody treat coming," Sharpe said. "Sorry, miss. Bad language. What we'll do is find him, take his money and give it to you. Simple, eh!" He grinned at her.

"I said you'd be all right," Harper said, as though the deed were already done.

Vicente had taken no part in this conversation, for a big man had come into the tavern and sat next to the Portuguese officer. The two had been talking and Vicente, his face worried, now turned to Sharpe. "This man is called Francisco," he said, "and he tells me there is a warehouse full of food. It is locked away, hidden. The man who owns it is planning to sell it all to the French."

Sharpe looked at Francisco. A rat, he thought, a street rat. "What does Francisco want?" he asked.

"Want?" Vicente did not understand the question.

"What does he want, Jorge? Why is he telling us?"

There was a brief conversation in Portuguese. "He says," Vicente translated, "that he does not want the French to get any food."

"He's a patriot, is he?" Sharpe asked skeptically. "So how does he know about this food?"

"He helped deliver it. He is, what do you say? A man with a cart?"

"A carter," Sharpe said. "So he's a patriotic carter?"

There was another brief conversation before Vicente interpreted. "He says the man did not pay him."

That made a lot more sense to Sharpe. Maybe Francisco was a patriot, but revenge was a much more believable motive. "But why us?" he asked.

"Why us?" Vicente was again puzzled.

"There's at least a thousand soldiers down at the quay," Sharpe explained, "and more marching through the city. Why does he come to us?"

"He recognized me," Vicente said. "He grew up here, like me."

Sharpe sipped his wine, staring hard at Francisco who looked, he thought, shifty as hell, but everything made sense if he really had been rooked out of his money. "Who's the man storing the food?"

Another conversation. "He says the man's name is Manuel Lopez," Vicente said. "I've not heard of him."

"Pity it's not bloody Ferragus," Sharpe said. "Sorry, miss. So how far is this warehouse?"

"Two minutes away," Vicente said.

"If there's as much as he says," Sharpe said, "then we'll have to get a battalion up there, but we'd best have a look at the stuff first." He nodded at Harper's volley gun. "Is that toy loaded?"

"It is, sir. Not primed, though."

"Prime her, Pat. If Mister Lopez don't like us then that should calm him down." He gave Vicente some coins for the wine and food, and the Portuguese officer paid while Francisco watched Harper prime the volley gun. Francisco seemed nervous of the weapon, which was hardly surprising for it was fearsome-looking.

"I need more bullets for this," Harper said.

"How many have you got?"

"After this load?" Harper patted the breech, then carefully lowered the flint to make the gun safe. "Twenty-three."

"I'll filch some from Lawford," Sharpe said. "His bloody great horse pistol takes half-inch balls and he never fires the bloody thing. Sorry, miss. He doesn't like firing it, it's too powerful. God knows why he keeps it. Perhaps to frighten his wife." He looked for Vicente. "You're ready?

Let's find this damn food, then you can report it to your Colonel. That should put you in his good books."

Francisco was anxious as he led them out of the tavern and down a stepped alleyway. Before arriving at the tavern he had been enquiring about the city for anyone who had seen two men dressed in green uniforms who were with Professor Vicente's clever son, and it had not taken long to discover they were in the Three Crows. Ferragus would be pleased. "Here, *senhor,*" Francisco told Vicente and pointed across the street at a great double doorway in a blank stone wall.

"Why don't I just tell my Colonel?" Vicente suggested.

"Because if you come back here," Sharpe said, "and find that this bastard has been lying to us, sorry, miss, you'll look like an idiot. No, we'll look inside, you go to your Colonel and we'll take Miss Fry down to battalion."

The door was padlocked. "Shoot it?" Vicente suggested.

"You only mangle the works if you do that," Sharpe said, "and make it harder." He felt through his haversack until he found what he wanted. It was a picklock. He had carried one since he was a child, and he unfolded the hooked levers, selected the one he wanted and stooped to the lock.

Vicente looked aghast. "You know how to do that?"

"I was a thief once," Sharpe said. "Earned my living that way." He saw the shock on Sarah's face. "I wasn't always an officer and a gentleman," he told her.

"But you are now?" she asked anxiously.

"He's an officer, miss," Harper said, "he's certainly an officer." He unslung the volley gun and cocked it. He glanced up and down the street, but there was no one taking any interest in them. A shopkeeper was stacking clothes on a handcart, a woman was shouting at two children, and a small group of people were struggling with bags, boxes, dogs, goats and cows downhill towards the river.

The lock clicked and Sharpe tugged it out of the staple. Then before opening the door, he took the rifle from his shoulder and cocked it. "Grab hold of Francisco," he told Harper, "because if there's nothing inside here I'm going to shoot the big bastard. Sorry, miss."

Francisco tried to pull away, but Harper held him fast as Sharpe dragged one of the huge gates open. He walked through into the darkness, watching for movement, seeing none, and as his eyes became accustomed to the shadows he saw the boxes, barrels and sacks piled up towards the beams and rafters of the high roof. "Jesus Christ!" he said in amazement. "Sorry, miss."

"Blasphemy," Sarah said, staring up at the huge stacks, "is worse than mere swearing."

"I'll try to remember that, miss," Sharpe said, "I really will. Good Christ Almighty! Just look at this!"

"Is it food?" Vicente asked.

"Smells like it," Sharpe said. He uncocked his rifle, slung it and drew his sword, which he jabbed into a sack. Grain trickled out. "Jesus wept, sorry, miss." He sheathed the sword and stared around the vast room. "Tons of food!"

"Does it matter?" Sarah asked.

"Oh, it matters," Sharpe said. "An army can't fight if it doesn't have food. The trick of this campaign, miss, is to let the Frogs march south, stop them in front of Lisbon, and watch them get hungry. This damn lot could keep them alive for weeks!"

Harper had let go of Francisco who backed away and suddenly darted out into the street and Harper, amazed at the piles of food, did not notice. Sharpe, Vicente and Sarah were walking down the central aisle, gazing up in astonishment. The stores were stacked in neat squares, each pile about twenty feet by twenty feet, and divided by alleys. Sharpe counted a dozen stacks. Some of the barrels were stamped with the British government's broad arrow, meaning they had been stolen. Harper was following the other three, then remembered Francisco and turned to see men coming from the house across the street. There were half a dozen of them and they were filling the warehouse's wide entrance and he saw, too, that they carried pistols in their hands. "Trouble!" he shouted.

Sharpe turned, saw the shadows in the entrance, knew instinctively that Francisco had betrayed them and knew too that he was in trouble. "Back here, Pat!" he shouted and at the same time he shoved Sarah hard, pushing her into one of the alleys between the sacks. The warehouse's open door was being tugged shut, darkening the huge room, and Sharpe was unslinging his rifle as the first shots came from the closing door. A ball thumped into a sack by his head, another ricocheted from an iron barrel hoop to smack into the back wall, and a third hit Vicente who spun back, dropping his rifle. Sharpe kicked the gun towards Sarah and dragged Vicente into the narrow space, then went back into the central aisle and aimed towards the door. He saw nothing, dodged back into cover. Some small light came through a handful of dirty skylights in the high roof, but not much. There was movement at the alley's far end and he turned, rifle going into his shoulder, but it was Harper who had sensibly avoided the central aisle by running around the flank of the high stacks.

"There's six of them, sir," Harper said, "maybe more."

"Can't stay here," Sharpe said. "Mister Vicente's hit."

"Christ," Harper said.

"Sorry, miss," Sharpe said on Harper's behalf and glanced at Vicente who was conscious, but hurt. He had fallen when the ball struck him, but that had been shock as much as anything else, and he was on his feet now, leaning against some boxes.

"It's bleeding," he said.

"Where?"

"Left shoulder."

"Are you spitting blood?"

"No."

"You'll live," Sharpe said and gave Vicente's rifle to Harper. "Give me the volley gun, Pat," he said, "and take Mister Vicente and Miss Fry to the back. See if there's a way out. Wait a second, though." Sharpe listened. He could hear small sounds, but they could have been rats or cats. "Use the side wall," he whispered to Harper, and he went there first and peered round the edge. A shadow in a shadow. Sharpe moved out into the open and the shadow sparked fire and a bullet scored along the wall beside him and he raised the rifle and saw the shadow vanish. "Now, Pat."

Harper shepherded Vicente and Sarah to the back of the warehouse.

Pray God there was a door there, Sharpe thought, and he slung the rifle on his left shoulder, put the volley gun on his right, and climbed the nearest stack. He scrambled up, jamming his boots into the spaces between the grain sacks, not caring about the noise he made. He almost lost his footing once, but anger drove him up and he rolled onto the top of the great pile where he took the volley gun from his shoulder. He cocked it, hoping that no one beneath would hear the click. A big cat hissed at him, its back arched and tail up, but then decided not to contest the lumpy plateau on top of the sacks and stalked away.

Sharpe edged across the sacks. He crawled on his belly, listening to a faint muttering of voices and he knew there were men in the alley beyond the sacks and knew they were planning how best to finish what they had started. He knew they would be fearful of the rifles, but they would also be confident.

But evidently not too confident. They wanted to avoid a fight if they could, for Ferragus suddenly shouted, "Captain Sharpe!"

No answer. Claws scratched at the far side of the warehouse and wheels clattered on the street cobbles outside.

"Captain Sharpe!"

Still no answer.

"Come out!" Ferragus called. "Apologize to me and you can go. That is all I want. An apology!"

Like hell, Sharpe thought. Ferragus wanted this food preserved until the French arrived, and the moment Sharpe or his companions appeared in the open they would be shot down. So it was time to spring an ambush on the ambushers.

He crept forward to the stack's edge and, very slowly, peered over. There was a knot of men down there. Half a dozen, perhaps, and none was looking up. None had thought to check the high ground, but they should have known they were up against soldiers and soldiers always sought the high ground.

Sharpe brought the volley gun forward. The seven half-inch balls had been rammed down on wadding and powder, but there was always a chance, a good chance, that some would roll out of the barrels the moment he pointed the gun downwards. There was no time to ram more wadding on top of the balls, so the trick of this was to shoot fast, very fast, and that meant he could not aim. He edged back, stood up, then froze as another voice spoke. "Captain Sharpe!" The speaker was not one of the men beneath Sharpe. His voice seemed to come from closer to the great doors. "Captain Sharpe. This is Major Ferreira."

So that bastard was here. Sharpe cradled the volley gun, ready to move forward and fire, but then Ferreira spoke again. "You have my word as an officer! No harm will come to you! My brother wants an apology, nothing more!" Ferreira paused, then spoke in Portuguese, presumably because he knew Jorge Vicente was with Sharpe, and Sharpe reckoned Vicente's neat, legal and trusting mind might just believe Ferreira and so he gave his own answer. In one fast movement he stepped to the edge, turned the gun's muzzles down into the alley and pulled the trigger.

Three of the balls were loose and had started to roll, and that reduced the gun's huge power, but the blast of the shots still echoed from the stone walls like thunder and the recoil of the bunched barrels almost threw the gun up and out of Sharpe's hands as the smoke billowed in the passage beneath him. There were screams in the passage too, and a hoarse shout of pain and the sound of feet scrambling as men ran from the sudden horror that had belched from above. A pistol fired, shattering a skylight, but Sharpe was already running towards the back of the warehouse. He jumped the next alley, landing on a pile of barrels that wobbled dangerously, but his momentum carried him on, scattering cats, then another jump and he was at the far end. "Found anything, Pat?"

"Bloody great trapdoor, nothing else."

"Catch!" Sharpe threw Harper the volley gun, then scrambled down, fumbling for footholds on the edges of boxes and jumping the last six feet. He looked left and right, but saw no sign of Ferragus or his men. "Where the hell are they?"

"You hit some of them?" Harper asked in a hopeful voice.

"Two, maybe. Where's the trapdoor?"

"Here."

"Jesus, it stinks!"

"Something nasty down there, sir. Lots of flies."

Sharpe crouched, thinking. To escape out the front of the warehouse meant going into the alleys between the piles of food, and Ferragus would have men covering all those passages. Sharpe could probably make it, but at what cost? At least one more wound. And he had a woman with him. He could not expose her to more fire. He lifted the trapdoor, letting out a gust of foul-smelling air. Something dead was down in the blackness. A rat? He peered down, saw steps going into darkness, but the shadows suggested there was a cellar down there, and once he was at the base of the steps he could fire up the stone stairway. Ferragus and his men would have to brave that fire to approach, and they would be reluctant to do that. And perhaps there was a way out of the cellar?

There were footsteps on the warehouse's far side, then more sounds from the top of the stacks. Ferragus had learned quickly and sent men to take the high ground and Sharpe knew he was trapped properly now and the cellar was the only option left. "Down," he ordered, "all of you. Down."

He went last, clumsily closing the trapdoor behind him, letting the heavy timber down slowly so that Ferragus might not realize his enemies had gone to earth. It was pitch black at the foot of the steps, and so foul-smelling that Sarah gagged. Flies buzzed in the dark. "Load the volley gun, Pat," Sharpe said, "and give me the rifles."

Sharpe crouched on the steps, one rifle in his hands, two beside him. Anyone opening the trapdoor now would be silhouetted against the warehouse's dim light and would fetch a bullet for their pains. "If I fire," he whispered to Harper, "you have to reload the rifle before the volley gun."

"Yes, sir." Harper could have reloaded a rifle blindfolded in Stygian darkness.

"Jorge?" Sharpe asked, and the answer was a hiss, betraying Vicente's pain. "Feel your way round the walls," Sharpe said, "see if there's a way out."

"Major Ferreira was up there," Vicente said, sounding reproachful.

"He's as bad as his brother," Sharpe said. "He was planning to sell the Frogs some bloody flour, Jorge, only I stopped it, so then he set me up for a beating at Bussaco." He had no proof of that, of course, but it seemed obvious. Ferreira had persuaded Hogan to invite Sharpe to supper at the monastery, and must have let his brother know that the rifleman would be alone on the dark path afterwards. "Just feel round the walls, Jorge. See if there's a door."

"There are rats," Vicente said.

Sharpe took his folding knife from his pocket, took out the blade, and whispered Sarah's name. "Take this," he said, and felt for her hand. He put the knife's handle into her fingers. "Be careful," he warned her, "it's a knife. I want you to cut a strip off the bottom of your dress and see if you can bandage Jorge's shoulder."

He thought she might protest at mangling her only dress, but she said nothing and a moment later Sharpe heard the ripping sound as she slashed and tore at the silk. Sharpe crept a small way up the stairs and listened. There was silence for a while, then the sudden bang of a pistol and another bang, virtually instantaneous, as the ball hammered into the trapdoor. The ball stuck there, not piercing the heavy timber. Ferragus was announcing that he had found Sharpe, but plainly the big man was unwilling to lift the hatch and rush the cellar, for there was another long silence. "They want us to think they've gone," Sharpe said.

"There's no way out," Vicente announced.

"There's always a way out," Sharpe said. "Rats get in, don't they?"

"But there are two dead men here," Vicente sounded disgusted. The smell was overpowering.

"They can't hurt us," Sharpe said in a whisper, "not if they're dead. Take your jacket and shirt off, Jorge, and let Miss Fry bandage you."

Sharpe waited. Waited. Vicente was hissing in pain and Sarah made soothing noises. Sharpe went closer to the hatch. Ferragus was not gone, he knew, and he wondered what the man would do next. Open the hatch and pour a pistol volley down? Take the casualties? Sharpe doubted it. Ferragus was hoping the fugitives would be deceived into thinking the warehouse was empty and would make their own way up the steps, but Sharpe would not fall for that. He waited, listening to the scrape of Harper's ramrod shoving down the seven bullets.

"Loaded, sir," Harper said.

"Let's hope the bastards come, then," Sharpe said, and Sarah gave a sharp intake of breath that he ignored, then there was a sudden, weighty thump that sounded as loud as a cannon firing and Sharpe flinched back, expecting an explosion, but the thump was followed by silence. Something heavy had been placed on the hatch. Then there was another thump, and another, followed by a heavy scraping sound and then a whole succession of bangs and scrapes. "They're weighting down the hatch," Sharpe said.

"Why?" Sarah asked.

"They're trapping us here, miss, and they'll come back for us when they're good and ready." Ferragus, Sharpe reckoned, did not want to attract more attention to his warehouse by starting another firefight while there were still British and Portuguese troops in the city. He would wait till the army was gone and then, in the time before the French arrived, he would bring more men, more guns and unseal the cellar. "So we've got time," Sharpe said.

"Time to do what?" Vicente asked.

"Get out, of course. All of you, fingers in your ears." He waited a few seconds, then fired the rifle up the stairs. The bullet buried itself in the trapdoor. Sharpe's ears were ringing as he found a new cartridge, bit off the bullet, spat it out, and then primed the rifle. "Give me your hand, Pat," he said, then put the rest of the cartridge, just the paper and powder, into Harper's palm.

"What are you doing?" Vicente asked.

"Being God," Sharpe said, "and making light." He felt inside his jacket and found the copy of *The Times* that Lawford had given to him and he tore the newspaper in half, put half back inside his jacket and screwed the other half into a tight spill that he laid on the floor.

"Ready, sir." Harper, who had guessed what Sharpe wanted, had twisted the cartridge paper into a tube in which he left most of the powder.

"Find the lock," Sharpe told him, and waited as Harper explored the rifle Sharpe was holding.

"Got it, sir," Harper said, then held the spill close by the shut frizzen.

"Glad you came with me today, Pat?"

"Happiest day of my life, sir."

"Let's see where we are," Sharpe said, and he pulled the trigger, the frizzen flew open as the flint struck it to drive the sparks downwards, there was a flare as the powder in the pan caught fire and Harper had the cartridge paper in just the right place, for a spark went into the tube and it fizzed up, suddenly bright, and Sharpe snatched up the newspaper spill and lit one end. Harper was licking his burned fingers as Sharpe let the tightly rolled paper flare up. He had about one minute now before the newspaper burned out, but there was little to see except the two bodies at the back of the cellar, and they were a foul sight, for the rats had been at the men, chewing their faces to the skulls and excavating their swollen bellies that were now crawling with maggots and thick with flies. Sarah twisted into a corner and vomited while Sharpe examined the rest of the cellar, which was about twenty feet square and stone-floored. The ceiling was of stone and brick, supported by arches made with narrow bricks.

"Roman work," Vicente said, looking at one of the arches.

Sharpe looked up the stairwell, but its sides were of solid stone. The newspaper guttered and he dropped it on the lowest step and looked around one more time as the flames flickered low.

"We're trapped," Vicente said gloomily. He had torn open his shirt and his left shoulder was now clumsily bandaged, but Sharpe could see blood on his skin and on the torn edges of the shirt. Then the flames went out and the cellar returned to darkness. "There's no way out," Vicente said.

"There's always a way out," Sharpe insisted. "I was trapped in a room in Copenhagen once, but I got out."

"How?" Vicente asked.

"Chimney," Sharpe said, and shuddered at the memory of that black, tight, lung-squeezing space up which he had fought, before turning in a soot-filled chamber to wriggle like an eel down another flue.

"Pity the Romans didn't build a chimney here," Harper said.

"We'll just have to wait and fight our way out," Vicente suggested.

"Can't," Sharpe said brutally. "When Ferragus comes back, Jorge, he won't be taking chances. He'll open that trapdoor and have a score of men with muskets just waiting to kill us."

"So what do we do?" Sarah, recovered slightly, asked in a small voice.

"We destroy that food up there," Sharpe said, nodding in the dark towards the supplies in the warehouse above. "That's what Wellington wants, isn't it? That's our duty. We can't spend all our time swanning around universities, miss, we have work to do."

But first, and he did not know how, he had to escape.

⁂

FERRAGUS, his brother and three of the men from the warehouse retired to a tavern. Two men could not come. One had been hit in the skull by one of the seven-barrel gun's bullets and, though he lived, he was unable to speak, control his movements or make sense and so Ferragus ordered him taken to Saint Clara's in hope that some of the nuns were still there. A second man, struck in the arm by the same volley, had gone to his home to let his woman splint his broken arm and bandage his wound. The wounding of the two men had angered Ferragus who stared morosely into his wine.

"I warned you," Ferreira said, "they're soldiers."

"Dead soldiers," Ferragus said. That was his only consolation. The four were trapped, and they would have to stay in the cellar until Ferragus fetched them out and he toyed with the idea of leaving them there. How long would it take them to die? Would they go mad in the stifling dark? Shoot each other? Become cannibals? Perhaps, weeks from now, he would open the trapdoor and one survivor would crawl blinking into the light and he would kick the bastard to death. No, he would rather kick all three men to death and teach Sarah Fry a different lesson. "We'll get them out tonight," he said.

"The British will be in the city tonight," Ferreira pointed out, "and there are troops billeted in the street behind the warehouse. They hear shots? They may not go as easily as those this afternoon." A Portuguese patrol had heard the shots in the warehouse and come to investigate, but Ferreira, who had not joined the fight, but had been standing by the door, had heard the boots on the cobbles and slipped outside to fend off the patrol, explaining that he had men inside killing goats.

"No one will hear shots from that cellar," Ferragus said scornfully.

"You want to risk that?" Ferreira asked. "With that big gun? It sounds like a cannon!"

"Tomorrow morning, then," Ferragus snarled.

"Tomorrow morning the British will still be here," the Major pointed out patiently, "and in the afternoon you and I must ride north to meet the French."

"You ride north to meet the French," Ferragus said, "and Miguel can go with you." He looked at the smaller man who shrugged acceptance.

"They are expecting to meet you," Ferreira pointed out.

"So Miguel will say he's me!" Ferragus snapped. "Will the damned French know the difference? And I stay here," he insisted, "and play my games the moment the British are gone. When will the French arrive?"

"If they come tomorrow," Ferreira guessed, "in the morning, perhaps? Say an hour or two after dawn?"

"That gives me time," Ferragus said. He only wanted enough time to hear the three men begging for mercy that would not come to them. "I'll meet you at the warehouse," he told Ferreira. "Bring the Frenchmen to guard it, and I'll be inside, waiting." Ferragus knew he was allowing himself to be distracted. His priority was to keep the food safe and sell it to the French, and the trapped foursome did not matter, but they mattered now. They had defied him, beaten him for the moment, so now, more than ever, it was an affair of pride, and a man could not back down from an affront to his pride. To do so was to be less than a man.

Yet, Ferragus knew, there was no real problem left. Sharpe and his companions were doomed. He had piled more than half a ton of boxes and barrels on the trapdoor, there was no other way out of the cellar and it was just a matter of time. So Ferragus had won, and that was a consolation. He had won.

MOST OF THE RETREATING BRITISH and Portuguese army had used a road to the east of Coimbra and so crossed the Mondego at a ford, but enough had been ordered to use the main road to send a steady stream of troops, guns, caissons and wagons across the Santa Clara bridge which led from Coimbra to its small suburb on the Mondego's southern bank where the new Convent of Saint Clara stood. The soldiers were joined by an apparently unending stream of civilians, handcarts, goats, dogs, cows, sheep and misery that shuffled over the bridge into the narrow streets around the convent and then went south towards Lisbon. Progress was painfully slow. A child was almost run over by a cannon and the driver only avoided her by slewing the gun into a wall where the offside wheel broke, and that took nearly an hour to repair. A handcart collapsed on the bridge, spilling books and clothes, and a woman screamed when Portuguese troops threw the broken cart and its contents into the river which was already thick with flotsam as the troops on the quays shoved shattered barrels and slashed sacks into the water. Boxes of biscuits were jettisoned and the biscuits, baked hard as rock, floated in their thousands downstream. Other troops had gathered timber and coal and were making a huge fire onto which they tossed salt meat. Still other troops, all Portuguese, had been ordered to break all the bakers' ovens in town, while a company of the South Essex took sledgehammers and pickaxes to the tethered boats.

Lieutenant Colonel Lawford returned to the quays in the early afternoon. He had slept well and enjoyed a surprisingly good meal of chicken, salad and white wine while his red coat was being brushed and pressed. Then, mounted on Lightning, he rode down to the quayside where he discovered his battalion hot, sweating, disheveled, dirty and tired. "The problem," Major Forrest told him, "is the salt meat. God knows, it won't burn."

"Didn't Sharpe say something about turpentine?"

"Haven't seen him," Forrest said.

"I was hoping he was here," Lawford said, looking around the smoke-wreathed quay that stank of spilled rum and scorched meat. "He rescued rather a pretty girl. An English girl, of all things. I was a little abrupt with her, I fear, and thought I should pay my respects."

"He isn't here," Forrest said bluntly.

"He'll turn up," Lawford said, "he always does."

Captain Slingsby marched across the quay, stamped to a halt and offered Lawford a cracking salute. "Man gone missing, Colonel."

Lawford touched the heel of his riding crop to the forward tip of his cocked hat in acknowledgement of the salute. "How are things going, Cornelius? All well, I hope?"

"Boats destroyed, sir, every last one."

"Splendid."

"But Sergeant Harper's missing, sir. Absent without permission."

"I gave him permission, Cornelius."

Slingsby bristled. "I wasn't asked, sir."

"An oversight, I'm sure," Lawford said, "and I'm equally sure Sergeant Harper will be back soon. He's with Mister Sharpe."

"That's another thing," Slingsby said darkly.

"Yes?" Lawford ventured cautiously.

"Mister Sharpe had more words with me this morning."

"You and Sharpe must patch things up," Lawford said hastily.

"And he has no right, sir, no right whatsoever, to take Sergeant Harper away from his proper duties. It only encourages him."

"Encourages him?" Lawford was slightly confused.

"To impertinence, sir. He is very Irish."

Lawford stared at Slingsby, wondering if he detected the smell of rum on his brother-in-law's breath. "I suppose he would be Irish," the Colonel finally said, "coming, as he does, from Ireland. Just like Lightning!" He leaned forward and fondled the horse's ears. "Not everything Irish is to be disparaged, Cornelius."

"Sergeant Harper, sir, does not show sufficient respect for His Majesty's commission," Slingsby said.

"Sergeant Harper," Forrest put in, "helped capture the Eagle at Talavera, Captain. Before you joined us."

"I don't doubt he can fight, sir," Slingsby said. "It's in their blood, isn't it? Like pugdogs, they are. Ignorant and brutal, sir. I had enough of them in the 55th to know." He looked back to Lawford. "But I have to worry about the internal economy of the light company. It has to be straightened and smartened, sir. Doesn't do to have men being impertinent."

"What is it you want?" Lawford asked with a touch of asperity.

"Sergeant Harper returned to me, sir, where he belongs, and made to knuckle down to some proper soldiering."

"It will be your duty to see that he does when he returns," Lawford said grandly.

"Very good, sir," Slingsby said, threw another salute, about-turned and marched back towards his company.

"He's very enthusiastic," Lawford said.

"I had never noticed," Forrest said, "any lack of enthusiasm or, indeed, absence of efficiency in our light company."

"Oh, they're fine fellows!" Lawford said. "Fine fellows indeed, but the best hounds sometimes hunt better with a change of master. New ways, Forrest, dig out old habits. Don't you agree? Perhaps you'll take supper with me tonight?"

"That would be kind, sir."

"And it's an early start in the morning. Farewell to Coimbra, eh? And may the French have mercy on it."

Twenty miles to the north the first French troops reached the main road. They had brushed aside the Portuguese militia who had blocked the track looping north around Bussaco's ridge, and now their cavalry patrols galloped into undefended and deserted farmland. The army turned south. Coimbra was next, then Lisbon, and with that would come victory.

Because the Eagles were marching south.

CHAPTER 8

THE FIRST IDEA was to break through the trapdoor and then work on whatever had been piled above. "Go through the edge of the hatch," Vicente suggested, "then perhaps we can break through the box above? Take everything out of the box? Then wriggle through?"

Sharpe could think of nothing else that might free them, so he and Harper set to work. They tried raising the trapdoor first, crouching beneath it and heaving up, but the wood did not move a fraction of an inch, and so they started to carve away at the timbers. Vicente, with his wounded shoulder, could not help, so he and Sarah sat in the cellar as far from the two decaying bodies as they could and listened as Sharpe and Harper attacked the trapdoor. Harper used his sword bayonet and, because that was a shorter blade than Sharpe's sword, worked farther up the steps. Sharpe took off his jacket, stripped off his shirt and wrapped the linen round the blade so he could grip the edge without being cut. He told Harper what he was doing and suggested he might want to protect his own hands. "Pity, though," Sharpe said, "this is a new shirt."

"A present from a certain seamstress in Lisbon?" Harper asked.

"It was, yes."

Harper chuckled, then stabbed the blade upwards. Sharpe did the same with his sword and they worked in silence mostly, gouging in the dark, splintering and levering out scraps of tough, ancient wood. Once in a while a blade would encounter a nail and they would swear.

"It's a real language lesson," Sarah said after a while.

"I'm sorry, miss," Sharpe said.

"You sort of don't notice when you're in the army," Harper explained.

"Do all soldiers swear?"

"All of them," Sharpe said, "all of the time. Except for Daddy Hill."

"General Hill, miss," Harper explained, "who's noted for his very clean mouth."

"And Sergeant Read," Sharpe added, "he never swears. He's a Methodist, miss."

"I've heard him swear," Harper said, "when bloody Batten stole eight pages from his Bible to use as . . ." He stopped suddenly, deciding Sarah did not want to know what use Batten had made of the book of Deuteronomy, then gave a grunt as a great splinter cracked away. "Be through this in no bloody time," he said cheerfully.

The timbers of the trapdoor were at least three inches thick, and reinforced by two sturdy beams on their underside. For the moment Sharpe and Harper were ignoring the beam on their side, reckoning it was best to break through the trapdoor before worrying how to remove the bigger piece of timber. The wood was hard, but they learned to weaken its grain by repeated stabbing, then they scraped and gouged and prised the loosened timber away. The broken wood came in thimblefuls, in dust, scrap by scrap, and the cramped area under the steps gave them little space. They had to rest just to stretch their muscles from time to time, and at other times it seemed that no amount of stabbing and scraping would loosen another piece, for the two weapons were ill suited to the work. The steel was too slender, so could not be used for brutal leverage for fear the blades would snap. Sharpe used his knife for a time, the sawdust sifting down into his eyes, then he rammed the sword up again, his linen-wrapped hand near the tip to brace the steel. And even when they broke through, he thought, they would only have a small hole. God knows how they were to enlarge it, but all battles had to be fought one step at a time. No point in worrying about the future if there was to be no future, so he and Harper worked patiently away. Sweat poured down Sharpe's naked chest, flies crawled on him, the dust was thick in his mouth, and his ribs were hurting.

Time meant nothing in the dark. They could have worked an hour or ten hours, Sharpe did not know, though he sensed that night must have fallen outside in the world that now seemed so far away. He worked doggedly, trying not to think about the passing time, and slowly he chipped and gouged, rammed and scraped, until at last he thrust the sword hard up and the blow jarred down his arm because the tip had hit something more solid than wood. He did it again, then swore viciously. "Sorry, miss."

"What is it?" Vicente asked. He had been asleep and sounded alarmed.

Sharpe did not answer. Instead he used his knife, gnawing at the small hole he had made in the upper part of the broken timber and, when he had widened the hole sufficiently, he probed with the knife blade to scratch at whatever lay immediately above the trapdoor and then swore again. "The bastards have put paving slabs up there," he said. He had broken through, but only to meet immovable stone. "Bastards!"

"Mister Sharpe," Sarah said, though tiredly, as if she knew she was fighting a losing battle.

"They probably are bastards, miss," Harper said, then rammed his sword bayonet up into the splintered hole he had made and was rewarded with the same sound of steel against stone. He uttered his opinion, apologized to Sarah, then slumped down.

"They've done what?" Vicente asked.

"They've put stones on top," Sharpe said, "and other stuff on top of the stones. The bastards aren't as daft as they look." He edged down the steps and sat with his back against the wall. He felt used up, exhausted and it hurt just to breathe.

"We can't get through the trapdoor?" Vicente asked.

"Not a bloody chance," Sharpe said.

"So?" Vicente asked tentatively.

"So we bloody think," Sharpe said, but he could not think of anything else to do. Hell and damnation was all he could think. They were bloody well trapped.

"How do the rats get in?" Sarah asked after a while.

"Those little bastards can get through gaps as small as your little finger," Harper said. "You can't keep a good rat out, not if he wants to get in."

"So where do they get in?" she persisted.

"Round the edge of the trapdoor," Sharpe guessed, "where we can't get out."

They sat in gloomy silence. The flies settled back on the corpses. "If we fired our guns," Vicente said, "someone might hear?"

"Not down here, they won't," Sharpe said, preferring to keep all his firepower for the moment when Ferragus came for them. He leaned his head against the wall and closed his eyes, trying to think. The ceiling? Bricks and stones. Hundreds of the buggers. He imagined himself breaking through, then he was suddenly in a field, bright with flowers, a bullet came past him, then another and he was struck on the leg and he woke suddenly, realizing that someone had tapped his right calf. "Was I asleep?" he asked.

"We all were," Harper said. "God knows what time it is."

"Jesus." Sharpe stretched himself, feeling the pain in his arms and legs that had come from working inside the cramped stairway. "Jesus," he said angrily. "We can't afford to sleep. Not with those bastards coming for us."

Harper did not answer. Sharpe could hear the Irishman moving, apparently stretching on the floor. He supposed the Irishman wanted to sleep again, and he did not approve, but he could not think of anything more useful Harper could do and so he said nothing.

"I can hear something," Harper spoke after a while. His voice came from the center of the cellar, from the floor.

"Where?" Sharpe asked.

"Put your ear on the stone, sir."

Sharpe stretched out and put his right ear against the floor. His hearing was not what it was. Too many years of muskets and rifles had dulled it, but he held his breath, listened hard, and heard the faintest hint of water running. "Water?"

"There's a stream down there," Harper said.

"Like the Fleet," Sharpe said.

"The what?" Vicente asked.

"It's a river in London," Sharpe said, "and for a long way it flows underground. No one knows it's there, but it is. They built the city on top of it."

"They've done the same here," Harper said.

Sharpe tapped the floor with the hilt of his sword, but was not rewarded with a hollow sound, yet he was fairly certain the noise of water was there, and Sarah, whose hearing had not been dulled by battle, was quite certain of it. "Right, Pat," Sharpe said, his spirits restored and the pain in his ribs even seeming less biting. "We'll lift a bloody stone."

That was easier said than done. They used their weapons again, scraping away at the edges of a big flagstone to work down between the slab and its neighbors, and Harper found a place where a chip the size of his little finger was missing from the stone's edge, and he delved down there, working the sword bayonet into the foundations. "It's rubble down there," he said.

"Let's just hope the bloody thing isn't mortared into place," Sharpe said.

"No," Harper said scornfully. "Why would you mortar a slab? You just lay the buggers on gravel and stamp them down. Move back, sir."

"What are you doing?"

"I'm going to lift the sod."

"Why don't we lever it up?"

"Because you'll break your sword, sir, and that'll put you in a really bad mood. Just give me space. And be ready to hold it when I've got the bastard up."

Sharpe moved, Harper straddled the stone, got two fingers underneath its edge and heaved. It did not move. He swore, braced himself again, and used all his vast strength and there was a grinding sound and Sharpe, touching the stone's edge with his fingers, felt it move a trifle upwards. Harper grunted, managed to get a third finger underneath and gave another giant pull and suddenly the stone was lifted and Sharpe rammed the muzzle of his rifle under the exposed edge to hold it up. "You can let go now."

"God save Ireland!" Harper said, straightening. The stone was resting on the rifle muzzle and they left it there while Harper caught his breath. "We can both do it now, sir," the Irishman said. "You on the other side? We'll just turn the bugger over. Sorry, miss."

"I'm getting used to it," Sarah said in a resigned voice.

Sharpe got his hands under the edge. "Ready?"

"Now, sir."

They heaved and the stone came up, and kept going to turn on its end so that it fell smack on the nearer corpse with a wet, squashing sound that released a gust of noxious vapor along with an unseen cloud of flies. Sarah gave a noise of disgust, Sharpe and Harper were laughing.

Now they could feel a square patch of rubble, a space of broken bricks, stones and sand, and they used their hands to scoop it out, sometimes loosening the packed rubble first with a blade. Vicente used his right hand to help and Sarah pushed the excavated material aside.

"There's no end to the bloody stuff," Harper said, and the more they pulled out, the more fell in from the sides. They went down two feet and then, at last, the rubble ended as Sharpe's battered and bleeding hands found a curved surface that felt like tiles stacked on edge. They went on scooping until they had bared two or three square feet of the arched surface.

Vicente used his right hand to probe what Sharpe thought were tiles. "Roman bricks," Vicente guessed. "The Romans made their bricks very thin, like tiles." He felt for a while longer, exploring the arched shape. "It's the top of a tunnel."

"A tunnel?" Sharpe asked.

"The stream," Sarah said. "The Romans must have channeled it."

"And we're going to break into it," Sharpe said. He could hear the trickle far more clearly now. So there was water there, and the water flowed to the river through a tunnel, and that thought filled him with a fierce hope.

He knelt at the edge of the hole, balancing on a slab that was unsteady because of the rubble that had fallen from beneath it, and began hammering down with the brass butt of a rifle.

"What you're doing," Vicente said, judging what was happening by the dull sound of the stock striking the bricks, "is hitting at the top of the arch. That will only wedge the bricks tighter."

"What I'm doing," Sharpe said, "is breaking the bugger." He thought Vicente was probably right, but he was too frustrated to work patiently on the old bricks. "And I hope I'm doing it with your rifle," he added. The butt hammered down again, then Harper joined in from the other side and the two rifles cracked and banged on the bricks and Sharpe could hear scraps dropping into the water, then Harper gave an almighty blow and a whole chunk of the ancient brickwork fell away and suddenly, if it was possible, the cellar was filled with an even worse smell, a stink from the foulest depths of hell.

"Oh, shit!" Harper said, recoiling.

"That's what it is," Vicente said in a faint voice. The smell was so bad that it was hard to breathe.

"A sewer?" Sharpe asked in disbelief.

"Jesus Christ!" Harper said, after trying to fill his lungs. Sarah sighed.

"It comes from the upper town," Vicente explained. "Most of the lower town just use pits in their cellars. It's a Roman sewer. They called it a *cloaca*."

"I call it our way out," Sharpe said and hammered the rifle down again, and the bricks fell more easily now and he could feel the hole widening. "It's time to see again," he said.

He retrieved the discarded half of Lawford's copy of *The Times* and found his own rifle, distinguishing it by the chip missing from the cheek rest on the left side of the butt where a French musket ball had snicked out a splinter. He needed his own rifle because he knew it was still un-loaded, and now he primed it while Harper twisted the newspaper into a spill. The spill caught on the second try, and the newspaper flared up, then the flames turned a strange blue-green as Harper moved the burn-ing paper close to the hole.

"Oh, no!" Sarah said, looking down.

The sound might be a trickle, but it came from a green-scummed liq-uid that glistened some seven or eight feet below. Rats, frightened by the sudden light, scuttled along the edge of the slime, scrabbling on the old bricks that were black and furred with growth. Sharpe, judging from the curve of the ancient sewer, reckoned the effluent was about a foot deep, then the flames scorched Harper's fingers and he let the torch drop. It burned blue for a second, then they were in the dark again. Thank God most of the richer folk were gone from Coimbra, Sharpe thought, or else the old Roman sewer would be brimming over its edge with filth.

"Are you really thinking of going down into that?" Vicente asked in a disbelieving voice.

"No choice, really," Sharpe said. "Stay here and die, or go down there." He took off his boots. "You might want to wear my boots, miss," he said to Sarah. "They should be tall enough to keep you out of the you-know-what, but you might want to take that frock off as well."

There were a few seconds' silence. "You want me to . . ." Sarah began, then her voice faded away.

"No, miss," Sharpe said patiently, "I don't want you to do anything you don't want to do, but if your dress gets in that muck then it'll stink to high heaven by the time we're through, and so far as I know you haven't got anything else to wear. Nor have I, and that's why I'm stripping."

"You can't ask Miss Fry to undress," Vicente said, shocked.

"I'm not asking her," Sharpe said, shuffling out of his French cavalry overalls. "It's up to her. But if you've got any sense, Jorge, you'll get undressed as well. Bundle everything inside your jacket or shirt and tie the sleeves around your neck. Bloody hell, man, no one can see! It's dark as Hades down there. Here, miss, my boots." He pushed them over the floor.

"You want me to go into a sewer, Mister Sharpe?" Sarah asked in a small voice.

"No, miss, I don't," Sharpe said. "I want you to be in green fields and happy, with enough money to last you the rest of your life. But to get you there I have to go through a sewer. If you like, you can wait here and Pat and I will go through and come back for you, but I can't promise that Ferragus won't come back first. So all in all, miss, it's your choice."

"Mister Sharpe?" Sarah sounded indignant, but was evidently not. "You're right. I apologize."

For a moment there was only the rustle of clothes, then all four rolled whatever they had stripped off into bundles. Sharpe was wearing his drawers, nothing else, and he wrapped his other clothes inside his overalls, then strapped the bundle tight with the shoulder straps. He laid the clothes beside the hole with his sword belt, which held his ammunition pouch, scabbard and haversack. "I'll go first," he said. "Miss? You follow me and keep your hand on my back so you know where I am. Jorge? You come next and Pat will be rearguard."

Sharpe sat on the edge of the hole, then Harper gripped his wrists and lowered him through the hole. Pieces of rubble and masonry splashed into the filth, then Sharpe's feet were in the liquid and Harper was grunting with the effort. "Just another two inches, Pat," Sharpe said, and then his wrists slid from Harper's grip and he fell those last inches and almost lost his balance because the bottom of the sewer was so treacherously slick. "Jesus," he said, filled with disgust and almost choking because of the noxious air. "Someone, hand down my sword belt, then my clothes."

He hung the buckled sword belt round his neck. His shako was tied to the cartridge box's buckle and the empty scabbard hung down his spine, then he knotted the overalls' legs over the belt. "Rifle?" he said, and someone pushed it down and he hung the weapon on his shoulder, then took his sword in his right hand. He reckoned the blade would be useful as a probe. For a moment he wondered which way to go, either uphill towards the university or down to the river, then decided the best hope of escape was the river. The sewer had to spew its muck out somewhere and that was the place he wanted. "You next, miss," he said, "and be careful. It's slippery as . . ." He paused, checking his language. "Don't be frightened," he went on as he heard her gasp as she negotiated the hole. "Sergeant Harper will lower you," Sharpe said, "but I'm going to hold on to you because I almost slipped when I got down here. Is that all right?"

"I don't mind," she said, almost breathless because the stench was so overpowering.

He put out his hands, found her bare waist and half supported her as she put her booted feet into the sewage. She lowered herself, but panic or horror still made her flail for balance and she gripped him hard and Sharpe put his arms round her narrow waist. "It's all right," he said, "you'll live."

Vicente handed down Sarah's bundle of clothes and, because she was shivering and frightened, Sharpe tied it around her neck while she clung to him. "You now, Jorge," Sharpe said.

Harper came last. Rats scrabbled past them, the sound of their claws fading up the unseen tunnel. Sharpe could just stand upright, but he stooped in hope of seeing even a glimmer of light farther down the sewer, but there was nothing. "You're going to hold on to me, miss," he said, deciding that the courtesy of calling her "miss" was really not needed now that they were both virtually naked and standing up to their calves in shit, but he suspected she would object if he called her anything else. "Jorge," he went on, "you hold on to Miss Fry's clothes. And we all go slowly."

Sharpe probed every step with the sword, then inched ahead before prodding the blade again, but after a while he became more confident and their pace increased to a shuffle. Sarah had her hands on Sharpe's waist, gripping him tight, and she felt almost light-headed. Something strange had happened to her in the last few minutes, almost as if by undressing and lowering herself into a sewer she had let go of her previous life, of her precarious but determined grip on respectability, and had let herself drop into a world of adventure and irresponsibility. She was, suddenly and unexpectedly, happy.

Nameless things hanging from the sewer roof brushed against Sharpe's face and he ducked from them, dreading to think what they were, and after a while he used his sword to clear the air in front of him. He tried to count the feet and yards, but gave up because their progress was so painfully slow. After a while the floor of the sewer rose, while the roof stayed at the same level and he had to crouch to keep going. More tendrils brushed against his hair. Other things dripped from the roof, then the bottom of the tunnel abruptly fell away and he was poking the sword into a stinking nothingness. "Hold still," he told his companions, then gingerly pushed the sword forward and found the bottom of the sewer again two feet away and at least a foot lower. There was some kind of sump here, or else the base of the tunnel had collapsed into a cavern. "Let go of me," he told Sarah. He prodded again, measured the distance and then, still bent into a crouch, took one long step and made the far side safely, but his foot slipped as he landed and he fell heavily against the sewer's side. He used the efficacious word. "Sorry, miss," he said, his voice echoing in the tunnel. He had managed to keep his clothes out of the muck, but the slip had scared him and his ribs were hurting again so that it was painful to draw breath. He straightened slowly and discovered he could stand up straight because the roof had risen again. He turned to face Sarah. "In front of you," he told her, "there's a hole in the floor. It's only a good pace wide. Find the edge of it with one of your feet."

"I've found it."

"You're going to take a long step," Sharpe told her, "two feet forward and one foot down, but take my hands first." He propped the sword against the wall, reached out and found her hands. "Are you ready?"

"Yes." She sounded nervous.

"Slide your hands forward," he told her, "hold on to my forearms, and hold hard." She did as he ordered and Sharpe gripped her arms close to her elbows. "I've got you now," he said, "and you're going to take one long step, but be careful. It's slippery as . . ."

"Shit?" Sarah asked, and laughed at herself for daring to say the word aloud, then she took a deep breath of the fetid air, launched herself forward, but her back foot slipped and she fell, crying aloud in fear, only to find herself being hauled to safety. Sharpe had half expected her to slip and now he pulled her hard into his body and she came easily, no weight on her at all, and she clung to him so that he felt her naked breasts against his skin. She was gasping.

"It's all right, miss," he said, "well done."

"Is she all right?" Vicente asked anxiously.

"She's never been better," Sharpe said. "There are some soldiers I wouldn't bring down here because they'd fall to pieces, but Miss Fry is doing well." She was holding on to him, shaking slightly, her hands cold on his bare skin. "You know what I like about you, miss?"

"What?"

"You haven't complained once. Well, about our swearing, of course, but you'll get over that, but you haven't once complained about what's happened. Not many women I could take down a sewer without getting an earful." He stepped back, trying to disentangle himself from her, but Sarah insisted on holding him. "You must give Jorge some room," he told her, and led her a pace down the sewer where she kept her arm around his waist. "If I didn't think it was a daft idea," Sharpe went on, "I'd guess you're enjoying yourself."

"I am," Sarah said, then giggled. She was still holding him and her face was against his chest so Sharpe, without really thinking about it, bent his head and kissed her forehead. For a second she went very still, then she put her other arm around him and lifted her face to press her cheek against his. Bloody hell, Sharpe thought. In a sewer?

There was a splashing sound and someone bashed into Sharpe and Sarah, then clutched at both of them. "You safe, Jorge?" Sharpe asked.

"I'm safe. I'm sorry, miss," Vicente said, deciding his hand had inadvertently groped something inappropriate.

Harper came last and Sharpe turned around and led on, conscious of Sarah's hands on his waist. He shuddered as he passed another sewer that came from the right-hand side. A dribble of something flopped from its outfall and splashed up his thigh. He sensed that their sewer was running more steeply downhill now. The filth was shallower here, for much of the sewage was stopped up behind the place where the floor had buckled upwards, but what there was ran faster and he tried not to think what might be bumping against his ankles. He was going in tiny steps, fearful of the slippery stones beneath him, though for much of the time his toes were squelching in jelly-like muck. He began using the sword as a support as much as a probe, and now he was sure that the fall was steepening. Where did it come out? The river? The sewer began to tilt downwards and Sharpe stopped, suspecting they could go no farther without falling and sliding into whatever horror lay below. He could hear the turgid stream splashing far beneath, but into what? A pool of muck? Another sewer? And how long was the drop?

"What is it?" Sarah asked, worried that Sharpe had stopped.

"Trouble," he said, then listened again and detected a new sound, a background noise, unstopping and faint, and realized it had to be the river. The sewer fell away, then ran to its outfall in the Mondego, but how far it fell, or how steeply, he could not tell. He felt with his right foot for a loose stone or fragment of brick and, when he found something, edged it up the curve of the sewer's side until it was out of the liquid. He tossed it ahead of him, heard it rattle against the sides of the sewer as it dropped, then came a splash.

"The sewer turns down," he explained, "and it falls into some kind of pool."

"Not some kind of pool," Harper said helpfully, "a pool of piss and shit."

"Thank you, Sergeant," Sharpe said.

"We have to go back," Vicente suggested.

"To the cellar?" Sarah asked, alarmed.

"God, no," Sharpe said. He wondered about lowering himself down, dangling on the rifle slings, but then remembered the terror of thinking himself trapped in the Copenhagen chimney. Anything was better than going through that again. "Pat? Turn around, go back slowly and tap the walls. We'll follow you."

They turned in the dark. Sarah insisted on going behind Sharpe, keeping her hands on his waist. Harper used the hilt of his sword bayonet, the dull clang echoing forlorn in the fetid blackness. Sharpe was hoping against hope that they would find some place where the sewer ran by a cellar, somewhere that was not blanketed by feet of earth and gravel, and if they could not find it then they would have to go back past the warehouse cellar and find some place that the sewer opened to the surface. It would be a long night, he thought, if it was still night time, and then, not ten paces up the sewer, the sound changed. Harper tapped again, and was again rewarded with a hollow noise. "Is that what you're looking for?" he asked.

"We'll break the bloody wall down," Sharpe said. "Jorge? You'll have to hold Sergeant Harper's clothes. Miss Fry? You hold mine. And keep the ammunition out of the sludge."

They tapped the wall some more, finding that the hollow spot was about ten feet long on the upper curve of the sewer. "If there's anybody up there," Harper said, "we're going to give them one hell of a surprise."

"What if it falls in on us?" Sarah asked.

"Then we get crushed," Sharpe said, "so if you believe in a God, miss, pray now."

"You don't?"

"I believe in the Baker rifle," Sharpe said, "and in the 1796 Pattern heavy cavalry sword, so long as you grind down the back blade so that the point don't slide off a Frog's ribs. If you don't grind down the back blade, miss, then you might as well just beat the bastards to death with it."

"I'll remember that," Sarah said.

"Are you ready, Pat?"

"Ready," Harper said, hefting his rifle.

"Then let's give this bastard a walloping."

They did.

⚜

THE LAST BRITISH and Portuguese troops left Coimbra at dawn on Monday morning. As far as they knew every scrap of food in the city had been destroyed or burned or tossed into the river, and all the bakers' ovens had been demolished. The place was supposed to be empty, but more than half of the city's forty thousand inhabitants had refused to leave, because they reckoned flight was futile and that if the French did not overtake them here then they would catch them in Lisbon. Some, like Ferragus, stayed to protect their possessions, others were too old or too sick or too despairing to attempt escape. Let the French come, those who stayed thought, for they would endure and the world would go on.

The South Essex were the last battalion across the bridge. Lawford rode at the back and glanced behind for a sign of Sharpe or Harper, but the rising sun showed the river's quay was empty. "It isn't like Sharpe," he complained.

"It's very like Sharpe," Major Leroy observed. "He has an independent streak, Colonel. The man's a rebel. He's truculent. Very admirable traits in a skirmisher, don't you think?"

Lawford suspected he was being mocked, but was honest enough to realize that he was being mocked by the truth. "He wouldn't just have deserted?"

"Not Sharpe," Leroy said. "He's got caught up in a mess. He'll be back."

"He mentioned something to me about joining the Portuguese service," Lawford said worriedly. "You don't think he will, do you?"

"I wouldn't blame him," Leroy said. "A man needs recognition for his service, Colonel, don't you think?"

Lawford was saved from answering because Captain Slingsby, mounted on Portia, clattered back across the bridge, wheeled the horse and fell in beside Lawford and Leroy. "That Irish Sergeant is still missing," he said reproachfully.

"We were just discussing it," Lawford said.

"I shall mark him in the books as a deserter," Slingsby announced. "A deserter," he repeated vehemently.

"You'll do nothing of the sort!" Lawford snapped with an asperity that even he found surprising. Yet, even as he spoke, he realized that he had begun to find Slingsby annoying. The man was like a yapping dog, always at your heels, always demanding attention, and Lawford had begun to suspect that the new commander of his light company was a touch too fond of drink. "Sergeant Harper," he explained in a calmer tone, "is on detached service with an officer of this battalion, a respected officer, Mister Slingsby, and you will not question the propriety of that service."

"Of course not, sir," Slingsby said, taken aback at the Colonel's tone. "I just like to have everything Bristol fashion. You know me, sir. Everything in its place and a place for everything."

"Everything is in its place," the Colonel said, except that it was not. Sharpe and Harper were missing, and Lawford secretly feared it was his fault. He turned again, but there was no sign of the missing men, and then the battalion was off the bridge and marching into the shadows of the small streets about the convent.

Coimbra was strangely silent then, as if the city held its breath. Some folk went to the ancient city gates that pierced the medieval wall and stared nervously down the roads, hoping against hope that the French would not come.

Ferragus did not worry about the French, not yet. He had his own sweet revenge to take first and he led seven men to the warehouse where, before he uncovered the trapdoor, he lit two braziers of coal. It took time for the coal to catch fire from its kindling, and he used the minutes to make barricades from barrels of salt beef so that if the three men came charging up the steps they would be trapped between the barriers behind which his men would be sheltered. Once the coal was billowing foul smoke he ordered his men to uncover the hatch. He listened for any sounds from beneath, but heard nothing. "They're asleep," Francisco, the biggest of Ferragus's men, said.

"They'll be asleep for ever soon," Ferragus said. Three men held muskets, four took away the barrels and boxes, and when they were all removed Ferragus ordered two of the four to get their muskets, and for the other two men to drag away the paving slabs that had covered the trapdoor. He chuckled when he saw the holes in the wood. "They tried, eh? Must have taken them hours! Careful now!" There was only one slab remaining and he expected the trapdoor to be pushed violently upwards at any second. "Fire down as soon as they push it up," he told his men, then watched as the last paving slab was hauled away.

Nothing happened.

He waited, watching the closed trapdoor and still nothing happened. "They think we're going to go down," Ferragus said. Instead he crept onto the trapdoor, seized its metal handle, nodded to his men to make sure they were ready, then heaved.

The trapdoor lifted a few inches and Francisco pushed his musket barrel beneath and lifted it some more. He was crouching, half expecting a shot to come blasting out of the darkness, but there was only silence. Ferragus stepped to the trapdoor and hauled it all the way back so that it crashed against the warehouse's rear wall. "Now," he said, and two men pushed the braziers over so that the burning coals cascaded down the steps to fill the cellar with a thick and choking smoke. "They won't last long now," Ferragus said, and drew a pistol. Kill the men first, he thought, and save the woman for later.

He waited to hear coughing, but no sound came from the darkness. Smoke drifted in the stairwell. Ferragus crept forward, listening, then fired the pistol down the steps before ducking back. The bullet ricocheted off stone, then there was silence again except for the ringing in his ears. "Use your musket, Francisco," he ordered, and Francisco stepped to the edge, fired down and skipped back.

Still nothing.

"Maybe they died?" Francisco suggested.

"That stench would kill an ox," another man said, and indeed the smell coming from the cellar was thick and foul.

Ferragus was tempted to go down, but he had learned not to underestimate Captain Sharpe. In all likelihood, he thought, Sharpe was waiting, hidden to the left or right of the stairwell, just waiting for curiosity to bring one of his enemies down the steps. "More flames," Ferragus ordered, and two of the men broke up some old crates and the fragments were set alight and tossed down into the cellar to thicken the smoke. More wood was hurled down until the floor at the foot of the steps seemed to be a mass of flame, yet still no one moved down there. No one even coughed.

"They have to be dead," Francisco said. No one could survive that turmoil of smoke.

Ferragus took a musket from one of the men and, very slowly, trying to make no noise, he crept down the steps. The flames were hot on his face, the smoke was fierce, but at last he could see into the cellar and he stared, not believing what he saw, for in the very center, edged with glowing coals and smoldering wood, was a hole just like a grave. He stared, not comprehending for a moment, and then, suddenly and rarely, he felt afraid.

The bastards were gone.

Ferragus stayed on the bottom step. Francisco, curious, went past him, waited a moment for the worst of the smoke to subside, then kicked aside the flames to peer down the hole. He made the sign of the cross.

"What's down there?" Ferragus asked.

"Sewer. Maybe they drowned?"

"No," Ferragus said, then shuddered because a hammering sound was coming from the fetid hole. The noise seemed to come from far away, but it was a hard-edged noise, threatening, and Ferragus remembered a sermon he had once endured from a Dominican friar who had warned the people of Coimbra about the hell that waited for them if they did not mend their ways. The friar had described the fires, the instruments of torture, the thirst, the agony, the eternity of hopeless weeping, and in the echoing noise Ferragus thought he heard the implements of hell clanging and he instinctively turned and fled up the stairs. The sermon had been so powerful that for two days afterwards Ferragus had tried to reform himself. He had not even visited any of the brothels he owned in the town, and now, faced with that noise and the sight of the fire-edged hole, the terror of the sinner came back to him. He was overcome with a fear that Sharpe was now the hunter and he the quarry. "Up here!" he ordered Francisco.

"That noise . . ." Francisco was reluctant to leave the cellar.

"It's him," Ferragus said. "You want to go down and find him?"

Francisco glanced down the hole, then fled back up the steps where he closed the trapdoor and Ferragus ordered the boxes piled back on top as if that could stop Sharpe erupting from the stinking underworld.

Then another hammering sounded, this one on the warehouse doors and Ferragus whipped around and raised his gun. The new hammering came again and Ferragus suppressed his fear and walked towards the sound. "Who's there?" he shouted.

"*Senhor? Senhor?* It's me, Miguel!"

Ferragus dragged open one of the warehouse doors and at least one thing was right with the world, for Miguel and Major Ferreira had returned. Ferreira, sensibly, had abandoned his uniform and was wearing a black suit, and with him was a French officer and a squadron of hard-looking cavalrymen armed with swords and short muskets, and Ferragus was aware of noises in the streets again: a scream somewhere, the clatter of hooves and the sound of boots. He was in the daylight, hell had been shut up and the French had arrived.

And he was safe.

⁂

THE RIFLE BUTTS HAMMERED the sewer wall and Sharpe was instantly rewarded by the grating sound of bricks shifting. "Richard!" Vicente called warningly and Sharpe looked around and saw tiny glimmers of light sparking in the far recesses of the sewer. The glints flared, flashed and faded, reflecting their eerie light from things that glistened on the sides of the brick tunnel.

"Ferragus," Sharpe said, "chucking fire into the cellar. Is your rifle loaded, Jorge?"

"Of course."

"Just watch that way. But I doubt the buggers will come."

"Why wouldn't they?"

"Because they don't want to fight us down here," Sharpe said. "Because they don't want to wade through shit. Because they're frightened." He smashed the rifle into the old brickwork, hitting again and again in a kind of frenzy, and Harper worked beside him, timing his blows to strike at the same time as Sharpe's, and suddenly the ancient masonry collapsed. Some of the bricks cascaded down to Sharpe's feet, splashing his legs with sewage, but most fell into whatever space was beyond the wall. The good news was that they fell with a dry clatter, not with a splash that would announce they had only managed to break into one of the many cesspits dug beneath the houses of the lower town. "Can you get through, Pat?" Sharpe asked.

Harper did not answer, but just clambered through the black space. Sharpe turned again to watch the tiny sparks of falling fire that he reckoned were no more than a hundred paces away. The journey through the sewer had seemed much longer. A larger scrap fell, flared blue-green and splashed into oblivion, but not before its sheen of light had flickered off the walls to show that the tunnel was empty.

"It's another damned cellar," Harper said, his voice echoing in the dark.

"Take these," Sharpe said, and pushed his rifle and sword through the gap. Harper took the weapons, then Sharpe climbed up, scratching his belly on the rough edge of the shattered brickwork, then wriggling over onto a stone floor. The air was suddenly fresh. The stench was still there, of course, but less concentrated and he breathed deep before helping Harper lift the bundles of clothes through the hole. "Miss Fry? Give me your hands," Sharpe said, and he lifted her through the gap, stepped back and she fell against him so that her hair was against his face. "Are you all right?"

"I'm all right," she said. She smiled. "You're right, Mister Sharpe, and for some reason I am enjoying myself."

Harper was helping Vicente through the hole. Sharpe lifted Sarah gently. "You must get dressed, miss."

"I was thinking my life must change," she said, "but I wasn't expecting this." She was still holding him and he could feel she was shivering. Not with cold. He ran a hand down her back, tracing her spine. "There's light," she said in a kind of amazement, and Sharpe turned to see that there was indeed the faintest strip of gray at the far side of the wide room. He took Sarah's hand and groped his way past piles of what felt like pelts.

He realized that the room stank of leather, though that smell was a relief after the thickness of the stench inside the sewer. The gray strip was high, close to the ceiling, and Sharpe had to clamber up a pile of leather skins to discover that one pelt had been nailed across a small high window. He ripped it down to see that the window was only a foot high and crossed with thick iron bars, but it opened onto the pavement of a street which, after the last few hours, looked like a glimpse of heaven. The glass was filthy, but it still seemed as though the cellar was flooded with light.

"Sharpe!" Vicente said chidingly, and Sharpe twisted to see that the small light was revealing Sarah's near nakedness. She looked dazzled by the light, then ducked behind a stack of pelts.

"Time to get dressed, Jorge," Sharpe said. He fetched Sarah's bundle and took it to her. "I need my boots," he said, turning his back.

She sat down to take the boots off. "Here," she said, and Sharpe turned to see she was still almost naked as she held the boots up. There was a challenge in her eyes, almost as if she was astonished at her own daring.

Sharpe crouched. "You're going to be all right," he said. "Anyone as tough as you will survive this."

"From you, Mister Sharpe, is that a compliment?"

"Yes," he said, "and so's this," and he leaned forward to kiss her. She returned the kiss and smiled as he rocked back. "Sarah," he said.

"I think we've been introduced properly now," she allowed.

"Good," Sharpe said, then left her to dress.

"So what do we do now?" Harper asked when they were all clothed again.

"We get the hell out of here," Sharpe said. He twisted as he heard boots in the street, then saw feet going past the small window. "The army's still here," he said, "so we get out and make sure Ferragus loses all that food in the warehouse." He buckled on the sword belt and shouldered the rifle. "And then we arrest him," he went on, "stand him against a wall and shoot the bastard, though no doubt you'd like him to have a trial first, Jorge."

"You can just shoot him," Vicente said.

"Well said," Sharpe commented and crossed the room to where

some wooden steps climbed to a door. It was locked, evidently bolted on the far side, but the hinges were inside the cellar and their screws were sunk into rotted wood. He rammed his sword under one of the hinges, levered it cautiously in case the hinge was stronger than it looked, then gave it a good heave that splintered the screws out of the jamb. A troop of cavalry clattered past outside. "They must be leaving," Sharpe said, moving the sword to the lower hinge, "so let's hope the French aren't too close."

The second hinge tore out of the frame and Sharpe pulled on it to force the door inwards. It tilted on the bolt, but opened far enough for him to see down a passageway that had a heavy door at its far end and, just as Sharpe was about to step through the half-blocked opening, someone began thumping that far door. He could see it shaking, could see the dust jarring off its timbers, and he held up a hand to caution his companions to silence as he backed away. "What day is it?" he asked.

Vicente thought for a second. "Monday?" he guessed. "October the first?"

"Jesus," Sharpe said, wondering whether the horses in the street had been French and not British. "Sarah? Get up close to the window and tell me if you can see a horse."

She scrambled up, pressed her face against the grimy glass, and nodded. "Two horses," she said.

"Do they have docked tails?"

"Docked?"

"Are their tails cut off?" The door at the passageway's end was shaking with the blows and he knew it must give way at any second.

Sarah looked through the glass again. "No."

"Then it's the French," Sharpe said. "See if you can block the window, love. Push a piece of leather against it. Then hide! Go back to Pat."

The cellar went dark again as Sarah propped a stiff piece of leather over the small window, then she went back to join Harper and Vicente in the far corner where they were concealed by one of the massive heaps of hides. Sharpe stayed, watching the far door shake, then it splintered inwards and he saw the blue uniform and white crossbelt and he backed away down the steps. "Frogs," he said grimly, and crossed the cellar and crouched with the others.

There was a cheer as the French broke into the house. Footsteps were loud on the floorboards above, then someone kicked at the half-broken cellar door and Sharpe could hear voices. French voices and not happy voices. The men evidently paused at the cellar door and one made a sound of disgust, presumably at the stench of sewage. "*Merde*," one of the voices said.

"*C'est un puisard.*" Another spoke.

"He says it's a cesspit," Sarah whispered in Sharpe's ear, then there was a splashing sound as one of the soldiers urinated down the steps. There was a burst of laughter, then the Frenchmen went away. Sharpe, crouching close beside Sarah in the cellar's darkest corner, heard the distant sounds of boots and hooves, voices and screaming. A shot sounded, then another. It was not the sound of battle, for that was many shots melding together to make an unending crackle, but single shots as men blew off padlocks or just fired for the hell of it.

"The French are here?" Harper asked in disbelief.

"The whole damn army," Sharpe said. He loaded his rifle, shoved the ramrod back in its hoops, then waited. He heard boots clattering down the stairs in the house above, more boots in the passageway and then there was silence and he decided the French had gone to find a wealthier place to plunder. "We're going up," he said, "to the attic." Perhaps it was because he had been underground too long, or perhaps it was just an instinct to get high, but he knew they could not stay here. Eventually some Frenchmen would search the whole cellar and so he led them through the stacked hides and up the steps. The outer door was open, showing sunlight in the streets, but there was no one in sight and so he ran down the passage, saw stairs to his right and took them two at a time.

The house was empty. The French had searched it and found nothing except some heavy tables, stools and beds, so they had gone to look for richer pickings. At the top of the second flight of stairs was a broken door, its padlock split away, and above it was a narrow staircase that climbed to a set of attic rooms that seemed to extend across three or four houses. The largest room, long, low and narrow, had a dozen low wooden beds. "Student quarters," Vicente said.

There were screams from nearby houses, the sound of shots, then voices down below and Sharpe reckoned more troops had come to the house. "The window," he said, and pushed the closest one open and climbed through to find himself in a gutter that ran just behind a low stone parapet. The others followed Sharpe who found a refuge at the northern gable end that was not overlooked by any of the attic windows. He peered over the parapet into a narrow, shadowed alley. A French cavalryman, a woman across his pommel, rode beneath Sharpe. The woman screamed and the man slapped her rump, then hauled up her black dress and slapped it again. "They're having fun and games," Sharpe said sourly.

He could hear the French in the attic rooms, but none came out onto the roof and Sharpe sat back on the tiles and stared uphill. The great university buildings dominated the skyline, and beneath them were thousands of roofs and church towers. The streets were flooding with the invaders, but none were up high, though here and there Sharpe could see frightened people who, like him, had taken refuge on the tiles. He was trying to find Ferragus's warehouse. He knew it was not far away, knew it had a high, pitched roof, and finally reckoned he had spotted it a hundred or more paces up the hill.

He looked across the alley. The houses on the far side had the same kind of parapet protecting their roof and he reckoned he could jump the gap easily enough, but Vicente, with his wounded shoulder, might be clumsy, and Sarah's long, torn frock would hamper her. "You're going to stay here, Jorge," he told Vicente, "and look after Miss Fry. Pat and I are going exploring."

"We are?"

"Got anything better to do, Pat?"

"We can come with you," Vicente said.

"Better if you stay here, Jorge," Sharpe said, then took out his pocket knife and unfolded the blade. "Have you ever looked after wounds?" he asked Sarah.

She shook her head.

"Time to learn," Sharpe said. "Take the bandage off Jorge's shoulder and find the bullet. Take it out. Take out any scraps of his shirt or jacket. If he tells you to stop because it's hurting, dig harder. Be ruthless. Dig out the bullet and anything else, then clean up the wound. Use this." He gave her his canteen that still had a little water in it. "Then make a new bandage," he went on, before laying Vicente's loaded rifle beside her, "and if a Frog comes out here, shoot him. Pat and I will hear and we'll come back." Sharpe doubted that he or Harper could recognize a rifle's bark amidst all the other shots, but he reckoned Sarah might need the reassurance. "Think you can do all that?"

She hesitated, then nodded. "I can."

"It's going to hurt like hell, Jorge," Sharpe warned, "but God knows if we can find you a doctor in this town today, so let Miss Fry do her best." He straightened up and turned to Harper. "Can you jump that alley, Pat?"

"God save Ireland." Harper looked at the gap between the houses. "It's a terrible long way, sir."

"So make sure you don't fall," Sharpe said, then stood on the parapet where it made a right angle to the alleyway. He gave himself a few paces to build up speed, then ran and made a desperate leap across the void. He made it easily, clearing the far parapet and crashing into the roof tiles so that agony flared in his ribs. He scrambled aside and watched as Harper, bigger and less lithe, followed him. The Sergeant landed right across the parapet, winding himself as its edge drove into his belly, but Sharpe grabbed his jacket and hauled him over.

"I said it was a long way," Harper said.

"You eat too much."

"Jesus, in this army?" Harper said, then dusted himself off and followed Sharpe along the next gutter. They passed skylights and windows, but no one was inside to see them. In places the parapet had crumbled away and Sharpe scrambled up to the roof ridge because it gave them safer footing. They negotiated a dozen chimneys, then slid down to another alley and another jump. "This one's narrower," Sharpe said to encourage Harper.

"Where are we going, sir?"

"The warehouse," Sharpe said, pointing to its great stone gable.

Harper eyed the gap. "It would be easier to go through the sewer," he grumbled.

"If you want to, Pat. Meet me there."

"I've come this far," Harper said, and winced as Sharpe made the leap. He followed, arriving safely, and the two clambered up the next roof and along its ridge until they arrived at the street which divided the block of houses from the building Sharpe reckoned was the warehouse.

Sharpe slid down the tile slope to the gutter by the parapet, then peered over. He pulled back instantly. "Dragoons," he said.

"How many?"

"Dozen? Twenty?" He was sure it was the warehouse. He had seen the big double doors, one of them ajar, and from the roof ridge he had just seen the skylights on the warehouse which was slightly higher up the hill. The street was too wide to be jumped, so there was no way of reaching those skylights from this roof, but then Sharpe peered again and saw that the dragoons were not plundering. Every other Frenchman in the city seemed to have been let off the leash, but these dragoons were sitting on their horses, their swords drawn, and he realized they must have been posted to guard the warehouse. They were turning French infantrymen away, using the flat of their swords if any became too insistent. "They've got the bloody food, Pat."

"And they're welcome to it."

"No, they're bloody not," Sharpe said savagely.

"So how in Christ are we supposed to take it away from them?"

"I'm not sure," Sharpe said. He knew the food had to be taken away if the French were to be beaten, yet for a moment he was tempted to let the whole thing slide. To hell with it. The army had treated him badly, so why the hell should he care? Yet he did care, and he would be damned before Ferragus helped the French win the war. The noise in the city was getting louder, the noise of screaming, of disorder, of chaos let loose, and the frequent musket shots were startling hundreds of pigeons into the air. He peered a third time at the dragoons and saw how they had formed two lines to block the ends of the small street to keep the French infantry away from the warehouse. Scores of men were protesting to the dragoons and Sharpe guessed that the horsemen's presence had started a rumor that there was food in the street, and the infantry, who had become ever more hungry as they marched through a stripped land, were probably desperate with hunger. "I'm not sure," Sharpe said again, "but I've got an idea."

"An idea for what, sir?"

"To keep those bastards hungry," Sharpe said, which was what Wellington wanted, so Sharpe would give it to his lordship. He would keep the bastards hungry.

CHAPTER 9

A CHIEF COMMISSARY CAME to inspect the food. He was a small man named Laurent Poquelin, short, stocky and bald as an egg, but with long mustaches that he twisted nervously whenever he was worried, and he had been much worried in the last few weeks, for l'Armée de Portugal had found itself in a land emptied of food and he was responsible for feeding sixty-five thousand men, seventeen thousand cavalry horses and another three thousand assorted horses and mules. It could not be done in a wasted land, in a place where every orchard had been stripped of fruit, where the larders had been emptied, the storehouses despoiled, the wells poisoned, the livestock driven away, the mills disassembled and the ovens broken. The Emperor himself could not do it! All the forces of heaven could not do it, yet Poquelin was expected to work the miracle, and his mustache tips were ragged with nerves. He had been ordered to carry three weeks of supplies with the army, and those supplies had existed in the depots of Spain, but there were not nearly enough draught animals to carry such an amount, and even though Masséna had reluctantly cut each division's artillery from twelve guns to eight, and released those horses to haul wagons instead of cannon, Poquelin had still only managed to supply the army for a week. Then the hunger had set in. Dragoons and hussars had been sent miles away from the army's line of march to search for food, and each such foray had worn out more horses, and the cavalry moaned at him because there were no replacement horseshoes, and some cavalrymen died each time because the Portuguese peasantry ambushed them in the hills. It did not seem to matter how many such peasants were hanged or shot, because more came to harass the foraging parties, which meant more horsemen had to be sent to protect the foragers, and more horseshoes were needed, and there were no more horseshoes and Poquelin got the blame. And the foragers rarely did find food, and if they did they usually ate most of it themselves, and Poquelin got the blame for that too. He had begun to wish he had followed his mother's tearful advice and become a priest, anything would be better than serving in an army that was sucking on a dry teat and accusing him of inefficiency.

Yet now the miracle had happened. At a stroke, Poquelin's troubles were over.

There was food. Such food! Ferragus, a surly Portuguese merchant who made Poquelin shiver with fear, had provided a warehouse that was as crammed with supplies as any depot in France. There was barley, wheat, rice, biscuits, rum, cheese, maize, dried fish, lemons, beans, salt meat, enough to feed the army for a month! There were other valuables too. There were barrels of lamp oil, coils of twine, boxes of horseshoes, bags of nails, casks of gunpowder, a sack of horn buttons, stacks of candles and bolts of cloth, none of them as essential as food, but all profitable because, though Poquelin would issue the food, the other things he could sell for his own enrichment.

He explored the warehouse, followed by a trio of *fourriers*, quartermaster-corporals, who noted the list of supplies that Ferragus was selling. It was impossible to list all of it, for the food was in stacks that would take a score of men hours to dismantle, but Poquelin, a thorough man, did order the *fourriers* to remove grain sacks from the top of one pile to make certain that the center of the heap was not composed of bags of sand. He did the same with some barrels of salt beef and both times was assured that all was well, and as the estimates of the food rose, so Poquelin's spirits soared. There were even two wagons inside the warehouse and, for an army short of all wheeled transport, those two vehicles were almost as valuable as food.

Then he began to worry at the frayed ends of his mustaches. He had food, and thus the army's problems seemed solved, but, as ever, there was a cockroach in the soup. How could these new supplies be moved? It would be no use issuing several days' rations to the troops, for they would gorge themselves on the whole lot in the first hour, then complain of hunger by nightfall, and Poquelin had far too few horses and mules to carry this vast amount. Still, he had to try. "Have the city searched for carts," he ordered one of the *fourriers*, "any cart. Handcarts, wheelbarrows, anything! We need men to haul the carts. Round up civilians to push the carts."

"I'm to do all that?" the *fourrier* asked in amazement, his voice muffled because he was eating a piece of cheese.

"I shall talk to the Marshal," Poquelin said grandly, then scowled. "Are you eating?"

"Got a sore tooth, sir," the man mumbled. "All swollen up, sir. Doctor says he wants to pull it. Permission to go and have tooth pulled, sir."

"Refused," Poquelin said. He was tempted to draw his sword and beat the man for insolence, but he had never drawn the weapon and was afraid that if he tried then he would discover that the blade had rusted to the scabbard's throat. He contented himself with striking the man with his hand. "We must set an example," he snapped. "If the army is hungry, we are hungry. We don't eat the army's food. You are a fool. What are you?"

"A fool, sir," the *fourrier* dutifully replied, but at least he was no longer quite such a hungry fool.

"Take a dozen men and search for carts. Anything with wheels," Poquelin ordered, confident that Marshal Masséna would approve of his idea to use Portuguese civilians as draught animals. The army was expected to march south in a day or two, and the rumor was that the British and Portuguese would make a last stand in the hills north of Lisbon, so Poquelin only needed to make a new depot some forty or fifty miles to the south. He had some transport, of course, enough to carry perhaps a quarter of the food, and those existing mules and wagons could come back for more, which meant the warehouse needed to be protected while its precious contents were laboriously moved closer to Lisbon. Poquelin hurried back to the warehouse door and looked for the dragoon Colonel who was guarding the street. "Dumesnil!"

Colonel Dumesnil, like all French soldiers, despised the commissary. He turned his horse with insolent slowness, rode to Poquelin so that he towered above him, then let his drawn sword drop so that it vaguely threatened the small man. "You want me?"

"You have checked that there are no other doors to the warehouse?"

"Of course I haven't," Dumesnil said sarcastically.

"No one must get in, you understand? No one! The army is saved, Colonel, saved!"

"*Alléluia*," Dumesnil said dryly.

"I shall inform Marshal Masséna that you are responsible for the safety of these supplies," Poquelin said pompously.

Dumesnil leaned from the saddle. "Marshal Masséna himself gave me my orders, little man," he said, "and I obey my orders. I don't need more from you."

"You need more men," Poquelin said, worried because the two squads of dragoons, barring the street on either side of the warehouse doors, were already holding back crowds of hungry soldiers. "Why are those men here?" he demanded petulantly.

"Because rumor says there's food in there," Dumesnil flicked his sword towards the warehouse, "and because they're hungry. But for Christ's sake stop fretting! I have enough men. You do your job, Poquelin, and stop telling me how to do mine."

Poquelin, content that he had done his duty by stressing to Dumesnil how important the food was, went to find Colonel Barreto who was waiting with Major Ferreira and the alarming Ferragus beside the warehouse doors. "It is all good," Poquelin told Barreto. "There is even more than you told us!"

Barreto translated for Ferragus who, in turn, asked a question. "The gentleman," Barreto said to Poquelin, his sarcasm obvious, "wishes to know when he will be paid."

"Now," Poquelin said, though it was not in his power to issue payment. Yet he wanted to convey the good news to Masséna, and the Marshal would surely pay when he heard that the army had more than enough food to see it to Lisbon. That was all that was needed. Just to reach Lisbon, for even the British could not empty that great city of all its supplies. A treasure trove waited in Lisbon and now the Emperor's Army of Portugal had been given the means to reach it.

The dragoons moved aside to let Poquelin and his companions through. Then the horsemen closed up again. Scores of hungry infantry-men had heard about the food and they were shouting that it should be distributed now, but Colonel Dumesnil was quite ready to kill them if they attempted to help themselves. He sat, hard-faced, unmoving, his long sword drawn, a soldier with orders, which meant the food was in se-cure hands and the Army of Portugal was safe.

SHARPE AND HARPER made the return run to the roof where Vicente and Sarah waited. Vicente was bent over in apparent pain, while Sarah, her black silk dress gleaming with spots of fresh blood, looked pale. "What happened?" Sharpe asked.

In reply she showed Sharpe the bloodstained knife blade. "I did get the bullet out," she said in a small voice.

"Well done."

"And lots of cloth scraps," she added more confidently.

"Even better," Sharpe said.

Vicente leaned back against the tiles. He was barechested and a new bandage, torn from his shirt, was crudely wrapped about his shoulder. Blood had oozed through the cloth.

"Hurts, eh?" Sharpe asked.

"It hurts," Vicente said dryly.

"It was difficult," Sarah said, "but he didn't make a noise."

"That's because he's a soldier," Sharpe said. "Can you move your arm?" he asked Vicente.

"I think so."

"Try," Sharpe said. Vicente looked appalled, then understood the sense in the order and, flinching with pain, managed to raise his left arm, which suggested the shoulder joint was not mangled. "You're going to be right as rain, Jorge," Sharpe said, "so long as we keep that wound clean." He glanced at Harper. "Maggots?"

"Not now, sir," Harper said, "only if the wound goes bad."

"Maggots?" Vicente asked faintly. "Did you say maggots?"

"Nothing better, sir," Harper said enthusiastically. "Best thing for a dirty wound. Put the little buggers in, they clean it up, leave the good flesh, and you're good as new." He patted his haversack. "I always carry a half-dozen. Much better than going to a surgeon because all those bastards ever want to do is cut you up."

"I hate surgeons," Sharpe said.

"He hates lawyers," Vicente said to Sarah, "and now he hates surgeons. Is there anyone he likes?"

"Women," Sharpe said, "I do like women." He was looking over the city, listening to screams and shots, and he knew from the noise that French discipline had crumbled. Coimbra was in chaos, given over to lust, hate and fire. Three plumes of smoke were already boiling from the narrow streets to obscure the clear morning sky and he suspected more would soon join them. "They're firing houses," he said, "and we've got work to do." He bent down and scooped up some pigeon dung that he pushed into the barrels of Harper's volley gun. He used the stickiest he could find, carefully placing a small amount into each muzzle. "Ram it down, Pat," he said. The dung would act as wadding to hold the balls in place when the barrels were tipped downwards, and what he planned would mean pointing the gun straight down. "Do many of the houses here have student quarters?" he asked Vicente.

"A lot, yes."

"Like this one?" He gestured at the roof beside them. "With rooms stretching through the attic?"

"It's very common," Vicente said, "they are called *repúblicas*, some are whole houses, others are just parts of houses. Each one has its own government. Every member has a vote, and when I was here they . . ."

"It's all right, Jorge, tell me later," Sharpe said. "I just hope the houses opposite the warehouse are a *república*." He should have looked when he was there, but he had not thought of it. "And what we need now," he went on, "are uniforms."

"Uniforms?" Vicente asked.

"Frog uniforms, Jorge. Then we can join the carnival. How are you feeling?"

"Weak."

"You can rest here for a few minutes," Sharpe said, "while Pat and I get some new clothes."

Sharpe and Harper edged back down the gutter and climbed through the open window into the deserted attic. "My ribs bloody hurt," Sharpe complained as he straightened up.

"Did you wrap them?" Harper asked. "Never get better unless you wrap them up."

"Didn't want to see the angel of death," Sharpe grumbled. The angel of death was the battalion doctor, a Scotsman whose ministrations were known as the last rites.

"I'll wrap the buggers for you," Harper said, "when we've a minute." He went to the doorway and listened to voices below. Sharpe followed him down the stairs, which they took slowly, careful not to make too much noise. A girl began screaming on the next floor. She stopped suddenly as if she had been hit, then started again. Harper reached the landing and moved towards the door where the screaming came from.

"No blood," Sharpe whispered to him. A uniform jacket sheeted with new blood would make them too distinctive. Men's voices came from the lower floor, but they were taking no interest in the girl above. "Make it fast," Sharpe said, edging past the Irishman, "and brutal as you like."

Sharpe pushed the door open and kept moving, seeing three men in the room. Two were holding the girl on the floor while the third, a big man who had stripped off his jacket and lowered his breeches to his ankles, was just getting down on his knees when Sharpe's rifle butt took him in the base of his skull. It was a vicious blow, hard enough to throw the man forward onto the girl's naked belly. Sharpe reckoned the man had to be out of the fight, drew the rifle back and hit the left-hand man on the jaw and he heard the bone crack and saw the whole jaw twist awry. He sensed the third man going down to Harper's blow and finished off the man with the broken jaw by another slam of the brass-sheathed butt to the side of his skull. By the feel of the blow he had fractured the man's skull, then he was gripped around the legs by the first man who had somehow survived the initial assault. The man, hampered by his lowered breeches, clawed at Sharpe's groin, unbalancing him, then the heavy butt of the volley gun slammed into the back of his skull and he slid down, groaning. Harper gave him a last tap as a keepsake.

The girl, stripped naked, stared up in horror and was about to scream again as Harper snatched up her clothes, but then he put his finger to his lips. She held her breath, gazing up at him, and Harper smiled at her, then gave her the clothes. "Get dressed, sweetheart," he said.

"*Inglês?*" she asked, pulling the torn dress over her head.

Harper looked horrified. "I'm Irish, darling," he said.

"For God's sake, lover boy," Sharpe said, "get the hell up the stairs and fetch the other two down."

"Yes, sir," Harper said and went to the door. The girl, seeing him go, gave a small cry of alarm. The Irishman looked back at her, winked at her, and the girl snatched up the rest of her clothes and followed him, leaving Sharpe with the three men. The big man, who had taken such a beating, showed signs of recovery, lifting his head and scrabbling on the floor with a calloused hand, so Sharpe drew the man's own bayonet and slid it up between his ribs. There was very little blood. The man gave a heave, opened his eyes once to look at Sharpe, then there was a rattling noise in his throat and his head dropped. He lay still.

The other two men, both very young, were unconscious. Sharpe reckoned the one whose jaw he had broken and dislocated would probably die from the blow on the skull. He was white-faced and blood was trickling from his ear, and he gave no sign of consciousness as Sharpe stripped off his clothes. The second, whom Harper had hit, groaned as he was stripped, and Sharpe thumped him into silence. Then he peeled off his own jacket and pulled on a blue one. It fitted him well enough. It buttoned to one side of the broad white facing that blazoned the front and which ended at his waist, though a pair of tails hung down behind. The tails had white turnbacks decorated with pairs of red flaming grenades, which meant the jacket's true owner was from a grenadier company. The high stiff collar was red and the shoulders had brief red epaulettes. He pulled on the soldier's white crossbelt that was fastened at the left shoulder by the epaulette's strap, and from which hung the bayonet. He decided against taking the man's white trousers. He already wore the overalls of a French cavalry officer, and though the mix of coat and overalls was unusual, few soldiers were uniformed properly after they had been on campaign for a few weeks. He strapped his own sword belt beneath the coat tails and knew that was a risk, for no ordinary soldier would carry a sword, but he assumed men would think he had plundered the weapon. He hung his rifle on his shoulder, knowing that to any casual glance the weapon resembled a musket. He emptied the man's oxhide pack and put in his own jacket and shako, then pulled on the soldier's shako, a confection of red and black blazoned on the front with a brass plate showing an eagle above the number 19, making Sharpe a new recruit to the 19th Infantry of the Line. The cartridge box, which hung beneath the bayonet at the end of the crossbelt, had a brass badge of a grenade mounted on its lid.

Harper came back and looked startled for a second at the sight of Sharpe in enemy blue, then he grinned. "Suits you, sir." Vicente and the two girls followed. Sharpe saw that the Portuguese girl was young, perhaps fifteen, with bright eyes and long dark hair. She saw the trace of blood on the shirt of the man who had been about to rape her, then spat on him and, before anyone could stop her, she snatched up a bayonet and stabbed the neck of one of the other two, making blood spurt high up the wall. Vicente opened his mouth to protest, then fell silent. Eighteen months before, when Sharpe had first met him, Vicente's legal mind had balked at such summary punishment of rapists. Now he said nothing as the girl spat on the man she had killed, then went to the second, who was lying on his back and breathing with a hoarse sound from his broken jaw. She stood over him, poising the bayonet above his twisted mouth.

"I never did like rapists," Sharpe said mildly.

"Scum," Harper agreed, "pure bloody scum."

Sarah watched, not wanting to watch, but unable to take her eyes off the bayonet that the girl held two-handed. The girl paused, reveling in the moment, then stabbed down. "Get yourselves dressed," Sharpe told Vicente and Harper. The dying man gurgled behind him and his heels briefly drummed against the floor. "Ask her name," Sharpe told Sarah.

"She's called Joana Jacinto," Sarah said after a short conversation. "She lives here. Her father worked on the river, but she doesn't know where he is now. And she says to thank you."

"Pretty name, Joana," Harper said, dressed now as a French sergeant, "and she's a useful sort of girl, eh? Knows how to use a bayonet."

Sharpe helped Vicente put on the blue jacket, letting it hang from the left shoulder rather than force Vicente's arm into the sleeve. "She says," Sarah had held another conversation with Joana "that she wants to stay with us."

"Of course she must," Harper said before Sharpe could offer an opinion. Joana's dark brown dress had been torn at the breasts when the soldiers stripped her, and the remnants had been splashed with blood when she killed the second soldier, and so she buttoned one of the dead men's shirts over it, then picked up a musket. Sarah, not wanting to appear less belligerent, shouldered another.

It was not much of a force. Two riflemen, two women and a wounded Portuguese cazador. But Sharpe reckoned it should be enough to break a French dream.

So he slung his rifle, hitched the sword belt higher, and led them downstairs.

⚜

MOST OF THE FRENCH INFANTRY in Coimbra were from the 8th Corps, a newly raised unit of young men fresh from the depots of France, and they were half trained, ill disciplined, resentful of an Emperor who had marched them to a war they mostly did not understand and, above all, hungry. Hundreds broke ranks to explore the university, but, finding little that they wanted, they took out their frustration by smashing, mangling and shattering whatever could be broken. Coimbra was renowned for its work on optics, but microscopes were of small use to soldiers and so they hammered the beautiful instruments with muskets, then wrenched apart the fine sextants. A handful of telescopes were saved, for such things were valued, but the larger instruments, too long to carry, were destroyed, while an unparalleled set of finely ground lenses, cushioned by velvet in a cabinet of wide, shallow drawers, was systematically broken. One room was filled with chronometers, all being tested, and they were reduced to bent springs, cogwheels and shattered cases. A fine assembly of fossils was pounded to shards and a collection of minerals, a lifetime's work carefully catalogued into quartzes and spars and ores, was scattered from a window. Fine porcelain was shattered, pictures torn from their frames and if most of the library was spared that was only because there were too many volumes to be destroyed. Some men nevertheless tried, pulling rare books from the shelves and tearing them apart, but they soon got bored and contented themselves with smashing some fine Roman vases that stood on gilded pediments. There was no sense in it, except the anger that the soldiers felt. They hated the Portuguese and so they took their revenge on what their enemy valued.

Coimbra's Old Cathedral had been built by two Frenchmen in the twelfth century and now other Frenchmen whooped with delight because so many women had taken shelter close to its altars. A handful of men tried to protect their wives and daughters, but the muskets fired, the men died and the screaming began. Other soldiers shot at the gilded high altar, aiming at the carved saints guarding the sad-faced Virgin. A six-year-old child tried to pull a soldier off his mother and had his throat cut, and when a woman would not stop screaming a sergeant cut her throat as well. In the New Cathedral, up the hill, voltigeurs took it in turns to piss into the baptismal font and, when it was full, they christened the girls they had captured in the building, giving them all the same name, *Putain*, which meant whore. A sergeant then auctioned the weeping girls, whose hair dripped with urine.

In the church of Santa Cruz, which was older than the Old Cathedral, the troops found the tombs of Portugal's first two kings. The beautifully sculpted sepulchers were wrenched apart, the coffins shattered and the bones of Alfonso the Conqueror, who had liberated Lisbon from the Muslims in the twelfth century, were hauled from their winding cloth and thrown across the floor. His son, Sancho I, had been buried in a white linen shift edged with cloth of gold, and an artilleryman ripped the shroud away and draped it about his shoulders before dancing on the remnants of the corpse. There was a gold cross studded with jewels in Sancho's tomb and three soldiers fought over it. One died, and the other two hacked the cross apart and shared it. There were more women in Santa Cruz and they suffered as the other women were suffering, while their men were taken into the Cloisters of Silence and shot.

Mostly the soldiers wanted food. They broke into houses, kicked open cellars and searched for anything they could eat. There was plenty, for the city had never been properly stripped of foodstuffs, but there were too many soldiers, and anger grew when some men ate and others stayed hungry, and the anger turned into fury when it was fuelled by the lavish supplies of wine discovered in the taverns. A rumor spread that there was a great stock of food in a warehouse in the lower town, and hundreds of men converged on it, only to find the hoard guarded by dragoons. Some stayed, hoping the dragoons would go away, while others went to find women or plunder.

A few men tried to prevent the destruction. An officer attempted to pull two artillerymen off a woman and was kicked to the ground, then stabbed with a sword. A pious sergeant, offended at what went on in the Old Cathedral, was shot. Most officers, knowing it was hopeless to try and stop the orgy of destruction, barricaded themselves in houses and waited for the madness to subside, while others simply joined in.

Marshal Masséna, escorted by hussars and accompanied by his aides and by his mistress, who was fetchingly dressed in a sky-blue hussar's uniform, found a billet in the Archbishop's palace. Two infantry colonels came to the palace and complained of the troops' behavior, but they got small sympathy from the Marshal. "They deserve a little respite," he said. "It's been a hard march, a hard march. And they're like horses. They go better if you ease the curb rein from time to time. So let them play, gentlemen, let them play." He made certain Henriette was comfortable in the Archbishop's bedroom. She disliked the crucifixes hanging on the walls so Masséna jettisoned them through the window, then asked what she would like to eat. "Grapes and wine," she said, and Masséna ordered one of his servants to ransack the palace kitchens and find both.

"And if there are none, sir?" the servant asked.

"Of course there are grapes and wine!" Masséna snapped. "Good

Christ Almighty, can nothing be done without questions in this army? Find the damned grapes, find the damned wine, and take them to mademoiselle!" He went back to the palace's dining room where maps had been spread on the Archbishop's table. They were poor maps, inspired more by imagination than by topography, but one of Masséna's aides thought better ones might exist in the university, and he was right, though by the time he found them they had been reduced to ashes.

The army's Generals assembled in the dining room where Masséna planned the next stage of the campaign. He had been rebuffed at Bussaco, but that defeat had not prevented him turning the enemy's left flank and thus chasing the British and Portuguese out of central Portugal. Masséna's army was now on the Mondego and the enemy was retreating towards Lisbon, but that still left the Marshal with other enemies. Hunger assailed his troops, as did the Portuguese irregulars who closed behind his forces like wolves following a flock of sheep. General Junot suggested it was time for a pause. "The British are taking to their ships," he said, "so let them go. Then send a corps to retake the roads back to Almeida."

Almeida was the Portuguese frontier fortress where the invasion had begun, and it lay over a hundred miles eastwards at the end of the monstrously difficult roads across which the French army had struggled. "To what end?" Masséna asked.

"So supplies can get through," Junot declared, "supplies and reinforcements."

"What reinforcements?" The question was sarcastic.

"Drouet's corps?" Junot suggested.

"They won't move," Masséna said sourly, "they won't be permitted to move." The Emperor had ordered that Masséna was to be given 130,000 men for the invasion, but less than half that number had assembled on the frontier and when Masséna had pleaded for more men, the Emperor had sent a message that his present forces were adequate, that the enemy was risible and the task of invading Portugal easy. Yet the Emperor was not here. The Emperor did not command an army of half-starved men whose shoes were falling apart, an army whose supply lines were non-existent because the damned Portuguese peasants controlled the roads winding through the hills to Almeida. Marshal Masséna did not want to return to those hills. Get to Lisbon, he thought, get to Lisbon. "The roads from here to Lisbon," he asked, "are better than those we've traveled?"

"A hundred times better," one of his Portuguese aides answered.

The Marshal went to a window and stared at the smoke rising from buildings burning in the city. "Are we sure the British are making for the sea?"

"Where else can they go?" a general retorted.

"Lisbon?"

"Can't be defended," the Portuguese aide observed.

"To the north?" Masséna turned back to the table and stabbed a finger onto the hatch marks of a map. "These hills?" He was pointing to the terrain north of Lisbon where hills stretched for over thirty-two kilometers between the Atlantic and the wide river Tagus.

"They're low hills," the aide said, "and there are three roads through them and a dozen usable tracks besides."

"But this Wellington might offer battle there."

"He risks losing his army if he does," Marshal Ney intervened.

Masséna remembered the sound of the volleys from the ridge at Bussaco and imagined his men struggling into such fire again, then despised himself for indulging in fear. "We can maneuver him out of the hills," he suggested, and it was a sensible idea, for the enemy's army was surely not large enough to guard a front twenty miles wide. Threaten it in one place, Masséna thought, and launch the Eagles through the hills ten miles away. "There are forts in the hills, yes?" he asked.

"We've heard rumors that he's making forts to guard the roads," the Portuguese aide answered.

"So we march through the hills," Masséna said. That way the new forts could be left to rot while Wellington's army was surrounded, humiliated, and defeated. The Marshal stared at the map and imagined the colors of the defeated army being paraded through Paris and thrown at the feet of the Emperor. "We can turn his flank again," he said, "but not if we give him time to escape. He has to be hurried."

"So we march south?" Ney asked.

"In two days," Masséna decided. He knew he needed that much time for his army to recover from its capture of Coimbra. "Let them stay off the leash today," he said, "and tomorrow we'll whip them back to the Eagles and make sure they're ready for departure on Wednesday."

"And what will the men eat?" Junot asked.

"Whatever they damn well can," Masséna snapped. "And there has to be food here, doesn't there? The English can't have scraped a whole city bare."

"There is food." A new voice spoke and the Generals, resplendent in blue, red and gold, turned from their maps to see Chief Commissary Poquelin looking unusually pleased with himself.

"How much food?" Masséna asked caustically.

"Enough to see us to Lisbon, sir," Poquelin said, "more than enough." For days now he had tried to avoid the Generals for fear of the scorn they heaped on him, but Poquelin's hour had come. This was his triumph. The commissary had done its work. "I need transport," he said, "and a good battalion to help move the supplies, but we have all we need. More! If you remember, sir, you promised to buy these supplies? The man has kept faith. He's waiting outside."

Masséna half remembered making the promise, but now that the food was in his possession he was tempted to break the promise. The army's treasury was not large and it was not the French way to buy supplies that could be stolen. Live off the land, the Emperor always said.

Colonel Barreto, who had come to the palace with Poquelin, saw the indecision on Masséna's face. "If we renege on this promise, sir," he said respectfully, "then no one in Portugal will believe us. And in a week or two we shall be governing here. We shall need cooperation."

"Cooperation." Marshal Ney spat the word. "A guillotine in Lisbon will make them cooperate quickly enough."

Masséna shook his head. Barreto was right, and it was foolish to make new enemies at the very brink of victory. "Pay him," he said, nodding to an aide who kept the key to the money chest. "And in two days," he went on to Poquelin, "you start moving the supplies south. I want a depot at Leiria."

"Leiria?" Poquelin asked.

"Here, man, here!" Masséna stabbed a map with his forefinger, and

Poquelin nervously edged through the Generals to look for the town which, he discovered, lay some forty miles south of Coimbra on the Lisbon road.

"I need wagons," Poquelin said.

"You will have every wagon and mule we possess," Masséna promised grandly.

"There aren't enough horses," Junot said sourly.

"There are never enough horses!" Masséna snapped. "So use men. Use these damned peasants." He waved at the window, indicating the town. "Harness them, whip them, make them work!"

"And the wounded?" Junot asked in alarm. Wagons would be needed to carry the wounded southwards if they were to stay with the army and thus be protected from the Portuguese irregulars.

"They can stay here," Masséna decided.

"And who guards them?"

"I shall find men," Masséna said, impatient with such quibbles. What mattered was that he had food, the enemy was retreating, and Lisbon was only a hundred miles to the south. The campaign was half complete, but from now on his army would be marching on good roads, so this was no time for caution, it was time to attack.

And in two weeks, he thought, he would have Lisbon and the war would be won.

⚜

SHARPE HAD NO SOONER GONE into the street than a man tried to snatch Sarah away from his side. She hardly looked beguiling for her crumpled black dress was torn at the hem, her hair had come loose and her face was dirty, yet the man seized her arm, then protested wildly as Sharpe pinned him against the wall with his rifle butt. Sarah spat at the man and added a couple of words which she hoped were rude enough to shock him. "You speak French?" Sharpe asked Sarah, careless that the French soldier could overhear him.

"French, Portuguese and Spanish," she said.

Sharpe thumped the man in the groin for a remembrance, then led his companions past the bodies of two men, both Portuguese, who lay on the cobbles. One had been eviscerated and his blood trickled ten feet down the gutter from his corpse which was being sniffed by a three-legged dog. A window broke above them, showering them with glittering shards. A woman screamed, and the bells in one of the churches began a terrible cacophony. None of the French soldiers took any notice of them other than to ask if they had finished with the two girls, and only Sarah and Vicente understood those questions. The street became more crowded as they went uphill and got closer to where, rumor said, there was food enough for a multitude. Sharpe and Harper used their size to bully past soldiers, then, reaching the houses that stood opposite Ferragus's warehouse, Sharpe went into the first door and climbed the stairs. A woman, blood on her face and clutching a baby, shrank from them on the landing, then Sharpe was up the last flight of stairs and discovered, to his relief, that the attic here was like the first, a long room that overlaid the separate houses beneath. There had been a score of students living up here, now their beds were overturned, all except one on which a French soldier slept. He woke as their footsteps sounded loud on the boards and, seeing the two women, rolled off the bed. Sharpe was opening a window onto the roof and turned as the man held out his hands to Sarah who smiled at him and then, with surprising force, rammed the muzzle of her French musket into his belly. The man let out his breath in a gasp, bent over, and Joana hit him with the stock of her musket, swinging it in a haymaker's blow to crack the butt onto his forehead, and the man, without a sound, collapsed backwards. Sarah grinned, discovering abilities she had not suspected.

"Stay here with the women," Sharpe told Vicente, "and be ready to run like hell." He was going to attack the dragoons from above, and he reckoned the cavalrymen would come after their assailants by using the stairs closest to the warehouse, ignorant that the attic gave access to four separate stairwells in the four houses. Sharpe planned to go back the way he had come, and by the time the dragoons reached the attic he would be long gone. "Come on, Pat."

They clambered out onto the roof, the same roof that they had reconnoitered earlier, and, by following the gutter behind the parapet, they reached the gable end from which, leaning over, Sharpe could again see the horsemen three floors below him. He took the volley gun from Harper. "There's an officer down there, Pat," he said. "He's on the left, mounted on a gray horse. When I give the word, shoot him."

Harper put some pigeon dung into his rifle's barrel and rammed it down to hold the bullet in place, then he edged forward and peered down into the street. There were dragoons at either end of the short roadway, using their horses' weight and the threat of their long swords to hold the hungry infantry at bay. The officer was just behind the left-hand group, easily distinguished because of the fur-lined pelisse that hung from his left shoulder and because his green saddle cloth had no pouch attached. None of the dragoons looked upwards, why should they? Their job was to guard the street, not watch the rooftops, and Harper aimed the rifle downwards and pulled back the cock.

Sharpe stood beside him with the volley gun. "Ready?"

"I'm ready."

"You fire first," Sharpe said. Harper had to be sure of his aim, but there was no need for Sharpe to aim the volley gun, for it had no accuracy. It was just a slaughtering machine, its seven bullets spreading like canister from the clustered barrels.

Harper lined the sights on the officer's brass helmet which had a brown plume trailing from its crest. The gray horse stirred and the Frenchman calmed it, then looked behind him and just then Harper fired. The bullet cracked open the helmet so that a jet of blood sprayed briefly upwards, then more blood flooded from beneath the helmet's rim as the officer toppled slowly sideways, and just then Sharpe fired into the other dragoons, the noise of the volley gun sounding like a cannon shot as it echoed from the warehouse's facade. Smoke filled the air. A horse screamed. "Run!" Sharpe said.

They went back the way they had come, through the window and down the far stairs, with Vicente and the women following. Sharpe could hear uproar at the other end of the house. Men were shouting in alarm, horses' hooves were loud on cobbles, and then he was at the front door and, with the two guns slung on his shoulder, he pushed into the crowd. Sarah held on to his belt. The infantrymen were surging forward, but over their heads Sharpe could see dismounted dragoons shoving into the far house. As far as Sharpe could see only one man had stayed in his saddle, and that man was holding a dozen reins, but the horses were being pushed aside by the rush of infantry who suddenly understood that the warehouse was unguarded.

The dragoons had done exactly what Sharpe had wanted, what he thought they would do. Their officer was dead, others of them were wounded and, lacking leadership, their only thought was to take revenge on the men who had attacked them, and so they swarmed into the house and left the warehouse unguarded except for a handful of dragoons who were powerless to stem the surge of men who charged at the doors. A dragoon sergeant tried to stop them by swinging the flat of his sword at the leading men, but he was hauled from the saddle, his horse was shoved aside, and the great doors were dragged open. A huge cheer sounded. The remaining dragoons let the men run past, intent only on saving themselves and their horses.

"It's going to be chaos in there," Sharpe said to Harper. "I'm going in alone."

"To do what?"

"What I have to do," Sharpe said. "You and Captain Vicente look after the girls." He pushed them into a doorway. "I'll join you here." Sharpe would have preferred to take Harper with him, for the Irishman's size and strength would be huge assets in the crowded warehouse, but the biggest danger would be that the five of them would be separated in the dark, confused interior, and it was better that Sharpe worked alone. "Wait for me," Sharpe said, then gave Harper his pack and his rifle and, armed only with his sword and the unloaded volley gun, he bullied and shoved his way up the street, past the dead officer's frightened horse and so, at last, into the warehouse. The entrance was crammed, and, once inside, he found men hauling down boxes, sacks and barrels, making it hard to get through, but Sharpe used the butt of the volley gun, savagely clearing the way. An artilleryman tried to stop him, throwing a wild punch, and Sharpe drove the man's teeth in with the brass-bound stock, then he scrambled across a sprawling mound of sacks pulled down from one of the great heaps, and found himself in a relatively uncrowded area.

From here he could work his way to the edge of the warehouse where he remembered seeing the supplies piled on the two carts parked beside the great timber wall that divided this warehouse from the next. Few men were back here, for the French were interested in food, not candles and buttons and nails and horseshoes.

One man was already at one of the wagons, sorting through the goods on its bed, and Sharpe saw he already had a full sack, presumably stuffed with food, and so he clouted the man on the back of the neck with the volley gun, kicked him when he was down, stamped on his face when he tried to move, then looked inside the sack. Biscuits, salt beef and cheese. He would take that, for all of them were hungry, and so he put the sack aside, then drew his sword and used the blade to break open two barrels of lamp oil. It was whale oil, and it gave off a rank stench as it spilled from the broken staves and dripped down to the wagon bed. There were some bolts of cloth at the far end of the wagon and he climbed up to discover what they were made of and discovered, as he had hoped, that they were linen. He shook two of the bolts out, letting the cloth lie loosely across the wagon's load.

He jumped down, sheathed the sword, then broke open a cartridge to make a paper spill filled with gunpowder. He primed the unloaded volley gun, then glanced around the warehouse where men were dragging at supplies like fiends. A stack of rum barrels collapsed, crushing a man, who screamed as his legs were broken by a full barrel that split apart to flood rum across the floor. A Frenchman beat at another barrel with an axe, then dipped a tin cup into the rum. A dozen others went to join him, and no one took any notice of Sharpe as he cocked the unloaded volley gun.

He pulled the trigger, the priming flared and the spill caught. It fizzed angrily; he let the flame grow until the spill was burning well, then he tossed it down into the oil on the wagon bed. For a second the paper burned on its own, then a sheet of flame spread across the wagon and Sharpe snatched up the sack of food and ran.

For a few steps he was unimpeded. The men around the rum barrels ignored him as he edged past, but then the linen caught the fire and there was a sudden flare of light. A man shouted a warning, smoke began to spread, and the panic began. A dozen dragoons were fighting their way into the warehouse, ordered to the hopeless task of ejecting the men stealing the precious food, and now a wave of terrified soldiers struck the dragoons, two of whom fell, and there was screaming and snarling, the sound of a shot, and then the smoke thickened with appalling rapidity as the wagon caught fire. The cartridges in the pouch of the man whose food Sharpe had stolen began to explode and a burning scrap of paper fell into the rum and sudden blue flames rippled across the floor.

Sharpe ripped men away from his path, stamped on them, kicked them, then drew his sword because he reckoned it was the only thing that would clear the way. He stabbed men with the blade and they twisted aside, protesting, then shrank from the anger on his face, and behind him a small barrel of gunpowder exploded and the fire sprayed across the warehouse as Sharpe fought his way through the crush, except there was no way through. Scores of terrified men were blocking the gaps between the heaps, so Sharpe sheathed his sword, threw his sack of food up to the top of a stack of boxes and clambered up the side. He ran across the top. Cats fled from him. Smoke billowed in the rafters. He jumped to a half-collapsed heap of flour sacks, crossed them towards the doorway, then slid down the far side. He put his head down and ran, trampling fallen men, using his strength to escape the smoke, and burst out of the doors into the street where, gripping the sack of food to keep it safe, he worked his way back down to the house where he had left Harper.

"God save Ireland." Harper was standing in the doorway, watching the chaos. Smoke was tumbling out of the great doors and more was spewing up from the broken skylight. Soldiers, scorched and coughing, were staggering out of the door. Screams sounded inside the warehouse, and then there was another explosion as the rum barrels cracked apart. There was a glow like a giant furnace in the doors now, and the sound of the fire was like the roaring of a huge river going through a ravine. "You did that?" Harper asked.

"I did that," Sharpe said. He felt tired suddenly, tired and ravenously hungry, and he went into the house where Vicente and the girls were waiting in a small room decorated with a picture of a saint holding a shepherd's crook. He looked at Vicente. "Take us somewhere safe, Jorge."

"Where's safe on a day like this?" Vicente asked.

"Somewhere a long way from this street," Sharpe said, and the five of them went out of the back door and, looking back, Sharpe saw that the warehouse next to Ferragus's had caught the fire and its roof was now burning. More dragoons were evidently coming because Sharpe could hear the hooves loud in the narrow streets, but it was too late.

They went down one alley, up another, crossed a street and went through a courtyard where a dozen French soldiers were lying dead drunk. Vicente led them. "We'll go uphill," he said, not because he thought the upper town was any safer than the lower town, but because it had been his home.

No one accosted them. They were just another band of exhausted soldiers stumbling through the city. Behind them was fire, smoke and anger. "What do we say if they challenge us?" Sarah asked Sharpe.

"Tell them we're Dutch."

"Dutch?"

"They have Dutch soldiers," Sharpe said.

The upper town was quieter. It was mostly cavalrymen quartered here and some of them told the interloping infantrymen to go away, but Vicente led them down an alley, through a courtyard, down some steps and into the garden of a big house. At the side of the garden was a cottage. "The house belongs to a professor of theology," Vicente explained, "and his servants live here." The cottage was tiny, but so far no French had found it. Sharpe, on his way uphill, had seen how some houses had a uniform coat hung in the doorway to denote that soldiers had taken up residence and that the place was not to be plundered, and so he took off his blue jacket and hung it from a nail above the cottage door. Maybe it would keep the enemy away, maybe not. They ate, all of them ravenous, tearing at the salt beef and hard biscuit, and Sharpe wished he could lie down and sleep for the rest of the day, but he knew the others must be feeling the same. "Get some sleep," he told them.

"What about you?" Vicente asked.

"Someone has to stand guard," Sharpe said.

The cottage had one small bedroom, little more than a cupboard, and Vicente was given that because he was an officer, while Harper went into the kitchen where he made a bed from curtains, blankets and a greatcoat. Joana followed him and the kitchen door was firmly shut behind her. Sarah collapsed in an old, broken armchair from which tufts of horsehair protruded. "I'll stay awake with you," she told Sharpe, and a moment later she was fast asleep.

Sharpe loaded his rifle. He dared not sit for he knew he would never stay awake and so he stood in the doorway, the loaded rifle beside him, and he listened to the distant screams and he saw the great plume of smoke smearing the cloudless sky and he knew he had done his duty.

Now all he had to do was get back to the army.

CHAPTER 10

FERRAGUS AND HIS BROTHER went back to the Major's house, which had been spared the plundering suffered by the rest of the city. A troop of dragoons from the same squadron that had ridden to protect the warehouse had been posted outside the house, and they were now relieved by a dozen men sent by Colonel Barreto who, when his day's work was complete, planned to billet himself in the house. Miguel and five others of Ferragus's men were at the house, safe there from French attention, and it was Miguel who interrupted the brothers' celebrations by reporting that the warehouse was burning.

Ferragus had just opened a third bottle of wine. He listened to Miguel, carried the bottle to the window and peered down the hill. He saw the smoke churning up, but shrugged. "It could be any one of a dozen buildings," he said dismissively.

"It's the warehouse," Miguel insisted. "I went to the roof. I could see."

"So?" Ferragus toasted the room with his bottle. "We've sold it now! The loss is to the French, not to us."

Major Ferreira went to the window and gazed at the smoke. Then he made the sign of the cross. "The French will not see it that way," he said quietly, and took the bottle from his brother.

"They've paid us!" Ferragus said, trying to get the bottle back.

Ferreira placed the wine out of his brother's reach. "The French will believe we sold them the food, then destroyed it," he said. The Major glanced towards the street leading downhill as if he expected it to be filled with Frenchmen. "They will want their money back."

"Jesus," Ferragus said. His brother was right. He glanced at the money: four saddlebags filled with French gold. "Jesus," he said again as the implications of the burning building sank into his wine-hazed head.

"Time to go." The Major took firm command of the situation.

"Go?" Ferragus was still fuddled.

"They'll be after us!" the Major insisted. "At best they'll just want the money back, at worst they'll shoot us. Good God, Luis! First we lost the flour at the shrine, now this? You think they'll believe we didn't do it? We go! Now!"

"Stable yard," Ferragus ordered Miguel.

"We can't ride out!" Ferreira protested. The French were confiscating every horse they discovered, and Ferreira's contacts with Colonel Barreto and the French would avail him nothing if he was seen on horseback. "We have to hide," he insisted. "We hide in the city until it's safe to leave."

Ferragus, his brother, and the six men carried what was most valuable from the house. They had the gold newly paid by the French, some money that Major Ferreira had kept hidden in his study and a bag of silver plate, and they took it all up an alley behind the stables, through a second alley and into one of the many abandoned houses that had already been searched by the French. They dared not go farther, for the streets were filled with the invaders, and so they took refuge in the house cellar and prayed that they would not be discovered.

"How long do we stay here?" Ferragus asked sourly.

"Till the French leave," Ferreira said.

"And then?"

Ferreira did not answer at once. He was thinking. Thinking that the British would not just march away to their boats. They would try to stop the French again, probably near the new forts he had seen being constructed on the road north of Lisbon. That meant the French would have to fight or else maneuver their way around the British and Portuguese armies, and that would provide time. Time for him to reach Lisbon. Time to reach the money secreted in his wife's luggage. Time to find his wife and children. Portugal was about to collapse and the brothers would need money. Much money. They could go to the Azores or even to Brazil, then wait the storm out in comfort and return home when it had passed. And if the French were defeated? Then they would still need money, and the only obstacle was Captain Sharpe who knew of Ferreira's treachery. The wretched man had escaped from the cellar, but was he still alive? It seemed more probable that the French would have killed him, for Ferreira could not imagine the French taking prisoners in their orgy of killing and destruction, but the thought that the rifleman lived was worrying. "If Sharpe is alive," he wondered aloud, "what will he do?"

Ferragus spat to show his opinion of Sharpe.

"He will go back to his army," Ferreira answered his own question.

"And say you are a traitor?"

"Then it will be his word against mine," Ferreira said, "and if I am there, then his word will not carry much weight."

Ferragus stared up at the cellar roof. "We could say the food was poisoned," he suggested, "say it was a trap for the French?"

Ferreira nodded, acknowledging the usefulness of the suggestion. "What is important," he said, "is for us to reach Lisbon. Beatriz and the children are there. My money is there." He thought about going north and hiding, but the longer he was absent from the army, the greater would be the suspicions about that absence. Better to go back, bluff it out and reclaim his possessions. Then, with money, he could survive whatever happened. Besides, he missed his family. "But how do we reach Lisbon?"

"Go east," one of the men suggested. "Go east to the Tagus and float down."

Ferreira stared at the man, thinking, though in truth there was nothing really to think about. He could not go directly south for the French would be there, but if he and his brother struck east across the mountains, traveling through the high lands where the French would not dare go for fear of the partisans, they would eventually reach the Tagus and the money they carried would be more than sufficient to buy a boat.

Then, in two days, they could be in Lisbon. "I have friends in the mountains," Ferreira said.

"Friends?" Ferragus had not followed his brother's thinking.

"Men who have taken weapons from me." Ferreira, as part of his duties, had distributed British muskets among the hill folk to encourage them to become partisans. "They will give us horses," he went on confidently, "and they will know whether the French are in Abrantes. If they're not, we find our boat there. And the men in the hills can do something else for us. If Sharpe is alive . . ."

"He's dead by now," Ferragus insisted.

"If he's alive," Major Ferreira went on patiently, "then he will have to take the same route to reach his army. So they can kill him for us." He made the sign of the cross, for it was all so suddenly clear. "Five of us will go to the Tagus," he said, "and then go south. When we reach our army we shall say we destroyed the provisions in the warehouse and if the French arrive we shall sail to the Azores."

"Only five of us?" Miguel asked. There were eight men in the cellar.

"Three of you will stay here," Ferreira suggested and looked to his brother for approval, which Ferragus gave with a nod. "Three men must stay here," Ferreira said, "to guard my house and make any repairs necessary before we return. And when we do return those three men will be well rewarded."

The Major's suspicion that his house would need repairs was justified for, just a hundred and fifty yards away, dragoons were searching for him. The French believed they had been cheated by Major Ferreira and his brother and now took their revenge. They beat down the front door, but found no one except the cook who was drunk in the kitchen and when she swung a frying pan at the head of a dragoon she was shot. The dragoons tossed her body into the yard, then systematically destroyed everything they could break. Furniture, pictures, porcelain, pots, everything. The banisters were torn from the stairs, windows were smashed, and the shutters ripped from their hinges. They found nothing except the horses in the stables and those they took away to become French cavalry remounts.

Dusk came, and the sun flared crimson above the far Atlantic and then sank. The fires in the city burned on to light the smoky sky. The first fury of the French had subsided, but there were still screams in the dark and tears in the night, for the Eagles had taken a city.

SHARPE LEANED ON THE DOOR frame, shadowed by a small timber porch up which a plant twined and fell. The small garden was neatly planted in rows, but what grew there Sharpe did not know, though he did recognize some runner beans that he picked and stored in a pocket ready for the hungry days ahead. He leaned on the door frame again, listening to the shots in the lower city and to Harper's snores coming from the kitchen. He dozed, unaware of it until a cat rubbed against his ankles and startled him awake. Shots still sounded in the city, and still the smoke churned overhead.

He petted the cat, stamped his boots, tried to stay awake, but again fell asleep on his feet and woke to see a French officer sitting in the entrance to the garden with a sketch pad. The man was drawing Sharpe and, when he saw his subject had woken, he held up a hand as if to say Sharpe should not be alarmed. He drew on, his pencil making quick, confident strokes. He spoke to Sharpe, his voice relaxed and friendly, and Sharpe grunted back and the officer did not seem to mind that his subject made no sense. It was dusk when the officer finished and he stood and brought the picture to Sharpe and asked his opinion. The Frenchman was smiling, pleased with his work, and Sharpe gazed at the drawing of a villainous-looking man, scarred and frightening, leaning in shirtsleeves against the doorway with a rifle propped at his side and a sword hanging from his waist. Had the fool not seen they were British weapons? The officer, who was young, fair-haired and good-looking, prompted Sharpe for a response, and Sharpe shrugged, wondering if he would have to draw the sword and fillet the man.

Then Sarah appeared and said something in fluent French and the officer snatched off his forage cap, bowed and showed the picture to Sarah who must have expressed delight, for the man tore it from his big book and gave it to her with another bow. They spoke for a few more minutes, or rather the officer spoke and Sarah seemed to agree with everything he said, adding very few words of her own and then, at last, the officer kissed her hand, nodded amicably to Sharpe, and disappeared up the steps through the far archway. "What was that all about?" Sharpe asked.

"I told him we were Dutch. He seemed to think you were a cavalry-man."

"He saw the sword, overalls and boots," Sharpe explained. "He wasn't suspicious?"

"He said you were the very picture of a modern soldier," Sarah said, looking at the drawing.

"That's me," Sharpe said, "a work of art."

"He actually said that you were the image of a people's fury released on an old and corrupt world."

"Bloody hell," Sharpe said.

"And he said it was a shame what was being done in the city, but that it was unavoidable."

"What's wrong with discipline?"

"Unavoidable," Sarah ignored Sharpe's question, "because Coimbra represents the old world of superstition and privilege."

"So he was another Crapaud full of . . ." Sharpe started.

"Shit?" Sarah interrupted him.

Sharpe looked at her. "You're a strange one, love."

"Good," she said.

"Did you sleep?" Sharpe asked her.

"I slept. Now you must."

"Someone has to stand guard," Sharpe said, though he had not done a particularly good job. He had been fast asleep when the French officer came and it had only been pure luck that it had been a man with a sketch book in-stead of some bastard looking for plunder. "What you could do," he sug-gested, "is see if the fire in the kitchen can be revived and make us some tea."

"Tea?"

"There are some leaves in my haversack," Sharpe said. "You have to scoop them out, and they get a bit mixed up with loose gunpowder, but most of us like that taste."

"Sergeant Harper's in the kitchen," Sarah said diffidently.

"Worried what you might see?" Sharpe asked with a smile. "He won't mind. There's not a lot of privacy in the army. It's an education, the army."

"So I'm discovering," Sarah said, and she went to the kitchen, but came back to report that the stove was cold.

She had moved as quietly as she could, but she had still woken Harper who rolled out of his makeshift bed and came bleary-eyed into the small parlor. "What time is it?"

"Nightfall," Sharpe said.

"All quiet?"

"Except for your snoring. And we had a visit from a Frog who chatted with Sarah about the state of the world."

"It's in a terrible state, so it is," Harper said, "a shame, really." He shook his head, then hefted the volley gun. "You should get some sleep, sir. Let me watch for a while." He turned and smiled as Joana came from the kitchen. She had taken off her torn dress and seemed to be wearing nothing except the Frenchman's shirt, which reached halfway down her thighs. She put her arms round Harper's waist, rested her dark head against his shoulder and smiled at Sharpe. "We'll both keep watch," Harper said.

"Is that what you call it?" Sharpe asked. He picked up his rifle. "Wake me when you're tired," he said. He reckoned he needed proper sleep more than he needed tea, but Harper, he knew, could probably drink a gallon. "You want to make some tea first? We were going to light the stove."

"I'll brew it on the hearth, sir." Harper nodded at the small fireplace where there was a three-legged saucepan designed to stand in the embers. "There's water in the garden," he added, nodding at a rain butt, "so the kitchen's all yours, sir. And sleep well, sir."

Sharpe ducked through the low door which he closed to find himself in almost pitch blackness. He groped to find the back door beyond which was a small enclosed yard eerily lit by moonlight filtered by the drifting smoke. There was a pump in the yard's corner and he worked the handle to splash water into a stone trough. He used a handful of straw to scrub the filth off his boots, then tugged them off and washed his hands. He unstrapped the sword belt and carried belt, boots and sword back into the kitchen. He closed the door, then knelt to find the bed in the darkness.

"Careful," Sarah said from somewhere in the tangle of blankets and greatcoat.

"What are you . . ." Sharpe began, then thought it was a stupid question and so did not finish it.

"I don't think I was really wanted out there," Sarah explained. "Not that Sergeant Harper was unwelcoming, he wasn't, but I had the distinct impression that the two of them could cope without me."

"That's probably true," Sharpe said.

"And I won't keep you awake," she promised.

But she did.

⚜

IT WAS MORNING when Sharpe woke. The cat had somehow got into the kitchen and was sitting on the small shelf beside the stove where it was washing itself and occasionally looking at Sharpe with yellow eyes. Sarah's left arm was across Sharpe's chest and he marveled at how smooth and pale her skin was. She was asleep still, a strand of golden hair shivering at her open lips with every breath. Sharpe eased himself from beneath her embrace and, naked, edged open the kitchen door just far enough to see into the parlor.

Harper was in the armchair, Joana asleep across his lap. The Irishman turned at the creak of the hinges. "All quiet, sir," he whispered.

"You should have woken me."

"Why? Nothing's stirring."

"Captain Vicente?"

"He crept out, sir. Went to see what was happening. Promised he wouldn't go far."

"I'll make some tea," Sharpe said, and he closed the door.

There was a basket of kindling beside the stove and a box of small logs. He worked as quietly as possible, but heard Sarah stir and turned to see her looking up at him from the jumble of bedclothes. "You're right," she said, "the army is an education."

Sharpe leaned against the stove. She sat up, clutching Harper's great-coat to her breasts, and he stared at her, she stared back and neither spoke until she suddenly scratched at her thigh. "When you were in India," she asked unexpectedly, "did you meet people who believed that after death they came back as another person?"

"Not that I know about," Sharpe said.

"I'm told they believe that," Sarah said solemnly.

"They believe all sorts of rubbish. Couldn't keep up with it."

"When I come back," Sarah said, tilting her head to rest against the wall, "I think I'll come back as a man."

"Bit of a waste," Sharpe said.

"Because you're free," she said, gazing up at the dried herbs hanging from the beams.

"I'm not free," Sharpe said. "I've got the army all over me. Like fleas." He watched her scratch again.

"What we did last night," Sarah said, and blushed very slightly and it was plain she had to force herself to speak of what had happened so naturally in the darkness, "doesn't leave you changed. You're the same person. I'm not."

Sharpe heard Vicente's voice in the parlor and, a heartbeat later, there was a knock on the kitchen door. "In a minute, Jorge," Sharpe called out. He looked into Sarah's eyes. "Should I feel guilty?"

"No, no," Sarah said quickly. "It's just that everything's changed. For a woman," she looked up at the herbs again, "it's not a small thing. For a man, I think, it is."

"I won't let you be alone," Sharpe said.

"I wasn't worried about that," Sarah said, though she was. "It's just that everything's new now. I'm not who I was yesterday. And that means to-morrow is different as well." She half smiled at him. "Do you understand?"

"You'll probably have to talk to me some more," Sharpe said, "when I'm awake. But for the moment, love, I have to let Jorge have his say, and I need some bloody tea." He leaned over and kissed her, then scooped up his clothes.

Sarah lifted her torn dress from the tangled bedding. She was about to pull it over her head, then shuddered. "It stinks," she said in distaste.

"Wear this," Sharpe said, tossing her his shirt, then he pulled on the overalls, shrugged the straps over his bare shoulders and tugged on the boots. "We'll have a make and mend day," he said. "Wash everything. I doubt the bloody French will leave today and we seem safe enough here." He waited until she had buttoned the shirt, then opened the door. "Sorry, Jorge, just making a fire."

"The French aren't leaving," Vicente reported from the door. He was in shirtsleeves and had made a sling for his left arm. "I couldn't go far, but I could see downhill and they're not making any preparations."

"They're catching their breath," Sharpe said, "and they'll probably march tomorrow." He twisted to look at Sarah. "See if Patrick's fire is going, will you? Tell him I need a flame for this one."

Sarah slipped past Vicente who stood aside to let her pass, then he looked from Sarah to Joana, both girls bare-legged and dressed in grubby shirts. He came into the kitchen and frowned at Sharpe. "It looks like a brothel in there," he said reprovingly.

"Greenjackets always were lucky, Jorge. And they're both volunteers."

"Does that justify it?"

Sharpe pushed more kindling into the stove. "Doesn't have to be justified, Jorge. It's life."

"Which is why we have religion," Vicente said, "to raise us above life."

"I was always lucky," Sharpe said, "in escaping law and religion."

Vicente looked miserable with that reply, but then saw the pencil portrait of Sharpe that Sarah had propped on a shelf and his face brightened. "That's good! It's just like you!"

"It's a picture, Jorge, of a people's anger let loose on a corrupt world."

"It is?"

"That's what the fellow who drew it said, something like that."

"Miss Fry didn't do it?"

"It was a Frog officer, Jorge. Did it last night while you were sleeping. Step aside, fire coming." He and Vicente made way for Sarah who was carrying a burning scrap of wood that she pushed into the stove, then watched to make sure the fire caught. "What we're going to do," Sharpe said as Sarah blew on the small flames, "is boil up some water, wash our clothes and pick off the fleas."

"Fleas?" Sarah sounded alarmed.

"Why do you think you're scratching, darling? You've probably got worse than fleas, but we've got all day to clean up. We'll wait for the Crapauds to go, which will be tomorrow at the earliest."

"They won't go today?" Sarah asked.

"That drunken lot? Their officers will never get them in march order today. Tomorrow if they're lucky. And tonight we'll have a look at the streets, but I doubt we can get out tonight. They're bound to have patrols. Best to wait till they've gone, then cross the bridge and head south."

Sarah thought for a second, then frowned as she scratched at her waist. "You just follow the French?" she asked. "How do you get past them?"

"The safest way," Vicente said, "would be to head for the Tagus. We must cross some high hills to reach the river, but once there we might find a boat. Something to take us downstream to Lisbon."

"But before that," Sharpe said, "there's another job to do. Look for Ferragus."

Vicente frowned. "Why?"

"Because he owes us, Jorge," Sharpe said, "or at least he owes Sarah. He stole her money, the bastard, so we have to get it back."

Vicente was plainly unhappy at the idea of prolonging the feud with Ferragus, but he did not voice any objections. "And what if a patrol comes here today?" he asked instead. "They'll be searching the town for their own troops, won't they?"

"You speak Frog?"

"Not well, but I speak some."

"So tell them you're an Italian, a Dutchman, anything you like, and promise we'll rejoin our unit. Which we will, if we can get out of here."

They made tea, shared a breakfast of biscuit, salt beef and cheese, then Sharpe and Vicente stood guard while Harper helped the two women do the laundry. They boiled the clothes to get the stench of the sewer out of the cloth and, when everything was dry, which took most of the day, Sharpe used a heated poker to kill the lice in the seams. Harper had torn down some curtains from the bedroom, washed them, torn them into long strips, and now insisted on bandaging Sharpe's ribs that were still bruised and painful. Sarah saw the scars on his back. "What happened?" she asked.

"I was flogged," Sharpe explained.

"For what?"

"Something I didn't do," Sharpe said.

"It must have hurt."

"Life hurts," Sharpe said. "Wrap it tight, Pat." His ribs were still painful, but he could take a deep breath without wincing, which surely meant things were mending. They were mending in the city too, for Coimbra was quieter today, though the plume of smoke, thinner now, still drifted up from the warehouse. Sharpe suspected the French would have rescued some supplies from the blaze, but not nearly enough to release them from the hunger that Lord Wellington had deployed to defeat their invasion. At midday Sharpe crept to the end of the tortuous alley and saw, as he had suspected, patrols of French soldiers rooting men out of houses, and he and Harper then filled the alley with garden rubbish to suggest that it was not worth exploring, and the ruse must have worked, for no patrol bothered to explore the narrow passage. At nightfall there were the sounds of hooves and iron-rimmed wheels on the nearby streets and when it was fully dark Sharpe negotiated the obstacles in the alley and saw that two batteries of artillery were parked in the street. A half-dozen sentries guarded the vehicles and one, more alert than the others, saw Sharpe's shadow in the alley's entrance and shouted a challenge. Sharpe crouched. The man called again and, receiving no answer, shot into the blackness. The ball ricocheted above Sharpe's head as he crept backwards. "*Un chien*," another sentry called. The first man peered down the alley, saw nothing and agreed it must have been a dog in the night.

Sharpe stood guard for the second half of the night. Sarah stayed with him, staring into the moonlit garden. She spoke of growing up and of losing her parents. "I became a nuisance to my uncle," she said sadly.

"So he got shot of you?"

"As fast as he could." She was sitting in the armchair and reached out to run a finger down the zigzag leather reinforcements on the leg of Sharpe's overalls. "Will the British really stay in Lisbon?"

"It'll take more than this pack of Frenchmen to get them out," Sharpe said scornfully. "Of course we're staying."

"If I had a hundred pounds," she said wistfully, "I'd find a small house in Lisbon and teach English. I like children."

"I don't."

"Of course you do." She slapped him lightly.

"You wouldn't go back to England?" Sharpe asked her.

"What can I do there? No one wants to learn Portuguese, but plenty of Portuguese want their children to know English. Besides, in England I'm just another young woman with no prospects, no fortune and no future. Here I benefit from the intrigue of being different."

"You intrigue me," Sharpe said, and got slapped again. "You could stay with me," he added.

"And be a soldier's woman?" She laughed.

"Nothing wrong with that," Sharpe said defensively.

"No, there's not," Sarah agreed. She was silent for a while. "Until two days ago," she went on suddenly, "I thought my life depended on other people. On employers. Now I think it depends on me. You taught me that. But I need money."

"Money's easy," Sharpe said dismissively.

"That is not the conventional wisdom," Sarah said dryly.

"Steal the stuff," Sharpe said.

"You were really a thief?"

"Still am. Once a thief, always a thief, only now I steal from the enemy. And some day I'll have enough to stop doing it and then I'll stop others thieving from me."

"You have a simple view of life."

"You're born, you survive, you die," Sharpe said. "What's hard about that?"

"It's an animal's life," Sarah said, "and we are more than animals."

"That's what they tell me," Sharpe said, "but when war comes they're grateful for men like me. At least they were."

"Were?"

He hesitated, then shrugged. "My Colonel wants rid of me. He's got a brother-in-law he wants to have my job, a man called Slingsby. He's got manners."

"A good thing to have."

"Not when fifty thousand Frogs are coming at you. Manners don't get you far then. What you need is sheer bloody-mindedness."

"And you have that?"

"Buckets of it, darling," Sharpe said.

Sarah smiled. "So what happens to you now?"

"I don't know. I go back, and if I don't like what's there then I'll find another regiment. Join the Portuguese, perhaps."

"But you'll stay a soldier?"

Sharpe nodded. He could imagine no other life. There were times when he thought he would like to own a few acres and farm them, but he knew nothing of farming and recognized the wish as a dream. He would stay a soldier, and he supposed, when he thought about it at all, that he would reach a soldier's end, either sweating in a fever ward or dead on a battlefield.

Sarah must have guessed what he was thinking. "I think you'll survive," she said.

"I think you will too."

Somewhere in the dark a dog howled and the cat arched its back in the doorway and spat at the sound. After a while Sarah fell asleep and Sharpe crouched beside the cat and watched the light slowly creep across the sky. Vicente woke early and joined him.

"How's the shoulder?" Sharpe asked him.

"It hurts less."

"It's healing then," Sharpe said.

Vicente sat in silence. "If the French do leave today," he said after a while, "wouldn't it be sensible to go ourselves?"

"Forget Ferragus, you mean?"

Vicente nodded. "Our duty is to rejoin the army."

"It is," Sharpe agreed, "but we rejoin the army, Jorge, and they'll give us black marks for being absent. Your Colonel won't be pleased. So we have to take them something."

"Ferragus?"

Sharpe shook his head. "Ferreira. He's the one they need to know about. But to find him we look for his brother."

Vicente nodded acceptance. "So when we go back we haven't just been absent, but doing something useful?"

"And instead of stamping all over us," Sharpe said, "they'll be thanking us."

"So when the French go, we look for Ferreira? Then march him south under arrest?"

"Simple, eh?" Sharpe said with a smile.

"I'm not as good as you at this."

"At what?"

"At being away from the regiment. At being on my own."

"You miss Kate, eh?"

"I miss Kate too."

"You should miss her," Sharpe said, "and you're good at this, Jorge. You're as good a damn soldier as any in the army, and if you give the army Ferreira then they'll think you're a hero. Then in two years you'll be a colonel and I'll still be a captain, and you'll wish we'd never had this conversation. Time to make some tea, Jorge."

The French left. It took most of the day for the guns, wagons, horses and men to cross the Santa Clara bridge, twist through the narrow streets beyond, and so out onto the main road that would lead them south towards Lisbon. All day patrols went through the streets, blowing bugles and shouting for men to rejoin their units, and it was late afternoon before the last bugle sounded and the noise of boots, hooves and wheels faded from Coimbra. The French were not wholly gone. Over three thousand of their wounded were left in the big Saint Clara convent south of the river and such men needed protection. The French had raped, murdered and plundered their way through the city and wounded soldiers made for easy vengeance, and so the injured were guarded by one hundred and fifty French marines reinforced by three hundred convalescents who were not fit enough to march with the army, but could still use their muskets. The small garrison was commanded by a major who was given the grandiose title of Governor of Coimbra, but the tiny number of men under his command gave him no control of the city. He posted most of his force at the convent, for that was where the vulnerable men lay, and put picquets on the main roads out of the city, but everything in between was unguarded.

And so the surviving inhabitants emerged into a ravaged city. Their churches, schools and streets were filled with bodies and litter. There were hundreds of dead and the wailing of the mourners echoed up and down the alleys. Folk sought revenge, and the convent's whitewashed walls were pitted with musket balls as men and women fired blindly at the building where the French cowered. Some foolhardy folk even tried to attack the convent and were cut down by volleys from windows and doors. After a while the madness ended. The dead lay in the streets outside the convent, and the French were barricaded inside. The small picquets on the outlying streets, none larger than thirty men, fortified themselves in houses and waited for Marshal Masséna to trounce the enemy and send reinforcements back to Coimbra.

Sharpe and his companions left their house soon after dawn. They wore their own uniforms again, but twice in the first five minutes they were cursed by angry women and Sharpe realized that the people of the city did not recognize the green and brown jackets and so, before someone tried a shot from an alleyway, they stripped off their coats, tied their shakoes to their belts and walked in shirtsleeves. They passed a priest who knelt in the street to offer the last rites to three dead men. A crying child clung to one of the dead hands, but the priest eased her grip from the stiff fingers and, with a reproachful glance at the gun on Sharpe's shoulder, hurried the girl away.

Sharpe stopped before the corner that opened onto the small plaza in front of Ferragus's house. He did not know whether the man was in Coimbra or not, but he would take no chances and peered cautiously around the wall. He could see the front door was off its hinges, every piece of window glass was missing and the shutters had been torn away or broken. "He's not there," he said.

"How can you tell?" Vicente asked.

"Because he'd have at least blocked the door," Sharpe said.

"Maybe they killed him," Harper suggested.

"Let's find out." Sharpe took the rifle from his shoulder, cocked it, told the others to wait, then ran across the patch of sunlight, took the house steps three at a time and then was inside the hallway where he crouched at the foot of the stairs, listening.

Silence. He beckoned the others over. The two girls came through the door first and Sarah's eyes widened in shock as she saw the destruction. Harper gazed up the stairwell. "They kicked the living shit out of this place," he said. "Sorry, miss."

"It's all right, Sergeant," Sarah said, "I don't seem to mind any longer."

"It's like sewers, miss," Harper said. "Stay in them long enough and you get used to them. Jesus, they did a proper job here!" Everything that could be broken had been smashed. Pieces of crystal from a chandelier crunched under Sharpe's boots as he explored the hallway and looked into the parlor and study. The kitchen was a mess of broken pots and bent pans. Even the stove had been pulled from the wall and taken apart. In the schoolroom the small chairs, low table and Sarah's desk had been hammered into splinters. They climbed the stairs, looking in every room, finding nothing except destruction and deliberate fouling. There was no sign of Ferragus or his brother.

"Bastards have gone," Sharpe said after opening the cupboards in the big bedroom and finding nothing except a pack of playing cards.

"But Major Ferreira was on the side of the French, wasn't he?" Harper asked, puzzled that the French would have destroyed the house of an ally.

"He doesn't know what side he's on," Sharpe said. "He just wants to be on the winning side."

"But he sold them the food, didn't he?" Harper asked.

"We think he did," Sharpe said.

"And then you burned it," Vicente put in, "and what will the French conclude? That the brothers cheated them."

"So the odds are," Sharpe said, "that the French shot the pair of them. That would be a good day's work for a bloody Frog." He slung his rifle and climbed the last stairs to the attic. He expected to find nothing there, but at least the high windows offered a vantage point from which he could look down at the lower town and see what kind of presence the French were maintaining. He knew they were still in the city for he could hear distant sporadic shots that seemed to come from close to the river, but when he stared through a broken window he could see no enemy, nor even any musket smoke. Sarah had followed him upstairs while the others stayed on the floor below. She leaned on the window sill and gazed south across the river to the far hills.

"So what do we do now?" she asked.

"Join the army."

"Just like that?"

"We have to walk a long way," Sharpe said, "and you're going to need better boots, better clothes. We'll look for them."

"How far will we have to walk?"

"Four days? Five? Maybe a week? I don't know."

"And where will you find me clothes?"

"By the road, my love, by the road."

"The road?"

"When the French left," he explained, "they were carrying all their plunder, but a mile or two of marching changes your mind. You start throwing things away. There'll be hundreds of things on the road south."

She looked down at her dress, torn, dirty and wrinkled. "I look horrid."

"You look wonderful," Sharpe said, then turned because two smart taps had sounded from the floor below and he held his finger to his lips and, moving as softly as he could, edged back to the stairwell. Harper was at the bottom of the flight and the Irishman held up three fingers, then pointed down the next stairs. So three people were in the house. Harper looked back down the stairs, then held up four fingers and rocked his hand from side to side, telling Sharpe there could be more than three. Plunderers, probably. The French had gone through Coimbra once, but there would be pickings left and enough folk ready to come up from the lower town to enrich themselves from the upper.

Sharpe had edged down the top stairs, stepping at the side of the treads, going very slowly. Vicente was behind Harper, his rifle pointing down into the hall while Joana was in the bedroom door, her musket at her shoulder. Sharpe reached Harper's side. He could hear voices now. Someone was angry. Sharpe cocked the rifle, flinching at the small noise the mechanism made, but no one below heard. He pointed to himself, then down the stairs and Harper nodded.

Sharpe took these stairs even more slowly. They were strewn with pieces of balustrade and littered with crystal drops and he had to find a clear space for his foot with every step and transfer his weight gently. He had got halfway down the flight when he heard the footsteps coming from the passage at the bottom of the stairs and he crouched, brought the rifle up, and just then a man came into view, saw Sharpe and gaped at him in astonishment. Sharpe did not fire. If Ferragus had come back then he did not want to alert him, and instead he gestured at the man to drop onto the floor, but instead the man twisted away, shouting a warning. Harper fired, the bullet blasting over Sharpe's shoulder to catch the man in the back and send him sprawling onto the hallway floor. Sharpe was moving now, taking the stairs four at a time. The wounded man was scrambling down the passage. Sharpe kicked him in the back, jumped over him and a second man showed in the dark entrance to the kitchen and Sharpe fired, the flame of the rifle flashing bright in the dim passageway before the smoke filled the space. Harper was downstairs now, the volley gun in his hand. Sharpe leaped down the few steps to the kitchen, found a body at the foot of the steps, ran to the back door and threw himself backwards as a man fired at him from the yard.

Harper ran to the back door, did not pause, but just raised his empty rifle and the threat was enough to send whoever was there running. Sharpe was reloading. Joana came into the kitchen and he took her musket, gave her the half-loaded rifle and ran back up the passage, jumped over the dead man and over the wounded man and pushed into the parlor because its window overlooked the yard. The sash, the broken glass glinting at its edges, was raised and Sharpe ran to it and saw no one beneath him. "Yard's empty," he called to Harper.

Harper appeared from the kitchen door, crossed the yard and closed the gate. "Plunderers?" he asked Sharpe.

"Probably." Sharpe was wishing he had not opened fire. The menace of the rifles would have been enough to frighten off plunderers, but he supposed he had been nervous and so had killed a man who almost certainly did not deserve it. "Bugger," he said in self-reproof, then went to collect his rifle from Joana, but Sarah was crouching beside the wounded man in the passageway.

"It's Miguel," she said.

"Who?"

"Miguel. One of Ferragus's men."

"You're sure?"

"Of course I'm sure."

"Talk to him," Sharpe said to Vicente. "Find out where those damn brothers are." Sharpe stepped over the wounded man and fetched his rifle. He finished reloading it, then went back to the passage where Vicente was questioning Miguel.

"He won't speak," Vicente said, "except to ask for a doctor."

"Where's he shot?"

"The side," Vicente said, pointing to Miguel's waist where the clothes were darkened by blood.

"Ask him where Ferragus is."

"He won't tell me."

Sharpe put his boot on the blood-soaked patch of clothing and Miguel gave a gasp of pain. "Ask him again," Sharpe said.

"Sharpe, you can't . . ." Vicente began.

"Ask him again!" Sharpe snarled and he stared into Miguel's eyes and then smiled at the wounded man, and there was a wealth of meaning in the smile. Miguel began talking. Sharpe left his boot on the wound, listening to Vicente's translation.

The Ferreira brothers reckoned Sharpe was probably dead, but also that he was unimportant so long as they reached the army first and gave their version of events. And they were trying to reach the army by crossing the hills, going towards Castelo Branco because the road to that city would be free of the French, but they planned to cut south as they neared the river. They wanted to get to Lisbon, because that was where the Major's family and fortune had found temporary refuge, and they had left Miguel and two others to watch over the property in Coimbra.

"Is that all he knows?" Sharpe asked.

"It is all he knows," Vicente said, then moved Sharpe's foot away from Miguel's wound.

"Ask him what else he knows," Sharpe said.

"You can't torture a man," Vicente reproved Sharpe.

"I'm not torturing him," Sharpe said, "but I bloody will if he doesn't tell us everything."

Vicente spoke with Miguel again, and Miguel swore on the blessed Virgin that he had told them everything he knew, but Miguel had lied. He could have warned them about the partisans waiting in the hills, but he reckoned he was dying and, as his final wish, he wanted death for the men who had shot him. Those men bandaged him, and promised they would try to find a physician, but no physician came and Miguel, abandoned in the house, slowly bled to death.

As Sharpe and his companions left the city.

THE BRIDGE WAS UNGUARDED. That astonished Sharpe, but he sensed that the French garrison was tiny, which suggested the enemy had decided to throw all their troops into an assault on Lisbon and risk leaving Coimbra barely protected. Folk on the street told them the convent of Santa Clara was full of troops, but it was easy enough to avoid, and by late morning they were well south of the town on the road to Lisbon.

The verges were indeed strewn with discarded plunder, but scores of people were raking through the leavings and Sharpe did not have time to search for clothes and boots for the women. Nor could he stay on the road, for it would lead only to the French rearguard, and so, when the sun was at its height, they struck eastwards across country. Sarah and Joana, neither of whom had robust shoes, went barefoot.

They climbed into steep hills. The few villages were deserted, and by mid-afternoon they were among trees. They stopped to rest where a great outcrop of rock jutted into the valley like the prow of a monstrous ship, and from its summit Sharpe could see French troops far below. He took out his telescope, found it was undamaged after his adventures, and trained it down into the shadows of the valley where he saw fifty or more dragoons searching a small village for food.

Sarah joined him. "May I?" she asked, reaching for the telescope. Sharpe gave it to her and she stared down. "They're just pouring water onto the ground," she said after a while.

"Looking for food, love."

"How does that help?"

"Peasants can't carry their whole harvest off to safety," Sharpe explained, "so sometimes they bury it. Dig a hole, put the grain in, cover it with soil and put the turf back. You could walk right across and never see it, but pour water on the soil and it drains faster where it's been dug."

"They're not finding anything," she said.

"Good," Sharpe said, and watched her, thinking what a fine face she had, and thinking, too, that she was a spirited creature. Like Teresa, he reflected, and wondered what the Spanish girl did, or whether she even lived.

"They're going," Sarah reported, and collapsed the telescope, noticing the small brass plate attached to the biggest barrel. "*In gratitude*," she read aloud, "AW. Who's AW?"

"Wellington."

"Why was he grateful to you?"

"It was a fight in India," Sharpe said, "and I helped him."

"Just that?"

"He'd come off his horse," Sharpe said. "He was in a bit of trouble, really. Still, he got out safe enough."

Sarah handed him the glass. "Sergeant Harper says you're the best soldier in the army."

"Pat's full of Irish wind," Sharpe said. "Mind you, he's a terror himself. No one better in a fight."

"And Captain Vicente says you taught him everything he knows."

"Full of Portuguese wind."

"Yet you think your captaincy is at risk?"

"The army doesn't care if you're good, love."

"I don't believe you."

"I wish I didn't believe me," Sharpe said, then grinned. "I'll get by, love."

Sarah was about to speak, but whatever she wanted to say went unspoken because there was a crackle of gunfire from across the valley. Sharpe turned, saw nothing. The dragoons in the village were remounting their horses and were gazing southwards, but they could evidently see nothing either for they did not move in that direction. The musketry went on, a distant splintering sound, then slowly died away. "There,"

Sharpe said, and he pointed across the wide valley to where more French horsemen were spilling out of a high saddle in the hills. Sarah gazed and could see nothing until Sharpe gave her back the glass and told her where to look. "They've been ambushed, probably," he said.

"I thought no one was supposed to be here. Weren't they ordered to Lisbon?"

"Folk had a choice," Sharpe explained, "they could either go to Lisbon or climb into high ground. My guess is these hills are full of people. We just have to hope they're friendly."

"Why wouldn't they be?"

"How would you feel about an army that says you must leave home? Which tears down your mills, destroys your harvest and breaks your ovens? They hate the French, but they've not much love for us either."

They slept under the trees. Sharpe did not light a fire, for he had no idea who was in these hills or how they regarded soldiers. They woke early, cold and damp, and set off uphill in the gray first light. Vicente led, following a path that climbed steadily eastwards towards a range of rocky peaks, the highest of which was crowned with the stump of an ancient tower. "An *atalaia*," Vicente said.

"A what?"

"*Atalaia*. A watchtower. They are very old. They were built to keep a look out for the Moors." Vicente crossed himself. "Some were turned into windmills, others just decay. When we get to that one we will be able to see the route ahead."

The sun, streaked with purple and pink clouds, was behind them. The day was warming, helped by a southern wind. Off to the south, far away, a ragged smear of smoke rose from a valley, evidence that the French were searching the countryside, but Sharpe was confident no horsemen would climb this high. There was nothing up here to steal except heather, gorse and rock.

Both girls were suffering. The path was stony and Sarah's bare feet were too tender for the hard going so Sharpe made her wear his boots, first wrapping her feet in strips of cloth that he tore from the ragged hem of what was left of her dress. "You'll still get blisters," he warned her, but for a time she made better progress. Joana, more used to hardship, kept going, though the soles of her feet were bleeding. And still they climbed, sometimes losing sight of the watchtower as the path twisted through gullies. "Goat paths," Vicente guessed. "Nothing else could live up here."

They dropped into a small high valley where a tiny stream trickled between mossy rocks and Sharpe filled their canteens, then distributed the last of the food he had taken from Ferragus's warehouse. Joana was massaging her feet and Sarah was trying not to show the pain of her newly forming blisters. Sharpe jerked his head to Harper. "You and me," he said, "up that hill." Harper looked at the hill looming to their left. It lay north of them, off their path, and his face showed puzzlement as to why Sharpe should want to climb it. "Give them a rest," Sharpe said, and he took his boots back from Sarah who gratefully put her feet into the water. "We can see a long way from that peak," Sharpe said. Perhaps not as far as they would from the watchtower, but going up the hill was an excuse to give the girls some time to recover.

They climbed. "How are your feet?" Harper asked.

"Cut to bloody pieces," Sharpe said.

"I was thinking I should give my boots to Joana."

"She'd probably think she was wearing a boat on each foot," Sharpe said.

"She's managing, though. A tough one, that."

"Needs to be if she's going to endure you, Pat."

"Soft as lights with women, I am."

They climbed straight up through the tangling heather, the slope every bit as steep as the one the French had assailed at Bussaco, and both stopped talking long before they reached the summit. They were saving their breath. Sweat was pouring down Sharpe's face as he neared the peak which was crowned with a scatter of rocks and he kept looking up, willing the rocks to get closer, and it was on his fourth or fifth glance that he saw the small movement, saw the foreshortened barrel moving and he threw himself sideways. "Down, Pat!"

Sharpe was pushing the rifle forward when the musket fired. The puff of smoke blossomed among the rocks and the bullet ripped through the heather between him and Harper, and Sharpe immediately stood and, his tiredness forgotten, ran diagonally up the hill, daring anyone else on the summit to take a shot at him, but no shot sounded. Instead he could hear the clatter of a ramrod on a barrel and he knew whoever had fired was reloading and he swerved uphill, always watching the rocks for the sight of another barrel, and then he saw the man, a young man, just rising from behind a boulder, and Sharpe stopped and brought the rifle up. The young man saw him then, saw the soldier fifty paces from where he had expected him to be, and he began to move the musket and then understood that one more inch of movement would mean that the green-jacketed soldier would pull the trigger and he went very still. "Put the gun down," Sharpe said.

The young man did not understand him. He looked from Sharpe to Harper, who was now climbing towards his other side. "Put the bloody gun down!" Sharpe snarled and walked forward, keeping the rifle at his shoulder. "Down!"

"*Arma!*" Harper called. "*Por terra!*"

The young man looked as if he would twist and run away. "Go on, son," Sharpe said, "give me an excuse." And then the boy put the musket down and looked terrified as the two green men came up either side of him. He dropped behind a boulder, cowering there, expecting to be shot.

"Jesus," Sharpe said, for now he was on the hilltop and he could see that the young man had been a lookout, and that on the long downwards sweep of the far slope there were a score of other men, some of them bunched where the path that Sharpe and his companions had been using crossed the hill's shoulder. A half-dozen others, evidently alerted by the young man, were climbing towards the hilltop, but they stopped abruptly when they saw Sharpe and Harper appear on the summit.

"You were sleeping, son, weren't you?" Sharpe said. "Didn't see us till it was too late."

The young man did not understand and just looked helplessly from Sharpe to Harper.

"That was good, Pat," Sharpe said, picking up the young man's musket and tossing it to one side. "You learned Portuguese quickly."

"Picked up a word or two, sir."

Sharpe laughed. "So what do these buggers want, eh?" He turned and gazed at the six closest men who were staring up the long slope.

They were all civilians, refugees or possibly partisans. They were two hundred paces away and one had a dog, almost a wolf, on a rope leash. The dog was barking and trying to get away from his master to attack up the hill. All the men had muskets. Sharpe turned away and looked down to where Vicente was gazing up the slope, and Sharpe beckoned him. He waited, then saw Vicente and the two women begin to climb. "Best if we're all in the same place," he explained to Harper, then turned back because one of the six men had fired his musket. The men down the hill could not see their companion, who was hidden by the boulder, and perhaps they assumed he had escaped and so one of them opened fire. The ball went wild. Sharpe did not even hear it pass, but then a second man fired. The dog, excited by the sound of gunfire, was howling now, howling and leaping. A third man fired and this time the ball snapped past Sharpe's head.

"They need a bloody lesson," Sharpe said. He strode to the young man, pulled him to his feet and put the rifle to his head. The muskets stopped firing.

"We could shoot the bloody dog." Harper suggested.

"You can be sure to kill it at two hundred paces?" Sharpe asked. "And not just wound it? Because if you just wing it, Pat, that dog will want a mouthful of Irish meat as revenge."

"Better to shoot this bastard, sir, you're right," Harper said, standing on the other side of their terrified prisoner. The six men were now arguing amongst each other, while the rest, those who looked as if they had been waiting in ambush where the path crossed the lower crest, began to climb to the summit.

"There's almost thirty of them," Harper said. "We'll be hard put to deal with thirty."

"Fifteen each?" Sharpe suggested flippantly, then shook his head. "It won't come to that." He hoped it would not, but first he needed Vicente on the hilltop so that he could talk with the men.

Who began to spread out so that Sharpe could not get past them.

They had been waiting for him and he had come to them. And they had orders to kill.

PART THREE

THE LINES OF
TORRES VEDRAS

VICENTE REACHED SHARPE and Harper first, outclimbing the two women, who were hampered by their ragged skirts and bare feet. Vicente glanced at the armed men watching them, then talked to the young man who sounded ever more reluctant to answer as Vicente's voice grew angrier. "They were told to look out for us," Vicente finally explained to Sharpe, "and kill us."

"Kill us? Why?"

"Because they say we're traitors," Vicente spat angrily. "Major Ferreira was here with his brother and three other men. They said we'd been talking with the French and were now trying to reach our army to spy on it." He turned back to the young man and said something in a furious tone, then looked back to Sharpe. "And they believed him! They're fools!"

"They don't know us," Sharpe said, nodding at the men down the hill, "and maybe they do know Ferreira?"

"They know him," Vicente confirmed. "He provided those weapons earlier in the year." He nodded towards the guns the men were holding, then turned back to the young man, asked a question, received a one-word answer and immediately started down the hill.

"Where are you going?" Sharpe called after him.

"To talk to them, of course. Their leader's a man called Soriano."

"They're partisans?"

"Every man in the hills is a partisan," Vicente said, then dropped the rifle from his shoulder, unbuckled his sword belt and, thus unarmed to show he meant no mischief, strode on down the hill.

Sarah and Joana arrived at the crest. Joana began questioning the young man, who seemed even more frightened of her than he had been of Vicente, who had now reached the group of six men and was talking with them. Sarah stood beside Sharpe and gently touched his arm as if reassuring herself. "They want to kill us?"

"They've probably got something else in mind for you and Joana," Sharpe said, "but they want to kill me, Pat and Jorge. Major Ferreira was here. He told them we were enemies."

Sarah asked the young man a question, then turned back to Sharpe. "Ferreira was here last night," she said.

"So the bastard's half a day ahead of us."

"Sir?" Harper was watching down the hill and Sharpe looked to see that the six men had taken Vicente hostage by pointing a musket at his head. The implication was obvious. If Sharpe killed the young man, they would kill Vicente.

"Shit," Sharpe said, not sure what he should do now.

Joana made the decision. She ran down the hill, easily evading Harper's attempt to stop her, and she screamed at the men holding Vicente. She stood twenty yards from them and told them what had happened in Coimbra, how the French had raped and stolen and killed, and said how she had been dragged to a room by three Frenchmen and how the British soldiers had saved her. She unbuttoned the shirt to show them her torn dress, then she cursed the partisans because they had been fooled by their true enemies. "You trust Ferragus?" she asked them. "Has Ferragus ever shown you a kindness? And if these men are spies, why are they here? Why do they not travel with the French?" One man evidently tried to answer her, but she spat at him. "You are doing the enemy's work," she said scornfully. "You want your wife and daughters to be raped? Or are you not man enough to have a wife? You play with goats instead, do you?" She spat at him a second time, buttoned the shirt and turned back up the hill.

Four men followed her. They came cautiously, their muskets held towards Sharpe and Harper, and they stopped a safe distance away and asked a question. Joana answered them.

"She's saying," Sarah translated for Sharpe, "that you burned the food in the city that Ferragus would have sold to the French." Joana was evidently telling the four men more than that for she went on, spitting out words like bullets, her tone scornful, and Sarah smiled. "If she was my pupil," she said, "I'd wash her mouth out with soap."

"Good job I'm not your pupil," Sharpe said. The four men, evidently shamed by Joana's passion, glanced up at him and he saw the doubt on their faces and, on impulse, he pulled the young man to his feet. The four muskets immediately twitched upwards. "Go," Sharpe told the young man, releasing his hold on the frayed collar, "go and tell them we mean no harm."

Sarah translated and the young man, with a nod of gratitude, ran down the hill to his companions, the tallest of whom slung his musket and walked slowly up the hill. He still asked questions that Joana answered, but eventually he offered Sharpe a curt nod and invited the strangers to talk with him. "Does that mean they believe us?" Sharpe asked.

"They're not sure," Sarah answered.

It took the best part of an hour's talking to persuade the men that they had been deceived by Major Ferreira, and it was only when Vicente put his right hand on a crucifix and swore on his life, on his wife's soul and on the life of his baby child that the men accepted that Sharpe and his companions were not traitors, and then they took the fugitives to a small, high village that was little more than a sprawl of hovels where goatherds stayed in the summer. The place was now crammed with refugees who were waiting for the war to pass. The men were armed, mostly with British muskets that Ferreira had supplied, and that was why they had trusted the Major, though enough of the fugitives were familiar with the Major's brother and had been worried when Ferragus came to their settlement. Others knew of Vicente's family, and they were helpful in persuading Soriano that the Portuguese officer was telling the truth. "There were five of them," Soriano told Vicente, "and we gave them mules. The only mules we had."

"Did they say where they were going?"

"Eastwards, *senhor*."

"To Castelo Branco?"

"Then to the river," Soriano confirmed. He had been a miller, though his mill had been dismantled and its precious wooden mechanism burned and he did not know how he was to make a living now that he was behind the French lines.

"What you do," Vicente told him, "is take your men southwards and attack the French. You'll find foraging parties in the foothills. Kill them. Keep killing them. And in the meantime you give us shoes and clothes for the women, and guides to take us after Major Ferreira."

A woman in the settlement looked at the wound in Vicente's shoulder and said it was healing well, then rewrapped it in moss and a new bandage. Shoes and footcloths were found for Sarah and Joana, but the only dresses were heavy and black, not garments suitable for traveling miles across rough country, and Sarah persuaded the women to give up some boys' breeches, shirts and jackets instead. There was little food in the village, but some hard bread and goat's cheese were wrapped in cloth and given to them and then, near midday, they set off. They had, so far as Vicente could gauge, some sixty miles still to travel before they reached the River Tagus where, he hoped, they could find a boat that would carry them downstream towards Lisbon and the British and Portuguese armies.

"Three days' walking," Sharpe said, "maybe less."

"Twenty miles a day?" Sarah sounded dubious.

"We should do better than that," Sharpe insisted. The army reckoned to march fifteen miles a day, but the army was encumbered with guns, baggage and walking wounded. General Craufurd, vainly trying to reach Talavera in time for the battle, had marched the Light Brigade over forty miles in a day, but that had been on half-decent roads and Sharpe knew his route would be across country, up hill and down dale, following the paths where no French patrol would dare to ride. He would be lucky, he thought, if they reached the river in four days, and that meant he would fail because the Ferreira brothers had mules and would probably complete the journey in two.

He thought about that as they walked eastwards. It was high, bare country, barren and empty, though they could see settlements far below in the valleys. It would be a long unrewarding walk, he thought, because by the time they reached the river and found a boat the brothers would be a long way ahead, probably in Lisbon, and Sharpe knew the army would never give him permission to pursue the feud into the city. "Is Castelo Branco," he asked Vicente, "the only route to the river?"

Vicente shook his head. "It's the safe route," he said. "No French. And this road leads there."

"Call this a road?" It was a track, fit for men and mules, but hardly deserving the name of road. Sharpe turned and saw that the watchtower close to where they had encountered Soriano was still visible. "We'll never catch the bastards," he grumbled.

Vicente stopped and scratched a rough map in the earth with his foot. It showed the Tagus curling east out of Spain, then turning south towards the sea and so narrowing the peninsula on which Lisbon was built. "What they are doing," he said, "is going directly east, but if you want to take a risk we can go south across the Serra da Lousã. Those hills are not so high as these, but the French could be there."

Sharpe looked at the crude map. "But we'd reach the river farther south?"

"We'll reach the Zêzere"—Vicente scratched another river, this one a tributary of the Tagus—"and if we follow the Zêzere then it will come to the Tagus well south of where they're going."

"Save a day?"

"If there are no French." Vicente sounded dubious. "The farther south we go the more likely we are to meet them."

"But it will save a day?"

"Maybe more."

"Then let's do it."

So they turned south and saw no dragoons, no Frenchmen and few Portuguese. On the second day after their encounter with Soriano's men it began to rain: a gray, Atlantic drizzle that soaked them all to the bone and left them chilled and sore, but it was downhill now, going from the bare hilltops into pastureland and vineyards and small walled fields. The three escorts left them, not wanting to go into the Zêzere valley where the French might be, but Sharpe, throwing caution to the wind, followed a road down to the river. It was dusk when they came to the fast-flowing Zêzere which was dappled by rain, and they spent the night in a small shrine beneath the outstretched hand of a plaster saint whose shoulders were thick with bird dung. Next morning they crossed the river at a place where the water foamed white across gaunt and slippery boulders. Harper made a short rope by joining the rifle and musket slings, then they helped each other from stone to stone, wading where they had to, and it took much longer than Sharpe had hoped, but once on the far bank he felt more secure. The French army was on the road to Lisbon and that was now over twenty miles to the west, on the river's opposite bank, and he reckoned any French foraging parties would stay on that side of the Zêzere and so he walked openly on the eastern bank. It was still hard going, for the river flowed fast through high hills, twisting between great rocky shoulders, but it became easier the farther south they went and by the afternoon they were following tracks which led from village to village. A few inhabitants were still in their cottages and they reported seeing no enemy. They were poor folk, but they offered the strangers cheese and bread and fish.

They reached the Tagus that evening. The weather was worse now. The rain was coming out of the west in great gray swathes that lashed the trees and turned small rivulets into streams. The Tagus was wide, a great flood of water being beaten by the seething rain, and Sharpe crouched at its edge and looked for any sign that there were boats and saw none. The Portuguese government had scoured the river, taking away any craft to prevent the French from using boats to circumvent the new defenses at Torres Vedras, but without a boat Sharpe was trapped, and by crossing the Zêzere he had put that river between himself and Lisbon and to recross it, in order to follow the Tagus's right bank down towards the army, he would have to go back upstream to find a place where the smaller river could be forded. "There'll be a boat," he said. "There was at Oporto, remember?"

"We were lucky there," Vicente said.

"It isn't luck, Jorge," Sharpe said. At Oporto the British and Portuguese had destroyed the vessels on the Douro, yet Sharpe and Vicente had found some boats, enough indeed to let the army cross. "It isn't luck," Sharpe said again, "but peasants. They can't afford new boats, so they'll have given the government their old wrecked boats and hidden the good ones, so we just have to find one." Ferreira and his brother, Sharpe thought sourly, would find it easier to secure a boat. They carried money and he stared upriver, praying that he had got ahead of them.

They spent the night in a shed that leaked like a sieve and next morning, cold and damp and tired, they walked upstream, coming to a village where a group of men, all armed, some of them with ancient matchlocks, met them at the end of the street. Vicente talked with them, but it was plain the men were in no mood to be friendly. These river settlements had been harrowed by the Portuguese army to make certain no boats were left for the enemy, and Vicente was unable to persuade them to reveal any that might be hidden, and the men's guns, old as most of them were, convinced Sharpe that they were wasting their time. "They're telling us to go to Abrantes," Vicente said. "They say there will be boats hidden there."

"There are boats hidden here," Sharpe grumbled. "How far is Abrantes?"

"We could be there by midday?" Vicente sounded dubious. And the Ferreira brothers, Sharpe thought, would surely be on the river already and floating south. He was fairly confident that, by following the Zêzere, he had managed to get ahead of them, but at any moment he half expected to see them float past and so escape him.

"I can talk to them." Vicente suggested, gesturing at the men. "If I promise to come back and pay for the boat, perhaps they'll sell us one."

"They won't believe a promise like that," Sharpe said. "No, we keep walking." They left the village, followed by seven men who were cheerful in their victory. Sharpe ignored them. He was going north now, the wrong direction entirely, but he said nothing until the villagers, sure they had seen the threat off, abandoned them with a shouted injunction to stay away. Sharpe waited till they were out of sight. "Time to get nasty," he said. "Those bastards have got a boat and I want it."

He led his companions off the road into the higher ground, then back towards the village, staying hidden in trees or behind the rows of vines that straggled on chestnut stakes. The rain kept coming down. His plan was simple enough: to find something that the villagers valued more than their boats and threaten that thing, but as they crept back towards the houses there was nothing obvious to take. There was no livestock, nothing except some chickens scratching in a fenced garden, but the men who had marched the strangers out of the village were celebrating in the tavern. Their boasting and laughter were loud and Sharpe felt his anger rise. "Fast in," he told Harper, "and scare the hell out of them."

Harper took the seven-barrel gun from his shoulder. "Ready when you are, sir."

"The two of us go in," Sharpe said to Vicente and the women, "and you three stand at the door. And look as if you're ready to use your guns."

He and Harper jumped a fence, ran across some rows of beans and threw open the tavern's back door. A dozen men were gathered in the room, clustered about a barrel of wine, and most still had guns on their shoulders, but Sharpe was across the floor before any could unsling a musket and Harper was bellowing at them from the empty hearth, his volley gun aimed at the group. Sharpe began by snatching muskets off shoulders and, when one man resisted, he slapped him around the face with his rifle's barrel, then he kicked the wine barrel off its small stand so that it crashed onto the stone floor with a noise like a cannon firing. Then, when the men were cowed by the noise, he backed to the front door and pointed the rifle at them. "I need a bloody boat," he snarled.

Vicente took over. He slung his rifle, walked slowly forward and spoke softly. He spoke of the war, of the horrors that had been visited on Coimbra, and he promised the men that the same would happen in their village if the French were not defeated. "Your wives will be violated," he said, "your houses burned, your children murdered. I have seen it. But the enemy can be beaten, will be beaten, and you can help. You must help." He was an advocate suddenly, the tavern his courtroom and the disarmed men his jury, and the speech he gave was impassioned. He had never spoken in a courtroom, his law had been practiced in an office where he enforced the regulations of the port trade, but he had dreamed of being an advocate, and now he spoke with eloquence and honesty. He appealed to the villagers' patriotism, but then, knowing what kind of men they were, he promised that the boat would be paid for. "In full," he said, "but not now. We have no money. But on my honor I shall return here and I shall pay you the price we agree. And when the French are gone," he ended, "you will have the satisfaction of knowing that you helped defeat them." He stopped, turned away and made the sign of the cross, and Sharpe saw that the men had been moved by Vicente's speech. It was still a near thing, for a promise of money in the future was the stuff of dreams, and patriotism struggled with cupidity, but finally a man agreed. He would trust the young officer and sell them his boat.

It was not much of a boat, merely an old skiff that had been used to ferry folk across the mouth of the Zêzere. It was eighteen feet long, big-bellied, with two thwarts for oarsmen and four sets of tholes for oars. It had a high, curving prow and a wide flat stern. The ferryman had hidden the boat by sinking it in the Zêzere, but the men of the village emptied it of stones, floated it, provided the oars and then demanded that Vicente repeat the promise to pay for the craft. Only then did they let Sharpe and his companions board the vessel. "How long to Lisbon?" Vicente asked them.

"It will drift there in a day and a night," the ferryman said, then watched as his boat was unhandily rowed out into the stream. Sharpe and Harper were at the oars and neither was used to such things and at first they were clumsy, but the current was doing the real work by swirling them downstream while they learned to control the long oars and at last they rowed steadily down the center of the Tagus. Vicente was in the bows, watching the river ahead, and Joana and Sarah were in the wide stern. If it had not been raining, if the brisk wind had not been kicking up the river to splash cold water into a boat that was perceptibly leaking, it might have been a jaunt, but instead they shivered beneath a dark sky as their small boat was swept southwards between the rain-darkened flanks of great hills. The river flowed fast, carrying its water from far across Spain to hurry them towards the sea.

And then the French saw them.

THE FORT WAS SIMPLY KNOWN as Work Number 119, and it was not much of a fort, merely a bastion built on the summit of a low hill, then given a stone-roofed magazine and six gun emplacements. The guns were twelve-pounders, taken from a flotilla of Russian warships that had taken shelter in Lisbon from an Atlantic storm and there been captured by the Royal Navy, while the gunners were a mix of Portuguese and British artillerymen who had ranged their unfamiliar weapons, determining that the shots would reach across the wide valley that was spread east and west beneath Work Number 119. To the east were ten more forts, reaching to the Tagus, while to the west, stretching more than twenty miles to the Atlantic, were over a hundred more forts and bastions that snaked in two lines across the hilltops. They were the Lines of Torres Vedras.

Three major roads pierced the lines. The principal road, halfway between the Tagus and the sea, was the main road to Lisbon, but there was another road, running beside the river and thus not far from Work Number 119, and that eastern road offered another route to the Portuguese capital. Masséna, of course, did not have to use either route, nor the third road which pierced the lines at Torres Vedras and was protected by the River Sizandre. He might choose to outflank the three roads and attempt to march overland, attacking through the wilder and lonelier country that lay between the roads, but he would only find more forts and bastions.

He would find more than the newly constructed forts. The northward-facing slopes of the hills had been scarped by thousands of laborers who had hacked at the soil to steepen the slopes so that no infantry could possibly attack uphill, and where the slopes were made of rock the engineers had drilled and blasted the stone to create new cliff faces. If the infantry ignored the scarped slopes and endured the artillery bombardment from the crests, they could march into the valleys between the steepened hills, but there they would find huge barriers of thorn bushes filling the low ground like monstrous dams. The thorn bush barricades were strengthened by felled trees, protected where possible by dams that flooded the valleys, and were flanked by smaller bastions so that any attacking column would find itself funneled into a place of death and under the flail of cannon and musket fire.

Forty thousand troops, most of them Portuguese, manned the forts, while the rest of the two armies were deployed behind the lines, ready to march wherever an attack might threaten. Some British troops were stationed in the lines and the South Essex had been given a sector between Work Number 114 and Work Number 119 where Lieutenant Colonel Lawford had summoned his senior officers to show them the extent of their responsibilities. Captain Slingsby was the last to arrive and the other men watched as he negotiated the steep, muddy steps that climbed up to the masonry firestep.

"A guinea says he won't make it," Leroy muttered to Forrest.

"I can't conceive that he's drunk," Forrest said, though without much certainty.

Everyone else believed Slingsby was drunk. He was mounting the steps very slowly, taking exaggerated care to place his feet in the exact center of each tread. He did not look up until he reached the top when, with evident satisfaction, he announced to the assembled officers that there were forty-three steps.

This news took Colonel Lawford aback. He alone had not watched Slingsby's precarious ascent, but now turned with a look of polite surprise. "Forty-three?"

"Important thing to know, sir," Slingsby said. He meant that it was important in case the steps had to be climbed in darkness, but that explanation vanished from his head before he had time to say it. "Very important, sir," he added earnestly.

"I am sure we shall all remember it," Lawford said with a touch of asperity, then he gestured towards the rain-soaked northern landscape. "If the French do come, gentlemen," he said, "then this is where we stop them."

"Hear, hear," Slingsby said. Everyone ignored him.

"We let them come," Lawford went on, "and permit them to break themselves against our positions."

"Break themselves," Slingsby said, but quietly.

"And it is possible they will attempt a breakthrough here." Lawford hurried on in case his brother-in-law added more words. The Colonel pointed west to where a small valley twisted southwards past Work Number 119 and then curled around the back of the hill. "Major Forrest and I rode north yesterday," he said, "and looked at our position from the French point of view."

"Very wise," Slingsby said.

"And from those hills," Lawford continued, "that valley is a temptation. It seems to penetrate our lines."

"Penetrate," Slingsby repeated, nodding. Major Leroy half expected him to take out a notebook and pencil and write the word down.

"In truth," Lawford went on, "the valley is entirely blocked. It leads to nothing except a barricade of felled trees, thorn bushes and flooded land, but the French will not know that."

"Ridiculous," Slingsby muttered, though whether that was a judgment on Lawford or the French it was hard to tell.

"But we must nevertheless expect such an attack," Lawford continued, "and be prepared to deal with it."

"Unleash the cat," Slingsby said obscurely, though only Leroy heard him.

"If such an attack develops," Lawford said, his cloak billowing in a sudden gust of wet wind that blew around the hilltop, "the enemy will be under artillery fire from this work and from every other fort within range. If they survive it they will be penned in the valley and we would offer volley fire from the shoulder of this hill. They cannot climb the hill, which means they can only suffer and die in the valley."

Slingsby looked surprised at this, but managed to say nothing.

"What we cannot do," Lawford went on, "is allow the French to establish batteries in the larger valley." He pointed to the low ground that lay ahead of Work Number 119. This was the wide valley which lay north of the lines and on the other side of which were the hills that would doubtless become the French positions. The stretch of lowland had once been rich and fertile, but the engineers had breached the embankment of the Tagus, letting the river flood much of the country beneath the fort. The floods came and went with the tide, which was high now, so that under Work Number 119 was a stretch of wind-rippled water that loosely followed the course of a stream that came from the west and meandered through the valley to its confluence with the Tagus.

The stream made a great double bend beneath the hill where Lawford spoke. It swerved from the northern side of the valley, almost reached the southern and then curved back to run into the Tagus. Inside the first bend, and on the British bank, was an ancient barn that was little more than a stone ruin in a grove of trees, while within the second curve, and thus on the French side of the stream, was what had once been a prosperous farm with a big house, some smaller cottages, a dairy and a pair of cattle sheds. All were abandoned now, people and livestock ordered south to escape the French, and the buildings looked forlorn in the inundated landscape. The farm itself was high and dry, perched on a small rise, so that it resembled an island in a wind-fretted lake, though as the tide ebbed the floods would slowly drain away, but the ground would still remain waterlogged and any French advance beside the Tagus would thus be forced to march westwards on the valley's far side until it reached the drier ground somewhere near the half-ruined barn. The enemy could cross the stream there and advance on the British works, a possibility that Lawford raised with his officers. "And if the devils manage to put some heavy guns in that barn," he went on, "or in those farm buildings," he pointed to the farm which lay a half mile east of the barn and was linked to the smaller building by an embanked track that was carried over the stream by a stone bridge, though the flooding meant that only the bridge's parapets were now visible, "then they can bombard these positions. That will not happen, gentlemen."

Major Leroy thought it a most unlikely proposition. To get to the dilapidated barn the French would have to cross the stream, while to reach the farm would mean negotiating a long stretch of waterlogged ground, and neither would make it easy to move guns and caissons. Leroy suspected Lawford knew that, but he also reckoned the Colonel did not want his men becoming complacent. "And to stop it from happening, gentlemen," Lawford said, "we're going to patrol. We're going to patrol vigorously. Company size patrols, down in the valley, so that any damned Frog who shows his nose will get it bloodied." Lawford turned and pointed at Captain Slingsby, "Your task, Cornelius . . ."

"Patrol," Slingsby said quickly, "vigorously."

"Is to establish a picquet in that barn," Lawford said, irritated at the interruption. "Day and night, Cornelius. The light company will live there, you understand?"

Slingsby stared down at the old barn beside the stream. The roof had partially fallen in and the place looked nothing like as comfortable as the billets that the light company had been given in the village behind Work Number 119, and for a moment Slingsby did not seem to entirely understand his orders. "We're taking up residence there, sir?" he asked plaintively.

"In the barn, Cornelius," Lawford replied patiently. "Fortify the place and stay there unless the whole damned French army attacks you, upon which eventuality you have my reluctant permission to withdraw." The other officers chuckled, recognizing a joke, but Slingsby nodded seriously. "I want the light company in position by nightfall," Lawford went on, "and you'll be relieved on Sunday. In the meantime our patrols will keep you supplied with provisions." Lawford paused because a nearby telegraph station had begun to transmit a message and the officers had all turned to watch the inflated pigs' bladders being hoisted up the mast. "And now, gentlemen," Lawford retrieved their attention, "I want you to walk this section of the line," he gestured to the east, "familiarize yourselves with every fort, every path, every inch. We might be here a long time. Cornelius? A word."

The other officers walked away, going to explore the line between Work Number 119 and Work Number 114. Lawford, when he was alone with Slingsby, frowned at the smaller man. "It pains me to ask this," he said, "but are you drunk?"

Slingsby did not answer at once, instead he looked indignant and it seemed as though he would return a sharp answer, but then words failed him and he just turned away and gazed across the valley. The rain on his face made it appear as though he were crying. "Drank too much last night," he finally confessed in an abject voice, "and I apologize."

"We all do from time to time," Lawford said, "but not every night."

"Good for you," Slingsby said.

"Good for me?" Lawford was lost.

"Rum deters the fever," Slingsby said. "It's a known thing. It's a feb—" He paused, then tried again. "A febri—"

"A febrifuge," Lawford said for him.

"Exactly," Slingsby said vigorously. "Doctor Wetherspoon told me that. He was our fellow in the West Indies and a good man, a very good man. Rum, he said, it's the only feb— The only thing that works. Died in their hundreds, they did! But not me. Rum. It's medicine!"

Lawford sighed. "I have offered you an opportunity," he said quietly, "and it is an opportunity most men would seize gladly. You have command of a company, Cornelius, and it's a very fine one, and it seems ever more likely that it will need a new captain. Sharpe?" Lawford shrugged, wondering where on earth Sharpe was. "If Sharpe doesn't return," he continued, "then I shall have to appoint another man."

Slingsby just nodded.

"You are the obvious candidate," Lawford said, "but not if you are inebriated."

"You're right, sir," Slingsby said, "and I apologize. Fear of fever, sir, that's all it is."

"My fear," Lawford said, "is that the French will attack in the dawn. Half light, Cornelius, a touch of morning mist? We won't be able to see much from up here, but if you're in the barn then you'll see them quickly enough. That's why I'm putting you there, Cornelius. A picquet! I hear your muskets and rifles firing and I know the enemy is out and that you're retreating here. So keep a good watch and don't let me down!"

"I won't, sir. I won't." If Slingsby had been more than a little drunk when he arrived at the bastion he was now stone-cold sober. He had not meant to be drunk. He had woken feeling cold and damp and he had thought a little rum might revive him. He never meant to drink too much, but the rum gave him confidence and he needed it for he was finding the light company very hard to manage. They did not like him, he knew that, and the rum gave him the drive to cope with their obdurate behavior. "We won't let you down, sir," he said, meaning every word.

"That's good," Lawford said warmly, "very good." In truth he did not need the picquet in the old barn, but if he was to keep the promise he had given to his wife then he had to make a decent officer out of Slingsby, so now he would give him a simple job, one that would keep him alert instead of idling behind the lines. This was Slingsby's chance to show he could manage men, and Lawford was generous in giving it to him. "And I insist on one last thing," Lawford said.

"Anything, sir," Slingsby said eagerly.

"No rum, Cornelius. Don't take your medicine to the picquet, understand? And if you feel you're getting the fever, come back and we'll let the doctor have at you. Wear flannel, eh? That's supposed to ward it off."

"Flannel," Slingsby said, nodding.

"And what you do now," the Colonel went on patiently, "is take a dozen men and reconnoiter the farm. There's a path down the hill behind Work Number 118," he pointed, "and meanwhile the rest of your company can get ready. Clean muskets, sharp bayonets, fresh flints and full cartridge boxes. Tell Mister Knowles you're drawing rations for three days and be ready to deploy this afternoon."

"Very good, sir," Slingsby said, "and thank you, sir."

Lawford watched Slingsby go down the steps, then he sighed and took out his telescope which he mounted on a tripod already placed on the bastion. He stooped to the eyepiece and gazed at the northern landscape. The hills across the valley were crowned with three broken windmills, nothing left of them but their white stone stumps. Those, he supposed, would become French watchtowers. He swung the glass to the right, coming at last to a glimpse of the Tagus which swept wide towards the sea. A Royal Navy gunboat was anchored in the river, its ensign hanging limp in the rain. "If they come," a voice spoke behind Lawford, "then they can't use the road because it's flooded, so they'll be forced to make a detour and come straight up here."

Lawford straightened from the glass and saw it was Major Hogan who was swathed in an oilskin cape and had a black oilskin cover over his cocked hat. "You're well?" Lawford greeted the Irishman.

"I can feel a cold coming on," Hogan said, "a damned cold. First of the winter, eh?"

"Not winter yet, Hogan."

"Feels like it. May I?" Hogan gestured at the telescope.

"Be my guest," Lawford said, and courteously wiped the rain from the outer lens. "How's the Peer?"

"His lordship thrives," Hogan said, stooping to the glass, "and sends his regards. He's angry, of course."

"Angry?"

"All those damned croakers, Lawford, who say the war's lost. Men who write home and get their block-headed opinions in the newspapers.

He'd like to shoot the whole damned lot of them." Hogan was silent for a few seconds as he gazed at the British gunboat in the river, then he turned a mischievous look on Lawford. "You're not writing home with a bad opinion of his lordship's strategy, are you, Lawford?"

"Good Lord, no!" Lawford said, honestly.

Hogan bent to the glass again. "The flooding isn't all we hoped for," he said, "or what Colonel Fletcher hoped for. But it should suffice. They can't use the road, anyway, so what the bastards will do, Lawford, is march inland. Follow the base of those hills," Hogan was tracking the possible French route with the telescope, "and somewhere near that abandoned barn they'll cross over and come straight at you."

"Exactly what I'd surmised," Lawford said, "and then they'll advance into that valley." He nodded to the low ground that curled about the hill.

"Where they'll die," Hogan said with an indecent satisfaction. He stood up straight and winced at a twinge in his back. "In truth, Lawford, I don't expect them to try. But they might get desperate. Any news of Sharpe?"

Lawford hesitated, surprised by the question, then realized that it was probably the reason Hogan had sought him out. "None."

"Bloody lost, is he?"

"I fear it's time to write him out of the books," Lawford said, meaning that he could officially declare Sharpe missing and so create a vacant captainship.

"A bit premature, don't you think?" Hogan suggested vaguely. "Your affair, of course, Lawford, your affair entirely, and no damned business of mine whether you write him out or not." He stooped to the glass again and stared at one of the broken mills that crowned a hilltop across the wide valley. "What was he doing when he went missing?"

"Looking for turpentine, I think. That and escorting an English woman."

"Ah!" Hogan said, still vaguely, then straightened from the glass again. "A woman, eh? That sounds like Mister Sharpe, doesn't it? Good for him. That was in Coimbra, yes?"

"In Coimbra, yes," Lawford confirmed, then added indignantly, "He never turned up!"

"Another fellow disappeared there," Hogan said, standing at the bastion's edge and staring through the rain at the northern hills. "A major, quite important. He does for the Portuguese what I do for the Peer. Be a bad thing if he fell into French hands."

Lawford was no fool and knew that Hogan did not just make vague conversation. "You think they're connected?"

"I know they're connected," Hogan said. "Sharpe and this fellow had what you might call a disagreement."

"Sharpe never told me!" Lawford was piqued.

"Flour? On a hilltop?"

"Ah. He did tell me. No details, though."

"Richard never wastes details on senior officers," Hogan said, then paused to take a pinch of snuff. He sneezed. "He doesn't tell us," he went on, "in case we get confused. But he coped, in a way, and got himself thoroughly beaten up as a result."

"Beaten up?"

"The night before the battle."

"He said he'd tripped."

"Well, he would, wouldn't he?" Hogan was not surprised. "So, yes, the two were connected, but whether they still are is very dubious. Very dubious, but not impossible. I have great faith in Sharpe."

"As do I," Lawford said.

"Indeed you do," Hogan said, who knew more about the South Essex than Lawford would ever have guessed. "So if Sharpe does turn up, Lawford, send him on to the Peer's headquarters, would you? Tell him we need his information about Major Ferreira." Hogan very much doubted that Wellington would want to waste a second on Sharpe, but Hogan did, and it did no harm for Lawford to think that the General shared that wish.

"Of course I will," Lawford promised.

"We're at Pero Negro," Hogan said, "a couple of hours' ride westwards. And of course we'll send him back as soon as we can. I'm sure you're eager for Sharpe to resume his proper duties." There was a faint stress on the word "proper" that did not escape Lawford who sensed the mildest of reproofs, and the Colonel was wondering whether he should explain just what had happened between Sharpe and Slingsby when Hogan suddenly gave an exclamation and put his eye to the glass. "Our friends are here," he said.

For a moment Lawford thought Hogan meant that Sharpe had turned up, but then he saw horses on the far hill and he knew it was the French. The first patrols had come to the lines, and that meant Masséna's army could not be far behind.

The Lines of Torres Vedras, built without the knowledge of the British government, had cost two hundred thousand pounds. They were the greatest, most expensive defensive works ever made in Europe.

And now they would be tested.

⚜

THEY WERE DRAGOONS, the inevitable, green-coated dragoons who rode along the river beneath the looming hills of the Tagus's western bank. There were at least thirty of them and they had plainly been foraging for they had two small cows tied to one man's horse, but now, in the wet afternoon, they saw the small boat with its three men and two women, and the chance for sport was too good for the dragoons to pass up. They began by shouting that the boat was to be brought to their bank, but they had no expectation that their words would be understood, let alone obeyed, and a few seconds afterwards the first man fired.

The carbine shot splashed into the water five paces short of the boat. Sharpe and Harper began rowing harder, steering the boat obliquely away from the horsemen towards the eastern bank, and the dragoons spurred on ahead, a dozen or more of the horsemen dismounting where a wooded spur projected into the river. "They're getting ready to fire at us," Vicente warned.

The river made a bend around the wooded headland and on its eastern bank, a hundred paces from the dragoons, a vast tree had fallen into the water where it lay, half in and half out, its gaunt, sun-whitened branches jutting into the drizzle. Sharpe, twisting on the thwart, saw the tree and tugged hard on his left oar to steer for it. The other dragoons had dismounted now and hurried to the river's edge where they knelt, aimed and fired. The balls skipped across the river and one drove a splinter out of the small boat's gunwale. "You see the tree, Pat?" Sharpe asked, and Harper turned on the thwart and grunted confirmation and the two pulled at the heavy oars as another ragged volley crackled from the far bank, then the high, tarred prow of the boat smashed into the dead branches that tangled the backwater formed by the huge, pale trunk. A carbine bullet smacked into the dead wood and another whip-cracked overhead as Vicente pulled the boat farther into the sanctuary made by the fallen tree. Now, so long as they kept their heads down, the dragoons could not see them and could not hit them, but that did not deter the French, who kept up a desultory fire, evidently convinced that sooner or later the boat must reappear.

Vicente got tired of it first. He stood and edged his rifle over the tree. "I must find out if I can still fire a rifle," he said.

"Your left shoulder won't stop you," Sharpe said.

"Fire it accurately, I mean," Vicente said, and bent to the sights. The dragoons were using smoothbore carbines that were even less accurate than a musket, but at this range Vicente's rifle was deadly and he aimed at a mounted man he presumed was an officer. The dragoons had seen him, though whether they saw his gun was doubtful, and a flurry of shots banged from the far bank. None came close. Sharpe was peering over the trunk, curious as to how good a marksman Vicente was. He heard the bang of the rifle and saw the dragoon officer twitch hard back to leave a spray of blood. The man fell sideways.

"Good shooting," Sharpe said, impressed.

"I practiced all last winter," Vicente said. He could fire the rifle well enough, but reloading hurt his wounded shoulder. "If I am to be a leader of a *tirador* company then I must be a good marksman, yes?"

"Yes," Sharpe said, as a volley of French carbine fire rattled through the dead branches.

"And I won every competition," Vicente said as modestly as he could, "but it was only because of practice." He rammed a new bullet down and stood again. "This time I will kill the horse," he said.

He did, too, and Sharpe and Harper both added bullets into the group of dismounted dragoons. The carbines retaliated with a furious rattle of shots, but all were wasted. Some thumped into the tree, some threw splashes from the river, but most flew harmlessly overhead. Vicente flinched as he reloaded, then calmly shot a man standing up to his knees in the river in hope of closing the range, and the dragoons at last realized that they were making idiots of themselves by offering easy targets to men who were using rifles, and so they ran back to their horses, mounted, and disappeared into the trees.

Sharpe watched the horsemen riding south through the trees as he reloaded. "They'll be waiting for us downstream," he said.

"Unless they're going back to their army." Harper suggested.

Vicente stood and peered over the tree, but saw no enemy. "I think they'll be staying on the river," he said. "They won't have found much food between here and Coimbra, so they'll be wanting to make a bridge somewhere."

"A bridge?" Harper asked.

"To reach this bank," Vicente said. "There will be plenty of food on this bank. And if they do make a bridge it will be at Santarém."

"Where's that?"

"South," Vicente said, nodding downstream, "an old fortress above the river."

"Which we have to pass?" Sharpe asked.

"I suggest we do it tonight," Vicente said. "We should rest here for a while, wait for dark, then float downstream."

Sharpe wondered if that was what the Ferreira brothers would be doing. He constantly stared northwards, half expecting to see them, and worried that he did not. Perhaps they had changed their minds? Maybe they had gone to the northern mountains, or else had crossed the Tagus much higher up and used their money to buy horses to carry them down the eastern bank. He told himself it did not really matter, that the only important thing was to get back to the army, but he wanted to find the brothers. Ferreira, at least, should pay for his treachery and Sharpe had a score to settle with Ferragus.

They lingered till dusk, making a fire ashore and brewing a can of strong, gunpowder-flavored tea with the last leaves from Sharpe and Harper's haversacks. Any dragoons would long have ridden back to their base for fear of the partisans who were at their most dangerous in the darkness, and as the light faded Sharpe and Harper pushed the boat out of their refuge and let it drift downstream again. The rain persisted: a soft drizzle that soaked and chilled them as the last light went. Now they were at the mercy of the stream, unable to see or steer, and they let the boat go where it wanted. Sometimes, far off, there was the misted gleam of a fire high in the western hills, and once there was a bigger fire, much closer, but who had lit it was a mystery. Once or twice they bumped into solid pieces of driftwood, and then they brushed past a fallen tree, and an hour or so later, after it seemed to Sharpe that they had drifted for hours, they saw a cluster of rain-hazed lights high up on the western bank. "Santarém," Vicente said softly.

There were sentries on the high wall, lit up there by fires behind the parapet, and Sharpe assumed they were French. He could hear men singing in the town and he imagined the soldiers in the taverns and wondered if the rape and horror that had raged through Coimbra was being visited on Santarém's townsfolk. He crouched low in the boat, even though he knew that any sentry on that high wall could see nothing against the river's inky blackness. It seemed to take forever to pass beneath the ancient ramparts, but at last the lights faded and there was only the wet darkness. Sharpe fell asleep. Sarah bailed the boat with a tin cup. Harper snored while, beside him, Joana shivered. The river was wider now, wider and faster, and Sharpe woke in the wolf light before dawn to see misted trees on the western bank and fog everywhere else. The rain had stopped. He unshipped his oars and gave a few tugs, to warm himself more than anything else. Sarah smiled at him from the stern. "I've been dreaming," she said, "of a cup of tea."

"None left," Sharpe said.

"That's why I was dreaming of it," she said.

Harper had woken and started rowing now, but it seemed to Sharpe they were making no progress at all. The fog had thickened and the boat seemed suspended in a pearly whiteness into which the water faded. He tugged harder at the oars and finally saw the vague shape of a twisted tree on the eastern bank and he kept his eyes on the tree, kept rowing as strongly as he could, and slowly became convinced that the tree was staying in the same place however hard he pulled.

"Tide," Vicente said.

"Tide?"

"It comes up the river," Vicente said, "and it's carrying us backwards. Or trying to. But it will turn."

Sharpe thought about going to the eastern bank and mooring the boat, but then decided that the Ferreira brothers, who could not be so very far behind, might slip past in the fog, so he and Harper pulled at the oars until their hands were blistered with the effort of fighting the flooding tide. The fog grew brighter, the tide at last slackened and a gull flew overhead. They were still miles from the sea, but there was a smell of salt and the water was brackish. The day was growing warmer, and that seemed to thicken the fog which drifted in patches like gun smoke above the swirling gray water. They had to go nearer the western bank to avoid the bedraggled remains of a fish trap made of nets, withies and poles that jutted far out from the eastern shore. There was no movement on the western bank so that they seemed to be alone on a pale river beneath a pearly sky, but then, from ahead, came the unmistakable bang of a cannon. Birds shot up from the trees on the bank and flew in circles as the sound echoed from some unseen hills, rumbled up the river's valley and faded.

"I can't see anything," Vicente reported from the bow.

Sharpe and Harper had rested on their oars and both twisted to see ahead, but there was only the fog over the river. Another cannon sounded and Sharpe thought he saw a patch of the mist thicken, then he rowed two more strokes and there, appearing like a ghost ship in the vapor, was a gunboat firing at the western shore. There were dragoons there, half seen in the mist, scattering from the gunfire. Another cannon blasted from the boat that was anchored in midstream, and a barrel-load of grapeshot threw down two horses and Sharpe saw a sudden spray of blood, almost instantly gone, discolor the fog, and then the gunboat's forward cannon fired and a round shot skipped across the water a score of yards ahead of the skiff. It had been a warning shot, and a man was standing in the gunboat's forepeak, shouting at them to come alongside.

"They're English," Vicente said. He stood in the skiff's bow and waved both arms while Sharpe and Harper pulled towards the gunboat that had one high mast, a low waist, and six gunports visible on its port side which faced upstream. A white ensign hung at the stern while a union flag drooped at the topmast.

"Here!" the man shouted. "Bring that bloody boat here!"

The two aft cannon fired at the retreating dragoons who were now galloping into the fog, leaving dead horses behind. Three seamen with muskets were waiting for the skiff, pointing their guns down into the boat.

"Any of you speak English?" another man called.

"My name's Captain Sharpe!"

"Who?"

"Captain Sharpe, South Essex regiment. And point those bloody muskets somewhere else!"

"You're English?" The astonishment might have come from Sharpe's appearance for he was not wearing his jacket and his beard had grown to a thick stubble.

"No, I'm bloody Chinese," Sharpe snapped. The skiff bumped against the tarred side of the gunboat and Sharpe looked up at a very young naval lieutenant. "Who are you?"

"Lieutenant Davies, commanding here."

"I'm Captain Sharpe, that's Captain Vicente of the Portuguese army, and the big fellow is Sergeant Harper and I'll introduce the ladies later. What we need, Lieutenant, if you'd be so kind, is some proper tea."

They scrambled aboard by using the chain plates which secured the ratlines for the big mast and Sharpe saluted Davies who, though he only looked about nineteen years old and was a lieutenant, nevertheless out-ranked Sharpe because, as an officer commanding one of His Majesty's vessels, he had the equivalent rank of major in the army. The seamen gave a small cheer as Joana and Sarah climbed over the side in their rain-shrunken breeches. "Quiet on deck!" Davies snarled and the seamen went instantly silent. "Secure the guns," Davies ordered. "Make fast that boat! Lively, lively!" He gestured that Sharpe and his companions should go to the boat's stern. "Welcome to the *Squirrel*," he said, "and I think we can supply tea. Might I ask why you're here?"

"We've come from Coimbra," Sharpe said, "and you, Lieutenant?"

"We're here to amuse the Frogs," Davies said. He was a very tall, very thin young man in a shabby uniform. "We come upstream on the tide, kill any Frogs foolish enough to appear on shore, and drift back down again."

"Where are we?" Sharpe asked.

"Three miles north of Alhandra. That's where your lines reach the river." He paused by a companionway. "There's a cabin below," he said, "and the ladies are welcome to it, but I must say it's damned poky. Damp as well."

Sharpe introduced Sarah and Joana who both elected to stay on the stern deck, which was cumbered by a vast tiller. The *Squirrel* had no wheel, and its quarterdeck was merely the after part of the maindeck which was crowded with seamen. Davies explained that his vessel was a twelve-gun cutter and that, though it could easily be managed by six or seven men, it needed a crew of forty to man its guns, "and even then we're short-handed," he complained, "and can only fire one side of guns. Still, one side is usually enough. Tea, yes?"

"And the loan of a razor?" Sharpe asked.

"And something to eat," Harper said under his breath, staring innocently up at the huge mainsail that was brailed onto a massive boom which jutted out over the diminutive white ensign.

"Tea, shave, breakfast," Davies said. "Stop gawking, Mister Braithwaite!" This was to a midshipman who was staring at Joana and Sarah and evidently trying to decide whether he preferred his women dark- or fair-haired. "Stop gawking and tell Powell we need breakfast for five guests."

"Five guests, sir, aye aye, sir."

"And might I beg you to keep an eye out for another boat?" Sharpe asked Davies. "I have a suspicion that five fellows are following us, and I want them stopped."

"That's my job," Davies said. "Stop anything that tries to float down river. Miss Fry? Might I bring you a chair? You and your companion?"

A breakfast was served on deck. There were thick white china plates heaped with bacon, bread and greasy eggs, and afterwards Sharpe blunted Davies's razor by scraping at the stubble on his chin. Davies's servant had brushed his green jacket, cleaned and polished his boots, and burnished his sword's metal scabbard. He leaned on the gunwale, feeling a sudden relief that the journey was over. In a matter of hours, he thought, he could be back with the battalion, and that spoiled his good mood, for he supposed he would be doomed to Lawford's continuing displeasure. The fog had thinned into a mist, and the tide was dropping, swirling past the *Squirrel*, which was anchored at bow and stern so that her small broadside pointed up river. Sharpe could see a chain of islands off the western bank, low-lying streaks of grassy sand that sheltered a smaller inshore channel, while down river, beyond a wide bend and just visible above the skeins of mist, Sharpe could see the masts of other ships. It was a whole squadron of gunboats, Davies said, posted to guard the flank of the defensive lines. Somewhere in the distance a cannon fired, its sound flat in the warming air.

"It's going to be a nice day for a change," Davies leaned on the gunwale beside Sharpe, "if this damn mist clears."

"I'm glad to be rid of the rain," Sharpe said.

"Rather rain than fog," Davies said. "Can't fire guns if you can't see the bloody target." He glanced up at the dim glow of the sun through the mist, judging the time. "We'll stay here for another hour," he said, "then drop down to Alhandra. We'll put you ashore there." He looked up at the union flag that stirred listlessly at the masthead. "Bloody south wind," he said, meaning that he could not sail down river, but would have to let the current take him.

"Sir!" There was a man at the crosstrees where the topmast met the mainmast. "Boat, sir!"

"Where away?"

The man pointed and Sharpe took out his glass and searched westwards and then, through a shimmer of mist, saw a small boat running down the inshore channel. He could only see the heads of the men in the boat. Davies was running down the deck. "Let go the after spring," he shouted, "man numbers one and two!"

The *Squirrel* swung on its bow anchor, the current hurrying her round until the guns bore and then the tension was taken up on the stern anchor line to steady the ship at a new angle. "Fire a warning shot when you can!" Davies ordered.

There was a pause as the *Squirrel* steadied, then the gun captain, who had been squinting down the barrel, leaped back and jerked his lanyard. The small cannon recoiled onto its breeching ropes and thick smoke clouded the gunwales. The second gun fired almost immediately, its round shot hissing above the low island to splash into the channel ahead of the fleeing boat.

"They ain't stopping, sir!" the man at the crosstrees called.

"Fire at them, Mister Combes! Directly at them!"

"Aye aye, sir!"

The next shot struck the island and bounced high over the fleeing boat which was traveling fast on the river's current and was helped by the ebbing tide. Sharpe doubted the gunfire would stop the boat. He scrambled a few rungs up the ratlines and used his telescope, but he could see little of the occupants who were obscured by the mist. Yet it had to be the Ferreira brothers. Who else could it be? And he thought, but could not be sure, that one of the men in the boat was unnaturally large. Ferragus, he thought.

"Lieutenant!" he called.

"Mister Sharpe?"

"There are two men in that boat who need to be captured. That's my duty." That was not really true. Sharpe's duty was to return to duty, not to prolong a feud, but Davies did not know that. "Can we borrow one of your boats to pursue them?"

Davies hesitated, wondering if granting such a request would contravene his standing orders. "The gunboats downstream will apprehend them," he pointed out.

"And they won't know they're wanted men," Sharpe said, then paused as the *Squirrel's* forward guns fired and missed again. "Besides, they're likely to slip ashore before they reach your squadron. And if that happens we need to be put ashore to follow them."

Davies thought for another second, saw that the fugitive boat had almost vanished in the mist, then turned on Midshipman Braithwaite. "The jolly boat, Mister Braithwaite. Look quick now!" He turned back to Sharpe who had regained the deck. "The ladies will stay here." It was not a question.

"We will not," Sarah answered firmly, and hefted her French musket. "We've come this far together and we'll finish it together."

For a second Davies looked as though he would argue, then decided life would be simpler if all his unbidden guests were off the *Squirrel*. The forward cannon fired a last time and smoke wreathed the deck. "I wish you joy," Davies said.

And they were over the side and in pursuit.

CHAPTER 12

MARSHAL ANDRÉ MASSÉNA was feeling numb. He was saying nothing, just staring. It was shortly after dawn, the day after his first patrols had reached the new British and Portuguese works, and now he crouched behind a low stone wall on which his telescope rested and he slowly panned the glass along the hilltops to the south and everywhere he saw bastions, guns, walls, barricades, more guns, men, telegraph stations, flagpoles. Everywhere.

He had been planning the victory celebrations to be held in Lisbon. There was a fine large square beside the Tagus where half the army could be paraded, and the greatest problem he had anticipated was what to do with the thousands of British and Portuguese prisoners he expected to capture, but instead he was looking at an apparently endless barrier. He saw how the lower slopes of the opposite hills had been steepened, he saw how the enemy guns were protected by stone, he saw flooded approach routes, he saw failure.

He drew in a deep breath and still had nothing to say. He leaned back from the wall and took his one eye from the telescope. He had thought to maneuver here, to show part of his army on the road to draw in the enemy forces who would think an attack imminent, and then launch the greater part of l'Armée de Portugal round to the west in a slashing hook that would cut off Wellington's men. He would have pinned the British and Portuguese against the Tagus and then graciously accepted their surrender, but instead there was nowhere for his army to go except up against those walls and guns and steepened slopes.

"The works extend to the Atlantic," a staff officer reported dryly.

Masséna said nothing and one of his aides, knowing what was in his master's mind, asked the question instead. "Not the whole way, surely?"

"Every last kilometer," the staff officer said flatly. He had ridden the width of the peninsula, protected by dragoons and watched all the way by an enemy ensconced in batteries, forts and watchtowers. "And for much of its length," he continued remorselessly, "the works are covered by the River Sizandre, and there is a second line behind."

Masséna found his voice and turned furiously on the staff officer. "A second line? How can you tell?"

"Because it's visible, sir. Two lines."

Masséna stared again through the glass. Was there something strange about the guns in the bastion immediately opposite? He remembered how, when he had been besieged by the Austrians in Genoa, he had put false guns in his defenses. They had been painted tree trunks jutting from emplacements and, from anything more than two hundred paces, they had more or less looked like cannon barrels, and the Austrians had dutifully avoided the fake batteries. "How far to the sea?" he asked.

"Nearly fifty kilometers, sir." The aide made a wild guess.

Masséna did the arithmetic. There were at least two bastions every kilometer, and the bastions he could see all had four cannon, some more, so by a cautious estimate there were eight guns to the kilometer, which meant Wellington must have assembled four hundred cannon for just the first line, and that was a ridiculous assumption. There were not that many guns in Portugal, and that encouraged the Marshal to believe that some of the guns were false. Then he thought of Britain's navy and wondered if they had brought ships' guns ashore. Dear God, he thought, but how had they done this? "Why didn't we know?" he demanded. There was silence in which Masséna turned and stared at Colonel Barreto. "Why didn't we know?" he demanded again. "You told me they were building a pair of forts to protect the road! Does that look like a pair of lousy forts!"

"We weren't told," Barreto said bitterly.

Masséna stooped to the glass. He was angry, but he curbed his feelings, trying to find a weakness in his enemy's careful defenses. Opposite him, beside the bastion which had the strangely dark guns, there was a valley that curled behind the hill. He could see no defenses there, but that meant little for all of the low ground was obscured by mist. The hilltops, with their forts and windmills, were in the bright sun, but the valleys were shrouded, yet he fancied that small valley, which twisted behind the nearest hill, was bereft of defenses. Any attack up the valley would be harassed by the high guns, of course, if they were real guns, but once through the gap and behind the hill, what was to stop the Eagles? Perhaps Wellington was deceiving him? Perhaps these defenses were more show than real? Perhaps the stone bastions were not properly mortared, the guns fake and the whole elaborate defense a charade to dissuade any attack? Yet Masséna knew he must attack. In front of him was Lisbon and its supplies, behind him was a wasteland, and if his army were not to starve then he must go forward. The anger bloomed in him again, but he thrust it away. Anger was a luxury. For the moment he knew he must show sublime confidence or else the very existence of these defenses would grind the heart from his army. "C'est une coquille d'oeuf," he said.

"A what?" An aide thought he had misheard.

"Une coquille d'oeuf," Masséna repeated, still gazing through the glass. He meant it was an eggshell. "One tap," he went on, "and it will crack."

There was silence except for the intermittent sound of cannon fire from a British gunboat on the River Tagus that lay a mile or so to the east. The aides and Generals, staring over Masséna's head, thought the defensive line a most impressive eggshell.

"They've fortified the hilltops," Masséna explained, "but forgotten the valleys between and that, gentlemen, means we shall prise them open. Prise them open like a virgin." He preferred that simile to the eggshell, for he repeated it. "Like a virgin," he said enthusiastically, then collapsed the glass and stood. "General Reynier?"

"Sir?"

"You see that valley?" Masséna pointed across the misted low ground to where the small valley twisted behind one of the fortified hills. "Send your light troops into it. Go fast, go before the mist vanishes. See what's there." He would lose some men, but it would be worth it to discover that the valleys were the weak point in Wellington's defense, and then Masséna could pick his valley and time and break this virgin wide open. Masséna chuckled at the thought, his spirits restored, and he held his telescope out to an aide and just then one of the dark guns on the opposite hill fired and the ball seared across the valley, struck the slope twenty paces below the wall and bounced up over Masséna's head. The British had been watching him, and must have decided that he had spent too long in one place. Masséna took off his cocked hat, bowed to the enemy in acknowledgment of their message, and walked back to where the horses waited.

He would attack.

☙

MAJOR FERREIRA HAD NOT FORESEEN THIS. He had thought the boat, which they had bought for too much money south of Castelo Branco, would take them all the way to the wharves of Lisbon, but now he saw that the British navy was blockading the river. It was the last of many difficulties he had faced on the journey. One of the mules had gone lame and that had slowed them, it had taken time to discover a man willing to sell a hidden boat, and then, once on the river, they had become entangled with a fish trap that had held them up for over an hour and next morning some French foragers had used them for target practice, forcing them to row into a tributary of the Tagus and hide there until the French got bored and rode away. Now, with the journey's end not so far away, there was the gunboat.

At first, seeing the boat in midstream, Ferreira had not been alarmed. He had the seniority and uniform to argue his way past any allied officer, but then, unexpectedly, the boat had opened fire. He had not known the *Squirrel* was warning him, ordering him either to heave to or else ground his boat on the island that edged the smaller channel; instead he believed he was under fire and so he snapped at his brother and his three men to row harder. In truth he panicked. He had been worrying about his reception in Lisbon ever since the army had retreated from Coimbra. Had anyone got wind of the food in the warehouse? He had a guilty conscience and that conscience made him try to outrun the gunfire, and he believed he had done it until he saw, dim through the mist layer that hung above the swathe of land encircled by the river's bend, the thicket of masts denoting a whole squadron of gunboats barring the river. He was standing in the sternsheets now, staring about him, and he saw, with a great pang of relief, the forts that guarded the main road north from Lisbon. A swirl of parting mist showed the forts on the hills and Ferreira saw the Portuguese flag flying above the nearest and so he impulsively pulled on the tiller ropes to carry the boat to shore. Better to deal with Portuguese soldiers, he thought, than British sailors.

"We're being followed," his brother warned him.

Ferreira turned and saw the jolly boat racing down the river's center. "We're going ashore," he said, "they won't follow us there."

"They won't?"

"They're sailors. Hate being on dry land." Ferreira smiled. "We'll go to the fort," he said, jerking his chin towards the new bastions dominating the road, "we'll get horses and we'll be in Lisbon by this afternoon."

The boat ran ashore and the five men carried their weapons and French coin up the bank. Ferreira glanced once at the jolly boat and saw it had turned and was making heavy going as it tried to cross the current. He assumed the sailors wanted to take his boat, and they were welcome to it for now he was safe, but when the five men broke through the bushes at the top of the bank they came across a further difficulty. The river was embanked here, but farther south the big earth wall must have been breached to let the water flood the road and Ferreira saw there would be no easy walk to the closest fort because the land was inundated and that meant they would have to go inland to skirt the floods. That was no great matter, but then he felt alarm because, somewhere in the mist ahead of him, a gun sounded. The echo rolled between the hills, but no shot came anywhere near them, and no second shot sounded, which suggested that there was no need to worry. Probably a gunner ranging his piece or testing a rebored touchhole. They walked westwards, following the line of the swamp-edged flood, and after a while, vague in the mist, Ferreira saw a farm standing on higher ground. There was a wide stretch of boggy land between them and the farm, but he reckoned if he could just reach those buildings then he would not be too far from the forts on the southern heights. That thought gave Ferreira a conviction that all would be well, that the tribulations of the last days would be crowned with unmerited but welcome success. He began to laugh.

"What is it?" his brother asked.

"God is good to us, Luis, God is good."

"He is?"

"We sold that food to the French, took their money and the food was destroyed! I shall say we tricked the French and that means we shall be heroes."

Ferragus smiled and patted the leather satchel hanging from his shoulder. "We're rich heroes."

"I'll probably be made Lieutenant Colonel for this," Ferreira said. He would explain that he had heard of the hoarded food and stayed behind to ensure its destruction, and such a feat would surely merit a promotion. "They were a bad few days," he admitted to his brother, "but we made it through. Good God!"

"What?"

"The forts," Ferreira said in astonishment. "Look at all those bastions!" The mist obscured the valley, but it was a low mist and as they breasted a gentle rise Ferreira could see the hilltops and he could see that every height had its small fort and, for the first time, he realized the extent of the new works. He had thought that only the roads were being guarded, but it was plain that the line stretched far inland. Could it cross the peninsula? Go all the way to the sea? And if it did then surely the French would never reach Lisbon. He felt a sudden surge of relief that he had been forced out of Coimbra for if he had stayed, if the warehouse had not been burned, then he would inevitably have found himself recruited by Colonel Barreto. "That damned fire did us a favor," he told his brother, "because we're going to win. Portugal will survive." All he had to do was reach a fort flying the Portuguese flag and it would all be over; the uncertainty, the danger, the fear. It was over and he had won. He turned, looking for the Portuguese flag he had seen flying above the mist, and when he turned he saw the pursuers coming from the river. He saw the green jackets.

So it was not over, not quite. And clumsily, weighed down by their money, the five men began to run.

⁂

GENERAL SARRUT ASSEMBLED four battalions of light infantry. Some were chasseurs and some voltigeurs, but whether they were called hunters or vaulters they were all skirmishers and there was no real distinction between them except that the chasseurs had red epaulettes on their blue coats and the voltigeurs had either green or red. Both considered themselves elite troops, trained to fight against enemy skirmishers in the space between the battle lines.

The four battalions were all from the 2nd regiment that had left France with eighty-nine officers and two thousand six hundred men, but now the four battalions were down to seventy-one officers and just over two thousand men. They did not carry the regiment's Eagle for they were not going to battle. They were carrying out a reconnaissance and General Sarrut's orders were clear. The skirmishers were to advance in loose order across the low land in front of the enemy forts and the fourth battalion, on the left of the line, was to probe the small valley and, if they met no resistance, the third would follow. They would advance only far enough to determine whether the valley was blockaded or otherwise defended and, when that was established, the battalions were to withdraw back to the French-held hills. The mist was both a curse and a blessing. A blessing because it meant the four battalions could advance without being seen from the enemy forts, and a curse because it would obscure the view up the smaller valley, but by the time his first men reached that valley Sarrut expected the mist would be mostly burned away. Then, of course, he could expect some furious artillery fire from the enemy forts, but as his men would be in skirmish order it would be a most unlucky shot that did any damage.

General Sarrut had been far more worried by the prospect of enemy cavalry, but Reynier had dismissed the concern. "They won't have horse-men saddled and ready," he had claimed, "and it'll take them half a day to get them up. If they bother to fight you in the valley it'll be infantry, so I'll have Soult's brigade ready to deal with the bastards." Soult's brigade was a mix of cavalry: chasseurs, hussars and dragoons, a thousand horse-men who only had six hundred and fifty-three horses between them, but that should be enough to deal with any British or Portuguese skirmishers who tried to stop Sarrut's reconnaissance.

It was mid-morning by the time Sarrut's men were ready to advance and the General was about to order the first battalion out into the mist-shrouded valley when one of General Reynier's aides came galloping down the hill. Sarrut watched the officer negotiate the slope. "It'll be a change of orders," he predicted sourly to one of his own aides. "Now they'll want us to attack Lisbon."

Reynier's aide curbed his horse in a flurry of earth, then leaned for-ward to pat the beast's neck. "There's a British picquet, sir," he said. "We've just seen it from the hilltop. They're in a ruined barn by the stream."

"No matter," Sarrut said. No mere picquet could stop four battalions of prime light infantry.

"General Reynier suggests we might capture them, sir," the aide said respectfully.

Sarrut laughed. "One sight of us, Captain, and they'll be running like hares!"

"The mist, General," the aide said respectfully. "It's patchy, very patchy, and General Reynier suggests if you head westwards you may slip around them. He feels their officer might have some information about the defenses."

Sarrut grunted. A suggestion from Reynier was tantamount to an order, but it seemed a pointless order. Doubtless the picquet did have an officer, though it seemed extremely unlikely that such a man would have any useful knowledge, yet Reynier had to be indulged. "Tell him we'll do it," he said, and sent one of his own aides to the front of the column and ordered half a battalion to curl around to the west. That would take them through the mist, probably out of sight of the barn, and they could head back to cut the picquet off. "Tell Colonel Feret to advance now," he told the aide, "and you go with him. Make sure they don't advance too far. The rest of the troops will march ten minutes after he leaves. And tell him to be quick!"

He stressed those last few words. The point of the exercise was merely to discover what lay behind the enemy hill, not to win a victory that would have the Parisian mob cheering. There was no victory to be won here, merely information to gather, and the longer his troops stayed in the low ground the longer they would be exposed to cannon fire. It was a job, Sarrut thought, that would have been done far more efficiently by a squadron of cavalry who could gallop across the valley in a matter of moments, but the cavalry was in poor shape. Their horses were worn out and hungry, and that thought reminded Sarrut that the British picquet in the old barn must have rations. That cheered him up. He should have thought to tell his aide to keep some back if any were found, but the aide was a smart young fellow and would doubtless do it anyway. Fresh eggs, perhaps? Or bacon? Newly baked bread, butter, milk yellow and warm from the cow? Sarrut dreamed of these things as the chasseurs and voltigeurs tramped past him. They had marched hard and long in these last few days and they must have been hungry, but they seemed cheerful enough as they went by the General's horse. Some had boot soles missing, or else had soles tied to the uppers with string, and their uniforms were faded, ragged and threadbare, but he noted that their muskets were clean and he did not doubt that they would fight well if, indeed, they were called on to fight at all. For most of them, he suspected, the morning would be a tiring tramp through sodden fields enlivened by random British artillery fire. The last company marched past and Sarrut spurred his horse to follow.

Ahead of him was a brigade of skirmishers, a misted valley, an unsuspecting enemy and, for the moment, silence.

⚜

LIEUTENANT JACK BULLEN was a decent young man who came from a decent family. His father was a judge and both his elder brothers were barristers, but young Jack Bullen had never shone at school and though his schoolmasters had tried to whip Latin and Greek into his skull, his skull had won the battle and stayed innocent of any foreign tongue. Bullen had never minded the beatings. He had been a tough, cheerful youngster, the sort who collected birds' eggs, scrapped with other boys and climbed the church tower for a dare, and now he was a tough, cheerful young man who thought that being an officer in Lawford's regiment was just about the finest thing life could afford. He liked soldiering and he liked soldiers. Some officers feared the men more than they feared the enemy, but young Jack Bullen, nineteen years old, enjoyed the rank and file's company. He relished their poor jokes, enthusiastically drank their sour-tasting tea and considered them all, even those whom his father might have condemned to death, transportation or hard labor, as capital fellows, though he would have much preferred to be with the capital fellows of his old company. He liked number nine company, and while Jack Bullen did not actively dislike the light company, he found it difficult. Not the men, Bullen had a natural talent for getting along with men, but he did find the light company's commanding officer a trial. It took a lot to suppress young Jack Bullen's spirits, but somehow Captain Slingsby had managed it.

"He's queer, sir," Sergeant Read said respectfully.

"He's queer," Bullen repeated tonelessly.

"Queer, sir," Read confirmed. To be queer was to be ill, but Read really meant that Captain Slingsby was drunk, but as a sergeant he could not say as much.

"How queer?" Bullen asked. He could have walked the twenty paces to discover for himself, but he was in charge of the sentries who lined the stream just outside the crumbling barn, and he did not really want to face Slingsby.

"Very queer, sir," Read said gravely. "He's talking about his wife, sir. He's saying bad things about her."

Bullen wanted to know what things were being said, but he knew the Methodist Sergeant would never tell him, so he just grunted in acknowledgment.

"It's upsetting the men, sir," Read said. "Such things shouldn't be said about women. Not about wives."

Bullen suspected Slingsby's outburst was amusing the men rather than upsetting them, and that was bad. An officer, however friendly, had to keep a certain dignity. "Can he walk?"

"Barely, sir," Read said, then amended the answer. "No, sir."

"Oh, dear God," Bullen said and saw Read flinch at the mild blasphemy. "Where did he get the liquor?"

Read sniffed. "His servant, sir. Got a pack filled with canteens and the Captain's been drinking all night, sir."

Bullen wondered what he should do. He could hardly send Slingsby back to battalion, for Bullen did not see it as his job to destroy his commanding officer's reputation. That would be a disloyal act. "Keep an eye on him, Sergeant," Bullen said helplessly. "Maybe he'll recover."

"But I can't take his orders, sir, not in the state he's in."

"Is he giving you orders?"

"He told me to put Slattery under arrest, sir."

"The charge?"

"Looking funny at him, sir."

"Oh dear. Ignore his orders, Sergeant, and that's an order. Tell him I said so."

Read nodded. "You're taking over, sir?"

Bullen hesitated, knowing the question was important. If he said yes then he was formally acknowledging that Slingsby was not fit to command, and that would inevitably result in an enquiry. "I'm taking over until the Captain has recovered," he said, which seemed a decent compromise.

"Very good, sir." Read saluted and turned away.

"And Sergeant?" Bullen waited till Read turned back. "Don't look funny at him."

"No, sir," Read said solemnly, "of course not, sir. I wouldn't do such a thing, sir."

Bullen sipped his mug of tea and found it had gone cold. He put it down on a stone and walked to the stream. The mist had thickened slightly, he thought, so that he could only see some sixty or seventy yards, though, perversely, the hilltops a quarter-mile away were clear enough, which proved that the mist was merely a low-lying layer blanketing the damp earth. It would clear. He remembered marvelous winter mornings in Essex when the mist would drift away to show the hunting field spread out in glorious pursuit. He liked hunting. He smiled to himself, remembering his father's great black gelding, a tremendous hunter, that always screwed left when it landed on the far side of a hedge and every time his father would shout, "Order in court! Order in court!" It was a family joke, one of the many that made the Bullen house a happy one.

"Mister Bullen, sir?" It was Daniel Hagman, the oldest man in the company, who called from a dozen paces upstream.

Bullen, who had been thinking how they would be readying the horses for the cubbing season at home, walked to the rifleman. "Hagman?"

"Thought I saw something, sir." Hagman pointed through the mist. "Nothing there now."

Bullen peered and saw nothing. "This mist will burn off soon enough."

"Be clear as a bell in an hour, sir. It'll be nice to have some sunshine."

"Won't it just?"

Then the shooting started.

SHARPE HAD FEARED that the Ferreira brothers would set up an ambush in the bushes at the top of the river bank and so he had asked Braithwaite to take the jolly boat downstream of the brothers' abandoned boat to a place where the river's edge was bare of trees. He had told Sarah and Joana to stay in the boat, but they had ignored him, scrambling ashore behind the three men. Vicente was worried by their presence. "They shouldn't be here."

"We shouldn't be here, Jorge," Sharpe said. He was gazing across the marshland, then saw the Ferreira brothers and their three companions in the mist. The five men were walking inland, looking as though they did not have a care in the world. "We shouldn't be here," Sharpe went on, "but we are, and so are they. So let's finish this." He unslung the rifle and made sure the priming was still in the pan. "Should have fired and re-loaded on board the *Squirrel*," he told Harper.

"You think the powder's damp?"

"Could be." He feared the mist might have moistened the charge, but there was nothing he could do about it now. They began walking, but, by landing farther south Sharpe had unwittingly put them deeper in the marshes and the going was hard. The ground, at best, was squelchy, at worst it was a glutinous mess and, because the tide was ebbing, the land was newly waterlogged. Sharpe cut north, reckoning that the land there was firmer, but the five fugitives were increasing their lead with every step. "Take your boots off," Harper recommended. "I grew up in Donegal," he went on, "and there's nothing we don't know about bog-land."

Sharpe kept his boots on. His came up to his knees and were not such an impediment, but the others pulled off their shoes and they made faster progress. "All we need to do," Sharpe said, "is get close enough to shoot the bastards."

"Why don't they look around?" Sarah wondered.

"Because they're dozy," Sharpe said, "because they reckon they're safe." They had reached the firmer ground, a very slight rise between the marsh and the northern hills, and they hurried now, closing the gap on the five men who still looked as carefree as if they were out for a day's rough shooting. They were strolling, guns slung, chatting. Ferragus tow-ered over his companions and Sharpe had an urge to kneel, aim and shoot the bastard in the back, but he did not trust the rifle's charge and so he kept going. Way off to his left he could see some buildings in the mist: a couple of cottages, a barn, some sheds and a larger house and he sup-posed it had been a prosperous farmstead before the engineers flooded the valley. He suspected the marshy ground extended almost to those half-seen buildings, which seemed to be on higher land, and he reck-oned Ferreira would try to reach the farm and then head south. Or else, if the brothers realized they were being followed, they would hole up in the buildings and it would be hell to get them out and Sharpe began to hurry, but just then one of the men turned and stared straight at him. "Bugger," Sharpe said, and dropped to his knee.

The five men began running, a clumsy run because they were carrying guns and coins. Sharpe lined the sights, pulled the cock all the way back and squeezed the trigger. He knew instantly he had missed because the rifle hesitated, then gave a wheezing cough instead of a bang, which meant that the mist-dampened charge had fired, but weakly, and the bullet would have dropped short. He began reloading as Harper and Vicente fired and one of their bullets must have struck a man in the leg because he fell. Sharpe was ramming a new charge down. There was no time to wrap the bullet in leather. He wondered why the hell the army did not issue ready-wrapped bullets, then he pushed the ramrod down onto the ball, primed, knelt and fired again. Joana and Sarah, even though their muskets were futile at this range, both fired. The man who had fallen was on his feet again, showing no sign of being wounded because he was running hard to catch up with his companions. Harper fired and one of the men swerved violently as if the ball had gone frighteningly close to him, and then all five were on the higher ground and running for the buildings. Vicente fired his second shot just as the men vanished among the stone walls.

"Damn," Sharpe said, ramming a new bullet down.

"They won't stay there," Vicente said quietly. "They'll run south."

"We'll go through the marsh, then," Sharpe said, and he set off, splashing into mud and waterlogged grass. He was aiming to get south of the farmstead and so cut off the fugitives, but almost at once he realized the attempt was probably futile. The ground was a morass, there were floods ahead, and when he was up to his knees in water he stopped. He swore because he could see the five men leaving the farm and heading south, but they were also balked by floodwater and turned west again. Sharpe put the rifle to his shoulder, led Ferragus with the sights and pulled the trigger. Harper and Vicente also fired, but they were shooting at moving targets and all three bullets missed, then the five men were gone in the persistent mist. Sharpe fished out a new cartridge. "We tried," he said to Vicente.

"They'll be in Lisbon by this evening," Vicente said. He helped Sharpe struggle free of a patch of mud. "I will report Major Ferreira, of course."

"He'll be long gone, Jorge. Either that or it'll be his word against yours and he's a major and you're a captain, so you know what that means." He stared into the western mist. "It's a pity," he said. "I owed that big bastard a beating."

"Is that why you followed him?" Sarah asked.

"As much as anything else." He rammed a new bullet down the rifle, primed the lock, closed the frizzen and slung the rifle. "Let's find dry land," he said, "and go home."

"They're not gone!" Harper said suddenly, and Sharpe turned to see, miraculously, that the five men were coming back to the farm. They were hurrying, looking into the mist behind them and Sharpe, unslinging the rifle, wondered what in hell was happening.

Then he saw the skirmish line. For a moment he was sure it had to be a British or a Portuguese company, but then he saw the blue coats and white crossbelts, saw the epaulettes, and saw that some of the men wore short sabers and he knew they were the French. And there was more than one company, for out of the mist a whole horde of skirmishers was appearing.

Then, from the west, came a splintering crackle of muskets. The skirmishers turned towards the sound, paused. The Ferreiras were in the farm buildings now. Harper cocked his rifle. "What in God's name is happening?"

"It's called a battle, Pat."

"God save Ireland."

"He can start by saving us," Sharpe said. For it seemed that, though his enemies were trapped, the French had trapped him.

※

A VAGARY OF THE MIST SAVED BULLEN. He was alert, all his men were alert, for shots had sounded to the east, somewhere out in the inundated land towards the river and Bullen had been about to order Sergeant Huckfield to take a dozen men to investigate the sounds when a swirl of wind, driven down from the southern heights, shifted a patch of whiteness on the western side of the ruined barn and Bullen saw men running. Blue-coated men, carrying muskets, and for a second or two he was so astonished that he did nothing. The French, he could hardly believe they were French, were already south of him, evidently running to get between the barn and the forts, and he understood instantly that he could not extricate the men back to the hills. "Sir!" one of the riflemen called, and the word jarred Bullen out of his shock.

"Sergeant Read!" Bullen was trying to think of everything as he spoke. "Redcoats to the farm. The place we went last night. Take your packs!" Bullen had led a patrol to the big farmstead in the dusk. He had followed the raised track at low tide, crossed the stream on the small stone bridge, poked around the deserted buildings, then explored a little way towards the Tagus until he was stopped by marshland. The farm was his best refuge now, a place with stone walls, marsh all around it, and only one approach: the track from the bridge. So long as he could reach that rough road before the French. "Riflemen!" he ordered. "Here! Sergeant McGovern! Pick two men and get Captain Slingsby out of here. Rifles? You're the rearguard! Let's go!"

Bullen went last, walking backwards among the riflemen. The mist had closed again and the enemy was hidden, but when Bullen was only thirty paces from the barn the French appeared there, charging into the ruins, and one of them saw the greenjackets off to the east and shouted a warning. Voltigeurs turned and fired, but their volley was a ragged effort because they were in skirmish order, although enough of the balls went dangerously close to Bullen and he backed away faster. He could see a half-dozen of the Frenchmen running towards him and he was about to turn and flee when some rifles snapped and two of the Frenchmen went down. Blood was bright on grubby white breeches. He turned and saw that the greenjackets were in skirmish order. They were doing what they were trained to do, and now some of them fired again and another Frenchman jerked backwards.

"We can manage them, sir," Hagman said. "Probably just a patrol. Harris! Watch left! You hurry on, sir." He spoke to Bullen again. "We know what we're doing and that pistol ain't much use." Bullen had been unaware of even drawing the pistol that had been a gift from his father. He fired it anyway and fancied that the small bullet struck a Frenchman, though it was far more likely the man had been thrown backwards by a shot from one of the riflemen. Another rifle fired. The greenjackets were going backwards, one man retreating while his partner kept watch. The French were firing back, but at too long a range. Their musket smoke made thicker patches of mist. By a miracle the voltigeurs were not following hard on Bullen's footsteps. They had expected to trap the picquet in the ruined barn and no one had given them orders to divert the attack eastwards, and that delay gave Bullen precious minutes. He realized that Hagman was right and that the riflemen did not need his orders so he ran past them to the bridge where Sergeant Read was waiting with the redcoats. Captain Slingsby was drinking from a canteen, but at least he was causing no trouble. The rifles fired from the mist and Bullen wondered if he should strike directly south, following the marshes by the stream, then he saw there were Frenchmen out in that open space and he ordered the redcoats across the bridge and back to the farm. The riflemen were hurrying back now, threatened by a new skirmish chain of voltigeurs who had come from the mist. Dear God, Bullen thought, but the Crapauds were everywhere!

"Into the farm!" he shouted at the redcoats. The farmhouse was a sturdy building that had been built on the western face of a small rise so that its front door was approached by stone steps and its windows were eight feet above the ground. A perfect refuge, Bullen thought, so long as the French did not bring artillery. Two redcoats hauled Captain Slingsby up the steps and Bullen followed into a long room, parlor and kitchen united in one, with the door and the two high windows facing down the track leading to the bridge. Bullen could not see the bridge in the mist, but he could see the riflemen retreating fast down the track and he knew the French could not be far behind. "In here!" he shouted at the greenjackets, then explored the rest of his makeshift fort. A second door and a single window faced the back where a yard was edged with other low-tiled buildings, while, at one end of the room, a ladder led to an attic where there were three bedrooms. Bullen split the men into six squads, one for each window facing the track, one for the door, and one each for the small rooms upstairs. He posted a single sentry at the back door, hoping the French would not reach the yard. "Break through the roof," he told the men he posted upstairs. The first voltigeurs were on the track now and their musket balls rattled on the farm's stone walls.

"There are men in the yard, sir," the sentry at the back door said.

Bullen thought he meant Frenchmen and snatched open the back door, but saw that one of the strangers was in the uniform of a Portuguese major and the others were all civilians, one of whom was the biggest man Bullen had ever seen. The Portuguese Major stared wide-eyed at Bullen, apparently as astonished to see Bullen as Bullen was to see him, then the Major recovered. "Who are you?" he demanded.

"Lieutenant Bullen, sir."

"There are enemy over there," the Major said, pointing east, and Bullen cursed, for he had been thinking that perhaps his men could wade towards the river and so put themselves under the protection of the British gunboat that he had heard firing in the dawn. Now, it seemed, he was surrounded, so he had no choice but to make the best defense he could. "We will join you," the Major announced, and the five men came into the farmhouse where Bullen, on the Major's advice, put a handful of men in the eastern window to keep a look out for the enemy the Major had seen in the direction of the river. There was a clatter as shattered tiles cascaded from the roof where men broke through from the attic, then a bellow of gunfire as the Portuguese civilians fired at men coming from the east. Bullen turned to see what they were shooting at, and just then a volley crackled from the west and glass shattered in the windows and a redcoat spun back, a bullet in his lung. He began coughing up frothy blood. "Fire!" Bullen shouted.

Another man was hit, this time in the farm's doorway. Bullen went to a window, peered over the shoulder of a redcoat and saw Frenchmen running to the left, more going right and still more coming up the track. Muskets and rifles fired from the roof, but he did not see a single Frenchman fall. The long, low room echoed with the bangs of the guns, filled with smoke, and then the British and Portuguese cannon on the ridge added their own noise. The men in the back windows were firing as hard as the men in the front.

"They're working their way around the sides, sir," Read said, meaning that the French were going to the flanks of the farmhouse where no windows pointed.

"Kill them, boys!" Slingsby suddenly shouted. "And God save King George."

"Bugger King George," a redcoat muttered, then cursed because he had been struck by a splinter of wood driven from the window frame by a musket ball. "'Ware left, 'ware left!" a man shouted and three muskets banged together. Bullen dashed to the back door, peered through and saw powder smoke at the far end of the farmyard where cottages and cattle sheds huddled together. What the hell was happening? He had somehow hoped the French would stay on the track, attacking only from the west, but he realized now that had been a stupid hope. The voltigeurs were surrounding the farm and hammering it with musket fire. Bullen could sense panic in himself. He was twenty years old and over fifty men were looking to him for leadership, and so far he had given it, but he was being assailed by the sound of enemy musketry, the unending rattle of balls against the stone walls and by Captain Slingsby who was now on his feet and shouting at the men to look for the whites of the enemies' eyes.

Then the Portuguese Major solved some of his problems. "I'll look after this side," he told Bullen, pointing east. Bullen suspected there were fewer enemy out there, but he was grateful that he could forget them now. He looked back to the west which was taking the brunt of the fire, though most of it was being wasted on the stone walls. The problem, Bullen saw, lay north and south, for once the French realized that he had no guns covering the flanks of the building, they were bound to concentrate there.

"Loopholes in the gable ends, sir," Hagman suggested, intuitively understanding Bullen's problem, and he did not wait for the Lieutenant's answer, but went up the ladder to try and prise out the masonry at the gable ends of the roof. Bullen could hear the French shouting to each other now and, for want of anything better to do, fired his pistol through the open door, and then another gust of wind swirled more mist away and he saw, to his astonishment, that the whole valley beyond the bridge was filled with Frenchmen. Most were going away from him, advancing in a huge skirmish line towards the forts, and the gunners were firing at them from the hilltops and their shells exploded above the grassland, thickening the mist with their smoke and adding to the noise.

A redcoat fell back from a window, his skull spurting blood. Another was hit in the arm and dropped his musket which fired and the bullet hit a rifleman in the ankle. The noise outside was unceasing, the sound of the balls hitting the stone walls a devil's drumbeat, and Bullen could see the fear on the men's faces, and it was not helped by the fact that Slingsby had now drawn his sword and was shouting at the men to fire faster. The front of Slingsby's red coat was spattered with dribble and he was staggering slightly. "Fire!" he bellowed. "Fire! Give them hell!" He had an open canteen in his left hand and Bullen, suddenly angry, pushed the Captain aside so that Slingsby staggered and sat down. Another man was hit in the doorway, this one wounded in the arm by a splinter from a musket stock that had been struck by a bullet. Some men were refusing to go to the door now, and there was more than just fear on their faces, there was sheer terror. The sound of the guns was magnified by the room, the French shouts seemed horribly close, there were the incessant, deeper bangs of the big guns on the ridge, while in the farmhouse there was smoke and fresh blood and the beginnings of panic.

Then the bugle sounded. It was a strange call, one that Bullen had never heard, and slowly the musket fire died away as the bugle called again, and one of the redcoats guarding a west-facing window called that a Frenchman was waving a white rag on the end of a sword. "Hold your fire!" Bullen shouted. "Hold your fire!" He stepped cautiously to the doorway and saw a tall man in a French coat, white breeches and riding boots approaching up the track. Bullen decided he did not want the men to hear the parley and so he stepped outside, taking off his hat. He was not quite sure why he did that, but he had no white cloth and taking off his shako seemed the next best thing.

The two men met twenty paces from the farm. The Frenchman bowed, swept off his cocked hat, put it back on, then took the handkerchief from the tip of his sword. "I am Captain Jules Derain," he announced in impeccable English, "and I have the honor to be an aide to General Sarrut." He put the handkerchief in his breast pocket, then sheathed the sword so hard that the hilt clashed against the scabbard throat. It was an ominous noise.

"Lieutenant Jack Bullen," Bullen said.

Derain waited. "You have a regiment, Lieutenant?" he asked after the pause.

"The South Essex," Bullen said.

"Ah," Derain said, a response that delicately implied he had never heard of the unit. "My General," he went on, "salutes your bravery, Lieutenant, but wishes you to understand that any farther defense is tantamount to suicide. You might like to avail yourself of this opportunity to surrender?"

"No, sir," Bullen said instinctively. He had not been brought up to give in so easily.

"I congratulate you on a fine sentiment, Lieutenant," Derain said, then drew a watch from his pocket. He clicked open the watch's lid. "In five minutes, Lieutenant, we shall have a cannon by the bridge." He gestured down the track that was misted and so crowded with voltigeurs that Bullen had no chance to see if Derain told the truth. "Three or four shots should persuade you," Derain went on, "but if you yield first then you shall of course live. If you force me to use the cannon then I shall not offer you another chance to surrender, nor will I be responsible for my men's behavior."

"In my army," Bullen said, "officers are held responsible."

"I daily thank my God that I am not in your army," Derain said smoothly, then took off his hat and bowed again. "Five minutes, Lieutenant. I wish you good day." He turned and walked away. A mass of voltigeurs and chasseurs were on the track, but, worse, Bullen could see more on either side of the farmhouse. If the farm was a virtual island in the marshes then it already belonged more to the French than to him. He pulled on his shako and walked back to the farmhouse, watched by the French soldiers.

"What did they want, Lieutenant?" It was the Portuguese officer who asked the question.

"Our surrender, sir."

"And your reply?"

"No," Bullen said, and heard the men murmuring, though whether they agreed with him or were grieved by his decision, he could not tell.

"My name is Major Ferreira," Ferreira said, drawing Bullen towards the hearth where they were assured of a little privacy, "and I am on the Portuguese staff. It is important, Lieutenant, that I reach our lines. What I wish you to do, and I know it will be hard for you, is to bargain with the French. Tell them you will surrender," he held up his hand to still Bullen's protest, "but tell them, too, that you have five civilians here and your condition for surrender is that the civilians go free."

"Five civilians?" Bullen managed to interrupt with the question.

"I shall pretend to be one," Ferreira said airily, "and once we have passed the French lines you will then yield, and I assure you that Lord Wellington will be told of your sacrifice. I also have no doubt you will be exchanged very soon."

"My men won't be," Bullen said belligerently.

Ferreira smiled. "I am giving you an order, Lieutenant." He paused to take off his uniform coat, evidently deciding the lack of it would disguise his military status. The big civilian with the frightening face came to stand beside him, using his bulk as an added persuasion, and the other civilians stood close behind, carrying their guns and their heavy bags.

"I recognize you!" Slingsby said suddenly from the hearth. He blinked at Ferragus. "Sharpe hit you."

"Who are you?" Ferreira demanded coldly.

"I command here," Slingsby said, and tried to salute with his sword, but only succeeded in striking the heavy wooden mantel. "Captain Slingsby," he said.

"Until Captain Slingsby recovers," Bullen said, ashamed to be admitting to a foreigner that his commanding officer was drunk, "I command."

"Then go, Lieutenant." Ferreira pointed to the door.

"Do as he says," Slingsby said, though in truth he had not understood the conversation.

"Best to do what he says, sir," Sergeant Read muttered. The Sergeant was no coward, but he reckoned staying where they were was to invite death. "Frogs will look after us."

"You can't give me orders," Bullen challenged Ferreira.

The Major restrained the big man, who had growled and started forward. "That is true," Ferreira said to Bullen, "but if you do not surrender,

Lieutenant, and we are captured then eventually we shall be exchanged and I shall have things to tell Lord Wellington. Things, Lieutenant, that will not improve your chances of advancement." He paused, then lowered his voice. "This is important, Lieutenant."

"Important!" Slingsby echoed.

"On my honor," Ferreira said solemnly, "I have to reach Lord Wellington. It is a sacrifice I ask of you, Lieutenant, indeed I beg it of you, but by making it you will serve your country well."

"God save the gracious King," Slingsby said.

"On your honor?" Bullen asked Ferreira.

"Upon my most sacred honor," the Major replied.

So Bullen turned to the door. The light company would surrender.

♛

COLONEL LAWFORD STARED INTO THE VALLEY. The mist was fast disappearing now, showing the whole area covered in French skirmishers. Hundreds of skirmishers! They were spread out so that the British and Portuguese guns were having little or no effect. The shells exploded, shrapnel burst in the air with black puffs of smoke, but Lawford could see no French casualties.

Nor could he see his light company. "Damn," he said quietly, then stooped to the telescope on its tripod and stared at the ruined barn that was half shrouded in the remaining mist, and though he could see men moving close to the broken walls he was fairly sure they wore neither green nor red coats. "Damn," he said again.

"What the devil are the benighted buggers doing? Morning, Lawford. What the devil do the bloody bastards think they're doing?" It was General Picton, dressed in a shabby black coat, who bounded up the steps and scowled down at the enemy. He was wearing the same tasseled nightcap he had worn during the battle on Bussaco's ridge. "Bloody silly maneuver," he said, "whatever it is." His aides, out of breath, followed him onto the bastion where a twelve-pounder fired, deafening everyone and shrouding the air with smoke. "Stop your damned firing!" Picton bellowed. "So, Lawford, what the devil are they doing?"

"They've sent out a brigade of skirmishers, sir," Lawford said, which was not a particularly helpful answer, but all he could think of saying.

"They've sent out skirmishers?" Picton asked. "But nothing heavy? Just out for a bloody stroll, are they?"

Musket fire crackled in the valley. It seemed to come from the big abandoned farm that was hidden by the mist, which lay thicker above the swampy ground, yet it was plain something was happening there, for three or four hundred of the French skirmishers, instead of advancing across the valley, were crossing the bridge and moving towards the farm. The floods were receding with the ebbing tide, showing the big curve of the stream that cradled the farm.

"They're there," Major Leroy announced. He had his own telescope propped on the parapet and was staring into the shredding mist. He could only see the farm's rooftops and there was no sign of the missing light company, but Leroy could see dozens of voltigeurs firing at the buildings. He pointed down into the valley. "They must be at the farm, sir."

"Who's at the farm?" Picton demanded. "What farm? Who the devil are you talking about?"

That was the question Lawford had dreaded, but he had no choice but to confess what he had done. "I put our light company out as a picquet, sir," he said.

"You did what?" Picton asked, his tone dangerous.

"They were in the barn," Lawford said, pointing at the ruined building. He could hardly explain that he had put them there as an opportunity for his brother-in-law to get a grip on the light company, and that he had supposed that even Slingsby would have the wit to retreat the moment he was faced with overwhelming force.

"Just the barn?" Picton asked.

"They were ordered to patrol," Lawford replied.

"God damn it, man," Picton exploded. "God damn it! One picquet's about as much use as a tit on a broomstick! Chain of picquets, man, chain of picquets! One bloody picquet? The bloody French quick-stepped round them, didn't they? You might as well have ordered the poor devils to line up and shoot themselves in the head. It would have been a quicker end. So where the hell are they now?"

"There's a farm," Leroy said, pointing, and just then the mist cleared enough to show the western face of the farm from which musket smoke spurted.

"Sweet Jesus bloody Christ," Picton grumbled. "You don't want to lose them, do you, Lawford? Looks bad in His Majesty's bloody army when you lose a whole light company. It reeks of carelessness. I suppose we'd best rescue them." The last words, spoken in an exaggerated Welsh accent, were scornful.

"My battalion's standing to," Lawford said with as much dignity as he could muster.

"What's left of it," Picton said. "And we have the Portuguese, don't we?" He turned to an aide.

"Both battalions are ready, sir," the aide said.

"Then bloody go," Picton ordered. "Draw them off, Lawford." Lawford and the other South Essex officers ran down the steps. Picton shook his head. "It's too late, of course," he said to an aide, "much too late." He watched the powder smoke thicken the lingering mist around the distant farmstead. "Poor buggers will be in the net long before Lawford has a chance, but we can't do nothing, can we? We can't just do nothing." He turned furiously on the gunners. "Why are you standing around like barrack-gate whores? Put some fire on those bastards." He pointed to the skirmishers threatening the farm. "Kill the vermin."

The guns were realigned, then bucked back and their smoke vented out into the valley as the shells screamed away, leaving their traces of fuse smoke behind. Picton scowled. "Bloody picquet in a barn," he said to no one in particular. "No Welsh regiment would have been so cretinous! That's what we need. More Welsh regiments. I could clear bloody Europe if I had enough Welsh regiments, instead of which I have to rescue the bloody English. God only knows why the Almighty made bloody foreigners."

"Tea, sir," an aide said, bringing the General a generous tin mug and that, at least, silenced him for the moment. The guns fired on.

CHAPTER 13

SHARPE STRUGGLED THROUGH the marsh to the edge of the higher ground where the farm stood. He expected to be shot at, but it seemed the Ferreira brothers and their three companions were not waiting for him at the eastern edge of the farmyard and, as he reached a corner of a cattle byre, he saw why. French voltigeurs, a swarm of them, were on the other side of the farmhouse which was evidently under siege. Frenchmen were coming towards him, though for the moment they seemed not to have noticed Sharpe and were plainly intent on infiltrating the buildings to surround the beleaguered farmhouse.

"Who's fighting who?" Harper asked as he joined Sharpe.

"God knows." Sharpe listened and thought he detected the crisper sound of rifles from the farmhouse. "Are those rifles, Pat?"

"They are, sir."

"Then those have to be our fellows in there," he said, and he slipped around the end of the byre and immediately muskets blasted from the farmhouse and the balls struck the byre's stone walls and thumped into the timber partitions that divided the row of open cattle stalls. He crouched behind the nearest timber wall that was about four feet high. The byre was open on the side facing the yard and the muskets kept firing from the house to snap over his head or crack into the stonework. "Maybe it's the Portuguese," he shouted back to Harper. If Ferreira had discovered a Portuguese picquet in the farmhouse then doubtless he could persuade them to fire at Sharpe. "Stay where you are, Pat!"

"Can't, sir. Bloody Crapauds are getting too close."

"Wait," Sharpe said, and he stood up behind the partition and aimed the rifle at the house and immediately the windows facing him vanished in smoke as muskets fired. "Now!" Sharpe called, and Harper, Vicente, Sarah and Joana came around the corner and joined him in the stall, which was crusted with ancient cattle dung. "Who are you?" Sharpe bellowed at the farmhouse, but his voice was lost in the din of constant musketry that echoed around the yard as the balls thumped home, and if there was any reply from the house he did not hear it. Instead two Frenchmen appeared between the cottages on the far side of the yard and Harper shot one and the other ducked away fast just before Vicente's bullet clipped a scrap of stone from the wall. The man Harper had shot crawled away and Sharpe aimed his rifle at the gap between the buildings, expecting another voltigeur to appear at any moment. "I'm going to have to reach the house," Sharpe said, and he peered over the partition again and saw what he thought was a red coat in the farmhouse window. There were no more voltigeurs on the far side of the yard and he thought briefly about staying where he was and hoping the French did not discover them, but inevitably they would find them in the end. "Watch for any bloody Frogs," he said to Harper, indicating across the yard, "and I'm going to run like hell. I think there are redcoats in there, so I just need to reach the buggers." He tensed, nerving himself to cross the bullet-stitched farmyard, and just then he heard a bugle blowing. It blew a second and a third time, and voices shouted in French, some of them horribly close, and the firing slowly died away until there was silence except for the boom of the artillery on the heights and the crack of exploding shells in the valley beyond the farm.

Sharpe waited. Nothing moved, no musket fired. He dodged around the partition into the next stall and no one fired at him. He could see no one. He stood up gingerly and gazed at the farmhouse, but whoever had been at the windows was now inside the house and he could see nothing. The others followed him into the new compartment, then they leapfrogged up the spaces where cattle had been kept and still no one

shot. "Sir!" Harper said warningly, and Sharpe turned to see a Frenchman watching them from beside a shed across the yard. The man was not
aiming his musket, instead he waved at them and Sharpe realized the
bugle call must have presaged a truce. An officer appeared beside the
French soldier and he gestured that Sharpe and his companions should
go back into the byre. Sharpe gave him two fingers, then ran for the next
building which proved to be a dairy. He banged open the door and saw
two French soldiers inside, who turned, half raising their muskets, then
saw the rifle aimed at them.

"Don't even bloody think about it," Sharpe said. He crossed the
flagged floor and opened the end door nearest the house. Vicente,
Harper and the two women followed him into the dairy, and Sarah
talked with the two Frenchmen, who were now thoroughly terrified.

"They've been told not to fire until the bugle sounds again," she told
Sharpe.

"Tell them they'd bloody well better not fire, then," Sharpe said. He
peered through the door to see how many voltigeurs were between the
dairy and the house and saw none, but when he looked around the corner there were a score of them, just yards away. They were crouching
well off to the side, then one turned and saw Sharpe's face at the dairy
door and must have assumed he was French for he simply yawned. The
voltigeurs were just waiting. A couple of the men were even lying down
and one had his shako over his eyes as if he was trying to catch a moment's sleep. Sharpe could not see an officer, though he was sure one
must be close.

Sharpe moved back out of the Frenchmen's sight and he wondered
who the hell was in the farmhouse. If they were British then he was safe,
but if they were Portuguese then Ferreira would have him killed. If he
stayed where he was he would either be killed or captured by the French
when the truce ended. "We're going to the house," he told his companions, "and there are a bunch of Frogs around the corner. Just ignore them.
Hold your weapons low, don't look at them and walk as though you own
the bloody place." He took a last look, saw no one in the farm window,
saw the voltigeurs chatting or resting, and decided to risk it. Just cross the
yard. It was only a dozen paces. "Let's do it," he said.

Sharpe, afterwards, reckoned the French simply did not know what to do. The senior officers, those who might have made an instant decision what to do about enemy soldiers patently breaking a truce, were at the front of the farm, and those who saw the three men and two women emerge from the dairy and cross the angle of the yard to the back door of the house were too surprised to react at once, and by the time any Frenchman had made up his mind, Sharpe was already at the farmhouse. One man did open his mouth to protest, but Sharpe smiled at him. "Nice day, eh?" he said. "Should dry out our wet clothes." Sharpe ushered the others through the door and then, going in last, he saw the redcoats. "Who the hell's been trying to kill us?" he demanded loudly and, for answer, an astonished Rifleman Perkins pointed wordlessly at Major Ferreira, and Sharpe, without breaking stride, crossed the room and smacked Ferreira across the side of the head with his rifle butt. The Major dropped like a poleaxed ox. Ferragus started forward, but Harper put his rifle muzzle to the big man's head.

"Do it," the Irishman said softly, "please."

Redcoats and greenjackets were staring at Sharpe. Lieutenant Bullen, in the front doorway, had stopped and turned, and now gazed at Sharpe as if he saw a ghost. "You bloody lot!" Sharpe said. "Of all people, you bloody lot. You were trying to kill me out there! Lousy bloody shots, all of you! Not one bullet came near me! Mister Bullen, isn't it?"

"Yes, sir."

"Where are you going, Mister Bullen?" Sharpe did not wait for an answer, but turned away. "Sergeant Huckfield! You'll disarm those civilians. And if that big bastard gives you any trouble, shoot him."

"Shoot him, sir?" Huckfield asked, astonished.

"Are you bloody deaf? Shoot him! If he so much as bloody twitches, shoot him." Sharpe turned back to Bullen. "Well, Lieutenant?"

Bullen looked embarrassed. "We were going to surrender, sir. Major Ferreira said we should." He gestured at Ferreira who lay motionless. "I know he isn't in charge here, sir, but that's what he said and . . ." His voice trailed away. He had been about to add that Slingsby had recommended surrender, but that would have been a disavowal of responsibility and so dishonorable. "I'm sorry, sir," he said miserably. "It was my decision. The Frenchman said they're fetching a cannon."

"The miserable bastard lied to you," Sharpe said. "They haven't got cannon. On ground as wet as this? It would take twenty horses to get a cannon over here. No, he just wanted to scare you, because he knows as well as anyone that we could all die of old age in here. Harvey, Kirby, Batten, Peters. Shut this door," he pointed to the front door, "and pile all the packs behind it. Block it up!"

"Back doorway too, sir?" Rifleman Slattery asked.

"No, Slats, leave it open, we're going to need it." Sharpe took a quick glance through one of the front windows and saw that it was so high from the ground that no Frenchman could hope to escalade the sill. "Mister Bullen? You'll command this side," he meant the two windows and the door at the front of the house, "but you only need four men. They can't get through those windows. Are there any redcoats upstairs?"

"Yes, sir."

"Get 'em down here. Rifles only up there. Carter, Pendleton, Slattery, Sims. Get up that ladder and try to look as if you're enjoying yourselves. Mister Vicente? Can you climb upstairs with your shoulder?"

"I can," Vicente said.

"Take your rifle up, look after the boys up there." Sharpe turned back to Bullen. "Keep your four men firing at the bastards. Don't aim, just fire. I want every other redcoat on this side of the room. Miss Fry?"

"Mister Sharpe?"

"Is that musket loaded? Good. Point it at Ferragus. If he moves, shoot him. If he breathes, shoot him. Perkins, stay with the ladies. Those men are prisoners, and you treat them as such. Sarah? Tell them to sit down and put their hands on their heads and if any one of them moves his hands, kill him." Sharpe crossed to the four men and kicked their bags to the side of the room and heard the chink of coins. "Sounds like your dowry, Miss Fry."

"The five minutes are up, sir," Bullen reported, "at least I think so." He had no watch and could only guess.

"Is that what they gave you? So watch the front, Mister Bullen, watch the front. That side of the house is your responsibility."

"I will command there." Slingsby, who had watched Sharpe in silence, suddenly pushed himself away from the hearth. "I am in command here," he amended his statement.

"Do you have a pistol?" Sharpe demanded of Slingsby, who looked surprised at the question, but then nodded. "Give it here," Sharpe said. He took the pistol, lifted the frizzen and blew out the priming powder so the weapon would not fire. The last thing he needed was a drunk with a loaded weapon. He put the gun back into Slingsby's hand, then sat him back down in the hearth. "What you're going to do, Mister Slingsby," he said, "is watch up the chimney. Make sure the French don't climb down."

"Yes, sir," Slingsby said.

Sharpe went to the back window. It was not large, but it would not be difficult for a man to climb through and so he put five men to guard it. "You shoot any bugger trying to get through, and use your bayonets if you run out of bullets." The French, he knew, would have used the last few minutes to reorganize, but he was certain they had no artillery so in the end they could only rush the house and he reckoned now that the main attack would come from the rear and would converge on the window and on the door he had deliberately left open. He had eighteen men facing that door in three ranks, the front rank kneeling, the others standing. The only last worry was Ferragus and his companions and Sharpe pointed his rifle at the big man. "You cause me trouble and I'll give you to my men for bayonet practice. Just sit there." He went to the ladder. "Mister Vicente? Your men can fire whenever you've got targets! Wake the bastards up. You men down here," he turned back to the large room, "wait."

Ferreira stirred and pushed up to all fours and Sharpe hit him with the rifle butt again, then Harris called from upstairs that the French were moving, the rifles cracked in the roof space and there was a cheer outside and a huge French volley that hammered against the outside wall and came through the open windows to thump into the ceiling beams. The cheer had come from the back of the house and Sharpe, standing beside the one window facing east, saw men come running from behind the byres on the one side and the cottages on the other. "Wait!" he called. "Wait!" The French still cheered, encouraged perhaps by the lack of fire, and then the charge came up the steps to the open back door and Sharpe shouted at the kneeling men. "Front rank! Fire!" The noise was deafening inside the room and the six bullets, aimed at three paces, could not miss. The front rank men scuttled aside to load their muskets and the second rank, who had been standing, knelt down. "Second rank, fire!" Another six bullets. "Third rank, fire!" Harper stepped forward with the volley gun, but Sharpe gestured him back. "Save it, Pat," he said, and he stepped to the door and saw that the French had blocked the steps with dead and dying men, but one brave officer was trying to lead men up between the bodies and Sharpe raised the rifle, shot the man in the head and stepped back before a ragged volley whipped up through the empty doorway.

That doorway was now blocked by corpses, one of whom was lying almost full length inside the house. Sharpe pushed the body out and closed the door, which immediately began to shake as musket balls struck the heavy wood, then he drew his sword and went to the window where three Frenchmen were clawing at the redcoats' bayonets, trying to drag the muskets clean out of their enemies' hands. Sharpe hacked down with the sword, half severed a hand, and the French backed off, then a new rush of men came to the window, but Harper met them with the volley gun and, as so often when the huge gun fired, the sheer noise of it seemed to astonish the enemy for the window was suddenly free of attackers and Sharpe ordered the five men to fire obliquely through the opening at the voltigeurs trying to clear a passage to the door.

A blast of musketry announced a second attack at the other side of the house. Voltigeurs were hammering on the front door, shaking the pile of packs behind it, but Sharpe used the men who had fired the lethal volleys at the back door to reinforce the musketry at the front of the house, each man firing fast through a window and then ducking out of sight, and the French suddenly realized the strength of the farmhouse and their attack ended abruptly as they pulled back around the sides of the house. That left the front empty of enemy, but the back of the house faced the farmyard with its buildings that offered cover and the fire there was unending. Sharpe reloaded the rifle, knelt by the back window and saw a voltigeur at the yard's end twitch back as he was struck by a bullet fired from the attic. Sharpe fired at another man, and the voltigeurs scuttled into cover rather than face more rifle fire. "Cease fire!" Sharpe shouted. "And well done. Saw the buggers off! Reload. Check flints."

There was a moment's comparative silence, though the cannon from the heights were loud and Sharpe realized that the artillery in the forts was shooting at the men attacking the farm because he could hear the shrapnel rattling on the roof. The riflemen in the attic were still firing. Their rate was slow, and that was good, signifying that Vicente was making sure they aimed true before pulling the triggers. He looked across at the prisoners, reckoning he could use Perkins's rifle and the muskets that Joana and Sarah carried. "Sergeant Harper?"

"Sir!"

"Tie those bastards up. Hands and feet. Use musket slings."

A half-dozen men helped Harper. As Ferragus was trussed he stared up at Sharpe, but he made no resistance. Sharpe tied the Major's hands as well. Slingsby was on his hands and knees, rooting at the packs piled behind the front door, and when he had found his bag with its supply of rum he went back to the hearth and uncorked the canteen. "Poor bloody bastard," Sharpe said, amazed that he could feel any pity for Slingsby. "How long has he been lushed?"

"Since Coimbra," Bullen said, "more or less continuously."

"I only saw him drunk once," Sharpe said.

"He was probably scared of you, sir," Bullen said.

"Of me?" Sharpe sounded surprised. He crossed to the hearth and went on one knee and looked into Slingsby's face. "I'm sorry, Lieutenant," he said, "for being rude to you." Slingsby blinked at Sharpe, confusion and then surprise on his face. "You hear me?" Sharpe asked.

"Decent of you, Sharpe," Slingsby said, then drank some more.

"There, Mister Bullen, you heard me. One apology."

Bullen grinned, was about to speak, but just then the rifles in the roof sounded and Sharpe turned to the windows. "Be ready!"

The French came at the back again, but this time they had assembled a large force of voltigeurs with orders to pour fire through the one window while a dozen men cleared the steps of bodies to make way for an assault party, who made the mistake of giving a huge cheer as they charged. Sharpe whipped open the door and Harper ordered the front rank to fire, then the second, then the third, and the bodies piled again at the foot of the steps, but the French kept coming, scrambling over the bodies, and a musket cracked just beside Sharpe's ear and he saw it was

Sarah, firing into the persistent attack. And still more Frenchmen came up the steps and Harper had the reloaded first rank fire, but a blue-coated man survived the fusillade and burst through the door where Sharpe met him with the point of the sword. "Second rank," Harper shouted, "fire!" and Sharpe twisted the blade out of the dying man's belly, pulled him into the house and slammed the door shut again. Sarah was watching the men reload and copying them. The door was shaking, dust flying from its bracing timbers with every bullet strike, but no one was trying to open it now, and the French musketry that had kept Sharpe's men away from the windows died down as the frustrated French retreated to the flanks of the house where they were safe from the fire. "We're winning," Sharpe said, and men grinned through the powder stains on their faces.

And it was almost true.

TWO OF GENERAL SARRUT'S AIDES completed the reconnaissance and, if sense had prevailed, their bravery would have finished the morning's excitement. The two men, both mounted on fit horses, had risked the cannon fire to gallop into the mouth of the valley that twisted behind the bastion the British called Work Number 119. Shells, rifle fire and even a few musket balls struck all around the two horses as they raced into the shadow of the eastern hill, then both riders slewed their beasts around in a flurry of turf and spurred back the way they had come. A shell banged close behind, spurting blood from the haunch of one horse, but the two exhilarated officers made their escape safely, galloped through the foremost skirmishers, jumped the small stream and reined in beside the General. "The valley's blocked, sir," one of them reported. "There are trees, bushes and palisades blocking the valley. No way through."

"And there's a bastion with cannon above the blockage," the second aide reported, "just waiting for an attempt on the valley."

Sarrut swore. His job was done now. He could report to General Reynier, who in turn would report to Marshal Masséna, that none of the guns was a fake and that the small valley, far from offering a passage through the enemy's line, was an integral part of the defenses. All he needed to do now was sound the recall and the skirmishers would retreat, the gun smoke dissipate and the morning would revert to silence, but as the two horsemen had returned from their excursion, Sarrut had seen brown-uniformed Portuguese cazadores coming from the blocked valley. The enemy, it seemed, wanted a fight, and no French general became a marshal by refusing such an invitation. "How do they get out of their lines?" he wanted to know, pointing at the Portuguese skirmishers.

"Narrow path down the backside of the hill, sir," the more observant of the aides answered, "protected by gates and the forts."

Sarrut grunted. That answer suggested he could not hope to assail the forts by the path used by the Portuguese, but he would be damned before he just retreated when the enemy was offering a fight. The least he could do was bloody their noses. "Push hard into them," he ordered. "And what the devil happened to that picquet?"

"Gone to ground," another aide answered.

"Where?"

The aide pointed to the farm that was ringed with smoke. The mist had just about gone, but there was so much smoke around the farm it looked like fog.

"Then dig them out!" Sarrut ordered. He had originally scoffed at the idea of capturing a mere picquet, but frustration had changed his mind. He had brought four prime battalions into the valley and he could not just march them back with nothing to show for it. Even a handful of prisoners would be some sort of victory. "Was there any damn food in that barn?" he asked.

An aide held out a lump of British army biscuit, twice baked, as hard as a round shot and about as palatable. Sarrut scorned it, then kicked his horse through the stream, past the barn and out into the pastureland where there was more bad news. The Portuguese, far from being hit hard, were driving his chasseurs and voltigeurs back. Two battalions against four and the two were winning, and Sarrut heard the distinctive crack of rifles and knew those weapons were swinging the confrontation in the Portuguese favor. Why the hell did the Emperor insist that rifles were useless? What was useless, Sarrut thought, was pitting muskets against skirmishers. Muskets were for use against enemy formations, not against individuals, but a rifle could pick the flea off a whore's back at a hundred paces. "Ask General Reynier to loose the cavalry," he said to an aide. "That'll sweep those bastards away."

It had started as a reconnaissance and was turning into a battle.

THE SOUTH ESSEX CAME from the eastern side of the hill on which Work Number 119 stood, while the Portuguese had come from its western side and those two battalions now blocked the entrance to the small valley. The South Essex was thus on the Portuguese right, a half-mile away, and in front of them was a stretch of pastureland edged by the flooded stream and the swamps which ringed the beleaguered farmstead. To Lawford's left was the shoulder of the hill, the flank of the Portuguese and, out in the valley in front of him, the swarm of voltigeurs and chasseurs whose scattered formations were punctuated by the exploding bursts of smoke from the British and Portuguese cannon. "It's a bloody mess!" Lawford protested. Most of the South Essex's officers had not had time to fetch their horses, but Lawford was up on Lightning and from the saddle's height he could see the track that crossed the bridge and led to the farmstead. That, he decided, was where he would go. "Double column of companies," he ordered, "quarter distance," and he glanced across at the farmhouse and realized, from the volume of fire and the thickness of the smoke, that the light company was putting up a stout resistance. "Well done, Cornelius," he said aloud. It might have been imprudent for Slingsby to have retreated to the farmhouse rather than to the hills, but at least he was fighting hard. "Advance, Major!" he told Forrest.

Each company of the South Essex was now in four ranks. Two companies were abreast, so that the battalion was arranged in two companies wide and four deep, with number nine company on its own at the rear. To General Picton, watching from the heights, it looked more like a French column than a British unit, but it allowed the battalion to keep itself in good close order as it advanced obliquely, the marshland to its right and the open land and the hills to its left. "We'll deploy into line as necessary," Lawford explained to Forrest, "sweep those men away from the farm track, capture the bridge, then send three companies up to the buildings. You can take them. Brush those damned Frogs away, bring Cornelius's fellows out, rejoin, and we'll go back for dinner. I thought we might finish that peppered ham. It's rather good, isn't it?"

"Very good."

"And some boiled eggs," Lawford said.

"Don't you find they make you costive?" Forrest asked.

"Eggs? Make you costive? Never! I try to eat them every day and my father always swore by boiled eggs. He reckoned they keep you regular. Ah, I see the wretches have noticed us." Lawford spurred Lightning up the narrow space between the companies. The wretches he had seen were chasseurs and voltigeurs who were gathering ahead of his battalion. The French had been attacking the right flank of the Portuguese, but now saw the redcoats approaching and turned to face the new threat. There were not enough of them to stem the battalion's advance, but Lawford still wished he had his light company to go out ahead and drive the skirmishers back. He knew he would have to take some casualties before he was in range to offer a volley that would finish the French nonsense and so he rode to the front so that the men saw him share their danger. He glanced over at the farm and saw the fighting was still fierce there. A shell cracked into flame and smoke a hundred yards ahead. A musket ball, fired at far too long a range, fluttered close above Lawford's head to strike the yellow regimental color, and then he heard the bugles and he stood in the stirrups and saw, way across the far side of the valley, columns of horsemen cascading out of the hills. He noted them, but did nothing yet, for they were too far away to pose any danger. "Go right!" Lawford shouted at Forrest who was by the grenadier company that was on the right flank at the front. "Head up! Head up!" He pointed, meaning that the battalion should march for the bridge. A man stumbled in the front rank, then stayed on the ground, holding his thigh. The files behind opened to march past him, then closed again. "Two men to help him, Mister Collins," Lawford called to the nearest Captain. He dared not leave an injured man behind, not with cavalry loose in the valley. Thank God, he thought, that there was no French artillery.

The horsemen had crossed the stream now and Lawford could see the bright glitter of their drawn sabers and swords. A mix of horsemen, he noted: green-coated dragoons with their long straight swords, sky-blue hussars and lighter green chasseurs with sabers. They were a good mile away, evidently intent on taking the Portuguese on their far flank, but a glance back showed that the cazadores were alive to the danger and were forming two squares. The horsemen saw it too and swerved eastwards, the soft turf flying up behind their horses' hooves. Now they were coming at the South Essex, but they were still far off and Lawford kept marching as voltigeurs scattered from the horsemen's path. Shells exploded among the cavalry and they instinctively spread out and Lawford had a mischievous impulse. "Half distance!" he shouted. "Half distance!"

The companies now increased the intervals between each other. Like the cavalry they were spreading out, no longer resembling a close column, but showing stretches of daylight between each unit and so inviting the cavalry to penetrate those gaps and rip the battalion apart from the inside. "Keep marching!" Lawford called to the nearest company which was looking nervously towards the cavalry. "Ignore them!" Less than half a mile now. The cavalry had spread into a line that thundered across the valley and the South Essex were marching across their front, the left flank of each rank exposed to the horsemen. Now it was all down to timing, Lawford thought, pure timing, for he did not want to form square too soon and so persuade the horsemen to sheer off. How many were there? Three hundred? More, he reckoned, and he could hear their hooves on the soft turf, see their pennants, and he saw the line go into the gallop and he reckoned they had committed themselves too soon because the ground was soft and their horses would be blown by the time they reached his battalion. A shell burst among the leading horsemen and a dragoon went down in a flurry of hooves, bridle, blood and sword. The second line of cavalry swerved around the thrashing horse and Lawford reckoned it was time. "Form square!"

There was something beautiful in good drill, Lawford thought. To watch the rearmost companies halt and march backwards, see the center companies swing out, the forward companies mark time, and all the separate parts come seamlessly together to make a misshapen oblong. Three companies formed the long sides, two were at the northern edge and a single company made the southern face, but what mattered was that the square was made and was impenetrable. The outside rank went onto one knee. "Fix bayonets!"

Most of the horsemen pulled away, but at least a hundred stayed straight and so rode directly into Lawford's volley. The western face of the square vanished in smoke, there were the screams of horses and as the smoke cleared Lawford could see men and beasts galloping away to leave a dozen bodies on the ground. Voltigeurs were firing at the square now, grateful to have such a huge target, and the casualties were being lifted into the square's center. The only answer to the skirmishers was half-company volley fire, and that worked, each blast driving a group of Frenchmen back and sometimes leaving one writhing on the ground, but, like wolves around a flock, they pressed back and the horsemen circled behind them, waiting for the redcoat battalion to open its ranks and give them a chance to attack. Lawford was not going to give it to them. His battalion would stay closed up, but that gave the skirmishers their target and he realized, slowly, that he had marched into a perilous dilemma. The best way of ridding himself of the voltigeurs was to open ranks and advance, but that would invite the cavalry to charge, and the cavalry was the greater danger so he had to stay closed up, yet that gave the French muskets a tempting target, and the voltigeurs were gnawing him to death one injury or death at a time. The artillery was helping Lawford. The shells were exploding steadily, but the ground was soft and the guns were firing from the heights so that many of the shells buried themselves before they exploded and their force was thus cushioned by the ground or wasted upwards. The shrapnel was deadlier, but at least one of the gunners was cutting the fuses too long. Lawford edged the battalion northwards. Moving in square was hard, it had to be done slowly, and the wounded men in the square's center had to be carried with the formation, and the battalion was forced to pause every few seconds so that another volley could blast out at the skirmishers. In truth, Lawford realized, he had been snared by the voltigeurs and what had seemed an easy task was suddenly bloody.

"I wish we had our rifles," Forrest muttered.

Lawford was irritated by the wish, but he also shared it. It was his fault, he knew, for sending the light company out as a picquet and trusting that they would not get into trouble, and now his own battalion was in trouble. It had begun so well: the march in close order, the beautiful drill-book example of forming square, and the easy defeat of the cavalry charge, but now the South Essex was near the center of the valley and had no support except for the distant guns, while more and more voltigeurs, smelling blood, were closing on the battalion. So far he had not suffered many casualties, only five men dead and a score wounded, but that was because the French skirmishers were keeping their distance, wary of his volleys, yet every minute brought another musket strike and the closer he went to the farm track, the more isolated he became. And Picton was watching, Lawford knew, which meant his battalion was on display.

And it was stuck.

⚜

VICENTE CAME DOWN THE LADDER to report that a redcoat battalion was marching to their rescue, but that it was threatened by cavalry and so had formed square a half-mile away. Sharpe looked through the window and saw from the regimental color that it was the South Essex, but the battalion might as well have been a hundred miles away for all the help they could offer him.

The French, after the repulse of their last attack, had concealed themselves behind the farm buildings, well out of sight of the rifles firing from the farmhouse roof. The track to the farm, which had been thick with voltigeurs, was empty now. Sharpe had brought two riflemen downstairs, placed them with himself and Perkins at the front windows and they had used the voltigeurs for target practice until the French, outranged and in the open, had either run into cover at the sides of the house or else gone back to the dryer part of the valley to help the attack on the beleaguered square. "So what do we do now, Mister Bullen?" Sharpe asked.

"Do, sir?" Bullen was surprised to be asked.

Sharpe grinned. "You did well to get the men here, very well. I thought maybe you had another good idea about how to get them out."

"Go on fighting, sir?"

"That's usually the best thing to do," Sharpe said, then peered quickly out of the window and drew no musket fire. "The Frogs won't last long," he said. That seemed an optimistic forecast to Bullen because, as far as he could see, the valley was full of Frenchmen, both infantry and cavalry, and the redcoat square was plainly balked. Sharpe had reached the same conclusion. "Time to earn all that money the King pays you, Mister Bullen."

"What money, sir?"

"What money? You're an officer and a gentleman, Mister Bullen. You've got to be rich." Some of the men laughed. Slingsby, sitting in the hearth with the canteen on his lap, was asleep, his head back against the masonry and his mouth open. Sharpe turned and looked through the window again. "They're in trouble," he said, nodding at the battalion. "They need our help. They need rifles, which means we've got to rescue them." He frowned at the prisoners, an idea half forming. "So Major Ferreira told you to surrender?" he asked Bullen.

"He did, sir. I know it wasn't his place to give orders, but . . ."

"It wasn't his place," Sharpe interrupted, more interested in why Ferreira would have been so willing to fall into French hands. "Did he say why you were to surrender?"

"I was to make a bargain with the French, sir. If they let the civilians go then we'd give up."

"Sneaky bastard," Sharpe said. Ferreira, utterly cowed and with a huge bruise on his temple, stared up at Sharpe. "So you want to get to the lines before us?" Sharpe asked him. Ferreira said nothing. "Not you, Major," Sharpe said, "you're a military man and you're under arrest. But your brother now? And his men? We can let them go. Miss Fry? Tell them to stand up."

The four men stood awkwardly. Sharpe had Perkins and a pair of redcoats point guns at them as Harper untied their feet, then their hands. "What you're going to do," he told them, letting Sarah translate, "is get out of here. There are no Frenchmen out front. Sergeant Read? Unblock the front door." Sharpe looked back at Ferragus and his three companions. "So you can go as soon as the door's open. Run like hell, cut across the marsh and you should make it to those redcoats."

"The French will shoot them if you make them go," Vicente protested, still a lawyer at heart.

"I'll bloody shoot them if they don't go," Sharpe said, then turned as there was a flurry of fire from the yard at the back of the house. The remaining riflemen in the roof answered it and Sharpe listened, judging from the noise whether another attack was coming, but it seemed to him the French were merely firing at random. The volleys of the South Essex came dull across the tongue of wetland while, farther away, the sound of the Portuguese rifles was crisper.

Major Ferreira, at the far end of the room, spoke in Portuguese to his brother. "He said," Sarah translated for Sharpe, "that you will shoot them in the back if they go."

"Tell them I won't. And tell them that if they go fast they'll live."

"The door's unblocked, sir," Read said.

Sharpe looked at Vicente. "Get all the riflemen out of the attic." He would miss their fire and he could only hope that the absence of powder smoke from the battered roof did not encourage the French, but he had an idea, one that could just do some real damage to the enemy. "Sergeant Harper!"

"Sir?"

"You're going to line up six riflemen and six redcoats, match them for size and make them change jackets."

"Change jackets, sir?"

"You heard me! Get on with it. And when the first six are done, do another six. I want every rifleman in a red coat. And once they're dressed they can put their packs on." Sharpe turned to look at the wounded men who were in the room's center. "We're going out," he told them, "and you're staying here." He saw the alarm on their faces. "The French won't hurt you," he reassured them. The British looked after French wounded and the French did the same. "But they won't take you with them either, so when this mess is over we'll come back for you. But the Frogs will steal anything valuable, so if you've got something that's precious give it to a friend to keep for you."

"What are you doing, sir?" one of the wounded men asked.

"Going to help the battalion," Sharpe said, "and I'll be back for you, that's a promise." He looked at the first riflemen reluctantly pulling on the yellow-faced red coats. "Get on with it!" he snapped, and just then Perkins, who had been helping to guard the civilian prisoners, gave a grunt of pain and surprise. Sharpe half turned, thinking an errant bullet must have come through the window, and he saw that Ferragus, released from his bonds, had hit Perkins, and that the redcoats dared not fire at the brute for fear of hitting the wrong man in the crowded room, and Ferragus, free, vengeful and dangerous, was now coming for Sharpe.

⁂

COLONEL LAWFORD WATCHED the voltigeurs thicken to the west and north. There were only a few to the south, and none to the east where the ground was flooded or waterlogged. The cavalry waited behind the voltigeurs, ready for the moment when the musket fire so weakened the South Essex's square that another charge would be possible. For now the French musketry was still at too long a range, but it was hurting and the center of the square was slowly filling with wounded men. The gunners on the hilltop were helping a little, for as the voltigeurs concentrated on the square they made a more inviting target for the shells and shrapnel, but the French skirmishers to the north, who were facing one of the square's narrower sides, were receiving less shell fire because the gunners feared striking the South Essex, and so those skirmishers pressed ever closer and inflicted increasing damage. More voltigeurs ran to that side, understanding that they would receive less volley fire there than from the longer side of the square that faced west.

"I'm not sure," Major Forrest came across to Lawford, "that we can reach the farm now, sir."

Lawford did not answer. The implication of Forrest's remark was that the attempt to rescue the light company should be abandoned. The way south, back to the fort on the hill, was clear enough and, if the South Essex moved back towards the heights, they would survive. The French would see it as a victory, but at least the battalion would live. The light company would be lost, and that was a pity, but better to lose one company than all ten.

"The fire is definitely slacking," Forrest said, and he was not talking of the incessant musketry of the voltigeurs, but of the action at the farm.

Lawford twisted in the saddle and saw that the farmhouse was virtually free of powder smoke. He could see a group of Frenchmen crouched behind a shed or barn, which told him the farmhouse itself had not fallen, but Forrest was right. There was less firing there and that suggested the light company's resistance was being abraded. "Poor fellows," Lawford said. He thought for a second of trying to reach the farm by cutting across the floods and the marshland, but a riderless horse, one of those whose saddles had been emptied by the South Essex square, was floundering in the swamp and, from its struggles, it was plain that any attempt to cross the waterlogged ground would be inviting trouble. The horse heaved itself onto a firmer patch and stood there, shivering and frightened. Lawford felt a flicker of fear himself and knew he must make a decision. "The wounded will have to be carried," he said to Forrest. "Detail men from the rear rank."

"We're going back?" Forrest asked.

"I fear so, Joseph. I fear so," Lawford said, and just then a voltigeur's bullet struck Lightning in the right eye and the horse reared, screaming, and Lawford kicked his boots from the saddle and threw himself to the left as Lightning twisted in the sky, hooves flailing. Lawford fell heavily, but managed to scramble clear as the big horse collapsed. Lightning tried to get up again, but only succeeded in kicking the ground and Lawford's servant ran to the beast with the Colonel's big horse pistol. Then he hesitated, for Lightning was thrashing. "Do it, man!" the Colonel called. "Do it!" The horse's eyes were white, its bloodied head was beating against the ground and the servant could not aim the pistol, but Major Leroy snatched the gun, rammed his boot onto the horse's head and then fired into Lightning's forehead. The horse gave a last great spasm, then was still. Lawford swore. Leroy threw the pistol back to the servant and, his boots glistening with the horse's blood, went back to the western face of the square.

"Give the orders, Major," Lawford said to Forrest. He felt close to tears. The horse had been magnificent. He ordered his servant to unbuckle the girth and remove the saddle, and he watched as those wounded who could not crawl or limp were lifted from the ground and then the South Essex began to retreat. It would be a painfully slow withdrawal. The square had to stay together if the horsemen were not to charge, and it could only edge its way cautiously, shuffling rather than marching. The French, seeing it move south, gave an ironic cheer, and pressed closer. They wanted to finish the redcoats and go back to their side of the valley with a fine haul of prisoners, captured weapons and, best of all, the two precious colors. Lawford looked up at the two flags, both now punctured with bullet strikes, and he wondered if he should strip them from the poles and burn the heavy silk, then dismissed that thought as panic. He would get back to the hills and Picton would be angry, and doubtless there would be mockery from other battalions, but the South Essex would survive. That was what mattered.

The route back to the hills was clear of all enemy now because the right-hand battalion of cazadores had moved closer to the South Essex. The French had been repulsed by the Portuguese, defeated by their rifles, and instead had concentrated on the vulnerable redcoats, and now the Portuguese battalion moved to its right and its rifles were working on the men assailing Lawford, and that cleared the way south, but the cavalry drifted that way and the Portuguese formed square again. The cavalry, harassed by the endless shells, moved back towards the center of the valley, but the Portuguese rifles still kept the way home clear for the South Essex. In another two or three hundred yards, Lawford thought, he would be close to the hill and the French would give up and retreat, except that they would console themselves by capturing the farm. Lawford glanced at the buildings, saw no smoke coming from the roof or windows and reckoned it was all too late. "We tried," he said to Forrest, "at least we tried."

And failed, Forrest thought, but said nothing. The northern-most files of the square divided to edge about Lightning's corpse, then closed up again. The voltigeurs, wary of the Portuguese rifles, were concentrating on that northern flank again and the half-company volleys were constant as the redcoats tried to drive the pestilential skirmishers away. The muskets flamed and the smoke thickened and the square shuffled south.

And the light company was alone.

SHARPE DUCKED, just evading a blow of Ferragus's right fist, and instead caught a left on his shoulder, which was like being hit by a musket ball. It almost knocked him over, and the following punch from Ferragus's right hand, which was supposed to half crush Sharpe's skull, only succeeded in glancing off the top of his head and knocking off his shako, but it still rocked Sharpe who instinctively rammed the butt of his rifle towards Ferragus and caught the big man on his left knee. The pain of that blow stopped Ferragus, and the second blow of the rifle caught him on his right fist which was still injured from the stone blow Sharpe had given him at the monastery. Ferragus flinched from the pain and two redcoats tried to haul him down but he shook them off like a bear shrugging off dogs, although they had slowed him for a second, giving Sharpe a chance to stand. He tossed the rifle to Harper. "Let him be," Sharpe said to the redcoats, "let him be." He unbuckled his sword belt and threw the weapon to Bullen. "Keep a watch out of the windows, Mister Bullen!"

"Yes, sir."

"A good watch! Make sure the men are looking out there, not in here."

"Let me murder him, sir," Harper suggested.

"Let's not be unfair to Mister Ferreira, Pat," Sharpe said. "He couldn't cope with you. And the last time he tried to deal with me he had to have help. Just you and me, eh?" Sharpe smiled at Ferragus who was flexing his right hand. Sarah was behind the big man and she cocked the musket, grimacing with the force needed to drag back the doghead. The sound of the ratchet made Ferragus glance behind and Sharpe stepped forward and drove his right knuckles into Ferragus's left eye. He felt something give there, the big head jerked back and Sharpe was out of range by the time he had recovered. "I know you'd like to kill him," Sharpe said to Sarah, "but it's not very ladylike. Leave him to me." He went forward again, aimed a blow at Ferragus's closing left eye and stepped back before he delivered it, moving to his left, making sure Ferragus followed him, and pausing just a heartbeat too long because Ferragus, faster than Sharpe expected, delivered a straight left. It did not travel far, it did not even look particularly powerful, but it struck Sharpe in his bandaged ribs and was like a cannonball's strike, and if he had not already decided to step back he would have been floored by the blow, but his legs were already moving as the pain seared up his ribs. He flicked out his own left hand, aiming again at the swollen eye, but Ferragus swatted it aside, released his left hand again, but Sharpe was safely back now.

Ferragus could see nothing from his left eye, and the pain of it was a flaring red agony in his skull, but he knew he had hurt Sharpe and knew if he could get close he could do more than just hurt the rifleman, who was now stepping back between the wounded redcoats and the big hearth. Ferragus hurried, reckoning to take Sharpe's best blows and then get close enough to murder the English bastard, but Slingsby, drunk as a judge and sitting in the hearth, stuck out his right leg and Ferragus tripped on it and Sharpe was back in his face, the left fist again pulping Ferragus's damaged eye and ramming the heel of his right hand into Ferragus's nose. Something broke there and Ferragus, swatting at Slingsby with his left hand, threw out his right to stop Sharpe, but Sharpe had stepped back again. "Let him be, Mister Slingsby," Sharpe said. "Are your men watching out the windows, Mister Bullen?"

"They are, sir."

"Make damn sure they are."

Sharpe was past the wounded men now, in the open space between the front and back windows where no one dared stand for fear of the French bullets, and he backed towards the window facing the yard, heard a bullet whack into the window frame, stabbed a quick left at Ferragus who swayed to let it pass and rushed at Sharpe. Sharpe stepped back, going to Ferragus's left because that was his blind side, and Ferragus turned to face Sharpe who knew he had to take the punishment now and he stepped into the big man's range and drove his fists one after the other into his enemy's belly and it was like punching an oak board. Sharpe knew those blows would not hurt and he did not care because all he wanted to do was drive Ferragus backwards. He rammed his head forward, banging his forehead into the bloody mess of Ferragus's face, and he heaved forward and his head rang as a blow struck him on the side of the skull. His vision went red and black. He pushed again and Ferragus's left hand hit him on the other side of the head and Sharpe knew he could not take more than one other such blow, and he was not even sure he would survive that for his senses were reeling and he gave a last heave, and felt Ferragus jar up against the window sill. Sharpe ducked then, trying to avoid the next blow, which glanced off the top of his head, but even that glancing blow was enough to send a stab of pain down through his skull, but then he felt Ferragus quiver. And quiver again, and now Sharpe staggered back and saw that Ferragus's remaining eye was dull. The big man was looking astonished and Sharpe, through his half daze, slashed out his left hand to hit Ferragus in the throat. Ferragus tried to respond, tried to plant two hammer-like blows into Sharpe's vulnerable ribs, but his broad back was filling the window and it was the first easy target the French had been given since the siege of the farm had begun, and two musket balls struck him and he shook again, then opened his mouth and the blood spilled out. "Your men aren't watching outside, Mister Bullen!" Sharpe said. A last bullet hit Ferragus, this one at the nape of his neck and he pitched forward like a felled tree.

Sharpe bent to recover his shako, took a deep breath and felt the pain in his ribs. "You want some advice, Mister Bullen?" Sharpe said.

"Of course, sir."

"Never fight fair." He took his sword back. "Detail two men to escort Major Ferreira and another two to help Lieutenant Slingsby. And those four men carry those bags." He pointed to the bags that had belonged to Ferragus and his men. "And what's inside, Mister Bullen, belongs to Miss Fry, so make sure the thieving bastards keep the bags buckled."

"I will, sir."

"And maybe," Sharpe said to Sarah, "you'll be kind enough to give Jorge some coins? He has to pay for that boat."

"Of course I will."

"Good!" Sharpe said, then turned to Harper. "Is everyone changed?"

"Almost, sir."

"Get on with it!" It took another moment, but finally every rifleman, even Harper, was in a red jacket, though the largest red coat looked ludicrously small on the Irishman. Sharpe changed coats with Lieutenant Bullen and hoped the French would really mistake the riflemen for men with muskets. He had not made the men change their breeches because he reckoned that would take too much time, and a sharp-eyed voltigeur might wonder why the redcoats had dark-green trousers, but he would risk that. "What we're going to do," he told the company, "is rescue a battalion."

"We're going out?" Bullen sounded alarmed.

"No, they are." Sharpe pointed to the three Portuguese civilians. He took his rifle from Harper and cocked it. "Out!"

The three men hesitated, but they had seen what the rifleman had done to their master and they were terrified of him. "Tell them to run to the square," Sharpe said to Vicente. "Tell them they'll be safe there." Vicente looked dubious, suspecting that what Sharpe was doing was against the rules of war, but then he looked into Sharpe's face and decided not to argue. Nor did the three men. They were taken to the front door and, when they hesitated, Sharpe leveled his rifle.

They ran.

Sharpe had not lied to them. They were fairly safe and the farther they went from the farmhouse, the safer they became. None of the French reacted at first, for the last thing they had expected was for anyone to break from the house, and it was a full four or five seconds before the first musket fired, but the voltigeurs were shooting at running men, men going away up the farm track, and the bullets went wild. After fifty yards the three men cut across the marshland, and the going was much harder for them, but they were also farther away from the French who, frustrated by their escape, tried to close the distance. They moved out from behind the farm buildings, going to the edge of the marsh, aiming their muskets at the three men who were trying to pick a path through the morass. "Rifles," Sharpe said, "start killing those bastards."

The French, by running from cover, had made themselves easy targets for rifles shooting from the farm windows. There were a few seconds of panic among the voltigeurs, then they ran back to the sides of the farm. Sharpe waited as the riflemen reloaded. "They won't do that again," he said, then told them what he planned.

The red-jacketed riflemen were to leave the farm first and, like the three Portuguese, were to run as fast as they could up the track and then angle across the swamp towards the flooded stream. "Except we're going to stop by the dungheap out front," Sharpe told them, "and give the others some covering fire." Major Ferreira, his escorts, Slingsby, Sarah and Joana would go next, shepherded by Vicente, and finally Lieutenant Bullen would bring the rest of the company out. "You're our rearguard," Sharpe told Bullen. "You hold off the voltigeurs. Proper skirmish work, Lieutenant. Fight in pairs, nice and calm. The enemy will see green jackets so they won't be eager to close, so you should be fine. Just retreat after us, get into the marsh, and go for the battalion. We'll all have to wade the stream and we'll drown if it's too bloody deep, but if those three make it then we know it's safe. That's what they're doing, showing us the way."

The three Portuguese were halfway across the boggy ground now, splashing into the receding floodwaters, and their flight had proved that once they were away from the farmhouse they were in no real danger from the voltigeurs. Sharpe reckoned he would be unlucky to lose two men in this foray. The French had been shocked by the volume of fire from the farm, and they were sheltering now, most of them just wanting to get back to their encampments. So give them what they wanted. "Rifles, are you all ready?"

He crowded them by the front door, told them they must get out of the farm fast, warned them to be ready to stop by the dunghill, turn there, and fight off any threat from the voltigeurs. "Enjoy yourselves, lads," Sharpe said. "And go!"

He went first, jumping down the steps, sprinting towards the track, stopping at the dunghill, turning and dropping to one knee, and the red-jacketed riflemen were spreading in the skirmish line either side of him as he aimed the rifle at the side of the house, looking for an officer, seeing none, but there was a voltigeur taking aim with his musket. Sharpe fired. "Jorge!" he bellowed. "Now!"

Rifles fired. The French were huddled on either side of the building, reckoning they were safe because none of the farm's garrison had succeeded in making a loophole in the gable ends, but they made easy targets now and the bullets tore into them as Vicente's group ran past Sharpe. "Keep going!" Sharpe called to Vicente, then looked back to the farm as a musket ball whipcracked past his head. "Mister Bullen! Now!"

Bullen's group, the largest, came out last and Sharpe bellowed at them to form the skirmish chain and start fighting. "Rifles, back! Back!" They were all there, eighteen men in red coats, running back up the track and then following Vicente as he angled into the wetland, behind the three Portuguese who were wading the stream close to the square now. So the stream could be crossed. The square had been retreating, edging away, but Sharpe saw it had stopped now, presumably because they had seen the light company break from the farm. The battalion's red files were edged with smoke that drifted past the two flags. Sharpe looked back, amazed again because time seemed to be slowing and everything was taking on a marvelous clarity. Bullen's men were too slow in making their skirmish chain and one man was down, struck in the knee, squealing with pain. "Leave him!" Sharpe shouted. He had stopped to reload his rifle. "Fight the bastards, Mister Bullen! Drive them in!" The French were starting to move from the shelter of the farmhouse and the muskets had to stop that, had to drive them back. Sharpe saw an officer shouting, gesturing with a sword, evidently encouraging men to come out of the farm buildings and charge down the track and Sharpe aimed, fired and lost the man in his rifle smoke. A ball struck the ground beside him, ricocheted upwards; another hissed past his head. Bullen had his men in hand now, had steadied them, they were fighting properly, retreating slowly, and Sharpe turned and ran after his disguised riflemen. They were in the marsh, waiting for him. "That way!" he shouted, pointing them towards the voltigeurs fighting the north face of the square. Vicente was close to the South Essex now, plunging into the flooded stream.

Sharpe angled into the march to join his riflemen. The going was easy enough at first for he could jump from tussock to tussock, but then his boots began to stick in the glutinous mud. A musket ball splashed near him and he saw, from the spray, that it had been fired from the west, from the voltigeurs harassing the square.

Those were the men Sharpe was heading for. He would let Bullen, Vicente and the rest of the company go towards the square, but he would take his red-jacketed riflemen up onto the flank of the voltigeurs who had been doing so much damage to the battalion. Only a few of those voltigeurs were worrying about him, and they were simply shooting wildly across the stream, firing at too long a range, and Sharpe knew they were seeing redcoats, not riflemen. They reckoned eighteen redcoats could do them no damage, and Sharpe wanted them to think that, and he led his men to the edge of the flooded ground where the range to the voltigeurs was under a hundred paces. "Officers," he told the riflemen, "sergeants. Look for them. Kill them."

This was why God had made rifles. Muskets could fight each other at a hundred paces and it was a miracle if an aimed shot hit, but the rifles were killers at that range, and the voltigeurs, who had thought themselves faced only with muskets, were ambushed. In the first few seconds Sharpe's riflemen had killed three Frenchmen and wounded another seven, then they reloaded and Sharpe edged them to the left, a few paces nearer the square, and they fired again and the voltigeurs, confused because they only saw red coats, fired back. Sharpe knelt, watched an officer running with a hand holding up his saber, waited for the man to stop and point out a target, and pulled the trigger. When the smoke cleared the officer was gone. "Slow and steady!" Sharpe called. "Make the bullets count!" He turned and saw that Bullen was safe in the marshland now, the voltigeurs had followed him up the track, but none was willing to splash into the morass.

He looked back west, loaded the rifle with its stock half submerged in water, saw a man taking aim with his musket and fired at him. The voltigeurs were at last realizing that they were fighting a cruelly unequal battle and they were running back out of the rifles' range, but the cavalry, farther away, saw only a scatter of red coats and a group of the horsemen turned, drove back their spurs, and burst past the retreating voltigeurs. "Back," Sharpe called, "gently back. And edge left!" He was taking his men closer to the square now, wading through water a foot deep. He still had to cross the stream, but so did the cavalry, and those Frenchmen seemed oblivious of the flooded obstacle. Perhaps they thought the sheet of water was all one depth, just a foot or so deep, and so they lowered their sabers, spurred their horses into a canter and rode for the kill. "Wait till they're floundering," Sharpe said, "then kill them."

The front rank splashed into the flooded land on the opposite bank, then one horse went down into the stream, pitching its rider over its head. The other horses slowed, struggling now to find their footing, and

Sharpe shouted at his men to open fire. A hussar, his pigtails hanging either side of his sunburned face, snarled as he wrenched at his reins and tried to force his horse on through the stream and Sharpe put a bullet straight through the sky-blue jacket. A shell exploded in the second rank of horsemen who had pulled up when they saw the first check. Sharpe reloaded, glanced around to make sure none of the voltigeurs from the farm were coming through the swampy ground, then shot a dragoon. This was easy killing and the horsemen understood it and turned their horses and raked back their spurs so that they struggled back to the firmer ground, still pursued by rifle fire.

And there was more rifle fire now, a storm of it from the far side of the South Essex where the cazadores had come to the redcoats' aid and were driving the voltigeurs back, then the north side of the square exploded into smoke as two companies fired a volley into the flank of the horsemen who were spurring away to safety. Sharpe slung his rifle on his shoulder. "Not a bad day's work, Pat," he said, then nodded at the lone cavalry horse that had crossed the stream and marooned itself in the marsh. "They still pay a reward for enemy horses, don't they? He's all yours, Sergeant."

The cavalry were no longer threatening and so the South Essex deployed into a four-rank line, twice as thick as they would use on a normal battlefield, but safer in case any of the hussars or dragoons decided to try one last attack. That was unlikely for there were Portuguese cazadores on the battalion's left flank now, and empty marshland on their right, while the French, harassed by the cannon fire, were retreating across the valley. Best of all the light company was back.

"It went well," Lawford said. He had mounted the horse Harper had brought to the battalion. "Very well."

"A nervous moment or two," Major Forrest said.

"Nervous?" Lawford said in a surprised tone. "Of course not! Everything went exactly as I thought. Quite exactly as I thought. Pity about Lightning, though." He looked with disgust at his brother-in-law who, plainly drunk, was sitting behind the color party, then he took off his hat as Sharpe walked down the line. "Mister Sharpe! That was very pretty what you did to those voltigeurs, very pretty. Thank you, my dear fellow."

Sharpe changed jackets with Bullen, then looked up at Lawford who was beaming with happiness. "Permission to rescue our wounded from the farm, sir," Sharpe said, "before I return to duty."

Lawford looked puzzled. "Rescuing the wounded is part of your duty, isn't it?"

"I mean being quartermaster, sir."

Lawford leaned from his captured saddle. "Mister Sharpe," he said softly.

"Sir?"

"Stop being bloody tedious."

"Yes, sir."

"And I'm supposed to send you to Pero Negro after this," the Colonel went on and, seeing Sharpe did not understand, added, "to headquarters. It seems the General wants a word with you."

"Send Mister Vicente, sir," Sharpe said, "and the prisoner. Between them they can tell the General everything he needs to know."

"And you can tell me," Lawford said, watching the French go back into the far hills.

"Nothing to tell, sir," Sharpe said.

"Nothing to tell! Good God, you've been absent for two weeks and you've nothing to tell?"

"Just got lost, sir, looking for the turpentine. Very sorry, sir."

"You just got lost," Lawford said flatly, then he looked at Sarah and Joana who were in muddy breeches and had muskets. Lawford looked as if he was about to say something about the women, then shook his head and turned back to Sharpe. "Nothing to tell, eh?"

"We got away, sir," Sharpe said, "that's all that matters. We got away." And they had. It had been Sharpe's escape.

THE FRENCH INVASION OF PORTUGAL in the late summer of 1810 was defeated by hunger, and it marked the last time that the French tried to capture the country. Wellington, by now commander of both the Portuguese and the British armies, adopted a scorched earth policy that brought huge hardship to the Portuguese people. Attempts were made to deny the invaders every scrap of food, while the inhabitants of central Portugal were required to leave their homes, either to take to the hills, go north to Oporto or south to Lisbon, which was to be defended by the extraordinary Lines of Torres Vedras.

The strategy worked, but at a very high price. One estimate reckons that forty to fifty thousand Portuguese lost their lives in the winter of 1811-1812, most from hunger, some from the French, but an appalling figure, amounting to about 2 per cent of the then Portuguese population. It was, by any reckoning, a hard-hearted strategy, throwing the burden of the war onto the civilian population. Was it necessary? Wellington conclusively defeated Masséna on the heights of Bussaco, and had he guarded the road around the north of the great ridge, he could probably have repulsed the French there and then, forcing them back to Ciudad Rodrigo across the Spanish border, but that, of course, would have left Masséna's army relatively undamaged. Hunger and disease were much greater enemies than redcoats and riflemen, and by forcing Masséna to spend the winter in the wasteland north of the lines, Wellington destroyed his enemy's army. At the beginning of the campaign, in September 1810, Masséna commanded 65,000 men. When he got back to Spain he had fewer than 40,000, and had lost half his horses and virtually all his wheeled transport. Of the 25,000 men he lost, only about 4,000 were killed, wounded or taken prisoner at Bussaco (British losses were about 1,000); the rest were lost because the Lines of Torres Vedras condemned Masséna to a winter of hunger, disease and desertion.

So why fight at Bussaco if the Lines of Torres Vedras could do the job better? Wellington fought there for the sake of morale. The Portuguese army did not have a sterling record against the French, but it was now re-organized and under Wellington's command and, by giving it a victory on the ridge, he gave that army a confidence it never lost. Bussaco was the place where the Portuguese learned they could beat the French and, rightly, it holds a celebrated place in Portuguese history.

The ridge is heavily forested now, so that it is difficult to imagine how any battle could have been fought up its eastern face, but photographs taken in 1910 show the ridge as almost entirely bare, and contemporary accounts suggest that was how it was a hundred years earlier. Those photographs can be seen in the splendid book, *Bussaco 1810*, by René Char-trand, published by Osprey. In most books about the battle the monastery on the reverse slope is referred to as a convent, a word which properly can be applied to communities of either monks or nuns, but common usage restricts it to nuns, and I have seen the building at Bussaco called the Convento dos Carmelitas Descalços and the Mosteiro dos Carmeli-tas, so I refer to it as a monastery to avoid giving the impression that nuns were present. It was occupied by the Barefoot Carmelites until 1834 when the Portuguese monasteries were dissolved. It still exists, as do the clay stations of the cross in their brick housings, and all can be visited. A massive hotel, built in the early twentieth century as a royal palace, now stands next to the monastery.

Masséna was indeed twenty-two miles behind Bussaco on the eve of the battle. He had visited Bussaco briefly, then returned to his eighteen-year-old mistress, Henriette Leberton, and Ney's aide, D'Esmenard, was forced to hold a conversation through their closed bedroom door.

Masséna managed to tear himself from Henriette's arms and rode back to Bussaco where he decided against any kind of reconnaissance and simply launched his troops into their attack. It was a foolhardy decision, for the ridge at Bussaco is a formidable position. Some of his generals advised against an attack, but Masséna was confident his troops could break the British and Portuguese line. It was an error born of over-confidence and, though the French columns did reach the crest as described in the novel, they were pinched off and defeated.

The French sack of Coimbra was every bit as nasty as its depiction in *Sharpe's Escape*. The first troops into the city were new conscripts, ill trained and undisciplined, and they ran wild. The city had 40,000 inhabitants at the beginning of the campaign, and at least half had decided not to retreat towards Lisbon, and of those that remained about a thousand were murdered by the occupiers. The university was plundered, the royal tombs in Santa Cruz opened and defiled, and, though the hungry French discovered plenty of food in the city, they managed to destroy most of it. Warehouses of supplies were put to the torch so that when Masséna's army marched south they were as hungry as when they arrived.

Masséna left his wounded in Coimbra under a totally inadequate guard. Their hold on the city lasted just four days after which Colonel Trant, a British officer leading Portuguese militia, captured Coimbra from the north and, having endured some difficulties protecting his new prisoners from the vengeance of the city's inhabitants, managed to march or carry them north to Oporto.

Masséna, meanwhile, had encountered the Lines of Torres Vedras and was astonished by them. Wellington and his chief engineer, Colonel Fletcher, had somehow managed to keep the massive construction project a secret (even from the British and Portuguese governments), and though Masséna had heard rumors about a line of forts, he was in no way prepared for the actuality. The lines comprised 152 defensive works (bastions or forts), mounting 534 cannon, and covering 52 miles of ground. The first two lines barred the French from approaching Lisbon, the third, far to the south, enclosed an emergency enclave into which Wellington could withdraw his troops if it became necessary to embark his army. A French officer said of the first two lines that they "were of such an extraordinary nature that I daresay there was no other position in the world that could be compared to them." Another Frenchman, a hussar officer, put it more graphically: "before them was a wall of brass and behind them a region of famine." Masséna stared at the lines through a glass and was driven off by a cannon shot, to which he responded by taking off his hat, which was polite of him, but in truth he was furious that he had not been warned of the new fortifications. It seems extraordinary that he had not heard of them, but they remained a secret. Thousands of men had worked on constructing the defenses, and thousands of others had passed the lines as they used the roads going through the works, yet the French were utterly surprised by them. Masséna made no serious attempt to breach them, indeed the only fighting at the lines themselves was a scrappy battle between two sets of skirmishers which took place at Sobral on 12 October, the day after the first French troops reached the lines. The fight at the end of *Sharpe's Escape* is loosely based on that fight, but I confess the operative word is loosely because I moved it the best part of twenty miles to put it nearer the Tagus and gave it to Sir Thomas Picton who was nowhere near Sobral.

Most of the 152 forts of the lines are still in existence, but many of them are so ruined and overgrown that they are not easily found. If the only chance of seeing them is a very swift visit then that should probably be to the town of Torres Vedras itself where, just to the north, the Fort of Saint Vincent has been restored. A longer visit should rely (as should any visit to a Peninsular battlefield) on Julian Paget's superb guide, *Wellington's Peninsular War* (Leo Cooper, London, 1990).

Masséna stayed in Portugal much longer than Wellington had hoped. The attempt to strip central Portugal of food never really worked, and the French discovered enough supplies to keep them well fed through October. They repaired the windmills and rebuilt the ovens, but by November they were on half rations, and then they were besieged by a winter that was unusually cold and wet. They left Torres Vedras in mid-November and retreated to where they hoped more food would be available, and somehow they lasted in Portugal until March when, hungry, dispirited and unsuccessful, they went back to their depots in Spain. It had been a bitter defeat for Masséna.

John Grehan's book, *The Lines of Torres Vedras*, published by Spellmount in 2000, was invaluable in writing *Sharpe's Escape*. It contains by far the best description of the lines themselves, but much more besides, including a gripping account of the battle of Bussaco, and I am indebted to it, though any mistakes are, of course, mine. Sharpe and Harper will march again.

BOOKS BY BERNARD CORNWELL

THE SAXON NOVELS

THE LAST KINGDOM
0-06-088718-4 (tp) • 0-06-075925-9 (cd)

THE PALE HORSEMAN
0-06-078712-0 (new in hc)

THE RICHARD SHARPE SERIES

SHARPE'S TIGER
Richard Sharpe and the Siege of
Seringapatam, 1799
0-06-093230-9 (tp) • 0-06-101269-6 (mm)

SHARPE'S TRIUMPH
Richard Sharpe and the Battle of Assaye,
September 1803
0-06-095197-4 (tp) • 0-06-074804-4 (mm)

SHARPE'S FORTRESS
Richard Sharpe and the Siege of Gawilghur,
December 1803
0-06-109863-9 (tp) • 0-06-101271-8 (mm)

SHARPE'S TRAFALGAR
Richard Sharpe and the Battle of Trafalgar,
October 21, 1805
0-06-109862-0 (tp)

SHARPE'S PREY
Richard Sharpe and the Expedition to
Copenhagen, 1807
0-06-008453-7 (tp)

SHARPE'S HAVOC
Richard Sharpe and the Campaign in
Northern Portugal, Spring 1809
0-06-056670-1 (tp) • 0-06-053275-0 (mm)

SHARPE'S ESCAPE
Richard Sharpe and the Bussaco Campaign,
1810
0-06-056155-6 (tp coming May 2006)
0-06-056095-9 (mm) • 0-06-059172-2 (cd)

SHARPE'S BATTLE
Richard Sharpe and the Battle of Fuentes de
Onoro, May 1811
0-06-093228-7 (tp) • 0-06-109537-0 (mm)

SHARPE'S DEVIL
Richard Sharpe and the Emperor, 1820-21
0-06-093229-5 (tp) • 0-06-109028-X (mm)

THE NATHANIEL STARBUCK CHRONICLES

REBEL
Book One: Bull Run, 1861
0-06-093461-1 (tp) • 0-06-109187-1 (mm)

COPPERHEAD
Book Two: Ball's Bluff, 1862
0-06-093462-X (tp) • 0-06-109196-0 (mm)

BATTLE FLAG
Book Three: Second Manassas, 1862
0-06-093718-1 (tp) • 0-06-109197-9 (mm)

THE BLOODY GROUND
Book Four: The Battle of Antietam, 1862
0-06-093719-X (tp) • 0-06-109198-7 (mm)

THE GRAIL QUEST SERIES

THE ARCHER'S TALE
0-06-093576-6 (tp) • 0-06-050525-7 (mm)
0-694-52609-6 (cd)

VAGABOND
0-06-093578-2 (tp coming April 2006)
0-06-621080-1 (hc) • 0-06-053268-8 (mm)
0-06-051080-3 (cd) • 0-06-051743-3 (lp)

HERETIC
0-06-074828-1 (tp coming June 2006)
0-06-053049-9 (hc) • 0-06-053284-X (mm)
0-06-056613-2 (cd) • 0-06-056998-0 (lp)

ALSO BY BERNARD CORNWELL

GALLOWS THIEF
A Novel
0-06-008274-7 (tp) • 0-06-051628-3 (mm)
0-06-009301-3 (cd)

STONEHENGE
A Novel
0-06-095685-2 (tp) • 0-06-109194-4 (mm)

REDCOAT
A Novel
0-06-051277-6 (tp) • 0-06-101264-5 (mm)

www.bernardcornwell.net